Dead Rich

Dead Rich

Katia Lief

W F HOWES LTD

This large print edition published in 2014 by
W F Howes Ltd
Unit 4, Rearsby Business Park, Gaddesby Lane,
Rearsby, Leicester LE7 4YH

1 3 5 7 9 10 8 6 4 2

First published in the United Kingdom in 2013
by Ebury Press

Copyright © Katia Spiegelman Lief, 2013

The right of Katia Lief to be identified as
the author of this work has been asserted by her
in accordance with the Copyright, Designs and
Patents Act, 1988.

A CIP catalogue record for this book is available
from the British Library

ISBN 978 1 47125 845 9

Typeset by Palimpsest Book Production Limited,
Falkirk, Stirlingshire
Printed and bound by
www.printondemand-worldwide.com of Peterborough, England

Mixed Sources
Product group from well-managed
forests, and other controlled sources
www.fsc.org Cert no. TT-COC-002641
© 1996 Forest Stewardship Council
FSC

PEFC Certified
This product is
from sustainably
managed forests
and controlled
sources
www.pefc.org
PEFC
PEFC/16-33-415

This book is made entirely of chain-of-custody materials

For my family, with love

PART I

CHAPTER 1

'This look all right?' Mac runs a hand down the length of his tie. The rarely excavated garment bag that houses his best suit lies puddled by the foot of the mirror. In his reflection, I see the ghost of a stain near the knee of his slacks, but decide not to mention it. The morning is rushing forward and we're low on time.

'You look handsome.' I smile at my husband from the edge of our bed. The stockings I just tugged on constrict like a sausage casing. I yank them off and toss them across the room, where they float to a landing beside the garment bag. 'Whoever invented these things should be hanged.'

'Then don't wear any.'

'It's summer. I don't know what I was thinking.' My linen dress will look better barelegged, anyway.

'You want to look nice for Ben's big day, that's what you were thinking.'

'I'm really excited about this.'

'So am I.'

Just then Dathi darts past our open bedroom

3

door: She has unpeeled her skinny jeans and put on a skirt and top for the occasion of her little brother's kindergarten 'stepping up.' It feels exciting and a little daunting, this gesture at a graduation ceremony aimed at launching an education everyone hopes will end with college. The idea of Ben not going straight to college after high school agitates me whenever the possibility drifts through my mind. I just turned forty, still haven't graduated college, and am beginning to think I never will.

Dathi comes into our room, barefoot, a pair of black flats dangling from one hand. 'My new shoes don't fit anymore.'

'You're growing like a weed.' And she's developing; you can see a curvaceous outline forming under her white blouse. Her face, though, hasn't changed much; despite two winters living with us in Brooklyn, the sun-soaked glow she brought with her from India makes her as radiant as ever.

'I can't even squeeze my feet in.' She demonstrates, dropping the left shoe and unsuccessfully jamming in her foot.

'Here, see if these fit.' I toss her the low-heeled sandals I had planned to wear.

'No, I couldn't.'

'Yes, you could, you can, and you will.'

She slips into my sandals, which are a little big, but will do.

Consulting his watch, Mac asks, 'Think I have time to swing by the office before we go? Mary texted me. She has a couple questions.'

'So text her back.'

'It's just down the street, Karin.'

'Twenty minutes,' I say to his back as he vanishes into the hallway. 'We'll ring the bell.'

Dathi and I finish getting ready. While she checks Facebook for the eighth time that morning, I pick up our cats' empty dishes and put them in the kitchen sink. Jeff and Justin, year-old brothers, always nap on the couch after breakfast. I steal a quick pet of Jeff's soft orange cheek, then Justin's silky black tail, as I cross the living room to the front door. Jeff coos but doesn't wake.

'Ready.' Dathi joins me at the door and out we step into the June morning. The tall old trees are in full leaf, casting welcome shade on an early summer just growing warm. Bergen Street is still as a portrait: the procession of brownstones with stoops tiered to the cracked uneven sidewalk, the sentinel watchfulness of the houses' gleaming windows awake to the life of the street.

The block is quiet except for a woman walking in our direction. She appears out of place, even in our gentrified neighborhood, with her soft pink sweater, creased slacks, and big diamond ring. She's more put together than the people you normally see this time of day, those left behind by the morning rush to the battlefields of corporate Manhattan. Anyone around here not swept away in the early commute is pretty much a jeans-and-bedhead freelancer, an at-home parent, or a student. Close to her now, I breathe in the luxuriant scent of a perfume I'd never be able to afford – an exquisite reduction of jasmine and roses – and feel an unwelcome spike of envy.

She turns in to ring the doorbell of the work-space Mac rents on the same block as our house – the ground-floor apartment cum office suite that MacLeary Investigations shares with a free-lance graphic designer named Andre. Andre rarely gets in before noon, and even if he did, his clients are never this posh. But then, neither are ours. I mentally scan today's calendar: No new clients are scheduled; the only thing of any impor-tance that's supposed to be happening is Ben's ceremony.

Mary's voice emanates from the intercom: 'Hello?'

'Is this MacLeary Investigations?'

'Yes.'

'I apologize, you're not expecting me, but—'

'Hang on. Be right out.'

The woman clutches her purse and glances over her shoulder at me and Dathi standing behind her. I decide not to take out my key because I don't want to go in, I want Mac to come out, or we'll be late.

'There's no sign,' she says. 'I wasn't sure I had the right address.'

'We should get a sign.' Immediately regretting the *we*. I've argued strenuously against adding myself to the company name yet can't help lumping myself in anyway. Sometimes I think Mac

6

is just waiting for me to break down and make it official, and some days I almost relent, but then I slip backward into a familiar yearning to disown this kind of work. It draws you deep inside. Masticates you. Dribbles you out like spit.

The door swings open before she can ask me any questions. She has that fraught look in her eyes new clients get when they first decide to take action and hire a private detective.

Mary glances at us and ekes out a smile for the unexpected visitor. 'How can I help you?' The purple canvas TOMS she keeps under her desk as slippers peek out beneath the frayed hems of her bell-bottoms. You can see she brushed her brown hair this morning but it didn't do much good.

Appearing behind her, Mac asks, 'Everything okay?'

'Are you—'

He offers a welcoming hand to the woman. 'Mac MacLeary. I'm sorry if . . . did we have an appointment?' He glances at Mary, who shakes her head.

'No,' she holds onto his hand, 'I'm Cathy Millerhausen. I'm sorry, I don't usually just show up.'

'You caught me at a bad time. I was on my way out the door.'

'Please, it won't take long. Please.' She squeezes his hand. Droplets gather on her upper lip, and she stares at him, waiting. Her desperation is palpable; you can practically see waves of anxiety waft off her like steam.

'We can make you an appointment for another day,' Mac offers.

'Please. I know I should have called first, but I'm just so . . . I just . . .'

His eyes shift between Cathy Millerhausen and me, and on impulse I wrest open a sliver of time for this woman I shouldn't care about, but for some reason do. 'If you get there by eleven,' I tell Mac, 'you won't miss anything.'

'Is fifteen minutes enough?' he asks her.

'I don't know how long something like this usually takes.'

'Well, it'll have to be.' Mac steps aside to invite her in.

'Have fun!' When Mary waves at us, the tattoo in the palm of her left hand catches Mrs Millerhausen's attention: a quarter-size smiley face. If Mary had raised her right hand, our visitor would have seen a lotus flower. Her expression doesn't shift, which almost surprises me; but when you're preoccupied, it takes a lot more than a silly tattoo to distract you. Whatever is on the woman's mind has her attention in a chokehold.

Mac steps into a pool of shadows in the outer vestibule so Cathy Millerhausen can pass. Under the fluorescent light her skin attains a fragility it lacked outside in the full-spectrum sun with all its hues. When she tries to smile, lines spray across her cheekbones. A knot forms in his stomach at the panic in her pale eyes.

8

He says, 'I'm at the end of the hall,' and leads her along a narrow passage off of which three offices blossom to the right: Andre's first, Mac's last, with the windowless room shared by Karin and Mary sandwiched between. As part-timers and last on board, the women landed the worst space, though no rationale has ever made the distinction comfortable for Mac. When he first rented office space here, the middle room was occupied by a woman novelist – he corrects himself: *novelist*. No one to his knowledge has ever called him a *man detective*. Through the open door he sees that Mary is back at her computer, working.

Mac sits at his desk, the window full of summer greenery open behind him, allowing a slight breeze. To combat the darkness of the ground floor rooms, the landlord painted this one a cooling yellow. From the ceiling a vintage fixture douses the room in agreeable light. A framed poster of windows flung open to an ocean hangs across from him so when he works he remembers there is more than this. Neatly stacked file folders documenting evidence of betrayal and paranoia and everything in between snake around two edges of the large desk, making him look busier than he is. He already knows he'll take her job as much as he knows he won't want to. He's seen it a hundred times, that despair in her eyes, and the truth is it no longer easily moves him. If Karin hadn't interceded, he would have turned Cathy Millerhausen away.

'How can I help?' he starts.

She sits across from him, back straight, hands folded on crossed knees, all tight angles that irritate and disturb him. 'It's my husband.'

He nods.

'I think he's unfaithful.'

Of course, what else? 'Go on.'

'He was unfaithful during his first marriage – unfaithful with me.' She clarifies: 'Godfrey left his first wife for me.' Her skin reddens violently. 'So I know he's quite capable of it.'

Mac sinks deeply into listening mode; nothing so far sounds all that unusual. He leans back, gets comfortable. She pulls her diamond ring up to her finger joint and then pushes it back down, twists it so the stone briefly vanishes before reappearing, dazzling as it catches the light.

'I suppose men like Godfrey always cheat.'

'What kind of a man is that?'

'Very rich, very powerful men.'

'You're his second wife, so I'm guessing he had you sign a prenup.'

She nods. 'But with a clause my lawyer insisted on: "If Godfrey Armstrong Millerhausen has sexual relations with another woman during the term of the marriage, if the marriage has lasted at least five years, and only if the infidelity occurs after five years of full-time marriage, then the prenuptial agreement is null and void." That's a quote.'

'And you've been married five years.'

'Nine.'

'Would the prenup leave you broke?'

'Not exactly. But without enough money to continue—'

He sees it coming and tries not to cringe: '. . . in the lifestyle to which I've become accustomed.' He thinks, *Who cares how pampered you've been, lady?* But that isn't what she says.

'– the care our son needs on a daily basis. We have twins, and one of them has special needs.' Her knuckles whiten as she grips one hand over the other.

Mac leans forward, and asks, 'What kind of needs?'

'He's intellectually disabled. I caught a virus when I was pregnant and it made Ritchie's brain development dysfunctional. Otherwise my boys are identical. Or would be, I mean. They're eight, and Bobby's fine, but Ritchie . . .' Her voice fades to silence.

'Bobby doesn't need any special care at all?'

'No. They both attend private school, of course, but Ritchie's school is particularly expensive. And his therapists *outside* school are exorbitant, but necessary to keep him moving forward, even incrementally. I would never be able to cover his costs on what the prenup would leave me.'

'And you don't believe your husband would cover his son's care?'

'I can't be sure. He doesn't pay much attention to Ritchie, and I know he blames me for the virus, irrational as it sounds. But it's the way Godfrey is: Someone is always at fault; someone always has to pay a price. Be accountable. That's Godfrey.'

'What makes you think the marriage is in jeopardy?'

'Are you married, Mr MacLeary?'

'Mac. And yes. In fact, you just met my wife.'

'Oh, the tall woman outside.'

'Karin. She works with me. Our son is graduating kindergarten this morning.' Mac glances at his watch, shifts in his seat. Eight minutes: That's all Mrs Millerhausen has left.

'I can feel it,' she tells him. 'There just isn't much between us anymore. He's lost interest in me . . . and the boys, too, I sometimes think.'

'Do you know for a fact he's got someone on the side?'

'Not for a fact, no. But I think he does. I'll need proof, of course, so when he hits me with the divorce I can void the prenup. That's all I want. I don't need to save the marriage – let him go to her, it's what he does. I can live without him, but my boys need to be raised.'

'I understand.'

'Ritchie will be all right, more or less, if he continues to get the best care. Godfrey once suggested institutionalizing him – but that breaks my heart, Mr MacLeary . . . Mac. Have you ever seen those places?'

'No.'

'They're horrible. I don't care if they're "state

12

of the art" or whatever other accolades they claim for themselves – no one loves you in those places. No one. You're alone, warehoused, for the rest of your life.' Her eyes water pitifully and Mac's whole body responds, melting. He steadies himself. 'How can I provide a normal life for Bobby, and give Ritchie what he needs, at the same time? I can't live two lives. I need to stay with both of them, make a normal life for Bobby and a special life for Ritchie.'

'That's a tough one.'

'You bet it is. And it takes a lot of money. And my husband *has* a lot of money.' She holds back her tears as if she has already cried enough. Leaning forward, she says, fiercely, 'Godfrey is *extremely* wealthy, partly inherited, partly earned. If he lost half his money, he'd still be filthy rich. I will pay you very well to get me the proof I need to void the prenup. Will you do it?'

'Why me?'

'Because no one knows you in our circles.'

A sarcastic snort escapes him. 'Sorry. It just sounds—'

'I know how it sounds, and I'm sorry. What I mean is that we live in a certain kind of world, where things are done in a certain way. In my circles we all go to the same places and hire the same people. We eat the same food and vacation in the same hotels. When we go to New York, trust me, we don't go to Brooklyn.'

'But you did.'

'Exactly.'

'How did you find me?'

'Random Internet search, to be honest. You seem to have the right background – former police detective, small business, and you have no sign out front, which is even better.'

'And you didn't call first because you don't want to risk Godfrey searching your phone records.'

She smiles, the lines fanning from her eyes again, making her less plastic, more attractive.

'You could have saved yourself a trip and used a pay phone.'

'Do you know I couldn't find a single working pay phone in Greenwich, Connecticut?' Her laugh is an intoxicating mixture of airy and bitter and hurt, and suddenly he wants to help her rob her husband blind.

Late morning blankets the brick school building with deep, comforting quiet. Mac rushes past the church, with its stone Madonna and her blank eyes watching and not watching but still getting under his skin every time he sees her – one of the many prices he pays for his Catholic upbringing. As soon as he flings open the door to the attached building, formerly a parochial school now leased to the city for public education, he is hit by the cacophony of little voices that always makes him smile. A boy about seven whizzes by, his sneakers leaving a black scuff mark on the polished floor as he takes the corner and bounds up the stairs, a high pitched 'Sorry, mister!' floating behind him like a sound bubble.

Mac passes through the cafeteria, echoing with pre-lunch silence, its cinder-block walls painted with a series of playful murals, and takes the back staircase down to a series of brightly painted rooms where kindergarten and pre-K are housed. Midway along the hall, he pulls open an apple-green door covered with construction paper leaves, each one bearing a student's name. He sees Ben's name on a blue leaf and feels a warm glow of pride ease onto his face.

The principal is speaking in front of a crowd of dressed-up parents arranged on folding chairs. When the classroom door squeals an announcement of Mac's arrival, heads turn. He waves an apology and catches Karin's eye, wincing. Her lips gather into a kiss and his smile broadens. But then he realizes that she isn't sending him a welcome kiss, she's shushing him. The ceremony has already begun.

CHAPTER 2

Mary Salter bursts out of the office bathroom while the toilet is still flushing, having barely had a chance to wash her hands before Mick Jagger's plea that he *ain't got no satisfaction* wails from her cell phone. It's Fremont's special ring, but he never calls during school hours. Ever since she got him his own phone when he was in fourth grade and started walking to school alone because she had to leave for work, she hasn't been able to respond to his rare school-day calls without a searing feeling of preemptory alarm.

The phone vibrates where she left it on her desk, bouncing in its rubbery skin in the direction of the pad where she'd started making notes on the new client, Cathy Millerhausen.

'Are you sick?'

A girl's voice asks, 'Hello?'

'Who *is* this?'

Silence.

'Why do you have my son's phone?'

'*Whose* phone?'

'My *son*, Fremont, why do—'

'Hey, Free,' she shouts, 'found your phone, called your number one, some lady thinks she's your *mother*. Catch!'

A braid of laughter includes strands of Fremont's voice, deep now in a way that still surprises Mary.

The girl hangs up and Mary is left floating in a blur of white noise that is her crashing thoughts: the daily existential crisis of every parent of a teenager. She speed-dials Fremont and her call goes straight to voice mail. She doesn't leave a message; what's the point? Fremont is a good boy but he still doesn't return her calls most of the time. She'll have to catch him later, ask casually about his day, the phone, that girl.

She closes her phone and puts it back on the desk but doesn't take her hand off it. Friends have told her she holds her only child too close, even other single-mother friends. How can she expect them to understand what it's like being a white mother raising a black teenage son in the city? Mary learned fast that, even in twenty-first-century New York, being a half-white boy means little when you're also half-black. As soon as Fremont had his first growth spurt, and especially when his voice sank and the faint mustache appeared, people routinely avoided him; she noticed it the first time when he walked ahead of her one day. Since then, she sometimes hangs back to test her theory, and it's always true: This charming boy who is her beloved son is also a member of that tribe of young-black-American-men who are marked as an

17

endangered species from puberty on. Now every time he steps out on his own, which is most of the time, worry claws at her from the inside.

Mary dials her son's phone again. And again, no one answers.

She shuts her eyes, takes a deep breath in and slowly lets it out with a long, throaty '*Aummmmmmm*.'

Hearing Andre laughing at her through their shared wall, she picks up Karin's squishy worry ball and throws it. It hits between the Adele concert poster and the dartboard. One of the darts plunks to the floor.

His chair scrapes, footsteps in the hall, and he's poking his head through her open door. His handlebar mustache is perfectly waxed as always, extending across his face in an extra smile. 'Lunch?'

'Give me half an hour. I have to finish this research for Mac.'

'You'll never be finished.' Andre has seen her work enough cases to know that she's an obsessive researcher. She's one of those people who the Internet helps *and* hinders, just by existing.

'Thirty minutes. I promise.'

So far, Mary has learned that Godfrey Millerhausen of Greenwich, Connecticut, and Park Avenue, New York, is the scion of Hauser International, which started with one Ohio food market more than a hundred years ago and grew into a massive national chain of supermarkets and liquor stores operating under the name Hauser.

18

The corporate headquarters was moved from Akron to Manhattan in 1925, reputedly (according to Wikipedia) managing to survive the crash and the Depression by bankrolling a bootlegging operation out of Toronto into Buffalo with a truck caravan relaying the illicit cargo straight into the thirsty veins of New York City. That's when and how Hauser landed in the liquor trade, growing even bigger and richer when Prohibition ended in 1933, by which time they had already cornered the local market. The only big difference being that now they didn't have to worry about getting arrested at the end of a typical workday. The supermarket business split off from the liquor side in the seventies, when Godfrey's father took over the food side and left the booze side to his brother Dean, who left it to his son Preston. Preston Millerhausen, (according to *Forbes*), is now the twenty-seventh wealthiest billionaire in the world. Godfrey Millerhausen lags behind, at ninety-second richest. *Boo hoo*, Mary thinks. What's a person to do with only 3.4 billion dollars when his cousin's got nearly 12 billion? Talk about tense family holidays.

These amounts of money are well past anything Mary can fathom. She lives in a slowly gentrifying slum in Clinton Hill, Brooklyn, and feels grateful, even lucky, for her rent-stabilized apartment. Reading through the online editions of *Forbes*, *Business Week*, and *Moneyedup*, she realizes that, compared to these people, she is certifiably poor.

Mrs Millerhausen didn't bat an eyelash when Mac said his retainer started at ten thousand dollars (double the usual) and had to be renewed every two weeks until he solved the case or she fired him. Apparently, it was chump change to her. He should have asked for twenty thousand, and given Mary a raise.

Her finger hits the down arrow hard, over and over, scrolling through an article called 'Billionaire Profile: Godfrey Millerhausen' that tells the story of how he grew up 'comfortable' and after Wharton Business School cultivated his inheritance into an even more substantial fortune. He's been married twice and has three children: a grown daughter from his first marriage, and the twin boys from his second.

Mary tries Fremont again, to no avail.

'*Aummmmmm*.'

'Ready?' Andre calls through the wall.

'Five more minutes.'

She compiles a list of data for Mac, including business names; office and home addresses; contact information for Dan Stylos, Hauser's chief operating officer and evidently Millerhausen's closest associate; and links to anything on the Internet Mary thinks Mac might want to look at himself. She hasn't been able to find anything on the ex-wife or grown daughter, though, no current addresses or any hard information since the divorce ten years ago. Mary is sure her boss will want to know where they are now and what they've been up to. Hoisting her purse strap over her shoulder and heading to lunch with Andre, she decides that if Mac isn't back when she returns, she'll go ahead and start trying to track them down. Skip tracing is her specialty, and she figures from experience he'll put her right on it. Why wait?

Tuesday, June 26

Across the street from 501 Madison Avenue, a huge clock above a storefront selling upscale watches yawns at Mac in a cruel reminder of how slowly time is passing. He's been standing outside the skyscraper, where Hauser International has eight floors split between the two sides of the business, for two hours and seven minutes. He wonders how many hundreds, if not thousands, of his lifetime's limited hours he's thrown away on stakeouts over the years. When he's stuck standing or pacing in front of a building, he wishes he could sit. When he's stuck sitting, he yearns to walk around. Greener grass, wherever he isn't. The cloying boredom is another painful reminder of how much he dislikes surveilling the unfaithful. Allegedly unfaithful. *Care*, he reminds himself. A client is paying you, and this one, for some reason he can't define, struck him as special. So *care*.

A brown UPS truck pulls up in front of the clock and Mac checks his watch as if the time might be running faster on his wrist. It isn't. He has been here since seven this morning; he always arrives

21

early on the first day of a stakeout to give the subject's habits ample margin for expression. But it turns out Godfrey Millerhausen doesn't get to work early, at least not today. Which makes sense if he's commuting in from Greenwich, unless he spent the night at the Park Avenue apartment, which is always a possibility. This time tomorrow they'll know a lot more about his weekday routines; they might even get the evidence Mrs Millerhausen wants by tonight. Mac hopes so.

He's into his third cup of coffee when a limousine pulls up in front of the revolving glass doors of 501 Madison. Godfrey Millerhausen gets out and strolls toward the building just after the flood of nine-A.M. secretaries and before the inevitable dribble of freelancers around ten.

Wearing an expensive-looking summer-weight suit, Millerhausen is taller than Mac expected from the wife's description: six-two, maybe six-three. Taller than Mac, and thinner. Neatly clipped brown hair. On the handsome side. Can't see the man's eyes from the obscured view of a quarter-block's distance and the steam rising from his coffee into his face, but Mary can get that kind of detail if they need it later, though Mac doubts they will.

Mac opens the calendar on his BlackBerry and keys in the license plate number of the limo, followed by *TOA 9:19 a.m.* After two plus hours standing on the sidewalk, logging time of arrival shouldn't feel like such a big accomplishment. But there have been jobs when Mac waited all day only to discover his subject decided not to come to work at all. Sometimes it was because the subject was booking time with his lover. Which meant Mac had wasted a day in exactly the wrong place.

At 12:36 Godfrey Millerhausen comes out of the building with another man in a suit and tie: shorter, stockier, with a halo of graying brown hair. Mac checks his BlackBerry to take another look at the photo of Dan Stylos, Hauser's COO, that Mary e-mailed him earlier: yup, it's him. The two men walk slowly, huddled in conversation. They eat lunch at a place down Fifty-third Street. Mac's stomach grumbles reading the menu posted outside: thirty-five-dollar hamburgers, thirty-dollar salads, ten-dollar cappuccinos. The late June afternoon gathers some serious heat and by the time the men reappear, an hour and a half later, the temperature has hit eighty and Mac is sweating down the back of his shirt. He follows them to 501 Madison, watches them enter the office building, and briefly retreats into the sweet air-conditioning of Crumbs Bake Shop next door, where the woman in the black hairnet and stained white apron already knows how he takes his iced coffee. He also orders a vanilla coconut cupcake. Returns to his post on the sidewalk.

At 5:23 the same limo returns and waits outside the building. At 5:44 Godfrey gets into the back of the long car. Mac steps to the curb and hails a taxi from the yellow armada crowding Madison Avenue to carry home middle managers who can afford to avoid the subway but can't come close to the kind of ride Millerhausen has at his disposal. Mac has no idea where they're going and doesn't really care. Cathy Millerhausen is paying for the cab, he's got all night, and he's glad to finally be off his feet.

Rush-hour traffic out of the city is murder on the Cross Bronx Expressway and barely lightens up on 87 north as they inch forward, two cars behind the limo. Apparently they're heading to the Connecticut house where Millerhausen lives with Cathy and the twins. Mac's stomach grips at the thought of how long and slow this drive is going to be, sitting in the back of a taxi that smells like spilled soda. He can picture Millerhausen stretched out in his limo, probably nursing a drink, maybe watching a Yankees game on a flat-screen TV. What do rich guys like that do during the times regular folk are inured to waiting? Mac, for one, reads. But Millerhausen already strikes him as a different breed of man. At that thought the detective's imagination wanders into the wilderness of all the possibilities of where a man with billions might go, what he might do. If you had enough money to satisfy your every whim, would you?

Ali Hussein Muhammad al-Adzharia (according to the Taxi and Limousine ID displayed on the dashboard) catches Mac's eye in the rearview mirror. 'Do this every day?'

'I'd have to be crazy.'

When a rap tune suddenly blasts on the radio, Ali grunts and turns the dial to 1010 WINS. A staccato of bad news pours out:

'Rare June hurricane forming off the Florida Panhandle!'

'U.S. high-school graduation rates drop dramatically!'

'Assistant football coach found guilty of raping young children for more than twenty years at Penn State!'

'Killer bees terrorize southern New Mexico, killing one man in his own home!'

'More help arrives in the hunt for the missing teen from Harrisburg, Pennsylvania! Says dad: "We won't give up hope of finding her alive."'

Leaning forward, Mac asks, 'Mind changing the station?'

Ali answers by searching for music, stopping on an auto-tuned cover of an old Joni Mitchell standard Mac used to love.

'Thanks,' Mac says.

'No problem.'

Mac closes his eyes and when he opens them, they're moving steadily along the leafy Hutchinson River Parkway, queuing for the Rye Brook/ Greenwich exit.

All of a sudden there's practically no traffic, and nearly all the cars on the road are new models of whatever's best on the market. They wind along pastoral byways aptly named Riversville Road and

Meadow Lane, until finding themselves alone behind the limo on Zaccheus Mead Lane. Mac chuckles aloud, thinking this has got to be someone's joke. He went to Bible school as a kid and remembers the story of Zacchaeus, the money-skimming tax collector who climbed a sycamore tree for a better view of Jesus. Whoever edited out the *a* to call this road Zaccheus instead of Zacchaeus wasn't fooling anyone. Greenwich is one of the richest towns in America; the last thing the robber barons living out here want to see is the taxman. Or a private investigator, for that matter.

The limo turns onto Ashton Drive and pulls into a driveway.

'Stop here,' Mac instructs Ali.

The taxi idles by a pair of stone columns into one of which is carved *Ashton Manor*.

'This your house?'

'You kidding?'

'What do I know?'

'Back up behind those trees and turn off the engine.'

Mac gets out, leaving the door cracked open, and walks quietly forward until he can see a long driveway lined with hedges all the way to a circular drive. He watches the limo glide to a halt in front of a brick mansion: big white portico, huge multi-paned windows, four chimneys sprouting from a tiled roof.

Millerhausen goes inside. The door shuts behind him.

'What now?' Ali asks, suddenly standing behind Mac.

'We wait.'

'How long?'

'No idea.'

'You know what this'll cost you?'

'You mean what it'll cost *him*.' Mac tilts his head toward the house.

Ali smiles: His yellow teeth are crooked, like they've been jammed into his mouth. 'You're crazy, man.'

They wait an hour. Two. Three. When the lights go off in the mansion, Mac decides that's it: Millerhausen is in for the night.

Wednesday, June 27

Squeezed into my little black dress which is really a little red dress, the one I only wear on stake-outs, I nod discreet thanks to the uniformed doorman who pulls open the entrance to Daniel, the restaurant Mac followed Godfrey Millerhausen to exactly fifty minutes ago. From the corner of my eye I watch my husband blend into the summer evening along Sixty-fifth Street in the direction of Park Avenue. It's his turn to go home tonight and get some rest, my turn to surveil Millerhausen.

The maître d', a wizened man in a dark suit, greets me with the obligatory stiff smile. 'How may I help you, madame?'

'I'm meeting a friend at the bar. I was asked to meet him here at seven.'

'It's a quarter to.'

'Is it?'

'His name?'

'I was asked not to give his name.' I smile, driving home the unspoken message: Master of the universe arranges assignation with paramour at bar of tony Manhattan restaurant. The maître d' eyes my camel pashmina as if he knows it cost me five bucks on the street.

'Come with me.'

I follow him through a series of rooms loosely delineated by archways and Grecian columns, spaces that are all creamy amber light, thick carpets, white tables, lacquered chairs, and whispered conversations. Waitstaff in black suits float through the luscious space like a band of helpful but otherwise invisible assistants whose only hope is to serve and please. As if they only exist here, and don't head home in sneakers afterward to the Bronx and Brooklyn and Queens and possibly even Staten Island. I make contact with no one as I'm led through rooms, past people all playing their parts, my gaze sliding over well-groomed heads and cashmere backs . . . and there he is, alone at a table with two dinner plates soiled with the remains of a meal.

Godfrey Millerhausen is seated at a low banquette so close to the bar, I have to swallow back the spike of adrenaline before it reaches my pulse or my face. You can't sweat, you can't blush, you can't show any sign that you're infiltrating a world where you don't belong.

He's handsomer than his photograph: forty-eight, looks closer to forty, with skin that appears just shaven and hair just cut. His silk tie is luminescent in the tawny restaurant light, but I doubt it's actually glimmering. His eyes, too, seem to glow. I notice him fiddling with his wedding ring, and wonder who left him alone at the table. All this I catch in a glance so quick it never settles on him.

One photograph showing something, anything, more than business or friendship – that's all I need. A stolen kiss. A hand touching a thigh beneath the table. A certain kind of smile.

A few steps down and I'm delivered to the small elegant bar with a bull's-eye view of the neat back of Godfrey's head, and a full frontal of whoever he's waiting for. The maître d' pulls out an unclaimed stool just the right number of inches for me to glide into place.

He nods politely. I nod politely. And off he goes.

I let the pashmina slump behind me onto the back of the stool. Unused to wearing heels, I'm grateful for the rush of blood to my feet as my four-inch patent leather pumps levitate off the floor. I subversively drop one shoe long enough to rub the sole of my foot back and forth on the lower bar connecting the stool's legs. Then I slip my foot back into the shoe.

'What white wine do you have by the glass?' I ask the bartender when he levels his patient smile on me. He lists them and I interrupt: 'The Pinot Grigio, thank you.'

The wine is cool and light on my tongue. Resting my chin in the palm of one hand, elbow perched on the bar – relaxed, waiting for my phantom date – my eyes stay on Godfrey. Times like this, it helps to be a long, lanky (albeit fake) blond. A spy in the world of the haves.

Not five minutes pass before Godfrey Millerhausen, still alone, stands and straightens the knot of his tie, lifts his chin slightly, adjusts his belt. I'm about to get up and follow him out, assuming he's given up on his dinner partner, when I see him coming down the steps into the bar area. I keep my cool. Sip my wine. In one fluid motion I take a deep breath, turn, glance at him, and subtly smile.

His eyes pause on me, and he nods.

'Jeremy?' he addresses the bartender.

'Whiskey sour?'

'Thanks.'

'He knows you,' I say, casually, to Millerhausen.

He glances at me sharply, but his voice is smooth when he says, 'I come here a lot. I don't recognize *you*, though.'

'My first time.' I giggle, like some other woman might, and feel certifiably stupid.

He checks his watch – the fat face of a Rolex on a band of heavy gold links – and then slips his watch hand, which is also his wedding-ring hand, into his pocket. 'Guy I'm having dinner with took a call ten, fifteen minutes ago.'

'They say time moves more slowly when you're waiting.'

'I'd say they're right – whoever they are.' That milk-chocolate voice. I like him without liking him, because I won't like him; I'm working for his wife.

'The thing about business dinners—' he starts to say, then sees that his dinner partner has returned to their table. He tips his chin at me, oozing a last-minute charmer of a smile that strikes me as more friendly than seductive, and takes his drink back up the steps to his spot on the banquette.

The man across from him has thick steel-gray hair and jowls that wobble as he shakes his head. I hear the words, 'Sorry about that,' hover in the air before being consumed by the dull cacophony of the other diners.

I finish my wine while Godfrey pays the men's bill. Then give it a couple of minutes before following them out.

The older man is halfway tucked into a taxi when I exit. Millerhausen's limo idles nearby. He waves it on. The long black car slides into traffic. Godfrey sticks both hands in his pockets and walks to the corner, turning uptown onto Park Avenue.

I feel invisible walking half a block behind him, my red dress cloaked by the pashmina, whose neutral color helps me blend into the hazily lit

31

darkness of the wide avenue. It's not too late, and there are enough well-heeled people filtering home from their evening events to make me one of many. Though we spoke, I don't feel as if he really noticed me at the bar, not the way hungry men notice available women. He'd seen me, vaguely; chatted with me; and moved along. I feel confident that, even if he turns around now, he won't know me at all.

But he doesn't turn around. He walks slowly, preoccupied gaze lowered, six blocks, until arriving at a gray awning that covers the entire width of the sidewalk. He briefly vanishes into a diagonal shadow before coming out the other side and proceeding into the building, failing to acknowledge the doorman's welcome. According to Mary, 740 Park is one of New York's most exclusive addresses, where the Millerhausens bought their classic six ten years ago for 9 million dollars, because they needed a pied-à-terre. Mary went a little crazy with her research and told us that the co-op apartment would market today for 20 million, easy. And that their maintenance is twelve grand – a month. Too much information, but no harm letting her get it out of her system.

I check my watch: 8:47. After noting the time in my BlackBerry, I phone Mac.

'He ate with an older man, and walked home alone. He seems kind of lonely.'

'What makes you think that?'

'I talked to him. At the bar.'

'About?'

'Nothing, really.'

'Take a taxi home.'

'It's not that late. The subway's fine.'

'No, Karin. Take a taxi. It's going on Millerhausen's tab.'

I step off the curb and raise my arm in a salute to the gods of Park Avenue, flashing enough red hem and creamy leg to spark a riot. Three taxis vie for me but, as with the way of the world, the fastest one wins.

CHAPTER 3

Monday, July 2

'**M**ary, meet me for lunch and we'll talk. If you get on the subway now, you'll be here in half an hour.' Mac would know: He's been commuting between Brooklyn and Madison Avenue every day for a week, getting nowhere on the Millerhausen case.

'Why don't we just talk on the phone? It'd be quicker.'

Mac sighs. 'Is Karin back?'

'Still with Ben at the playground. I think she wants to relieve you this afternoon.'

'She can't – she talked to Millerhausen, he knows her.'

'Right.'

'What else is happening there?'

'I called the camps again. No openings.'

Already the tag team operation of working and entertaining an active five-year-old over what promises to be a long summer break is wearing on everyone's patience, especially Karin's. Back in the early spring and late winter, when all the camps

34

suitable for a kid Ben's age were filling up despite their exorbitant cost, the MacLeary-Schaeffer family had been in a financial pinch. Now, thanks to the generosity of Cathy Millerhausen's paranoia, camp is suddenly affordable. But it has proven too late, and to make matters worse, all Ben's friends are either at camp or away for the summer. Dathi is doing some babysitting for her little brother, and so is Fremont, but the teenagers sleep until almost noon and are sometimes hard to pin down.

'Thanks, Mary.'

'Hear back from Dan Stylos yet?'

'No.' Six messages, six days. All left with a secretary who seems to buy Mac's story about being an acquaintance of Cathy Millerhausen who told him to call Dan about a job interview. Either Stylos is the meanest son of bitch to grace a corporate helm, with the nerve to blow off someone referred by his own boss's wife, or he's actively avoiding Mac in particular, even though Mac didn't use his real name.

'Want me to try?' Mary offers.

'Couldn't hurt.'

'You sound bored.'

'Out of my mind.'

An hour later, Mary stands beside Mac in front of Crumbs Bake Shop on sweltering, bustling Madison Avenue. They both know that he summoned her here for no other reason than to break up his day and keep him company. They share a chocolate cupcake and sip not-so-iced-anymore coffees in plastic cups that sweat profusely in the heat.

'There he is,' Mac checks his watch as Godfrey Millerhausen strides past them, 'just on time. He'll eat at one of three places in a two-block radius, either alone or with a colleague. He'll be back within an hour and a half. We could go to a movie now and we wouldn't miss a thing.'

'A short movie.'

'Granted.'

In the week he's been standing on Madison Avenue, sitting in rush-hour traffic to Connecticut, or waiting outside 740 Park Avenue, Mac has almost finished Charles Dickens's *Bleak House*, eight hundred pages of blessed distraction. He carried the thick paperback with him on day two of the stakeout, surreptitiously dipping into it when he thought it was safe to stop looking out for a man who rarely appeared. Reading on the job breaks every protocol of surveillance, but Mac is past caring. He doesn't think he can handle the tedium much longer, an acknowledgment that worries him more than he allows himself to actively consider. He has since replaced the heavy novel with a brand-new e-reader that rides almost weightlessly in his pocket. The night he bought it, on his way home, he downloaded *Bleak House* during the cab ride back to Brooklyn. Though he already owns the paper book, he paid for his electronic copy, willfully ignoring the hacked free version vying for his attention. Even though Dickens is long dead, on principal Mac just won't steal.

Shifting between the chaotic monotony of a twenty-first-century Manhattan sidewalk and nineteenth-century Yorkshire, Mac can practically feel the cool lift of humidity off his skin. Above all else what he has learned this past week, besides the vagaries of Chancery law, is that for all Millerhausen's wealth, and all his access, the man does not break rank with his schedule. Why his wife thinks he's cheating on her is a total mystery.

Mary's tongue emerges to swipe a brown crumb off her bottom lip. For a brief moment she looks embarrassed – a rare emotion for a woman with more inner confidence than just about anyone he's ever known. Then she's right back to business.

'Found the Millerhausen daughter on Facebook. Blaine. Twenty-two years old. I think she uses her dad's famous name to open doors.'

'How so?'

'She calls herself a documentary filmmaker. Not that she's ever made a film. But it looks like she's always working on one, or intending to work on one. She officially lives in Paris but she travels a lot. Here.' From her purse, she hands him a folded-up printout of a snapshot taken from Blaine Millerhausen's Facebook page: young, halfway pretty, a short dark choppy haircut.

'Easy to be an ex-pat when you can afford to. Anything on her mother?'

'Just that her name is Liz, otherwise still looking. Didn't want to friend Blaine trying to find out. Didn't seem like a good idea.' Mary balls the cupcake bag and slam-dunks it into the garbage can on the corner.

'So what do we learn from it?' Mac asks. 'About Godfrey Millerhausen, I mean.'

'He funds his grown-up kid. Doesn't seem like a dad who turns his back. Makes me wonder why Cathy's so nervous about getting cut off.'

'Not cut off. Cut *down*. It's all about Ritchie's disabilities.'

'Yeah, but with his kind of money, he could pay for whatever the kid needs and he wouldn't even feel it. What's Cathy *really* worried about?'

'Could be she's more hurt about the marriage ending than she claims.'

'But he hasn't ended it.'

'Yet. I wouldn't mind getting Wife One's scoop on how *her* divorce went down. How, exactly, Millerhausen hid his cheating. Because he's either really good at it or this time it isn't happening. If we don't find a mistress, maybe we could at least put Cathy's mind at ease. She could be over-reacting to something else. We could get paid and move on.'

Just then, Godfrey Millerhausen strolls right by them. Mac's pulse leaps; it's the first time he didn't see the man coming from a distance. They watch his gray-suited back disappear into 501 Madison with other office workers returning from lunch.

'He seems . . .' Mary searches for the right word: 'Dull.'

'He isn't cheating on Cathy, but I might keep working on it a while, just to be sure.'

Mary eyes him as if she knows what he's up to: stretching out a healthy payday. Normally he doesn't like to extend a case past its natural life, but for all he knows, Godfrey's lover is simply out of town, and another week of surveillance could present a different story. And yes, Mac needs the income. Badly.

Mary impulsively remembers, 'Someone called the office this morning.'

'Who?' Landline calls mean either an unwanted sales pitch or a new client who's looked them up online.

'Some lady, can't remember her name, but I wrote it down back at the office.'

Mac snickers: another lonely wife in search of answers.

'I remember where she works, though: Kroll Consulting. You guys redecorating?'

'What?'

'Kroll Consulting – interior designers.'

'They're *investigators*, mostly white-collar crime. Why would they call us?'

'Sounded like a professional call.'

'Kroll's a huge outfit. There's nothing we could possibly do for them.'

'Maybe they heard about our stellar reputation. Maybe they want to absorb us – buy us out for a million bucks.'

They both laugh.

'Actually I got the vibe the woman really wants to talk to you. She made me promise you'd call back by the end of the day.'

'Why didn't you tell me all that on the phone?'

'Because when I called you, you said you wanted me in person. So here I am, boss. And now you know.'

Tuesday, July 3

A trio of uniformed receptionists guards the beige marble lobby at 600 Third Avenue, making sure no one gets past them unnoticed. Mac is wearing his good suit, cleaned and pressed since Ben's stepping up last week. His stint at Quest Security, two years ago, taught him always to attend corporate meetings in full armor even if – especially if – you don't know why you're there. Lacie Chen, the Kroll executive whose call he returned yesterday afternoon, insisted on seeing him as soon as possible while refusing to explain the reason. She did, however, promise that it would be 'worth your while.' He paces in front of an enormous abstract painting in acid green, lilac, and teal, waiting.

Finally, a trim man, young but prematurely gray, appears from the elevator banks just beyond the security turnstiles. He scans the visitors milling

40

around the lobby, his focus settling on Mac. 'Mr MacLeary?'

Mac steps forward.

The young man smiles without showing any teeth. 'I'm Ms. Chen's assistant. Sorry for the wait.'

'No problem.'

With a swipe of the assistant's identification card, the turnstile's arm swings down. The elevator takes them to the fourth floor, where Mac is deposited in a generic conference room in front of an untouched pad of lined yellow paper, a pen, and a glass of water with a single ice cube floating at the top. Beside the pad is a glossy folder announcing *Kroll: When You Need to Know*. Catchy motto, Mac thinks, feeling more like a potential client than a fellow investigator. He pushes away that uncomfortable sensation.

When he told Karin about the meeting, her interest was sparked as much as his was, primarily because it was unexplained.

'Curiosity killed the cat,' she said.

'But I'm going.'

'Of course you're going.'

They are so alike that way: tempted by anything without an answer. A key element of what led them both into police work. And partly what drew them to each other.

But still, waiting in the chilly reconstituted air, he feels a little foolish. What *is* he doing here? A flat-screen TV hanging on the wall reflects him back to himself. He turns away, wishing for a window instead.

The crisp entrance of a small, heavily pregnant woman breaks his reverie. When he rises to greet her, he is surprised first that she's wearing stiletto heels in her state, and second that the shoes manage only to elevate her to shoulder level. He makes a conscious effort not to stoop, instinctively knowing she won't like being looked down on. She puts her file folder on the conference table and shakes his hand.

'Lacie Chen.' She smiles. 'Please, have a seat.'

They face each other across one end of the long table. Despite her last name, with her styled blond hair, freckled skin, and blue-green eyes, Ms. Chen appears anything but Chinese. She wears a large diamond ring alongside a platinum wedding band on a manicured hand whose forefinger is streaked with black ink. She opens the folder and reviews something inside. Burps.

'Excuse me.' She blushes, hand held daintily to her mouth. 'My stomach's out of room, I think. My daughter keeps kicking me. I can't even take a sip of water without, well . . . you don't want to hear this.'

He smiles, thinking back to when Karin was pregnant with Ben, and refuses the memory of her other, later pregnancy that miscarried at six months' gestation. A girl. Lacie Chen is right: He doesn't really want to hear it. Leaning forward, he asks, 'Mind if we cut to the chase?'

'You want to know why I asked you here.' Her smile shrinks to a wry grin as she pulls her attention away from the paperwork inside the file.

'Like I said on the phone, I specialize in small, mostly domestic jobs.'

'Do you know who we are here at Kroll? What we do?'

'Of course. Corporate intelligence – due diligence, fraud, all that.'

'And you know that Kroll is fairly well known in the corporate intelligence community.'

'I'd say so.' In fact, they are one of the largest global enterprises dealing in all manner of white-collar crime.

'Then you can understand how delicate undercover work can be for us. Once an operative is linked to Kroll, in any way, he or she is out of the game. It's that simple.'

'You out of bodies?' Now he understands: Though rare, small outsiders are occasionally subcontracted when the giants need help with a particularly delicate assignment.

'No.'

'Then why am I here?'

'We wanted an independent American investigator with excellent skills and a low profile.'

'Low profile.' Mac grins; what a nice way of saying his career has turned to shit. If it hadn't he wouldn't be here; they both know that. But Chen either doesn't get the irony or is too polite to acknowledge it.

'We feel your unique blend of experience – your distinguished career as a police detective, your in-house knowledge of corporate security, and your skill as a private investigator – could be just what we need on a particular aspect of a case we're working on now. We think you might be the perfect person to take on a simple, one-off, undercover job for us.'

Before responding, he pauses to weed through her laudatory description of his background; sweet talk tends to trigger his suspicions. 'If it's simple, why not do it yourselves?'

'Our people are already all over this case, but for this one thing, we'll need a deeper level of discretion.'

Ah, *discretion*. So what she likes about him is that he's a total no one. His insides cringe reflexively; this is one element of his professional independence that he still hasn't adjusted to. Without an institutional affiliation, you're free but you're also alone.

'We need someone who can move with complete autonomy but knows exactly what he's doing.'

Lay it on, lady. Mac leans back in his chair and listens, drinking in the praise for whatever it's worth, trying not to express amusement. Truth is, he knows he's as good as she's saying, but hearing compliments spoken aloud makes his skin crawl. Growing up with loving but strict Catholic parents fresh off the boat from Ireland, he and his siblings were taught that pride is a sin.

'The assignment itself will take just a few hours, and our client is prepared to pay quite well.'

Greed is a sin, too. But he's a grown man in the modern world and his parents are both dead. Times are tough. And he has a growing family to support. He leans forward and asks, 'How well?'

'What would you say to ten thousand dollars?'

'I'd say it's a starting point.'

'Our client is willing to go up to twenty.'

An alarm goes off in Mac's mind: That's too much money for half a day's work. He is well aware of how much damage a man can do in hours or even minutes. How little time it takes to kill someone, for instance – or get killed. Are they looking for someone relatively invisible to make an undercover hit? Is that what this is about? If she thinks his ethics, integrity, *and* morality are for sale, she is out of her mind.

'It's been nice meeting you,' he lies, pushing back his chair and standing to leave.

Incredulity spreads across her face. 'Don't you want to know what the job is?'

'I think I know what it is.'

'Do you think—? Mr MacLeary, I promise you, we're not in that business. *Ever.*'

Now that's a lie, and he knows it. She herself pointed out that he'd once worked in corporate security. They both know that neither one of them has ever met an unbreachable boundary or an unbuyable death.

'I've got things to do.' Mac heads for the door,

but before he can reach for the handle she tries again.

'It's an AML investigation. In London. Our client will go up to thirty thousand, and you can take your wife, all expenses paid. Half the fee in advance, half upon completion of the job. It will be the easiest money you've ever made and you won't have to get your hands dirty at all. That's a promise.'

Mac turns around. 'How do you know I have a wife?'

'You're wearing a wedding ring.'

'I could have a husband, for all you know.'

'Your wife's a pretty good investigator, herself. She won't get in your way.'

Mac stops pretending to be surprised. Obviously, Lacie Chen wouldn't have so much as dialed his number before finding out just who he is, how he lives, and whom he lives with.

'Anti-money laundering is a growing field, Mr MacLeary. Ever since 2008, when the banks started having trouble, we've seen more and more of these cases.'

Mac turns his back to the door and faces her, hands in his pockets. 'I've read about some, yes. People are hiding their money, especially now.'

'*Especially* now,' she repeats. 'So you can imagine how short-staffed we might be to handle every AML investigation up to our standards, which are high.'

'Thirty grand – for what, exactly?'

'Will you please sit down?'

'I can listen standing.'

'Please.'

Knowing that sitting down will shift the conversation back her way – that now all that money will be doing the talking, and Mac's desire to move away from the precipice of debt will be doing the listening – he returns to the chair facing Lacie Chen's. He doesn't like her, nor does he particularly trust her, but pride and greed are powerful bedfellows, and he long ago recognized the weakness of his humanity.

'That's a ridiculous amount of money,' he points out.

'I'm aware of that. But to our client, it isn't as much as you'd think.'

'Who's the client?'

'First you'll need to accept the job.'

'Like I said, I'm listening.'

'It's basic, really. A senior executive who has worked closely with us on investigations is himself under investigation now.'

'And he doesn't know it.'

'Not yet. But we worry that he's too familiar with our operations for us to get away with sending one of our own.'

The way she says it, so blithely: *get away with*. But that's always the litmus test in any investigation. If you can't get away with it, the game is over before it's called.

'What exactly can I do to help you?'

'That will be explained to you, in more detail, when you meet the client.'

'So I can't know the job. And I can't know the client.'

Chen shrugs. 'Sorry, but that's how they want it.'

A hiss of frustration escapes Mac. 'I don't like this.'

'But you'll do it.'

'When do you need it done?'

'Yesterday would be great.'

'Look, I don't know . . . I'm finishing up another case right now.' But as soon as he takes his righteous position, he chafes at the prospect of standing on Madison Avenue for more endless days, another week, perhaps two weeks. Of the early July heat turning to late July muggy suffocation. Of sinking again into that existential hell of waiting for something that may never happen.

'Well, if your other job is urgent, then that's your decision, of course.'

As she calls his bluff, a final thought forces itself into his consciousness: One more chapter and he'll be done reading *Bleak House*. The thought of finishing the book that's kept him sane all week, that has allowed him to escape to the cool green hills of England, fills him with despair. He could go to London and bring Karin along, *all expenses paid*. Earn a ridiculous sum of money for a day of work. Maybe even sidetrack briefly to the English countryside and soak up some of that chilly fog Dickens conjured so vividly for Mac as he sweated it out during the dog days of a New York City summer. The stupidity of passing that up weighs too heavily to ignore.

'We're probably about finished with it, actually. I'll speak with my client, see if we can wrap it up quickly, and get back to you.'

They smile at each other nakedly now, suddenly partners in an undefined venture Mac is too tired, too curious, and too broke to resist. Reaching to shake her hand, he smiles and asks, 'So when are you due?'

'August twenty-ninth. I hope she holds off a little, though, because there's a lot to get done first.'

'Sorry to tell you, but that feeling will never go away.'

Her laugh is airy, a release from the business part of their meeting. 'I'm up for a promotion and I'd feel more secure if it comes through first, you know? And my husband's still wrapping up his semester.'

'Where does he teach?'

'Rochester Institute of Technology – at the Dubai campus.'

'That's what I call a commute.'

'We never see each other. And now, well, we've had this home exchange planned for months, my husband was supposed to meet me in Italy next week, but yesterday my doctor said I can't fly.'

'The third trimester's a tricky time to travel.'

'I was stupid to plan it in the first place. I had

to promise the couple I'd help find a last-minute replacement to trade houses, because they already bought their tickets. What a hassle.'

'Sounds like it.'

'Everything about a long-distance marriage is nothing *but* a hassle. Once I get this promotion, my husband can come home, take his time looking for a teaching job here. That's the goal.'

'What's his subject?'

'Chemical engineering. We met in grad school, but I decided it wasn't for me. I've been at Kroll five years and I love it here, I—' Another burp stops her. Another blush reminds them both that there's only so much they need to share.

Mac stands and when she struggles to get out of her chair, he stops her. 'Don't get up. Good luck with everything. I'll be in touch.'

Just out of the elevator, halfway through the lobby, his BlackBerry vibrates with an incoming e-mail from Lacie Chen. He pictures her tapping out a message as she wobbles on her spike heels back to her office, and wonders what could be so urgent.

The subject line reads, *Have you ever been to Italy?*

'Great to meet you, Mac,' her message reads, 'and I look forward to hearing back that you've decided to take the job. Meanwhile, no sooner did you leave just now, than I had a brainstorm. If you go to London, why not consider tagging on a personal vacation to Sardinia? Because the home exchange is already arranged, there'd be very little for you to do. The house comes with a car. It's got three bedrooms. You could take your family. Here's the link if you decide to consider it.'

Trade homes with strangers? Even if he could spare the time, he'd never risk it, and neither would Karin. He feels a clip of outrage that Lacie Chen would cross a personal boundary with someone she just met; but then again, she came right out and said she was desperate.

On impulse, he opens the link on his phone and sees a couple in front of a sun-dappled white stucco house with red-flowering trellises. The man is tall and thin, with a charcoal pencil tucked behind one ear. The woman is short and plump, olive skinned, smiling. The caption beneath their photo reads, *Hello, we are Mario and Maria Rossi. Mario is a graphic novelist. Maria is a homemaker. We hope you will enjoy our beautiful house in Sardinia!* The Rossis look happy. Mac has to admit, the house is tempting. He logs off.

London, maybe, with Karin, *if* he takes the Kroll job.

CHAPTER 4

Wednesday, July 4

T he kids, the TV, the late-afternoon summer sunshine taunting from outside the windows. The tedious buzzing of the air conditioner. Why do these days feel (to me) as if they weigh a hundred pounds? Especially today – the Fourth of July – when, without plans, the city feels especially empty.

Dathi, Ben, and Fremont occupy the couch with stalwart quietude, their attention fixed on *The Invisibles*, a movie they've all seen before, but it's the only one they can agree on given their range of ages and interests. Dathi, on the left, the straps of her sleeveless shirt flopping over her sharply angled shoulders. Ben, in the middle, propped on a pillow for added height. Fremont, on the right, his dandelion-round Afro blocking half my view of the screen, waiting for Mary, his mother, to intercept him for their evening plans. Between them, atop Ben's small lap, sits a shared bowl of homemade popcorn into which their various-sized hands mindlessly dip. You can just barely hear their subtle crunching below the din of animation and dubbed voices of vaguely recognizable movie stars.

Standing in the kitchen doorway, my eyes stop on the back of Ben's bright red neck. I can't understand how I could have forgotten to put sunblock on him today.

'More!' he suddenly shouts.

Fremont lifts the empty popcorn bowl above Ben's head to show me.

Jumping up, Dathi says, 'I'll make it – but pause the movie.'

'I'll do it.' I take the bowl and return to the kitchen. Pour vegetable oil and organic kernels together into the bottom of a casserole dish I've used countless times to heat up anything I can cook from a jar. Slam shut the microwave – the crisp smash of the door feels irrationally satisfying – and stand there watching the carousel turn in the weak interior light. Gradually the kernels start to pop, and as the explosions accelerate so does my frustration.

How did I come to be the full-time caretaker of children whose relentless energy irritates me unless they're plugged into a television or computer or game? And then, when they are plugged in and quiet, I feel guilty that they're wasting their brains.

Why can't I relax and enjoy the small pleasures of domestic life?

Why am I here, stuck at home, instead of trading stakeout shifts with Mac? Working. Breaking up the days and the nights. Sharing the pain. Suffering the edgy discomfort that makes me feel alive. I realize that, if Mac had taken the day off like everyone else, my frustration wouldn't feel so acute.

I jam my fists into the front pockets of my jeans. Wait. Watch. A growing mountain of popcorn raises the lid off the dish as the seconds count down on the timer.

True, Mac complains about the tedium of the Millerhausen case, but I can't help regretting the moment I broke my cover by looking into Godfrey Millerhausen's eyes at the Daniel bar. What was I thinking, allowing myself to speak to the man? Did I really think I could divine something essential about his character? Find out if he is the kind of man who would betray his second wife? Did I think he would confess to me? Hit on me? Stick his hand up my skirt or his tongue down my ear? Reveal himself as a super-sleaze, just so we could deliver the goods to a suspicious wife?

It was stupid of me, and as a result Mac and Mary have had to share the surveillance between them, with Mac doing most of the legwork since Mary's talents lie in the background and not in the field. An ace researcher, Mary being pulled out of the office is counterproductive.

Two more months before school starts again. Whose bright idea was it to call it vacation? Vacation for who? Even the kids seem bored out of their minds.

The microwave times-out but the popping continues. I wait half a minute before reaching in with potholders to remove the hot bowl. Steam blasts into my face when I lift off the top and a scorching piece of popcorn hurls itself at my right eye. I cry out and cover my face with both hands, dropping the glass cover on the floor. It cracks apart, spewing shards of glass and greasy stuck-on, still-simmering bits of popcorn. As the panicked ringing in my ears subsides, I feel sobered by the aftermath of – nothing. Dull threads of cartoon voices drift in from the living room.

Ben runs in, saying, 'Mommy! Is the popcorn ready?'

Only now do I realize that I'm crying. I lift Ben up so he won't cut his bare feet on the broken glass and attempt a smile that probably looks more ghoulish than comforting.

'What's wrong, Mommy?'

'I broke something.'

'We'll fix it. Don't be sad.'

'I'm not sad, honey. I just got scared for a minute.'

He kisses and hugs me, just as I do when he's upset. I carry him to the threshold of the kitchen and set him down beyond the minefield of slivered glass. 'Wait here.' Refilling the bowl, I hand it to him. 'Careful not to spill any, but if you do—'

'I'll pick it right up.'

We smile at each other and off he goes. I watch

my little son carry the large bowl back to the couch, intrepid in his determination not to drop a morsel. I'm so proud of him. And then I remember.

Ben's sunburned skin.

I *know* why I was so preoccupied earlier today: the prospect of London, and all that money, which we sorely need. I've been stuck between school and work and family for so long now. Not finishing my degree. Not rebuilding my career. Not quite figuring out how to be a mother and do everything, or anything, else.

Like Mac, I don't care for the mysterious nature of the Kroll job: not knowing exactly what it will be until we get there. But thirty thousand bucks? Half up front? With an all-expenses-paid European trip for both of us thrown into the bargain? He lost more sleep than I did last night, mulling that over.

Digging my phone out of my pocket, I speed-dial my husband up on Park Avenue, where he's waiting it out to see if Godfrey Millerhausen will head out to Connecticut to spend the holiday with his family, or hide out in the city alone (or with company). Giving it another day, just to make sure he doesn't shortchange Cathy Millerhausen. Mac's a good man. A good detective. Too good, sometimes, I think with a twist of annoyance.

'Hey,' he answers.

'If he comes out, if he goes to Connecticut, don't follow.'

56

Mac's silence is threaded with a dissonance of honking horns, muddled voices, the whine of a siren.

'Nothing's going to happen,' I say, 'whether he comes out or not. This is a waste of time. You should be home with us today.'

Finally, Mac says, 'You're probably right.'

'Did you call Cathy?'

'I'm seriously thinking about it.'

'Don't think. Just do it.'

'Here he comes.' Mac stops talking and I imagine him retreating into a shadow where Millerhausen won't notice him. After a moment, Mac says, 'And there he goes, into his limo.'

'Don't get in a cab. Don't follow. We'll grill something for dinner and go see the fireworks later.'

'What time do they start?'

'Nine o'clock on the East River.'

'Sounds good.'

'Let's go to London.'

Another pause, and then, 'I'll call Cathy Millerhausen right now and give her our results. Hopefully she'll stop worrying. Then I'll e-mail Lacie Chen at Kroll and get the ball rolling.'

Before I press *end*, exhilaration replaces the dreariness of monotony. Today *is* Independence Day. I get the broom and start sweeping the floor, thinking, *London*. And then I feel a sharp edge of irony as I recall the title of a novel Mac was recently reading, a title I kept noticing with a sense of unease, though at the time I couldn't figure out why: *Anywhere But Here*.

Floor swept clean, mess on the counter wiped away, I stand in the kitchen doorway and distractedly watch the kids watching TV. Ben and Dathi, sitting with their heads tilted together. Suddenly the two older children laugh at something I missed on the screen. Fremont glances over Ben's head at Dathi and smiles mischievously. She rolls her eyes.

The kids.

London.

How long can Mac and I reasonably leave the kids to travel so far away?

Am I going to have to stay behind, after all?

What if my mother, or even Mary, agrees to move into the house while we're gone?

What will it take for all of us to get what we need from the vista of summer stretched out before us?

I do the calculations in my mind.

One week feels reasonable, but is that really enough for all the trouble of traveling overseas? You wouldn't even be over jet lag after a week. Two weeks would be a nice break. Three, even better.

As if reading my mind, Ben swivels around and catches my eye, grabs my heart. 'Hi, Mommy!' He turns back to the movie. But the deed is done. I won't be able leave my little boy for long enough to enjoy the trip, so what's the point?

58

I call Mac.

'You just caught me. I'm about to head into the subway.'

'I can't go to London with you.'

His sigh is the whoosh of a dying balloon. 'I thought you were excited about it.'

'I am. I was. But the kids—'

'We'll bring them,' with a snap in his tone, as if he's just decided something.

'To London? While you work?'

'I'll be working less than a day, but that's not what I mean. We'll take a real vacation.'

'It kind of defeats the purpose if we spend half the money you'll earn from the job. Our credit-card bill alone—'

'No. Just listen . . . better yet, I'm going to forward something to you right now. It's a leap of faith but we'll discuss it when I get home. I'm sorry I didn't share this with you before, but I thought it was an insane idea. Now I'm not so sure.'

'What idea?'

'Read the e-mail and you'll understand.'

Fifteen minutes later, having perused the home-exchange link sent to Mac by Lacie Chen, and having skipped through a range of doubt, I have started to see, really see, the beauty of the idea. I even have the gumption to write to her and ask if she's found someone to take her end of the trade (hoping she carries a smartphone and is a compulsive checker of e-mails, like half the New Yorkers

I've met). She answers immediately: She has not. Then I contact the Rossis in Sardinia, and the e-mails fly. By the time Mary walks in to meet up with Fremont, I'm nearly jumping out of my skin with plans. Getting up from my laptop, I stand in the kitchen doorway and wait for her attention.

'Come on, or we'll be late,' she tells her son, by way of hello. They have plans to go to see a free concert in Battery Park.

'But Mom.' He speaks without looking at her, eyes glued to the screen. 'It won't be over for like half an hour.'

'How many times have you seen that movie, sonny boy? But hey, if you'd rather watch it again instead of seeing the Fleet Foxes, it's fine with me.' She skewers her fingers into his Afro and sets the whole mass wiggling.

'Yo – not the hair.'

'Mary, come here just a minute,' I say.

She follows me into the kitchen. 'What burned?'

'Popcorn. It didn't burn exactly but I broke part of the dish . . . never mind. Have you talked to Mac recently?'

'Yep. So he's taking the Kroll mystery case – wow.'

'Did he mention how Cathy Millerhausen reacted?'

'She isn't convinced her husband's life is as boring as it seems. Mac promised to get back on the case when he's home, if she wants him to.'

'Sounds like a good compromise.'

'That guy's not cheating on his wife.' Mary picks up a baby carrot from a bowl on the table and pops the whole thing into her mouth. Chewing, she says, 'Mac asked me to book your flights tomorrow, but don't worry, I'll run all the options by you first. You must be psyched for London.'

'What do you think about Italy?'

'I've always wanted to go there. You guys thinking about a side trip? I can stay with the kids longer if you—'

'What if you took a trip this summer, too, and it wasn't counted as vacation time?'

Her eyebrows shoot up. 'Keep talking.'

'Italy – all of us.'

I turn my laptop screen to face her, and she peruses the Sardinian house's details as I fill her in on the possibilities, her whole face curling upward into a smile. We beam at each other like opposing headlights hurtling toward a meeting point.

'All the flights to Europe connect in Heathrow,' she says. 'You guys could peel off in London. I could take the kids straight to Italy.'

'Good idea.'

'I have a lot of miles saved up on my credit card, Karin, and so do you. We can probably buy flights for me and the kids with miles. The extended vacation would cost you close to nothing. You can bank nearly all of Mac's thirty-thousand-dollar fee. This is *genius*.'

'Exactly my thinking. There's just one thing we

61

have to do before we make it official: I want references on the Rossis.'

'I'm on it. As soon as I get home later tonight,
I'll start.'

'I'll do some checking, too.'

'What about Mac?'

'He's had this link in his phone since yesterday.
He finally told me about it. That means he's in.'

Saturday, July 7

Mac notices the letters and catalogs piled on the
foyer floor with a sharp stab of irritation. He had
already checked bills and paperwork off his list;
he hadn't thought of Saturday mail, which means
there are now more loose ends to take care of
before he can finish packing for their morning
flight to Heathrow.

Noise drifts upstairs from the bedrooms below,
where Karin and the kids are getting ready. The
tension in her tone unnerves him. He can't help
wondering if it's really worth the extreme hassle
of merging a family vacation with his business trip,
but having agreed to the plan – in fact, having
instigated it with his own suggestion – there is no
turning back. As Karin and Mary researched the
Rossis' background and references, all excellent,
lingering doubts were swept aside as the plans
evolved. And Lacie Chen was so relieved to be off
the hook for her home exchange, she upped his
fee another five grand.

He picks up the prodigious pile of mail and carries it to the kitchen where he tosses half of it into recycling, separates out the bills so everything can be paid before they leave, and stands there looking at the final envelope. This one stumps him: an overnight letter addressed to Mario Rossi with a return address from Barclays Bank in London.

Why would someone who lives in Italy receive mail in New York from a bank in London? Has the global economy spiraled even more tightly around everyone than he's realized?

And why would anyone receive mail on vacation?

It also catches Mac's attention because, as Lacie Chen finally divulged after he formally accepted the Kroll job, his meeting in London is with someone from Barclays who is to give him further instructions. All Chen told Mac was, 'You'll meet with Ian Gelson at Barclays headquarters. Mr Gelson will tell you the rest. Get the goods on the guy in question, be discreet, and report back – quietly. Shouldn't take more than a few hours.' On Wednesday he'll meet with Ian Gelson and take it from there.

Mac sets the letter atop the stapled list of home instructions Karin typed up for the Rossis. Barclays is a huge, global financial institution with a strong retail operation. Rossi probably lost his credit card or something right before his trip to New York. It happened to Mac once and he remembers how accommodating his own bank was in making sure a replacement card was waiting for him when he arrived at his destination. That has to be it. Because Lacie Chen had already used her Kroll contacts to vet the Rossis, and because Mario sounded so nice on the phone when they spoke last night, Mac reassures himself that any anxiety he feels is about the huge effort of sudden travel, nothing else.

He makes a pile of mail to go over to the office later, where he'll pay the bills, prepare an invoice for Cathy Millerhausen, and give her one last call to make sure she's comfortable with how they left things.

'The plan is this,' he told her on the phone when he broke the news that he was suspending her case, 'We'll be gone three weeks, and if you need anything, you can reach me by e-mail. If it's urgent, I'll get someone on it right away.' Mac is confident that Godfrey Millerhausen isn't cheating on his wife. But on the off chance that he's wrong, he'll ask his good friend Billy Staples, a detective with the Eighty-fourth Precinct, to do a little moonlighting for MacLeary Investigations and find out.

Thinking about the Millerhausen case, Mac remembers why he took the Kroll job – the other reason, besides the money. Boredom, restlessness, the craving for a challenge. For something new. He thinks of Dickens, and *Bleak House*, and the way he had so viscerally imagined, *felt*, the cool, damp air of Yorkshire. How, while he knows now that their hastily put together itinerary won't take them to Yorkshire, it will take them north of that, to Cumbria, for a couple of days alone together before the London meeting. He feels a spark of exhilaration at the thought that tomorrow at this time they'll be on their way across the Atlantic Ocean.

PART II

CHAPTER 5

A single road splits into two at an intersection that crests a bucolic slope, one slicing with smooth ease toward the nearest village, the other with jagged difficulty. Standing at the serene junction of Kirkstone Pass in Cumbria, England, Mac doesn't doubt which road they'll take when the choice is made: It will be the steep, curvy one with inclines and dips, twists, and turns so severe that it was named the 'Struggle' centuries ago by some long-dead resident or traveler-through. Karin stands beside him in the chilly summer air, gazing into the valley where the roads tumble apart like twins determined to express their differences: to the left, a smooth ribbon of pavement unfurls into the distance; and to the right, the treacherous Struggle with its neurotic bends and the clearly worded danger sign posted at its beginning above the ironically tempting promise that this route will, nonetheless, get you fastest to town.

Mac would prefer the road to the left, the easy

69

one. But lately Karin has been edgy . . . herself, but more so. How can a person be so deeply rooted and yet so inconsistent? But just as he thinks it, he recognizes that this is partly why he fell out of love with his first wife and into love with Karin years before she realized it. With Karin, he never knew quite what to expect. There was something exciting, ineluctable, about her that he found himself pulled in the direction of, as if compelled by gravity.

'You decide,' Mac says, guessing how her instincts will swing.

'Hmm.' She assesses the Struggle, and then the easy road, and then him. Her pupils widen when their eyes meet and the hint of a smile appears. Since they've been in England without the kids, he has noticed the way she incrementally relaxes just looking at him, and it makes him happy. 'Let me try them one more time,' she says, 'then we'll see.'

She makes her third call of the afternoon to the house in Sardinia, where Mary went ahead with the children after they parted ways at Heathrow yesterday. Mary called to say they'd landed safely in Cagliari, but that was the last they heard from her. Since then, cellular networks have completely failed them, despite having purchased all kinds of expensive overseas data packages to keep the family connected.

Mac watches Karin's fingers turn bloodless-white the harder she presses the ringing BlackBerry to her ear. She squints at the rolling green hills misted with cool humidity, then snorts frustration and ends the unanswered call with a jab of her fingertip. He knows which road she'll choose like he knows the inside of his own mind.

'That way.' She points to the Struggle with the battered red edge of her phone.

Both roads cross the same loping, gentle hills in various shades of green – vivid here, faded there, like a beloved old sweater. The shroud of fog that obfuscates the horizon makes it impossible to see very far. Mac wishes he could at least see the edge of the village so he'd have a sense of what they were in for. If it was worth the trip. This morning their host at the B and B mentioned that there was a good place for tea in the village. Karin has made it clear that she finds the idea of tea as an event both ludicrous and tempting, and has decided to make a sport of it while they're here. Karin on vacation is something Mac has only rarely experienced, so he's taking it as it comes. And he wants her to be happy; sometimes he thinks he wants that more than he wants anything else.

'Fine,' he says, wanting the smooth road, but choosing his battles.

'Let me drive.' I hold out my hand for the keys to the rental car. Mac looks at me without even making a move for his pocket. Just looks at me a second before speaking.

71

'Really?'

I can't help the smile that breaks over my face, the rush of anxiety that sometimes masquerades as joy or excitement. 'I *really* want to drive,' I tell him.

'When was the last time you drove on the left side of the road?'

'Let me think.' Never. Which he knows. I haven't traveled abroad as much as he has, so haven't had the opportunity.

'Karin, it's tricky.'

'There's no one around. The roads are nearly deserted. It's the perfect place for me to practice.'

'Not on *that* road, you don't.' He gives me one of his hard, probing looks, reading me. 'You can drive if you take the easy road.'

'What are you, my father?' I lunge for his pants and stick my hand in his front left pocket, where he always stashes keys. (Wallet in the front right.) A small blush darkens his face. He doesn't fight me when I pull the keys out of his pocket. I toss them in the air and they land in my palm with a jangle, along with the plastic Eurocar tag the agent forced onto the ring before handing them over, and grin at my dear husband. I turn and walk to the car – a black two-door Peugeot. He follows me, sighing, a familiar breathy sound I recognize as patience, love, forbearance, desire – a unique emotional reduction special to our marriage. I hear him chuckle behind me when I almost walk to the left side of the car before correcting myself and veering to the driver's side on the right.

'This is what I'm talking about,' he says. 'Are you sure you want to drive?'

'Just get in, sweetheart.' I wink at him like I'm a lecherous old man and he's my girlie. He ignores me. He fiddles with his iPod while I crank the engine and pull slowly off the gravel shoulder onto the road. A Raconteurs' song beats out of the speakers into the car: *Steady, As She Goes* . . .

'Too bad that place is closed.' Mac glances at the Kirkstone Pass Inn, the sprawling old house whose sign reads *Open* but whose doors and windows are all shuttered. 'Would have been a nice spot for *tea*.'

The way he says it: poking fun at me for my rant this morning about all the tea they serve in this country when maybe what you really want is a good strong espresso. How apparently here 'tea' doesn't necessarily mean a cup of tea but a whole elaborate spread involving scones, clotted cream, jam, and maybe sandwiches. How we are going to find some really good tea so we can know what all the fuss is about.

'Yup,' I say, 'tea,' and gun it so fast to the right, straight into the Struggle, that by the time Mac's expression shows betrayal it's too late to turn back.

'Jesus fucking Christ, Karin!'

I pat his knee and glance at him. 'But you love me.'

'Two hands on the wheel. Eyes on the road.'

73

I take the slopes, the curves, the surprises as they come, holding a steady speed. Not too fast, because it's tricky driving on the wrong side of the road, navigating from what inevitably feels like the passenger seat. But not too slow, either, because we're the only car around. Though the shifts in direction are jagged, sudden, the loamy edges of the road promise a soft enough landing if we crash. Which we won't. I don't sense danger here. If I did, I wouldn't take the risk; I do realize we're parents. I just need to burn off some of this agitation, make myself forget all the unanswered calls to Mary and the kids, because the more I think about it the more it bothers me. Really upsets me. It's one thing for our calls not to reach them. But why haven't they tried to reach us? That's what I can't understand. It's been twenty-seven hours since we parted ways at Heathrow.

I press the accelerator as we near a blind turn.

'Slow down!' Mac thrusts an arm in front of me, and I jam on the brakes as the dormant end of a long snake of traffic curls into view.

A gray-haired woman in the passenger seat of the car up ahead, the glittering-clean white Audi they very nearly hit, turns sharply and glares at Mac as if he is the one driving too fast. He in turn looks at Karin – who smiles and waves.

'Cup of tea?' Karin says to the windshield. Mac is sure the woman can't hear it, but nonetheless her expression hardens before she turns away. He

74

switches off the music and allows silence to hang heavily between them. Finally Karin rests her forehead on the top of the steering wheel, and mutters, 'Ugh. Sorry.'

'Yup.'

The zigzag line of cars and vans doesn't move; this traffic jam has the settled feel of a parking lot. Up ahead people chat in their cars. One couple sits on the roadside eating sandwiches, their doors hanging open to the fresh air. A man wearing a brown cable-knit sweater and a checkered cap is walking in from the distance, stopping to lean into each car. Apparently he's seen the trouble ahead and is reporting it to his fellow traffic jammers. Behind them another car screeches to a stop.

'Be right back.' In one quick move Karin unbuckles her seat belt, opens her door and gets out.

'Wait.' Why does she feel she needs to go to the man, when he'll get to them eventually?

But she acts as if she doesn't hear him and keeps going. Mac watches his tall, thin wife stride forward, her gray-blond hair (a fading dye job) pulled into a messy ponytail that flops over the collar of her black fleece hoodie. Her tight jeans make her legs look even longer. The laces of her left sneaker have come undone.

Just as he's hoping she won't pause at the old woman's window to say something snarky, she does worse than that: She stops and approaches the car. The man with the information, up ahead, is three cars away, speaking to the next driver in line. Mac watches the gray-haired woman turn at the sound of Karin's voice. Karin leans into the window. The woman responds. This seems to go on several minutes but is probably over in seconds. Mac's pulse gallops but then, when the woman smiles, slows down. The two women share a quick laugh. Karin pulls out of the window. She stands there and listens as the man stops to speak with the woman, then returns to the car to report in to Mac.

'He says a caravan is stuck up ahead. It can't make a turn. The road's been blocked for over half an hour.'

'Caravan?'

'That's what I thought – circus caravan or some kind of convoy. But no, here a caravan's an RV.'

'Some idiot drove an RV along the Struggle?'

'Apparently so.'

The man skips their car when Mac waves him on and delivers the news to the last car in line, just behind them. It turns around and drives in the opposite direction.

'Not a good idea,' Mac says. 'But . . . he said the road's been like this for half an hour?'

'And counting.' Karin puts the car into reverse, backs up and turns around. 'This might be our last chance, we better take it. I'm pretty sure I saw a turnoff a ways back.'

Mac hadn't noticed any other roads off this one; he was focused on staying alive. Now they're racing wrong-way on this treacherous road and he's tempted to close his eyes and take what comes but won't allow himself to. He forces himself to keep looking ahead, as if the vigilance of his personal attention can keep them safe despite the impulses of the inexperienced driver at the wheel. His wife. His eyes swerve between the road and her profile – bony and sharp, with the usually faded blue of her eyes darker, nearly denim, shadowed by the dense fog blocking out half the sunlight. She focuses on the road with such intensity it's as if her eyes are drinking in the asphalt, its gloomy color leeching into hers with an ominousness that frightens Mac.

They hear the motor before seeing its source, up ahead, coming toward them: a truck. Or what they'd call a lorry here.

'Shit,' Karin mutters.

There's the turnoff – right there! The words are on the tip of Mac's tongue but he doesn't have time to say them before Karin makes a sharp right off the Struggle onto a dirt road that funnels them into a cornfield. The lorry swooshes past them. Moments later, an enormous crash boomerangs into the sky.

She keeps driving, but slowly now, her expression dense with shock. He suspects she regrets the whole strand of decisions that led to this moment: how she allowed her frustration to lead her recklessly – to lead both of them – into a near collision. How many times over the years has she wept in his arms, chastising herself for doing something 'stupid'?

The car bumps along the ragged narrow road, towering cornstalks on either side of them. The fog clears and suddenly the sky above the cornfield is blue.

'Weird,' Karin says.

'Do you think this is a one-way road?'

'If it is, I hope we're going the right way.'

Mac picks up his iPod and with trembling fingers chooses something mellow, a classical violin concerto, as their little car meanders along a road that might be more of a farming path, taking them in an unknown direction. They don't speak at all because at this point there is really nothing to say. Nothing matters but finishing this outing – completing it, somehow.

Finally, they emerge from the cornfield into a juncture where the dirt road meets two paved roads. Directly across from them is an inn, freshly painted white clapboards with a glossy black sign announcing *The Drunken Duck Inn and Restaurant*. Without asking, Karin pulls into the parking lot around back.

'Screw tea,' she says.

Sitting at a table on the inn's covered porch, they order locally brewed beer, two huge steins. The sun has burned off most of the chill. They slough off their sweaters and order a plate of salty crackers and goat cheese to have with their second beers.

A siren breaks the thick country quiet and then an ambulance races past.

Is it her – the gray-haired woman in the car in front of us? Or her husband? Or both of them – strapped to gurneys in the back of the ambulance?

'Oh I've *had* it sitting in this bloody traffic half the day,' she said to me when I stuck my head in her window to apologize. 'Sorry for what?' she said. 'For getting stuck in this, too? It's not *your* fault, dear.' So her dirty look hadn't been directed at me, after all; it was directed at the traffic jam, the caravan up ahead no one could see; the pure frustration of being trapped on a one-way country road. We chatted and laughed and it was over. 'I'm thinking we might turn around and get out of here,' I said. She glanced at the man in the driver's seat, who stared glumly ahead with his hands perched on the wheel – her husband, clearly, as they wore matching gold wedding rings. 'We'll probably just stay right here,' she said a little sulkily; but it had nothing to do with me, I knew that.

'I should have asked her name.'

'It might not be her,' Mac tries to reassure me, but his guess is only as good as mine. And then, before the wail of the siren fades, the shiny white Audi noses out of the cornfield, pauses to check for traffic, turns left and drives away. As they pass I glimpse the woman turn to her husband, see him nod but otherwise not respond.

79

'Who was in front of them in the line?' I ask Mac.
'Didn't notice.'
'Neither did I.'

He takes a long drink of his beer, leaving a residual streak of foam across his upper lip.

'*God* that was a close one. I'm so sorry, Mac.'

He licks his lip. Puts out his hand. 'The keys.'

'You're not driving now, either. We're both tipsy.'

'There's a vacancy sign. If we have to, we'll rent a room here for the night.'

'We have a room in Penrith.'

'Doesn't matter.'

'We're not made of money.'

'I don't care.'

'Mary won't know where to find us.'

'Mary's in Italy. She has our cell numbers. She can find us.'

'I hope you're right.'

'Food here looks pretty good.' His face is blotted by shadow. You can see from the deep slant of the sun over the fields across the road that afternoon is fading.

After a delicious dinner at a small round table in a corner of the inn's restaurant, after cups of good strong 'American coffee' (the offering of which on the otherwise high-end menu feels uncanny, considering our day) we are ready for the hour's drive north.

Night deepens as they make their way back from Ambleside to Penrith, the mostly unlit roads illuminated sporadically by quiet villages before plunging them back into velvet darkness. When the mist grows thick on the windshield Mac switches on the wipers long enough to clear his vision, then turns them off, and the deep quiet returns. Karin, beside him, is perhaps also lost in that strange undertow of inspiration and collapse and pleasure and disorientation that gather into the unique sensation that is jet lag. Every now and then she pulls her BlackBerry out of her purse and speed-dials Mary, listens and waits, hangs up. Every time she does this, something cringes inside Mac, though he isn't sure what the uncomfortable sensation means. He's not sure if he's worried about Mary and the kids, or disturbed by how upset Karin has allowed the pause in their communication to make her. This is supposed to be Mac and Karin's alone time, their two days of (romantic) togetherness before rejoining the family.

They arrive at Penrith's Market Square, where a handful of restaurants enliven the otherwise sleepy town, and make their way to Portland Place. Their B and B is down toward the end of the street, last in a row of quaint brick guesthouses that have helped make this hub town a good launching point for tourists visiting Cumbria and possibly continuing north to Scotland.

Mac glances at Karin as she unfolds herself from the car, stands on the sidewalk, lifts a hand to stifle a yawn – and feels himself quicken from the inside out until all at once his skin is tingling.

81

Later, their bodies jumbled together in their big bed with cast-off sheets and kicked-away blankets, in the beige-on-beige room that is all softness and glow, she picks up her phone from the bedside table and it starts again.

The calling.

The not answering.

His mind moves outward to the sharp edges of their day, and then wanders backward to the day before, the day before that, and the week before that.

Sunday: the frenetic rush to get to JFK on time.

Yesterday: landing at Heathrow, the rowdy good-byes as Mary hustled the three children to their connection to Milan.

Tomorrow, London.

Thursday, Sardinia.

He smiles to himself in the dark, thinking how quickly and effectively the tedium of the Millerhausen case was thrust thousands of miles into his past. He looks at Karin. Rubs his hand along her arm to see if the damp heat from a quarter hour ago still lingers on her skin. She feels cool now, dry.

'Where are they?' she whispers.

Wednesday, July 11

In the morning, in the B and B's calico-and-lace dining room, they are served a full English breakfast of fried eggs, sausage, mushrooms, beans, tomatoes, tea, and strong hot coffee that Karin gulps almost as fast as their host, John, can pour it. There is an English couple across the smallish room, and no one talks above an occasional whisper, except for John, who sparks pleasantries each time he enters to deliver or remove a dish. When he vanishes to the kitchen, where his wife is busy cooking, the lull returns. Mac doesn't mind the quiet, he only wishes he had a newspaper to read.

When Karin's cell phone goes off in her pocket, everyone jumps. Her groggy eyes light when she looks at the screen. 'Mary,' she whispers, and hurries upstairs to their room to take the call in privacy.

'We're in Carrefour!' I pull the phone away from my ear; I can hear that it's noisy behind Mary but she doesn't need to shout.

'Where?'

'Carrefour – one of those huge hypermarkets. Kind of like Walmart, but Italian style, if you can imagine that.'

'I can't.' When I think of Sardinia I see images from guidebooks: palm trees and dishes of earthy pasta and Italian grannies in aprons. Not big-box shopping. 'What are you doing there?'

'*Long* long story, but in a nutshell, I'm looking for a locksmith. My Italian sucks as you know but they have a key-copying station and one of the guys working there speaks some English and he got me all set up. A locksmith's coming by the house tomorrow. Guy named Dante. Can you believe that – Dante the locksmith!'

'Slow down, Mary. I'm totally confused. Why do you need a locksmith?'

'Sorry. My head is spinning a little bit. So much is going on and the kids are keeping me busy – but don't worry, Karin, everything's fine. The house is great, the beaches are fabulous, the food is wonderful.'

'Did you get locked out of the house or the car? What happened?'

'The shed in the yard, where the fuse box is located – haven't been able to find the key. It was supposed to be in a basket on top of the fridge, but it wasn't there. A fuse blew practically as soon as we got to the house, so nothing works. That's why you haven't been able to reach me: All our cell phones died and we can't charge them, plus, even if we could, the Wi-Fi's out. But I'm working on it. Dante will get us into the shed tomorrow and I'll take care of the fuse.'

'You called the Rossis?'

'I tried e-mailing them before my phone totally died, but all my e-mails are probably just going out now that I finally have a connection. Everything got stuck in my phone. I mean now I've got my phone plugged in here at Carrefour, they've got these charging stations you can rent, but now I've got Dante coming tomorrow so I don't need to bother the Rossis. I'll e-mail them again to tell them I worked it out. Anyway, I just wanted to get in touch with you as soon as I could to let you know everything's okay, not to worry about anything. The kids are fine, the house is great, it's beautiful here, and everyone's really happy. Hold it – Ben's right here, he wants to talk to you.'

'Mommy.' The sound of his voice! I can feel my blood flowing warm again.

'Ben, sweetie, I miss you so much. Is Italy nice?'

'I miss you too Mommy and I'm having so much fun and we have pizza every night. Today we were at the beach and Fremont and me we dug a castle and Dathi wouldn't swim with us, she was reading.'

'Fremont and *I*.'

'No, me and him, you weren't there.'

'Never mind, it doesn't matter. Daddy and I are coming to Italy tomorrow so I'll be able to read you a book and tuck you in tomorrow night, okay? I love you so much.'

'Can we read *Moonshot*?'

'Did we pack that one?'

'Mary read it to me last night. Liftoff! *Vroooom!*'

'Then we can and we will.'

Suddenly he's gone, and Dathi is on the line.

'Karin, hello!'

'Dathi, honey, how's it going?'

'It's very hot here. Mary said if you agree, I might buy a bikini. They have them here at Carrefour, not expensive at all.'

'Sure, tell her to get you one and I'll pay her back.'

'Thank you. How is London?'

'We won't be there until this afternoon, but Cumbria's been really nice. Except I miss you.'

Her laugh: a steady ringing of bells. 'Don't miss me, Karin. Just have a nice time with Mac. If you know what I mean.' At thirteen, after a year and a half in America and by now a veteran jaded seventh-grade graduate, Dathi's antenna is tuned to an operatic channel of human relations. Man + woman = romantic. Someday she'll grow up and see the nuances.

'I've been trying to call you guys but haven't been able to get through to anyone. Mary told me about the lost key.'

'Fremont tried to pick the lock with a hanger, but it didn't work, which I think is a good thing – teenage boys shouldn't know how to break in. Especially . . .' She doesn't finish. Another American convention she's picked up is that you're not supposed to openly point out that black teenage boys are an especially endangered species, perfect targets for trigger-happy cops looking to bust someone. Or half-black boys, in Fremont's case, as his sperm donor was black because, according to Mary, she and her then-partner checked all the boxes for paternal race and took what came.

'You guys enjoying yourselves?' I ask Dathi.

'Yes, it's quite nice here. Hot all the time. The

86

beaches are lovely – we try a new one every day. And we have pizza every night – I don't think Mary can read the menu.'

'I hear the pizza's good there.'

'Quite good. We found a restaurant called Su Marigu, not far from the house. If we go at eight o'clock, when it opens, we're the only ones there. No one goes out to eat until ten o'clock here, but by then, Ben is sleeping across the chairs and we have to carry him to the car.'

'I can't wait to eat there with everyone. I miss you.'

'You already said that, Karin.' But her tone is kind. 'Shall I put Mary back on?' Unlike many girls her age, Dathi would never openly admit to being bored by a conversation with me. I almost wish she would; it might erase that final breach of awkwardness that sometimes reminds me we aren't blood.

'Sure, honey. See you tomorrow.'

'I should go help Dathi find a bikini,' Mary says, returning to the phone. 'Everything takes ten times longer in Italian. We'll see you soon.'

'If all goes well in London later today.'

'Why wouldn't it? Mac's appointment should be a piece of cake.'

'Should be. Good luck getting out of that store in one piece. Good luck with Dante. See you in paradise tomorrow.'

Mary laughs sharply and so do I at the divine comedy of getting snagged in a shopping hell in the middle of a world-renowned paradise. Obviously nothing stays pure forever, and whatever we've both read online and in the guidebooks about the exquisite beauty of Sardinia will be tempered by modern reality. Already has been, for Mary. My plan is to shut out the ugly parts, unplug from reality, and vacate.

Mac appears in our room. 'All well?' He hands me a fresh mug of coffee.

'A fuse blew. They got locked out of the shed where the fuse box is kept. Mary's got a locksmith coming tomorrow. They sound happy. I can't wait to get there.'

Mac smiles patiently. 'Let's get the most out of London, first. What do you want to do with yourself while I'm at the meeting?'

Good question. 'I'm not sitting in the hotel, that's for sure.'

'Hold on a sec,' Mary tells Dathi. 'Keep an eye on Ben while I send an e-mail, then we'll find you a bikini.'

'Can I have one of those cookies please?' Ben, at her hip, gazes up with his soft eyes.

'Sure, sweetie.' Digging into her purse, she opens the bag of biscotti she brought in case the errand took a long time. 'You want one, too, Dathi?'

Dathi accepts one of the long almond cookies. 'Thanks.'

'Five minutes and I'll be with you,' Mary promises.

Dathi leads Ben to a rack of Italian video games for younger children. Fremont's hair fluffs up from the other side of the rack. Incomprehensible chatter echoes through the giant store, giving Mary an intensified version of the overwhelmed feeling she always suffers at megastores back home. Luckily they'll be out of here fast and back to the house for lunch, then a new beach to try. There are so many beaches here, all different, each one spectacular in its own way.

Standing at the charging kiosk, she taps out an e-mail to the Rossis on her laptop.

Dear Maria and Mario,

Good news: We've got a locksmith coming tomorrow, so we'll be able to turn on the electricity soon.

I hope you don't mind, but when I was searching for the shed key again this morning, I opened a lot of drawers and cabinets and some stuff fell out. Putting it all back, I found a photo of someone I know. Well, I don't know her, but I recognize her. It's really an amazing coincidence.

Before finishing the e-mail, Mary retrieves the photo from her purse and takes another close look, making sure she didn't imagine it.

Four people sit on a verandah overlooking a crystalline emerald sea. The sun is vividly bright.

Sitting beside Mario Rossi, Maria shadows her eyes with a hand. One of the other two women, whose blond streaks look painted on in the intense light, has a smile bracketed by deep lines in a leathery face, and a large blue gem dipping into over-tanned cleavage. The other woman is young, with short dark hair and a diamond toe ring that catches a luminous spark from the sun: *She* is the person Mary is sure she's seen before, conjuring a disturbing connection. Certain aspects of the women's faces are too similar to ignore: the sad slopes of their eyes; the matching thumbprint clefts on their chins. Mary hopes the Rossis can put her doubts to rest and convince her that this really is a coincidence. But she doubts it. Before she rings any bells, though, before she even mentions this to Mac or Karin and wrecks their few days alone, Mary wants to be sure.

Her name is Blaine Millerhausen, and long story short, I'm wondering if the other woman in the picture is her mother, Liz. If I'm right, would you mind letting me know where to find her? If I'm wrong, just forget it, and have a great time in New York.

Ciao,
Mary

Mary's going to see what kind of answer she gets, and then she'll take it from there. Mac won't be

90

thrilled to be back on the Millerhausen case before his vacation has really started, especially not with this new, strange twist. But she knows how he and Karin think: They'll both be as curious as Mary is about how it came to pass that the strangers whose house they're staying in, on a far-flung island in the Mediterranean Sea, happen to know Godfrey Millerhausen's daughter and possibly his ex-wife. In a world where six degrees of separation is the norm, on rare occasions you might find yourself separated by a single degree. But Mary knows it's a leap of faith to think that Mac jettisoned a Millerhausen job for a too-convenient home exchange *with a Millerhausen friend*. What are the odds?

CHAPTER 6

Mary joins the kids in the front yard, where they have carried out lunch to eat on the house's only table large enough for everyone. The white plastic surface is hidden by plates, glasses, utensils, trays of prosciutto, cheese, bread, olives, grapes, butter cookies, and a pitcher of what was iced tea in the kitchen when she made it about five minutes ago but now looks more like tepid tea. How did all those ice cubes melt so fast? The kids are lined up on a bench under a wedge of shade, a good yard from the table where their food appears to be dissolving in the blazing sun. They hold their plates on their knees, looking miserable, eating as fast as they can. Mary pulls a chair into a shadow but even now, half protected from the sun, the heat isn't easy to take.

'Wow, it's brutal out here at this time of day,' she says. Yesterday for lunch they had a picnic on the beach, where the heat was tolerable, even enjoyable. 'Why don't we bring this back into the kitchen and eat there?'

Ben shakes his head. Dathi makes a face. Only

Fremont is willing to bark a direct complaint at his mother: 'Mom, that's an idiotic idea.'

'Free, *honestly*.'

But he has a point. If you had to make one complaint about this beautiful white stucco house in the sleepy Mediterranean village of Capitana, near Cagliari – the medieval city at the heart of southern Sardinia – it would be the kitchen: small, airless, with a tiny table suitable for two people, maybe three, to sit down to a meal. Definitely not commodious enough for four or, soon, six people.

More troublesome, as she learned within a few hours of their arrival on Monday, is that you can't run the washing machine, tucked into a corner of the kitchen, and the hot water heater, stowed under the sink, and make toast at the same time without blowing a fuse. Not a huge deal until night falls and thrusts you into total darkness, by which time you've realized that you can't see *or* cook *or* charge your phones and laptop *or* entertain three bored American kids by turning on the TV. By which point you fully understand what a modern creature you really are. When Mary found the stash of candles so easily that first night, right on a kitchen shelf where the Rossis' instructions said they'd be, she understood why they highlighted the part about where to locate the circuit breakers in the garden shed out front. If only they had been as conscientious about making sure the shed key was where they'd said it would be, in a dish on top of the fridge. 'To hell with it,' she said to herself in the kitchen that night. 'The laundry can wait. The dishes can wait. We're on vacation.' After all, they didn't come all this way to Sardinia to do household chores.

Aside from the small kitchen and gimpy electricity, the rest of the house is perfect: airy, earthy, and cozy, with lots of books and cats. For the life of her, Mary can't recall if anyone asked the Rossis how many cats they had, so she was a little surprised to find seven – two cats and five kittens – waiting for them at the house. But no matter. Feeding a bunch of cats is not a problem. And they use the big cactus garden out front as their litter box, so that's easy, too.

As in paradise, it never seems to rain; heat and blue skies are constant. Mary has already learned to enjoy the peaceful morning routine of an early breakfast at the outside table with Ben, watching the kittens frolic among the cactuses, while the teenagers sleep. In the cool early mornings, Mary has studied the front yard's flowering arbor, and learned that there are such things as short palm trees with bulbous trunks that look like pineapples, having counted three of them in the yard. The novelty of that alone – the pineapple palms in a cactus yard – is enough to make her happy to have come. For her, travel is all about learning and stretching and growing, seeing new things, and thinking new thoughts sparked by those new things, being open and available to experiences and feelings you simply wouldn't encounter at home. She feels perfectly satisfied, even joyful, here at the Rossis' house, where they've got everything you need despite a few inconveniences. And it's good for the kids to do without sometimes; it will make them stronger and better people in the long run.

But still, the brutality of the midday heat at the outdoor table feels like a little too much suffering.

'How about we picnic on the living-room floor?' Mary suggests. '*When in Rome.*'

'We're not in Rome,' Fremont says with a note of haughty sarcasm that momentarily silences Mary.

She looks at the handsome man-boy who is her sixteen-year-old son, who can't seem to decide if she's Mommy or Mom, if she's an idiot or an angel, if he still needs her or if he's through with her. His Afro is pulled off his face with a rolled up red bandana, creating a buoyant puffball atop his head. Shirtless in the sizzling heat, his mocha skin is speckled with droplets of perspiration that create an illusion that he's glowing. His skinny torso has lately developed sinewy muscles that remind her that her boy is in fact quickly becoming a man, that his body is probably changing faster than his mind, and regardless of how he might think of himself on any given day, her job is still to present him with boundaries. He recently shot up to nearly six feet tall, he's looking buff, and he's sitting next to Dathi, suddenly a teenager, looking pretty good herself in white hot pants and her new orange bikini top.

Mary says, 'Free, go put on a shirt.'

'I'm not exactly free, am I?' he snarks.

'*Fremont*, go put on a shirt, *please*. And take some of the lunch stuff with you on your way.'

He picks up the no-longer-iced-tea pitcher and a pair of empty glasses, and heads inside. Dathi follows with the platter of sweating cheeses, promptly appearing at the living-room window overlooking the table to say, 'I'll have to stay in here to guard the food or the kittens will jump all over it.'

'Right,' Mary says. 'We can handle the rest, right Benster?'

Ben carries a plate in his little hands, carefully, like it's a stick of dynamite. Mary balances as much as she can and follows.

Sitting on a blanket on the living-room floor, they eat their lunch in the cool shade of indoors, shooing away a relentless barrage of enthusiastic kittens that finally huddle in a furry black-and-tabby ball on the couch and fall asleep for their afternoon nap.

Standing back, Mary points her phone's camera at the scene: the scantily clad children lounging on the floor surrounding a casual feast like a trio of Caesars; the pile of sleeping kittens behind them; and the big bright square of window, suspended in the unlit room, with shutters flung open to a tableau of brilliantly lit palm fronds, twists of cactus, and dripping bougainvillea beneath a lush blue sky.

We found the right place, Mary writes to Karin in an e-mail that zaps to nowhere with the photo attached. *You're going to love it here*. Mary knows her messages won't send until tomorrow, when Dante the locksmith comes, or later today if they happen to pass through a Wi-Fi zone on their way to the beach. Stranger things have been known to happen. A few hours since her first slew of messages and photos shot out into the ether from Carrefour, she has already compiled a new batch, mostly for Karin, who sounded so worried on the phone. Mary is well aware that one of the functions she serves in Karin's life is to assure her that everything is running smoothly; she realized from the beginning that they hired her as much for her optimism as her competence. She decides that if she doesn't happen into a hotspot this afternoon, she'll find one somewhere, both so Karin can get her new batch of e-mails and pictures, and so Mary can see what kind of answer she gets from the Rossis. A stone of anxiety has weighed in her stomach ever since she saw that photo of them with Blaine Millerhausen and, possibly, the ex-wife.

She forces herself back to the moment with a cheerful command to the children: 'Okay, everyone, let's clear up these dishes and get ready for the beach. Meet you out front.'

Dathi helps Ben get slathered with sunblock while Fremont shakes sand out of yesterday's towels and shoves them into the big beach bag. Mary sits on the front steps with a map open across her lap, learning the route to Mari Pintau beach as she traces it with her fingertip. There seems to be an endless choice of beaches here, each one better than the next. They have decided to try a new one every day. They've also explored Cagliari, the medieval city, where Fremont convinced Ben that they were in the village near Hogwarts. The plan has been that, when Mac and Karin get here, they'll branch out and do some real sightseeing. Meanwhile, at night, when Ben's asleep and Dathi and Fremont are sprawled on the couch chatting or cross-legged on the floor playing cards by candlelight, Mary has been tucked in her bed with her *Lonely Planet* and a flashlight, researching and creating itineraries. She realizes quickly, and regretfully, that even in the unlikely event that the Millerhausen connection turns out to be innocuous, and they can continue innocently with their vacation as planned, three weeks will allow them to see just a small part of this nine-thousand-square-mile island.

She hears Dathi and Ben fussing in the bathroom. 'Free, would you please go see what's taking them so long?' Mary asks.

'Ben doesn't like sunscreen.'

'Go tell him a joke or something, okay? Distract him so Dathi can finish.'

Just as Fremont goes back inside the house, the doorbell rings. Because the yard is enclosed by a tall fence with a locked gate, outside of which the Rossis' car is parked, you can't know who's at the door without consulting the intercom. Mary goes inside and tries, in her scant Italian, '*Pronto!*'

A man rattles something off that she doesn't begin to understand. Then it hits her: Dante the locksmith has come a day early. Unless she misunderstood and he was always supposed to come today. Not knowing how to tell him she'll be right out, she hurries across the yard and opens the front gate.

A wiry young man with a black goatee and bright blue eyes is waiting, a battered toolbox at his feet. Behind him, a white SUV with a company logo featuring a key. With a tilt of his head, he says something that sounds pretty but makes no sense to her.

'I'm sorry,' she says, 'I don't speak any Italian. You must be Dante. I'm Mary. Come on, I'll show you the problem.' She steps away from the gate, into the yard, points to the locked shed and gestures for him to follow. Grabbing the shed's handle, she pulls and pulls, pretends to use a key that doesn't exist, and dolefully shakes her head, saying, 'No key. Key lost. No key. Change lock.'

Dante has a charming smile: a flash of white that competes with the sunshine. She puts him at about twenty-five. A likable young man with a wedding band and a steady job. She stands back and watches him find the right tool and *voila*: The door groans open, coughing stale air into the fresh afternoon.

'You make it seem so simple!'

He smiles at her, getting the gist if not the meaning. Pausing to wipe a sheen of sweat off his forehead with the back of his hand, he gets to work installing a new lock. When he's done, he stands, and gives her a brand-new key.

'We won't lose it this time,' she promises.

He shrugs, smiles, nods.

'*Grazie*,' she says, hoping to reassure him she's grateful, '*Grazie*,' because with so few words at her disposal she tends to overuse the ones she knows.

'*Di niente*.' You're welcome, she assumes, because he follows up by handing her a bill. She gets her purse from the house and methodically counts out lire until Dante says, '*Perfetto*.' He crosses the yard and pulls shut the gate behind him.

Mary goes into the shed, crowded with boxes and old furniture. Squeezing through a narrow path toward the fuse box on the far wall, she opens the metal box and flips the rogue circuit breaker back into position.

'All fixed!' Mary calls to the kids. 'Let's see if everything's working now.'

The three big globes hanging from the living room ceiling glow brightly. The downstairs bedroom lights flick on. From the kitchen, Mary hears the long-delayed ding of the toaster, as if anyone still wants toast. It occurs to her she can put in a load of laundry before they head out to the beach; the dirty clothes have piled up in the last two days and, given that there is no dryer and everything has to be hung on the line, getting through it is going to be a project. This time, she makes sure the under-sink hot-water heater is switched off before starting the washing machine. She's learning.

After plugging in the laptop charger – they charged their phones at Carrefour earlier – she calls out, 'Everyone ready to go?'

'Mom!' Fremont shouts from outside. 'We're waiting for *you*.'

Dathi and Fremont are standing by the front gate, watching Ben tickle the tiny black kitten he has named Midnight. Mary pulls the door shut behind her, not bothering to lock it since they're out in the middle of nowhere and the heavy gate out front makes this place a fortress.

The big kids disappear onto the dirt road, while Mary collects Ben's hand and drags him away from Midnight. 'Come on sweetie-pumpkin, let's go have fun at the beach.'

'But pumpkins are for Halloween and this is summer.'

'You got me there.'

A piercing sound stops Mary in her tracks. A sudden gasp from Dathi.

'What the *fuck*.' Fremont's voice is tighter, more afraid, than Mary has ever heard it.

'Wait here, Benny, okay?'

She steps into the road, alarm spiraling through her at the sight of a strange man standing beside Dante's SUV. A dusty maroon van, its side door gaping, blocks the road. The man is tall, in jeans, sneakers, and a crisp blue shirt, with a tattoo of a snake curling up his neck, its forked tongue licking the side of his jaw. A shiver of dread runs through Mary. She looks at Fremont and Dathi, huddled together, too afraid to move or speak. In a moment of disbelief, she watches the man raise a silencer-outfitted gun at the frightened teenagers. And then Mary notices Dante's motionless legs flopping over the lip of the open trunk. Blood dribbles down the white rear of the SUV, curving onto the silver bumper.

'*Sali sul furgone*,' the man shouts at Fremont and Dathi.

Only when she feels Ben leaning against her leg does she realize he's left the relative safety of the enclosed yard. She reaches down and his small hand creeps into hers.

'*Sali sul furgone!*' The man gestures sharply at the van's open door.

Mary's heart jumps. 'We don't know what you're saying.' But she does: He wants them to get into the van. *Never*, she thinks. Before she can warn Dathi and Fremont not to comply, they hurry across the dusty road and duck into the van, half disappearing into shadows.

'You shouldn't have done that,' she tells them, too late.

Now the gun pivots to her and Ben, and the man repeats: '*Sali sul furgone. Sali sul furgone.*'

'What do you want?'

'*Smettere di parlare! Sali sul furgone.*'

'We don't have much money, but you can have it all.'

Sweat drips into his eyes, and he blinks.

'Show us what you want us to do.' She raises her hand as if to pantomime showing.

'*Sali sul furgone!*' he shouts, rushing at her.

Mary drops Ben's hand and steps in front of him, protecting him, frantically calling, 'Stop! Stop *now*.'

But the man keeps coming and suddenly Ben darts away.

'Ben, run *that* way.' Mary points down the dirt road toward the intersection where someone might stop to question the small child, alone and crying, and hopefully bring help.

Instead, Ben scrambles into the van and presses himself between Fremont and Dathi. They wrap their arms around his tiny shoulders, try to comfort him.

The man, now an arm's length from Mary, holds the gun on her, repeating, '*Sali sul furgone!*' The cold circle of metal burning into her temple.

'*Sbrigati, nel furgone!*' Yanking Mary's elbow, he drags her forward. In the strangest way, knowing that whatever happens she can't let herself be separated from the children, she feels queasy with something akin to relief.

CHAPTER 7

'Mr MacLeary?' A young woman in a stylish black suit extends a cool hand, and smiles, but doesn't introduce herself. 'Come with me, will you?'

She leads them alongside artfully placed potted trees twice as tall as he is. Mac feels dwarfed in the enormous lobby; and as he walks, it strikes him that its most notable feature is the temerity to have been built in the first place. The impossibly large space would threaten existential crisis if not for grounding markers suggesting human scale: the trees, the variegated coloring of the marble floor, the hollow columns of turquoise netting hanging from the distant ceiling in a sly nod to gravity.

Bankers, he thinks, following the woman across the modernist savanna in the direction of the elevator banks, *don't mind letting their egos show.*

He is reminded of how abstract finance is, when you come right down to it. How creative and open to interpretation it is on the executive level, yet how it can punch a regular working guy in the face if the smallest calculation goes wrong. He thinks of the Occupy movement that seeded on Wall Street and blossomed around the world. His neck starches stiff with resentment that he pushes away: He is here for a job; no one forced him to work for these people. Still, as he steps into the elevator with his escort and her equally well turned out colleagues, he can't help wondering if that bald discrepancy – between the rich and the poor, the 1 percent and the 99 – that has thrust America into a battle for its capitalist soul and risen to torment the European Union in its own complicated ways, has anything to do with why he was summoned here. Are the powers that be finally earnest about trying to identify corruption in the higher realms of their business, soul-searching their way toward making connections, accepting responsibility?

He stifles the urge to laugh at that ridiculous idea. And then it hits him: *intelligence*. It operates differently from the kind of police work and private investigation Mac has mostly built his career on, the on-the-ground investigations in which eyeballs and the continuity of *being there* matter. He got a glimpse of it during his brief stint at Quest, when he worked in corporate security. When the kinds of information you have to collect are harder to grasp, you find unusual ways to get to it.

'This way.' The young woman's voice is crisp, but not unfriendly, as she leads him out of the elevator onto the thirtieth floor. He follows her along a wide hall decorated with museum-quality art. Forcing his jaw not to drop, he waits while she opens a glass door floating in a glass wall, and directs him inside.

'Mr Gelson will be right with you, if you don't mind waiting a moment.'

'Not at all.'

As soon as she's gone, he realizes he can't recall her face, and feels uneasy. It's as if the blank modernism of the spaces here defy the stickiness of detail that allow you to build memory. An interesting, almost inhuman approach to a work-place, he thinks. Efficient. Transparent, literally. Antiseptic.

The atmosphere inside the glass cube of a conference room feels weightless; any hint of the sweltering heat he carried in with him from outside has evaporated in the perfectly calibrated air-conditioning. Turning to face the glass wall, he looks down over the urban vista of Canary Wharf, roads curving through a landscape of squat old buildings studded with gleaming towers, and to the right, an elbow of gray-green canals that bends into the thick artery of the Thames. On either side of the massive river London is a caldron of activity that, from this height and distance, looks surreal. He wonders where Karin is right now. She said she planned to walk from their hotel in the direction of the Globe Theatre with the intention of taking a tour, unless something else caught her eye; that he should call her when his meeting is over and they'll convene somewhere near the

London Bridge. It's their last night alone together and he's looking forward to it.

'Well.' A man's voice startles him. He stands and faces the door, which hangs open on soundless invisible hinges. '*MacLeary* – Irish, of course.'

'My parents were. Name still is.' Mac shakes Ian Gelson's hand: soft, damp, smaller than you'd expect from a man who is relatively tall. His neatly combed hair is either greased or greasy, a fringe of it feathering his neck in the back and popping out over his ears. Otherwise, in a trim gray suit with a white pocket square and a red tie, he's immaculate, pretty much what you'd expect of a high-end banker. Mac pushes that thought away: expectations, assumptions, are his enemy.

They sit across from each other at one end of the black stone table, light sparking off chips of granite reacting to the bright sun. Mac folds his hands atop the table, his wedding ring sending up a beam that turns into a gold puddle on the ceiling. Ian Gelson ignores it but Mac's eyes can't help following the shaft of light.

'Some place,' Mac says. 'Kind of outer spacey.'

'Occasionally visitors find it a bit intimidating here, but one adapts.'

'I guess one would.'

'We appreciate your traveling so far to meet with us.'

'What can I do for you?'

Leaning back, crossing his legs at the knee and swinging one of his polished leather shoes, Gelson says, 'We understand you used to work in corporate security.'

'For a couple of years, yes.'

'And you've worked on AML cases?'

'Not me, specifically, but my team. Yes.' When the global economy boomed, anti-money laundering investigations boomed along with it. And now that the global economy is in bust mode, money-laundering schemes that went undetected before are starting to show their fracture lines.

'We have an in-house concern regarding one of our wealth clients.'

Mac thinks it's a funny way to put it: not wealthy, but wealth, indicating a whole other category of money. He knows that all the big banks cater to major wealth with separate departments and individual care. But he himself has rarely come near those people, their money, or their lives. These aren't the people who fly first class; they're the ones who own their own planes. Who own mansions in Greenwich and co-ops on Park Avenue, like the Millerhausens. An elite club of billionaires. Mac thinks of Cathy Millerhausen, and how the longer they spoke, the more he glimpsed her humanity. Fifteen minutes – is that all it takes for a person to peek out from behind a mask?

'Who's the client?'

'The client's identity isn't important at the moment. It's his liaison, here at the bank, we're interested in right now. A Mr Simon McLaughlin. He's a relatively junior member of our wealth group but he's become a key member of this client's team.'

'You think he's taking kickbacks?'

'Possibly.'

'Why?'

'Most notably because he appears to spend beyond his means. And lately there have been news reports that the client may have ties to organized crime. He also has close ties to government. We must be careful.'

'Of course.'

'We want to avoid any suggestion whatsoever of an investigation, which is why we contracted Kroll here in London. They had the idea to reach out to their office in New York. They thought it best to add yet another layer by subcontracting you. An American. With no ties to the UK.'

'But I'm Irish.' Mac smiles.

'Irish-American.' Gelson returns the smile. 'And so tonight, when you take your lovely wife out to dinner at the Ivy, and you meet Simon McLaughlin at the bar, you'll have ancestry to discuss.'

Mac almost laughs, but doesn't. 'Sounds easy, as long as we're wearing name tags.'

'Simon meets his mistress at the Ivy every Wednesday night. They have a few drinks, spend an hour or two at a nearby hotel, and then he returns home.'

'To his wife and kids.' Mac's stomach drops. Has he been brought all the way to London for another unfaithful-husband gig?

'To his wife. He has no children. But we don't care about his private life. Why would we? The Puritans left for America a long time ago.' Gelson's lips gather into a pinched, ironic smile.

'Well, that's always something we could discuss, if the Irish thing doesn't do it.'

'You'll find a way to spark a conversation, I'm sure.'

'And then what?'

'Feel him out.'

'On?'

'Try to steer it to business. Get a sense of his ethics. See if he drops any names.'

'And then?'

'Call me before you get on the plane to Italy tomorrow. Report back.'

'How do you know I'm going to Italy?'

'Kroll mentioned it, I believe. They mentioned you were bringing your family over for holiday. A brilliant idea, by the way.'

'Thanks. What time am I having dinner?'

'Eight o'clock. The reservation is under your given name, Seamus MacLeary.'

'My given name is Seamus Cian Benjamin MacLeary.'

Gelson offers his first authentic smile of the meeting, letting actual humor loosen his careful expression. The crack in his composure is all it takes for Mac's suppressed laugh to finally escape; he knows the two men aren't laughing about the same thing, but it doesn't matter. Gelson is

111

laughing at the Irish and the verbosity of their clan-centric names, and the Americans and their uptight sexual mores. Mac is laughing at the strangeness of finally knowing the double-barreled reason he was hired for this job: his *low profile* and his name. They want an invisible Irish American to cozy up to an Irish corporate scoundrel, see what happens, and then slip away into the night. Bond over drinks, *the way the Irish do*. Well, if they'd wanted a *drunken* Irish American they should have called Mac's brother Danny, whose struggles between sobriety and the bottle have become family legend. Mac kicks away that bitter digressive thought and reminds himself how much they're paying him for this assignment: a lot of seriously easy money. A lot of money for *him*. Looking through the glass wall, into another glass-enclosed conference room, through the side of the glass building into a blue sky streaked violet with the shadows of late afternoon, he reminds himself that what they're paying him is nothing to them, in the scheme of things; a windfall to him, it still doesn't qualify as wealth.

'Fine.' Mac stands. 'Eight o'clock at the Ivy. And I'll call you tomorrow.'

'And then you're done, Mr MacLeary. You can wash your hands of London and enjoy your holiday.'

On my way to take a tour of the Globe, the rebuilt version of Shakespeare's original open-air

112

theater-in-the-round that burned down in the seventeenth century, my BlackBerry comes alive with a batch of photos from Mary. I step out of sidewalk traffic into a doorway, sit on a step and open the attachments one by one. This is the second set of photos I've received today, the first having arrived soon after our conversation, when Mary had finally powered up her phone at Carrefour. Those first glimpses of the family's Sardinian vacation had shaken off any remnants of concern:

Ben covered in sand head to foot, grinning up at the camera phone.

Fremont in a yellow bathing suit, bent over, digging a moat with cupped hands around a drip-sand castle. Ben standing to the side holding a plastic bucket.

Dathi on her stomach under a shade tree, reading.

All three children splashing in the ocean together, shimmering wet in a sun-bleached lens.

Now, a new set of more recent photos warms my heart:

All three kids lounging on a floor in front of a couch, having an indoor picnic that looks so good it makes me hungry. My eyes light on Ben, sweet little son of mine, in his green sea-turtle bathing suit and blue T-shirt, reaching for something on Dathi's plate. Dathi, slapping his hand away but laughing, in an orange bikini top that must be the one she just bought at Carrefour. Fremont, in shorts and a T-shirt, leans back against the couch, long legs stretched beside the picnic, his bony fingers caught mid-strum on an air guitar. A furry pile of sleeping kittens rests on the couch behind them. Everyone looks relaxed and comfortable in the Rossi house in Capitana.

Tomorrow, we join them. I can hardly wait.

After a sandwich at the nearest tourist spot stills my hunger, I resume my walk toward the Globe. Mac recommended it, obviously wishing he could join me but satisfied with the thought that at least I would see the theater created by one of his literary heroes.

But then I spot something even better, and I can't resist: a round blue plaque on a stone wall announcing *The Clink, 1151–1780, Most notorious medieval prison*. I stand there and gape, digesting the idea of a prison nearly a thousand years old. Walking through the streets of London, a city as bustling and cosmopolitan as New York, what has surprised me most are the constant reminders of the comparative antiquity of this city's history. I've never thought much about history, aside from a long-simmering interest in jails and graveyards, but today it has me captivated. Here, the tangled roots of storied pasts reach farther and deeper than I had ever actively imagined. Somehow, America popped out of this place, borrowing a language but little else.

The oldest American prison I know of is Newgate, built less than three hundred years ago in late-eighteenth-century Manhattan, around the time the Clink was closed. Newgate was where you got *sent up the river* to, from the courthouse on Wall Street. I'd heard about Newgate and then one day, waiting on the Christopher Street subway platform in Manhattan, I happened to notice the only thing left in the city memorializing the old prison: a small mosaic showing a bulky-looking building on an open plain that now comprises the skewed streets of Greenwich Village. I went home that day and Googled it, learning that Newgate closed in 1828, when, according to legend, it was no longer feasible to march the prisoners through Washington Square Park and string them up on Hangman's Elm. Imagine that. As urban development crawled northward, so did the city's prisoners who were shipped upstate to the newer Sing Sing.

I want to see the Globe Theatre because I want to report back to Mac that I've been there, and I want to pick the kids up some fun loot. But I *really* want to step foot inside the Clink. I get a little shiver thinking about the long, dark shadows of crime and punishment from a time when barbers performed surgery on people whose illnesses were believed to have sprung from sin.

And so into the Clink I go, smiling at suddenly knowing where that slang comes from. The clammy darkness feels authentic until I read another plaque informing me that the museum was built on the original site of the prison . . . and a swell of

115

disappointment nearly turns me around. But then I spot the vicious foot-crushing iron boot, and I'm back on board. I wander among unimaginably brutal torture devices, finally coming to a chopping block with a well-worn neck rest and a giant axe chained to its base.

In this museum you're allowed to touch and so I run my hand along the dip of smooth wood and then, when no one's looking, lean in to cradle my neck in the wooden sling and close my eyes. A choking sensation creeps up my throat. I breathe, imagining the smells in thousand-year-old air – blood, urine, sweat, contagion – and just when I feel a gagging reflex forming I hear the rattle of the chain. Blinking open my eyes, I see a twiggy old man with a sinister smile raising the huge axe above my head as if to decapitate me. Rising off the block, I laugh a little nervously.

He chuckles, 'Had you there, missy, now didn't I?' The swagger of his Cockney accent tells me that he's as much a tourist as I am, albeit in his own country.

His name is Robin and next we chain each other into the interrogation chair, which is more fun than it looks. We take each other's pictures with our respective phones. As soon as I'm in the gift shop, I send the picture to Mary with a note: *They got me!*

I wander around by myself for another fifteen minutes, reading about some of the prisoners who lived and died here: the harlots and debtors, scoundrels and blasphemists, who had the bad luck to be born in a brutal time. After a stop at the gift shop, I'm back on the street with a bag full of miniature shackles, rubber rats and plastic skulls, and a strong feeling of gratitude to live in the modern world.

Since I still haven't heard anything from Mac, I wander over to the Globe, which is nearby. The next tour isn't for another thirty minutes, and then it will last a full hour, so I default to browsing the gift shop, where I add Shakespearean-themed knickknacks to my collection of souvenirs to bring with me to Italy tomorrow, and also buy a postcard and stamp to send my mother old-fashioned greetings from abroad.

Back on the sidewalk with a take-out coffee, I manage to carve some space among the thicket of fellow tourists occupying a low wall overlooking the Thames like a row of pigeons. Balancing the coffee between my knees, I scrawl a note to Mom: *Having lots of fun in England but miss the kids. I hear Sardinia is gorgeous – will arrive tomorrow and keep you posted. Hope all is well in Brooklyn! Xoxoxo Karin*

Finally my BlackBerry buzzes and vibrates with a text from Mac letting me know he's out of his meeting. A quick phone call, and we agree to meet at our hotel room to change for a dinner that's been prearranged for us.

'I thought we were going to do something romantic tonight.' Like champagne and room service in our hotel room.

'I'll explain when I see you,' Mac says in a voice infused with a familiar mix of determination and disappointment that tells me it will be a working dinner, after all.

'I think that's him, over there, at the bar.' Sitting across from Karin at the small table where they've been put to wait for their dinner reservation, Mac lifts his chin to indicate the man he suspects is Simon McLaughlin, based on the corporate photograph Ian Gelson showed him: close-cut ginger hair, sprinkled with silver, above a clean-shaven face; medium height and build; wearing a gray suit. He keeps checking his watch in between sips of whiskey, his eyes scanning the room, clearly eager for the arrival of his mistress.

'Maybe this is a good time to buy ourselves a couple of drinks,' Karin says. 'Get him now, before his girlfriend arrives.'

'Good idea.'

Mac stands, straightens his suit jacket, and walks past a half-wall of harlequin glass to approach the bar. All the green leather seats are taken, and since he has to squeeze in to catch the bartender's attention, he does it between McLaughlin and another man with his back turned to them.

'Excuse me,' Mac says.

'Not at all.' McLaughlin shifts back, allowing a view to the busy bartender, and then goes further and summons the man himself. 'Greg, you've got a customer, a Yank from the sound of it.' By the timbre of his voice, it's obvious McLaughlin's already had a few. His thick brogue reminds Mac of his parents' accents, sending an aural memory, and a sadness, through him.

'What'll it be?'

'Scotch on the rocks, and a wine – Pinot Grigio, if you have it.'

'We do.'

Turning to McLaughlin, Mac smiles and says, 'Actually, I'm not much of a Yankee – my family hasn't been there all that long. Seamus MacLeary, first-generation American.' He puts out a hand, which McLaughlin heartily shakes.

'One of our own, are you?'

'My parents grew up in Dublin.' The man whose back Mac avoided slides off his stool, opening the field. Mac takes the seat. 'In some ways they missed it, but they weren't sorry they left. Where are you from?'

'Won't she want her wine?' McLaughlin asks.

Mac glances at the empty table where Karin had been waiting. 'Looks like my wife's gone to the loo.'

'Ahh, right. Well then. Fellow Dubliner, since you asked. And you're from?'

'New York City.'

'The Rotten Apple.'

'The Big Apple,' Mac corrects him.

'Yes, I know.' McLaughlin's laugh reveals neat rows of cosmetically improved teeth. 'I suppose you could say I spent a bad week in New York last year and came away disillusioned.'

119

'What happened?'

'The usual – got mugged in the subway.'

'Sorry to hear that. Where were you?'

'Somewhere or other in East New York. Not really sure.'

'White guy in a business suit? Bad call.'

'We were trying to find a nightclub in Williamsburg that *Time Out* said was a must do. The pair of thugs took my wallet and left me with a black eye as a parting salvo.'

'Williamsburg by way of East New York – that's a new one.'

'Well, look at me. I'm a working stiff. I'm no good at culture. I should stay at my desk.'

'They bother your wife?' Glancing at McLaughlin's wedding ring, he chafes his fingers against his own in solidarity.

'Thankfully, she wasn't with me. It was a working trip.'

'What business are you in?'

McLaughlin offers a tight grin. 'You know, they say Americans ask that question right off, whereas Europeans don't consider it polite.'

'Sorry.'

'That's more like it.'

'So . . . what business are you in?'

They both laugh. McLaughlin nods at Greg, who brings them fresh drinks.

'Don't shoot me: I'm a banker.'

'I'm not armed.' With a casual laugh. Mac very well could be, but McLaughlin doesn't know that.

'And you?'

Mac sips his drink, its poignant smokiness jostling his brain into a higher gear, and reinvents himself for the moment: 'professor.' Which is what he might have been if he hadn't been lured by the practical realities of police work. The chance to actually do some good.

'Of?'

'Literature. Do you read?'

'Not too heavily outside of the newspaper.'

Mac says, 'I teach the nineteenth-century Russian novel,' confident now that McLaughlin won't follow him there, won't ask too many tough questions. 'Tolstoy, Dostoyevsky, Chekov, and so on.'

'Sounds fascinating.' McLaughlin steals a glance at his watch.

Leaning in, Mac says, 'Actually, I could use some banking advice.'

'Do you have a billion pounds?'

'Not on me.'

'Then I'm afraid I'm not your man.' McLaughlin smiles politely. 'Sorry. What I mean is, I'm a wealth manager.'

'I see,' Mac says, 'wow,' trying to sound cowed, American style. 'So if I'm not on the *Forbes* One Hundred, you won't work for me?'

'The Rich List, here. You have your *Forbes*, we have our *Sunday Times*.'

'So what's it's like? Must be hard on some level, coming so close to that kind of money, I mean *major* money, knowing you'll never have it yourself.'

'I do remember reading *Crime and Punishment* at university, and I can assure you that temptation, guilt, and remorse are not even in my realm of emotion. Banking is a science, if you do it right. It's a job, and trust me, we're paid a bit more than professors. There's absolutely no room for envy in my line of work.'

'Sour grapes?'

McLaughlin's eyes flash at him, appearing shocked, then angry, then amused as they pull a web of fine wrinkles across his temples. 'Certainly not.' The way he levels his empty glass on the bar like a stroke of punctuation tells Mac it's over, he's pushed the conversation as far as it will go. He wishes he hadn't had that second drink; with hard alcohol, he usually stops at one.

CHAPTER 8

Thursday, July 12

With a layover in Milan, it's five hours and early afternoon before we land at Cagliari-Elmas Airport, a hanger of a building surrounded by palm trees and embraced by ocean on one side and a tangle of roads on the other. Given that we arrived on a half-empty airbus, customs is a breeze. In twenty minutes, we are dragging our luggage across the main terminal's shiny stone floor.

'She's still not answering. Where is she?' After a third failed attempt to reach Mary, who promised to pick us up, I drop my phone back into my purse. 'Here we go again.'

'Maybe she forgot.'

'Forgot?'

'We'll take a taxi.'

'Do you know how expensive that will be?'

'We can afford it now.'

He's right. This morning, after we'd checked out of our hotel and were waiting in the foggy English morning for a cab, Mac's phone buzzed with an e-mail from our bank confirming that a large wire transfer had been received. Kroll, or Barclays, or whoever, had paid him the second half of his fee. He'd reported honestly that the conversation with Simon McLaughlin was a waste of time, that the guy had been a little arrogant but nothing to trigger any suspicions or leads. Of course, Mac never expected such a brief and casual meeting to yield much, if any, information, but it was what the client wanted, so it was what they got. A strange job but a paid job – and now a finished job – and we are on our way to two blissful weeks of vacation.

Peeling off the layers that kept me warm in a vastly different climate, I wait outside in the sweltering heat of the Mediterranean summer afternoon while Mac attempts to find us a taxi driver who speaks enough English to make the transaction. I roll my jeans up as far as they'll go, take off my socks and jam them into my purse, going barefoot in my sneakers. Pull my hair back and wind it into a knot as far off my neck as I can get it. Walk under the overhang into a deeper pocket of shade, and cool off beside a lone news seller with a stack of papers on a small folding table. The grizzled old man, in aviator sunglasses beneath an ink-stained white cap, waits silently for someone to come buy the afternoon edition of *L'Unione Sarda*, assumedly the local paper.

Mac is talking with a driver but I can't tell if he's making any progress. Pacing, the newspaper's

124

banner headline catches my eye: OMICIDIO! Homicide. You don't have to speak Italian to understand that. Beneath is a grainy photo of a young Italian man with a black goatee, copying a key in a locksmith's workshop. A caption I can barely understand beyond a few words nonetheless makes me uneasy: *Dante Serra, un fabbro di Quartu Sant'Elena, è stato trovato assassinato il Mercoledì.* Dante, a locksmith, *assassinato . . . omicidio.* The locksmith Mary told me about was named Dante; she'd joked about it. Panic bristles in my chest. How many locksmiths called Dante could there be on one isolated island in the Mediterranean Sea?

Mac waves me over to an air-conditioned minivan. The driver catches my eye in the rearview mirror. 'Capitana, yes?' he says, as if to assure me he knows where we're going.

'Yes.'

We slide into traffic.

I lean forward, the seat belt cutting into my neck. 'Excuse me, but I'm wondering – is Dante a common name around here?'

'Dante? Oh, yes. My cousin is Dante, my wife's father is Dante, my friend is Dante.'

'Do you know a Dante who is a locksmith?'

Mac looks at me quizzically, and I shake my head, begging his patience. Roads and palm trees and bright blue skies fly past us and we're on a highway, speeding away from the airport.

'You saw the news,' our driver says. 'It's very

125

sad, but I didn't know him. *Sardinia* is a big place.'

'When did it happen?'

'Yesterday, it was the top news this morning. Tomorrow they will be onto something else.'

'What happened to him?'

'His wife calls the police: her husband, he doesn't come home. His boss, he's worried, too. They find his car parked on the side of a road. Later they open the back of his car and there he is, dead. Shot. This is all they know.'

'What road?'

'Far away, in Seulo – as you say, in the middle of nowhere.'

Mac asks me, 'What's going on?'

'A guy named Dante,' I tell him, 'a locksmith, was murdered yesterday. What are the odds—'

'You heard what he said, there are a lot of Dantes around here. I'm sure there are a lot of locksmiths, and plenty of them are named Dante.'

'Really?' A bite in my tone, in exchange for his impatience.

'Joe the Plumber.' A bite in his. 'Mike the Mover. Jose the Gardener. Come on.'

'It's just that—'

'Give it a rest, Karin. You worry too much. We're on vacation.'

'I guess so. Maybe you're right.'

He takes my hand and squeezes it. I squeeze back. We ride in silence until we pass a sign saying we've entered Capitana and turn onto Via Degli

126

Oleandri, the quiet dirt road leading to the Rossis' house. The car kicks up a powdery cloud as it pulls to a stop in front of a fence blocking the view of the front yard. The Rossis' black Audi is parked out front, just like in the pictures on the home-exchange Web site.

'The gate's open,' I notice. 'Look, a few of the kittens are out.' They're incredibly cute but it worries me the way they're wandering loose on the road. Directly across the street from the house is a low wall abreast an open field. It's pretty remote here, with no traffic on the road except for us.

'Looks safe enough.' Mac cracks open the door, letting in a blast of damp heat.

The first thing I do when my feet hit the dirt is bend down and scoop up the nearest kitten, a black one. I nuzzle its tiny face and gently set it back on the ground. While Mac and the driver take our luggage out of the van, I push open the gate, calling, 'Mary! Dathi! Ben! Fremont! We're here!'

No one answers.

'Hello! *Ciao!*'

Footprints of various sizes are scattered on the dry ground beneath an arbor of blossoming vines. And kitten prints, everywhere, adding chaotic texture to the lacework of shadows draping the otherwise sunny yard. A rupture of gladness delivers me to the moment in a way that makes me want to sing. How could I have felt suffocated by the obligations of parenthood, even for a moment? Me, of all people, for whom motherhood has been so hard-won. I suck back the wave of emotion. Where are they?

Since the car is here and the gate is unlocked, I assume they're in the house. Four steps lead to a covered porch shading the front door. I knock twice, then wiggle the handle. The door springs open.

'The front door's unlocked, too,' I call to Mac, who is pulling our suitcases through the front yard.

'They're inside.' Spoken with confidence, as if he knows. But the subtext is louder than his words; yet another rebuke to *keep calm and carry on*, that suddenly ubiquitous slogan revived from a British governmental public relations campaign at the start of World War II. Last Mother's Day, Mac gave me a red mug with the motto below a royal crown. Cute. Ironic. But somehow, I didn't appreciate it.

I enter the living room, which I recognize most recently from yesterday's indoor picnic photos: dark wood floor littered with dusty kitten prints; long curved couch covered in orange bedspreads; big hanging lanterns; floor-to-ceiling shelves crammed with books. With the shutters closed, the room is bathed in shade.

Mac comes in behind me, dropping the suitcases with a *thlunk* on the floor. 'Where is everyone?'

'It's too quiet, Mac.'

'Let's take a look around – they're probably

napping. This sun is powerful, it would knock anyone out.'

He follows me into the small, windowless kitchen where dishes are piled in the sink. A door off the kitchen leads to an office. Then we check the two downstairs bedrooms – by the luggage and kind of mess, you can tell which one was claimed by Mary and which one by the two boys – and the bedrooms on the second floor. Dathi's room is first off the upstairs hall, her suitcase with its neatly folded clothes open on the floor, a single bed tucked into a corner. The unused bedroom awaiting our arrival is farthest from the staircase: a double bed with a yellow blanket, a ceiling fan, a big square window with vented shutters blocking out the light. I crank the handle and throw open the windows onto the view of a lone cypress tree reaching for a blue sky. Leaning out, I look straight down onto a white plastic table bathed in sun.

'All the windows are closed.' Mac sits on our bed, trying it out. 'They must have gone somewhere.'

'But the car is here and the doors were unlocked. I don't like it.'

'We're in the middle of nowhere, Karin – in Italy. It's probably safe here. Maybe no one locks their doors.'

'But they knew we were coming.'

'Is there a beach in walking distance?'

I remember from the Rossis' notes that there *is*

a beach nearby. 'They must have lost track of time. Want to go find them?'

'In a little while.' Mac reaches for me across the bed.

'What if they come home? What if they walk in and we're—'

'What if they don't?'

After, we lie naked beside each other, holding hands, our window open to the sky, allowing in the barely moving warm air.

'I love you, Karin.'

'I love you, too.'

'Let's put on our bathing suits and go find them.'

I'm first out of bed and into the bathroom, while he hoists our suitcases up the stairs to our room. We change and go downstairs in search of beach towels. In the kitchen, I grab a liter of bottled water from a case beside the refrigerator, and take in details I missed before. The dishes piled in the sink are green. A bowl of bananas and oranges sits on the small table. In a cubby of the white wall shelves is a big open bag of *Bistefani Krumiri Classici* (cookies), two kinds of cereal, a six-pack of boxed milk. A basket heaping with dirty laundry sits on the floor by a top-loading washing machine in the corner: Fremont's jeans, the linen skirt Mary wears a lot, the purple T-shirt Dathi bought last summer, the plaid shorts Ben had on when we said good-bye at Heathrow. I lift the top of the washer and stick my hand in. 'The clothes are still wet.'

'What's that?' Mac is carrying two neatly folded towels.

'Mary's in the middle of doing laundry. She must have put it in before they went out. Where's the dryer?'

'I don't see one.'

We locate a long clothesline on the baking-hot roof, along with a drying rack. The simple act of working together to hang our family's laundry feels almost as restorative as the sex. The harsh rooftop sun pounds my exposed skin, and each time I attach a clothespin to the line, a calmness glides through me. When all the clothes are hung, we return to the kitchen to figure out the washing machine and put in a new load. It's three o'clock. Nearly an hour has passed since our arrival. After consulting the stapled printout of the same home-exchange information packet the Rossis had e-mailed us, we realize that the nearest beach, Is Mortorius, is two miles away.

'They couldn't have walked that far in this heat,' I say.

'Mary's nothing if not intrepid. And she's always reminding the kids they're spoiled.'

'Which they are. Even Dathi, a little, though she wasn't when she came to us.'

'True.'

As per the house instructions, we find the spare set of house and car keys in the bowl atop the fridge. The short drive out of Via Degli Oleandri brings us onto Via Leonardo da Vinci, a busy two-laner with blue-skied palm-treed vistas, occasional little shops, and finally the gas station our instructions say is at the turnoff for Is Mortorius.

When Mac makes the turn, the gear slips and the car slows precipitously. My pulse races: Another car is coming up fast behind us. Mac deftly re-engages the gear and makes the turn just in time to avoid being back-ended by a red Fiat that whizzes past.

'That was a close one,' he says.

'Maybe there's someone at that gas station who can take a look.'

'With manuals, they have to put it on a lift and look underneath. I didn't see a service bay.'

'Let's hope that was just a fluke.'

'Unless it's why Mary and the kids walked to the beach instead of driving.'

'If they're even at the beach,' I say.

With no obvious place to park the car, we leave it edged off the side of the road and walk along a dirt pathway lined with tall oleander bushes bursting with lush white flowers to the beach.

'Should have worn a hat.' Mac visors his eyes with a hand to block the blinding sun. The broad brim of my sunhat throws enough shade across my face to allow me to see far down the beach, which is surprisingly narrow, just ten or twelve feet between the shore and a crude stone wall. The sand is packed with sunbathers lying on towels beneath a random array of colorful umbrellas.

Children and adults play and swim in the ocean. In the distance, boats.

'Where are they?'

'Let's walk down a bit,' Mac suggests.

'Now that I think of it, none of the pictures Mary sent showed them at this beach. I can see why: It's not very nice here. The beaches in their pictures all looked . . .'

'Better.' Mac finishes my sentence. He sees it, too: This is a beach of convenience for people without the means, or the time, to travel farther afield.

'I don't like this beach,' I say. 'I don't see them anywhere.'

We walk what must be a mile in the relentless sun until we reach the end of the sand, where a suddenly rocky beach truncates the ribbon of sun worshippers. I take another long swig from our water bottle, then hand it to Mac. 'They're not here.'

He nods, gazing back in the direction we came from, an expression of disquiet galvanizing his sunburned face. 'We'll go back and wait for them at the house. Give it a few hours. Then we'll see.'

I go upstairs to hang the second load of laundry on the roof, only to realize that the first load is still heavily damp. Right. The sun doesn't operate in sixty-minute cycles. I carry the plastic basket of wet clothing back into the house and shove it into a corner by the door, regretting the loss of a calming task to support me through another quarter hour of waiting. Each clothespin a meditation. A hope that at any moment, my family will arrive home.

By almost five o'clock the sun has finally waned enough to allow us to sit comfortably outside, nursing the glasses of water we've been swilling in an effort to rehydrate after the punishing walk on the beach. By six, we switch to wine. In the gentle evening, the kittens and their parents begin to reemerge from wherever they've been huddling out of the heat.

Mac leans down to pick up a little calico fluff ball we decide to call Luciano. 'How many times a day do they eat?'

'Good question.' I go inside and get the house instructions. Outside, I flip through the section on caring for their pets. 'They get canned food in the mornings and dry food the rest of the day. Their dry food bowl looks pretty full, so they're set.'

'Did you check their water?'

'No.' But I'm already sitting back down at the table, pouring my second glass of wine. Mac gets up to check the water bowl. I decide to read through the instructions from the first page. Inside the house, I hear the water running. Little footsteps scampering toward the sound. Mac chuckling.

He sits back down at the table. 'Six thirty-five,' he says in a heavy tone. *And they still aren't home.*

'We should call the Rossis' friend.' I lay the

instructions on the table, my fingertip under-scoring the name, and read aloud: 'Giulia Porcu, my dear friend who lives in Capitana, will happily answer questions and offer assistance. She speaks English.'

'Mary probably called her about the lock. She's probably the one who told her to go to Carrefour.'

'You'd think she'd know a locksmith to refer directly.'

'Well, maybe she didn't. Let's call and find out.'

The instructions suggest we use the landline for local calls. We find it on a side table in the living room, by the couch. Mac reads the numbers from the page and I dial. The soft, foreign ringing sends a nervous thrum through me. Finally, a woman answers, '*Pronto!*'

'Hello,' I begin.

'Is that Mary?'

'No, Giulia . . . this is Karin, Mary's friend.'

'Ah, Karin. How is England?' She has a throaty voice, as if she smokes, or used to.

'We're here in Capitana.'

'Today?'

'Mary was supposed to meet us at the airport but she didn't show up. We were wondering if you have any idea where she is. We're concerned because the car is here, and—'

'Ah, yes. Karin, listen to me, Mary she thought you were coming *tomorrow*. Not today. I loaned her my extra car because Mario's car is difficult.'

'We noticed.'

135

Giulia has the easy laugh of someone who enjoys life. 'Oh, yes, sorry. It works, but you know, he must fix his . . . his . . .'

'Transmission.'

'It slips sometimes, yes?'

'Yes.'

Why, then, I silently wonder, did he loan it to us? Fixing a transmission is expensive, not something we want to take on for strangers. Why didn't the Rossis let us know so we could have rented something more reliable?

'Do you have any idea where they went today?'

'Yes – they took the long drive to Su Nuraxi, in Barumini. It's quite far, and Mary wasn't comfortable with Mario's car, so she's driving mine. I have two. I was happy to loan one.'

Pulling the phone away from my mouth, I whisper to Mac: 'They took a day trip in a borrowed car.' He smiles and pats my shoulder. Relief flows through me like cooling water.

'Giulia, do you remember what time they left?'

'Of course. I brought them the car and Mary drove me back home. It was about eleven in the morning. They won't be home until late, I'm sure. So relax and enjoy, you and your husband – maybe have a romantic evening.' The sweet laugh again.

'Thanks, Giulia. Thanks so much.'

'Your children are *adorabile*.'

'I can't wait to see them.'

'Soon they'll be home.'

After the call, Mac and I hug. 'Wish we called her sooner,' he says.

'Me too.'

I try all their cell phones again – first Mary's, then Dathi's, then Fremont's – just to prove to myself that there's no service over in Su Nuraxi, wherever that is.

'Relax,' Mac reminds me.

Jet-lagged from the time change, wrung out from the stressful afternoon, we go upstairs and collapse into a nap. A couple of hours later we wake to the rattle of cicadas through the open window. The sight of a heliotrope sky makes me lurch out of bed.

'Look at that.'

'It's incredible.' Mac joins me at the window, resting a lazy arm around my shoulders. We kiss.

'Think they're home?'

Downstairs, silence hangs like fog. You can hear the sound of the kittens playing outside the front door, the cicadas, but nothing else.

Mac feels palpably relieved to be driving in the left side of the car on the right side of the road. Now that they have an answer for the family's whereabouts, he finds he's able to notice small things, like the relative ease of driving in the right lane, despite the gimpy transmission. The fact that road signs are already starting to look a bit familiar, though this is just their third time on the road, after being driven in from the airport and then their trip to the beach. According to the house instructions, the restaurant Dathi had mentioned to Karin, Su Marigu, is just up Via Leonardo da Vinci.

'There it is.' Karin points to a sprawling white-washed restaurant across the street.

He drives until he finds a reasonable turnaround and then backtracks to the parking lot beside a festive outdoor garden. White lights are strung from palm tree to palm tree surrounding two dozen tables, all empty.

'It doesn't look open,' Mac says.

'Dathi said people eat late here.'

When they're shown to their outdoor table, they are the only ones until eventually another couple arrives, and then a large family. Gradually the patio fills up, as does the inside of the restaurant. The mood grows vibrant and the night air lulls into a soft warmth. Waiting for their food, Mac is suddenly taken by how serene Karin looks. He reaches across the table for his wife's hand.

'We made it. We're here.'

She smiles. 'It's starting to feel good. If only—'

'Nope, let's not go there. Once they're back, we'll be wishing we could be alone again.'

Karin lifts her glass of red wine. 'A toast. To the leap of faith that brought us here.'

Mac touches his glass to hers. 'Here to Italy? Or *here* here?' Meaning their marriage, their family, their complicated and sometimes combustible but generally happy life together.

'You need me to define it?' She smiles, her teeth glowing almost-white in the sparkling darkness.

He wants to lean over the table and kiss her – and then he does, whispering, 'Maybe later, if they're still not home, we can, you know, again.'

'Greedy man.' But she smiles. 'They better be home, though.'

At the moment, Mac feels two ways about that. Of course he wants the rest of the family to be home, safe and sound. But another few hours alone with Karin would be good, too. Their dynamic changes, relaxes, when they're alone together without worries, which so rarely happens. The past few days in England were tenser than he'd expected. But now, sitting here with her, everything feels different and suddenly good. It's as if, by traveling the distance, they've managed to unglue themselves from a stasis that keeps everyone stuck in place back home. He's glad they did it. Glad they came this far. He'd had his doubts but now he sees that Karin and Mary were right about this trip. Now that the London piece of it is behind them, now that no one's working and they're on the same piece of soil as the rest of the family (even if a different part of it), now that they're sitting in Mary's and the kids' favorite (so far) Sardinian restaurant, they've found an equilibrium they wouldn't have otherwise. Away from home. Away from work. Away even from the children for a little while longer, but close to them. For now, just the two of them,

Mac and Karin, alone in a place they've never been.

'They'll be back,' Mac says. 'But meanwhile – this is good.'

Dinner is pizza with what they'd thought was sausage when they'd ordered it but now aren't so sure; it's tougher than anything they've had before. Mac remembers reading somewhere that horse meat is commonly eaten in Sardinia, and wonders if that's what this is, but decides not to share the possibility with Karin. She keeps twisting around when new people arrive. He knows she's checking to see if it's Mary and the kids – imaging the celebratory reunion – but by the time they've eaten as much as they can and nearly finished their wine, it's still just the two of them.

'Too bad.' He winks at her, after she signs their credit-card chit and rests it on the edge of the table for the waiter. She smiles, and Mac reads a promise in the smile, a promise that fifteen minutes from now, at home, if they're still alone, maybe they can find each other again in their bedroom. Twice in one day: It hasn't happened since before Ben.

It's so dark when we pull up in front of the house on Via Degli Oleandri that it would be possible for a black or navy car to be parked there invisibly. I jump out before Mac has the engine turned off. Walk up and down the road, looking, but there are no other cars tucked into the darkness. It

140

occurs to me that Mary might have pulled her car inside the gate. I push it open with a sharp squeal that bites into the hush of the front yard. The kittens run up in a pack.

There is no car.

I turn to Mac, feeling my face twist in panic, watching his eyes cloud as he looks at me. His energy seems to bleed away as his mood shifts from relaxed to frightened.

'Maybe Giulia dropped them here and drove back home with her car,' he suggests.

'But all the lights are off in the house.'

'Maybe they're asleep.'

'Wouldn't they have waited up for us? Seeing our stuff? Knowing we're here?'

'Not if they're tired, Karin. At least not the kids.'

But Mary would have waited up, I know that deep inside. And no lights are on.

'We'll call Giulia again if no one's home,' Mac says.

A gaggle of kittens follows us into the dark house. I flick on the overhead lights: Nothing is different from when we left for dinner. Not a speck of dust is out of place.

Mac finds Giulia's number in the house instructions, and dials. Her phone rings and rings and rings, the long rolling tones thwarted and far away and unanswered.

'We should call the Rossis,' Karin suggests, 'see if they have any idea where Giulia might be.'

'Right.' No one answers their Brooklyn landline, so Mac tries Mario's cell.

'*Pronto.*'

'Mario, it's Mac. The house is fine, but listen, there's been a problem.' He regurgitates the story.

'I am stunned, really,' Mario says. '*Sardinia* is a safe place. I don't understand how this could happen. You've been to the police?'

'Not yet. Mary borrowed Giulia's car, that's what Giulia told us. We've been trying to call her again but there's no answer.'

'If you leave a message, she will call you later.'

'What about the car? Any information you can give us – make, color, license plate number – would help.'

'Of course. Giulia has two cars – I will guess she gave them the Peugeot, it is big enough for more people. Her Fiat can carry just two.'

'Do you know the models and years of the cars?'

'The Peugeot is blue, the Fiat white. Does that help?'

'It helps a little. Mario, if you can think of anything else, call me, please. We're losing it.'

Mario pauses, confused.

'We're upset,' Mac clarifies. 'Scared. Worried.'

'Yes, I understand.'

'If you hear from Giulia—'

'I will tell her to call you right away. She's one of our best friends. She will help you.'

'Thank you.'

'It will be okay, I promise.'

Ending the call, Mac says to Karin, 'I hate it when people promise everything will be okay. It feels like the kiss of death.' He searches for another number on the list.

'Who are we calling now?'

'*Polizia.*'

As the phone rings, he becomes aware that his heart is beating too fast. And the bright panic in Karin's eyes – he can read her so well, it hurts. Panic: to be here again, not in this place but in this sensation of your skin slipping away. Panic: to hear the word *police*, even in another language.

'We can't do this in Italian, Mac.'

'We have no choice.'

'I have an idea.'

She hurries upstairs and returns with the laptop. Meanwhile, a woman answers, '*Polizia municipale, come posso aiutarla?*'

Karin pulls up the translation page and takes Mac's dictation, typing it into the English box on the left: 'Please, can you tell me if there were any car accidents today?' Feeling like a bumbling idiot, he repeats the Italian translation, from the box on the right, into the phone as best he can: '*Per favore, mi puoi dire se ci fossero incidenti stradali oggi?*'

The woman rattles something off. Mac feels his forehead compressing into the grid that settles on him to provide headaches and age him prematurely. He listens to the woman with his eyes pinned to Karin's and dictates, in a whisper: 'I don't understand.'

143

'*Non capisco.*'

'*Non parla italiano?*'

He's pretty sure she's asking if he speaks Italian, so takes a shot at an answer. 'I speak English.'

'Okay, *inglese. Aspetti, per favore.*'

Holding his hand over the phone, he whispers to Karin, 'I think she put me on hold.'

Karin nods, her gaze pinned anxiously to Mac. He knows where this is sending her emotionally and runs a gentle finger along her cheek. She breathes. He makes himself smile a little, even though he doesn't feel it, but he wants to reassure her that this is not going in the direction she obviously fears. It can't be. She lost a child to murder once, another to late-term miscarriage. The shock of those disasters have gradually diminished but they both know that resonant echoes will always circle her.

A man's voice comes onto the phone. 'How may I help you?'

'Hello,' flooded with relief, 'this is Mac MacLeary, we're visiting Capitana and part of our group, including our children, didn't come home. They drove to Su Nuraxi this morning. Please, can you tell me if there were any car accidents on the island today?'

'Sardinia is a mountainous island. Unhappily, we have accidents every day.'

'Between Capitana and Su Nuraxi,' Mac rephrases the question. 'Were any tourists reported injured in an accident on that road? We're staying in

Capitana, and we were told our family left for Su Nuraxi this morning.'

'You were told?'

'We just arrived this afternoon. Our children came a few days ago, ahead of us, with a friend of ours, while we took care of some business in London.'

'You are English.'

'No, American. They borrowed someone's car and took off for Su Nuraxi and they're still not back. We can't reach them. We're really worried.'

'Whose car did they borrow? I'm just a little bit confused. They borrowed a car and someone told you . . . Please, help me understand.'

'Giulia Porcu, she's a friend of our host's in Capitana, Mario Rossi. He and his wife are staying in our house in New York – it's a home exchange. Our friend borrowed Giulia's car to drive to Su Nuraxi because Mario's car . . . Listen, can you just find out if there were any accidents?'

'*Sì, sì* – will you wait a moment?'

'He's finding out now.' Mac catches Karin's eyes, waiting with her.

'Sir?'

'Yes?'

'I'm happy to tell you that there were no accidents on any roads between Capitana and Su Nuraxi. There were two accidents on the island today, but both in the North, and so even if your friend and children are lost, it wasn't them. You may breathe, Mr . . .'

145

'MacLeary,' Mac reminds him.

'Mr MacLeary. Please, be patient. Your family will return, I'm sure.'

How many times in his long career has Mac reassured worried families with the same empty promise? 'And if they don't?'

The man releases a long breath Mac recognizes as a prelude to what no cop wants to acknowledge unless he has to: the possibility that this isn't just another instance of human error, something gone wrong that will right itself in time. *Wait*, they always say; and everyone waits. The billion-dollar question is always: How long?

'Write this down,' the man instructs.

Mac whispers to Karin, 'Something to write with,' and she dashes into the kitchen for a pen and the pad of paper on which Mary had started a shopping list: olive oil, cereal, grapes.

'Enzio Greco, Quartu Sant'Elena, via Firenze Fifty-two. Call me, or come see me. I am easy to find. If you need me, I will help you.'

'Thank you.'

They bid each other good-bye.

'Who is he?' Karin asks the moment Mac hangs up.

'Enzio Greco. Works for the police. Speaks English. He sounds nice but hopefully we'll never have to talk to him again.'

CHAPTER 9

Friday, July 13

*P*olizia di Stato Commissariato, reads a simple square sign next to the entrance of a beige stucco building at via Firenze, 52. Just inside the glass door sits a slender woman behind a reception desk. Her tan arms etched with veins, she smiles at us from beneath a black nest of a hairdo. I won't be surprised if a little sparrow flies out, and let that thought evaporate. I feel dizzied by that off-key sensation when you've barely slept. All night long, we awoke to the slightest sound let in through our flung-open bedroom window. Any random chirp, the nighttime orchestral sawing of crickets, the soft growling of kittens play-fighting – every sound registered as the possibility of a car driving up, and every sound wasn't.

'*Come posso aiutarla?*'

'Enzio Greco,' Mac answers.

'*Gli americani, sì.*'

The woman rises briskly from her desk and disappears through a door, releasing a whisper of classical music. Violins. We are left alone in the modest reception area. A Most Wanted poster hangs on the wall directly behind her desk: an array of mug shots beneath the word *iLatitanti*. Taped on the wall beside it is a travel poster boasting of the historical monuments of Sardinia. An earthy fragrance, rosemary, floats in the air, making me wonder if someone is cooking in a back room before I remind myself with weighty disappointment that we're in a police station, and remember why.

The music again, and she's back, followed by a tall man, thin except for a conspicuously round belly and a flagrant double chin. His thick white hair bounces when he walks, giving him a jolly demeanor. He extends a hand toward Mac, smiling with gentle sympathy – obviously, he knows why we've come.

'Mr MacLeary. I am Enzio Greco. Welcome.'

While they greet each other, just before Mac turns the introductions to me, I notice that the employee ID hanging from Greco's neck identifies him as *Commissario di Polizia*. Commissioner? Never in the States would the police commissioner appear so casually to greet a visitor, and it throws me a moment before I get my bearings and remember that we're in a different country with different rules and presumably different professional titles. For all I know, here 'police commissioner' means 'office manager.' But I doubt it.

'Karin Schaeffer,' I introduce myself when Greco's attention turns to me. 'Mac's wife.'

'Please, please, come in.' He gestures for us to follow him through the door. The violin music grows more insistent as we approach his office, a tangle of bright sound at the far corner of what appears to be a detectives unit. A spate of plain-clothes officers work their trade, Italian style, at metal desks distinctly unfamiliar for their sleek design. Nothing like the decades-old clunkers cops work on back home, with an accidentally vintage look no one could have planned. And the chairs: molded orange wheeled seats that could be out of a magazine. One workspace in particular catches my attention: Atop the desk sits a blue pencil cup that looks like a piece of twisted paper, a bright purple plastic stapler, a shiny silver globe that is a magnetic paper-clip holder. The skinny jeans and tinted lenses of half the cops in this room make me feel like I've accidentally wandered into a hip neighborhood in a world-class cosmopolitan city, not a relatively backwater cop shop in a Mediterranean island town. Crossing the room to Greco's office in the far corner, I swallow back a certainty that these are not real police. We've come to the wrong place. If we don't hurry, we'll lose time finding out where we really need to go for help locating Mary and the kids.

'Have a seat, please.' Greco gestures to the matching black seats facing his neat desk. He walks around to his ultramodern ergonomic lime green executive chair. The name plate on his desk reads

149

Enzio Greco, Commissario, Polizia di Stato, Sant'Elena Provincia.

This can't be real. I want it to not be real. I want to close my eyes and then wake up all over again, go downstairs into the small kitchen of our Italian vacation house and find the chaotic remnants of children's breakfasts.

'We're sorry to bother you.' Mac folds his hands together over crossed knees, leaning forward. 'We didn't realize who you are.'

'Who I am?' Greco's smile reveals unusually long canines in his upper row of teeth. The detail unnerves me and I look away toward a half-empty green mesh recycling basket on the floor beside his desk: tight wads of paper like snowballs, a take-out coffee cup, a tattered inter-office envelope. 'I am the only one who speaks English enough for this conversation we must have. I am happy to talk with you. No, not happy – your children, they're not home?'

'No,' I say. 'And we haven't heard anything. We're losing our minds with worry.'

'*Signora,*' both his hands clasp his heart, 'of course you are worried.'

Mac asks, 'If you'll just tell us where we need to go to file a missing persons report, we can get started.'

'You are in the right place. Excuse me, I will check on the accident reports since last night. We'll start there.' Greco lifts his phone, presses an intercom button, and says something in Italian.

150

While we wait, he explains, 'We have many tourists visiting our island every summer, visitors from all nationalities. Every day someone is getting lost. In some towns there are homes that provide sleep and breakfast just for these travelers – *viaggiatore albergo perso*. For a small fee, of course. And in the morning, the lost traveler is on his way. There are many such stories. Later, you will laugh.'

No we won't. We squeeze out polite smiles. Suddenly I think of Dante the locksmith and my pulse hammers.

'Yesterday, at the airport, I saw a newspaper article about a murder – a locksmith named Dante.'

Greco shakes his head. Sighs. 'Yes, of course. It was terrible. But I can assure you, that kind of thing is very rare here. *Sardinia* is safe for our visitors. Our crime rate here is very low, please believe me.'

'The thing is,' I lean forward, willing him not to look away or change the subject, 'there was a locksmith named Dante who was supposed to fix a lock at our house.'

'And did he?'

'He must have. The electricity had gone off. The circuit breaker box is in a shed and the key was lost. We know the electricity came back on on Wednesday because I got a bunch of e-mails and pictures from our friend Mary that day. They suddenly flooded in. There was wet laundry in the washing machine when we arrived yesterday, and

151

the electricity was working. I thought Mary told me the locksmith was coming yesterday, on Thursday, but he must have come on Wednesday instead.'

Greco nods, listening, his eyes – vaguely green under sagging lids – watching me closely as I speak.

'And so you can see why we'd be concerned. Our family doesn't come home. And a man was murdered the same day he went to fix a lock at our house.'

An expression of alarm animates Greco's face. 'You're sure it was this same Dante Serra?'

'His name was Dante,' Mac says. 'That's all we know.'

'The victim was a locksmith from Villesimus, twenty-five years old. A tragic loss to his wife and mother. What makes you think your locksmith was Dante *Serra*?'

'Well, we don't—'

'Karin,' Mac interrupts me, 'we never knew the locksmith's last name. We have no idea if it was the same Dante,' he tells Greco in that let's-be-rational-man-to-man tone I hate whenever I hear it.

'We will find out,' Greco says, 'if Dante *Serra* was at your house, what day and what time.' He makes a note. 'We'll ask records from our electric company so we can know specific the time the electricity went back on. Let us hope it wasn't *this* Dante at your home, because then it will be . . . complicated, yes?'

'Yes.' I twist my fingers into a knot on my lap. 'Exactly.'

Mac releases one of his long breaths and I won't so much as glance at him. He can think what he wants, but as a detective, he should know better than to look away from any possibilities, no matter how long the shot. If I am too quick to decide, too impulsive, sometimes judgmental, he's too unwilling to move on instinct. We sit there, in front of Enzio Greco, deadlocked in marital silence.

Finally Greco's phone rings and he listens for a long minute. 'Okay,' he reports to us, 'just one accident on the road from Su Nuraxi last night, an Italian couple, no one injured. Good news, yes?'

Is it? I'm not sure. My craving for answers makes me feel unbearably restless. There's too much we still don't know. 'What about the . . . what did you call it? The lost-traveler network.'

'*Viaggiatore albergo perso*. We can try, but it will take time. We make some calls to police in the villages, we find out if anyone is there.'

'I'm not sure if I mentioned on the phone that my wife and I are both retired police detectives,' Mac says. 'We're private investigators now.'

'No, I don't think you did.' Greco's eyebrows contract into a fat white caterpillar. 'So you'd like to know our procedure for missing persons. Of course.'

'Yes, that would help.'

'Let me explain.' Greco leans forward, elbows atop desk, chin resting in a hammock of clasped fingers. A wedding band on one hand, a heavy school ring on the other. 'We don't wait. I am going to take your full report, learn about the missing persons involved. I am going to issue an alert across the island, to all the police, and to hotels as well. All eyes will be looking for your family, I promise you. And you will let me know the moment you hear from them. We work together, yes?'

Suddenly I swing from doubt to confidence: Maybe this *is* a real police station, maybe he *is* a real commissioner, despite all the hints to the contrary. The whimsical decor. The boss's accessibility. None of it makes sense to me, but if Mary and the kids don't return soon, we're going to have to work with the Italian police and we'd better get with their program. The alert system he's describing sounds credible and right.

'Okay,' Mac says, and I echo, 'Good.'

'What are you thinking?' Mac asks me, driving out of Quartu S'Elena: pale buildings cloaked in sunshine. I look at his face in profile, the slight curve of his nose, the feathered lines beside his eyes, the furrows across his forehead. I know he's worried, and I know he wants us on the same page, and I want that, too. But I won't lie.

'I felt like you ganged up on me in there.'

'Ganged up on you?'

'You didn't want to push Greco as hard as I wanted to, and you made me feel like an idiot for asking about the locksmith.'

154

'Look, they're putting out a bulletin as we speak. If I didn't think the guy was good for his word, I—'

Suddenly the transmission slips (again). Mac struggles to reengage the gear while nearly driving through a red light. Back on track, his face flushed from panic, he says, 'Okay, that's enough of this bullshit.'

My heart is beating so fast, I can't answer at first. By the time I realize he means the car, and not my complaint of a moment ago, I wholeheartedly agree. 'Let's see if we can rent a safer car.'

We stop at the first rental agency we see, and then try two more, only to hear the same discouraging response repeated: 'No.' A word we easily understand. Apparently, with tourist season in full swing, nothing is available – not a car, van, truck, or even motorcycle. Standing in the windy heat of a parking lot beside a busy street, I wrinkle my nose against the gas fumes collecting from a row of cars waiting at a light. Flatten a hand to shelter my eyes from the burning sun. And look out into the gas-wavy horizon of a town blending into countryside.

'How are we going to do this with an unreliable car?'

Mac knows exactly what I mean, because no way are we sitting still and waiting anymore.

'We'll master it,' he says, as if he actually believes that willpower can overcome mechanical failure.

I watch him anxiously as he pulls his gaze across the distance. Our quest feels uniquely impossible, here in a foreign island, without language, with half-broken wheels. I realize I've stopped breathing when Mac rests a hand on my arm and air suddenly fills my lungs.

'Let's go see if we can get ourselves a GPS,' he says. 'It'll be easier than a map, and we'll know where we're going.'

'I saw a sign for Carrefour on our way in to town. That's where Mary went to find the locksmith.'

Mac nods; of course: Why should we wait for the commissioner to learn what we can find out ourselves right now?

We delve into the monolithic belly of Carrefour and head straight for the locksmith station, which we locate first by a drawing of a lock beneath an arrow, and finally by the cawing grind of a key being cut. We follow the noise to a counter where a fiftyish man with a halo of salt-and-pepper hair is just finishing the copy of a key.

He looks at us. '*Di cosa hai bisogno?*'

I show him a photograph of Mary on my phone. 'My friend.'

He smiles. Shrugs. Looks at me with the strained patience a parent would show a babbling child.

'Have you seen her?' I ask, pushing the phone closer to his face in the hope that he'll understand. 'She was here two days ago.' Mac gently pulls my hand back, just an inch, but I get the point and he's right. I'm coming on too strong, and raising our voices won't help us understand each other. I drop the phone back into my purse.

'Dante,' Mac tries. 'Did he work here? Dante Serra. *Omicidio*.'

The man's eyes cloud. The loose muscles of his face contract in sadness. He shakes his head mournfully. '*Dante era un uomo giovane, sua moglie aspetta il loro primo bambino*.'

What did he just tell us? 'His last job,' I try, 'was it in Capitana? Via Degli Oleandri?'

But the man turns away, irritated, it seems, that two strangers are hurling a foreign language at him in the wake of his colleague's death.

'Greco will have to do this.' Mac takes the commissioner's card from his pocket, and dials. He's put right through. But when Mac offers to hand the phone to the locksmith, apparently Greco declines, because suddenly the call is over.

'What was that?'

'He wants to do it in person. He's sending someone now.'

We look at each other, and I say, 'I don't think we should wait. We can't understand them, anyway. Let's drive to the place Giulia said Mary took the kids yesterday. I wrote it down at home.'

We choose one of the simpler TomTom GPS units. As we head to a distant cluster of cash registers, passing through crisply air-conditioned aisles, the canyons of stacked merchandise loom with an

157

overwhelming sensation of claustrophobia. I want out of here, fast. The need to start our search claws from the inside, and I pick up my speed. Mac follows suit. We pay, and quickly we're back in the car, suctioning the GPS onto the windshield. As Mac drives, I program the unit to deliver directions in an American female voice I call Jane, which (I decide) is what Mary's sister would be called, if she had one.

On the way back to the house, I try Giulia Porcu for the second time that morning. When I get her voice mail, I don't bother leaving another message. 'I wish she'd call us back.'

'She would if she knew something.'

'She could call, anyway.'

This time, we're not surprised to find the house empty. My note from yesterday reads *Su Nuraxi, Barumini*. Mac finds it on a map, unfurled across his knees for a broad view of the island, while I make coffee and pack water.

'Hot coffee.' I set his on the side table. 'Just what you need.'

'I'll take the caffeine.' Perspiration dribbles down his forehead, a drop of it jumping off an eyebrow onto the map like a daredevil skier. 'Here.' His fingertip presses on a spot due north of the southern coastal village of Capitana, which is part of the province of Quartu S'Elena, which is just east of Cagliari, the island's capital. I'm startled to see how close southern Sardinia is to northern Africa; you could practically swim to Tunisia. The truth is, I'd been so fixated on organizing our home exchange and packing for the family that I hadn't studied Sardinia's geography until now.

'Foolish American tourist,' I mutter, bitterly, to myself.

'What?' Mac glances at me, somewhere between startled and offended.

'Nothing.'

'Su Nuraxi of Barumini.' He redirects his attention back to the map. 'That's what we have to plug into the GPS.'

A kitten suddenly runs underfoot and I startle, spilling hot coffee over the back of my hand. Tears flood my eyes. Mac sets aside the map and rises to take the cup from me so I can wipe my hand on my jeans. With his free hand he takes mine, lifts it to his lips, kisses it. 'The police will come up with something.'

'I hope so.'

'Should we pack sandwiches for the road?'

'Let's not take the time,' I say. 'We can stop for something if we need to.' Though it's hard to imagine this gnawing sensation inside me as the kind of hunger that can be appeased by food.

Outside, Mary hears voices speaking in Italian and wishes she knew what they were saying. The woman who appears to be their main captor, and whose name is Emiliana, is talking to the man who arrived yesterday at about the same time: a tall, older man with thick white hair.

Why, Mary keeps wondering, does Emiliana look so familiar?

Emiliana's linen slacks billow in a sharp gust of wind from the ocean. Standing barefoot on the beach, her bony toes dig clawlike into the sand. She shields her eyes from the bright midday sun with a liver-spotted hand that sends a milky shadow over her upper half. The low buttoned blouse shows tanned, sagging cleavage. Frazzled bleached blond hair whips around her face and she ignores it, listening to the man.

Peering through the window, half hidden behind the billowing curtains, Mary can't see Emiliana's eyes but she knows them: empty and cold, as depthless as the thin line between ocean and sky that refuses any indication of where they are. After two nights of inexplicable lockdown, Mary still has no idea why they were brought here.

'Play with me, Mary!' Ben hurtles into the room from one of the bedrooms, where Dathi and Fremont were supposed to be keeping him entertained while Mary makes lunch. Some of the groceries Emiliana supplied them with are out on the kitchen counter of the all-purpose living/dining room.

'Shhh!' Mary admonishes Ben, pulling away from the window to hide herself against the wall. Dropping to her knees, she catches him in her arms and reflexively covers his mouth with her hand. Guilt surges through her with this act of suppression, but boundaries and priorities have shifted dramatically: Safety, survival, come first.

Mary doesn't know where they are except that it took hours to get here. Three or four hours, but she can't be sure. The cruel man who snatched them at gunpoint – *who shot the locksmith* – took away her watch along with all their cell phones, but not before an e-mail of Karin appeared on Mary's phone with the horrifying message *They got me!* and a picture showing Karin chained up somewhere cavernous and dark. When Mary saw that, she sucked back her horrified reaction to avoid frightening the children any more than they already were. They didn't need to know.

Regardless of how much she tries to understand this, she can't. Why would someone want to kidnap her and the children? Why would someone want to hold Karin hostage? And where is Mac?

A flourish of helplessness grips Mary: They are completely cut off now.

After the man took their phones, he crushed them with the heel of his shoe on the floor of the van, and then scattered them along the highway as he drove, or so she guesses. He'd blind-folded all of them but the sharp crackling sounds of something being tossed out of the van's open window, coupled with the rush of air, told her he'd disposed of the evidence. She hasn't seen him since he delivered them here to this remote house on the edge of who knows where. Nor has she seen the van, or heard the coming

161

and going of any vehicle except the one driven by the white-haired man, and the little red Fiat driven occasionally by Emiliana that is otherwise kept parked beside the house.

Emiliana, the old man, the disembodied voice of a second woman who has yet to be seen, and a pair of armed guards who never speak or make eye contact. That's it for company. Thank God for the children. Mary pulls Ben closer, whispering, 'Shhh,' noticing a new, salty smell to his skin. 'We have to be quiet. After lunch I'll play with you, okay?'

He nods, head bobbing once, dutifully, under the tight bond of her hand.

'Are you ready to be super quiet?' she whispers in his ear.

Another nod. She lets go. When he turns to look at her, his face is bright red, holding back tears. Her heart breaks: He's too young to know how to do that. She pulls him into her arms, holds him, rubs his small back. She knows how awful this is for him, that he yearns to shout, run, play, go outside, see his parents. But her job is to keep the children safe and that's what she'll do, whatever it takes.

Dathi shuffles into the main room, looking exhausted; she hasn't been able to sleep well since they arrived. Behind her, Fremont looks too thin, his eyes hollow with thwarted rebellion. The normally rambunctious teenagers caught on quickly that silence and submission are the name of this game. Mary hasn't had to repeat her initial admonishment that they keep quiet and take her lead while she figures out what's going on and what, if anything, they can do about it. 'First and foremost,' she instructed them on their first night of captivity, 'is survival.' With the bigger kids, she didn't see the point of mincing words.

From what Mary can tell, the house is completely isolated between the sea on one side with miles of open land on the other three sides. Perfect for someone who wants to vacation in solitude, which she suspects is just the purpose of this house. Fully equipped with linens and pots and pans, it has everything you need to just walk in and live, including hotel amenities like shampoo and soap. Even a washing machine and dryer, not that that helps much considering that none of them has a change of clothes.

To the left of the house is another, smaller one, where Emiliana appears to live. Mary doesn't get the sense that the guards live anywhere, because they are omnipresent and alert. She thinks there are just the two of them, unless there are more and they're working in shifts. Dressed in black from head to toe, each armed with a machine gun strapped over one shoulder and a pistol holstered on the opposite hip, the guards look to Mary like interchangeable stock characters from action-adventure movies.

The house has two doors, front and back, both locked from the outside. All the windows are protected by white curlicues of ironwork. You'd be safe here, as a tourist, sleeping in the isolated house in the middle of nowhere, on the edge of an island floating between Europe and Africa. No one could possibly get to you, locked in the house at night. Or in the day. No one would know you were here. Not for the first time, that thought sends a shiver of despair through Mary.

Holding Ben close to her side, she rises to peer through the window. The white-haired man is gone. She hears a car drive away, but the red Fiat is still there. Emiliana turns to glance at the house with eyes blanched by the scorching sun, hard lines bracketing a frown cold with shadow. Again, it haunts her: that feeling; the riptide sensation she's seen that face before.

CHAPTER 10

The road to Barumini is mostly an open topography of farmland stretching flat for eighty kilometers, or fifty miles. To help pass the time, and also prepare them for where they're going, Mac listens as Karin reads aloud from her Web browser, which weaves in and out of reception as they drive along. '"Su Nuraxi is an archeological site centered around a three-story tower built in the fifteenth or sixteenth century B.C. Italian archaeologist Giovanni Lilliu discovered the underground remains of a fortified village beneath what had become, over time, a hill. It served as a castle, a village, and a fortress. Lilliu's excavations in the 1950s revealed a new chronology of Sardinian prehistory."'

Of course Mary would have wanted to bring the kids there. But why, Mac wonders, didn't she wait for them to arrive from England so they could all go together? If only Mary had waited for them, if only . . .

Distracted, he realizes they've missed their turn when Jane-the-GPS announces, 'Rerouting,' with mild irritation.

They find themselves climbing into the mountains.

'This isn't right,' Karin informs him, as if in cahoots with Jane.

'I realize that.' His pulse spikes when a turn in the road shows them a steep drop off an unprotected cliff.

'We have to turn around.'

'I realize that, too.' Monitoring his tone. This is not the time for an argument. She has to realize that there's no place to turn around on this narrow uphill road.

'Jesus!' Mac shouts.

Karin's body slams against his, shifting suddenly away from the cliff as the car stalls out and Mac struggles to steer away from the sheer drop down and revive the transmission in time to get ahead of a car coming up behind them.

'Got it, got it, got it,' he chants, guiding the car into the middle of the narrow road as, finally, their speed picks up. He forces himself to breathe deeply as the roar in his ears and the urge to vomit subside. Karin's hand unclenches his knee. Evidently, if they were going over, she wanted to die touching him.

'Fucking car.'

'Too fast,' Karin says, 'slow down.'

'Trying to find the right speed. Too slow and it stalls out and someone rams us from behind. Too fast and we fly off a fucking cliff.'

With the cliffside road growing steeper as they

166

ascend the mountain, the lulls between each sharp bend grow fewer and farther between until finally it feels like lurching deaf, dumb, and blind around a roller coaster. Surrounded by a cacophony of stone and blue sky, discordant threats of pulverization and the abyss.

'I don't like this,' Karin says in a tight whisper.

A car zooms around a bend in front of them, racing past in the opposite direction, and Mac resists a powerful centrifugal force threatening his control of the car. The other car recedes and he steadies them in the middle of the winding road, saying, 'I don't like this, either.'

Suddenly Karin bursts into laughter, uncontrollable, weepy-eyed fits of hysteria. Mac can't help laughing, too.

'Stop,' he begs. 'My eyes are tearing and I have to see.'

'I'm going to wet my pants,' she cries.

'Stop.'

The moment passes and a survivalist quiet descends between them. Hush. Concentrate. Drive. The road calms as they pass through a village so sleepy it seems abandoned.

'Siesta time,' Karin notes.

The village burps them back onto the road. Up they drive, ears popping, until they come to a large, nearly empty parking lot with a breathtaking view of gently sloping green-on-green fields that belie the treachery of the road that gets you there.

The air is thin and earthy. They cross the parched

lot to speak with two old men sitting on folding chairs under a shade tree, beside a few haphazardly piled saddles and some jumbled bridle. The men stop talking as Mac and Karin approach, Karin in her sunglasses, Mac shielding his eyes from the extravagant brightness of high noon. A conspicuous smell of horse manure hangs in the air. In the far distance, down a long dirt road that appears to lead nowhere, a line of horseback riders vanishes into the distance like a swallowed chain.

'Hello,' Mac launches in, speaking English, hoping for the best. 'Su Nuraxi?'

One man tilts his leathery head back in amusement. The other man smiles with what's left of his teeth and says, '*Laggiù, verso gli altri, sei venuto troppo lontano.*'

Mac and Karin smile politely.

'Go back,' the toothless man says. 'Go back.'

'Since we're here,' Karin says. Pulling out her phone, she opens her photos, and finds one with Mary and the children taken last year at Christmas. Showing it to the men, she asks, 'Have you seen them?'

They scrutinize the photograph and look at her, shrugging their shoulders, either because they don't recognize the family or they have no idea why they're being shown the picture.

'Thank you,' Mac tells the men. '*Ciao.*'

'*Ciao, ciao,*' both men mutter, returning to their conversation.

'I think this might be the end of the world.' Karin

168

pauses to sweep her gaze across the vista. 'I think we found it.'

'It's beautiful,' Mac agrees.

'And kind of creepy.' She looks at him. 'Do you know what I mean?'

'Wouldn't want to get lost here.'

They drive back down the steep, twisting road, their hearts in their throats, until they reach the intersection where they made their mistake. There is only one other way to go.

Finally, there it is, Su Nuraxi, an imposing mass of stones off the side of the road, fronted by a modest parking lot and gift shop. With only the smallest sign, the place looks as unheralded as it must have been way back when it served its purpose ushering history out of the Middle Ages.

While Mac parks, Karin twists in her seat, searching the distance in every direction. 'I don't see a blue Peugeot.'

They walk through the dusty parking lot, through visible waves of heat, to the gift shop and adjoining visitors' entrance. Mac reaches out for Karin's hand, which is so cold, so clammy, a sudden, deep sadness fills him. He squeezes tight and she responds without looking at him. He can feel her wish to take off and run to the small building up ahead. With her free hand she thumbs to the photo in her phone, getting ready.

'Hello,' Karin begins with a girl selling tickets through a window cut out of a booth at the entrance. 'I'm sorry but I only speak English.'

'Yes,' the girl answers sweetly. 'English is okay with me.'

'Oh, good.' Karin smiles and brings forth her phone, pointing the screen at the girl. 'This is my family. Have you seen them? Were they here yesterday?'

'Ah, yesterday. I no work yesterday. Please wait a moment.' The girl leans out the window and calls, 'Luisa!' issuing a stream of Italian that summons a middle-aged woman with dark hair pulled off her face by a barrette. Her khaki pants and white T-shirt appear to be a uniform; a name tag pinned to her shirt reads *tour guide* in several languages.

'English please, Luisa,' the girl indicates Mac and Karin.

'How may I help you?' Luisa's smile sprays friendly lines from the edges of her eyes.

'Were you working here yesterday?' Mac asks.

'Yes, all day.'

Karin taps her phone to refresh the picture. 'Our family was here yesterday. Did you see them?'

Luisa looks over the photograph carefully. Shaking her head, she says, 'No, I don't remember them. Are these your children?'

'Two of them are,' Karin answers. 'The little boy and the girl. The other boy and the woman are our friends.'

'I also have a daughter this age.' Luisa's smile fades to concern. 'You're looking for them?'

'How many other tour guides were working yesterday?' Mac asks.

'Just two of us, me and Niccolo – *mi scusi*.' She turns to a man just returning from a tour, followed by a group of Japanese tourists. 'Niccolo!'

'*Si?*' A young man with thick brown ringlets to his shoulders and a tattoo of the Virgin Mary on his bicep, he wears the same khaki pants, white T-shirt, and tour-guide pin as Luisa.

'A question, please.'

Smiling, Niccolo joins them. 'Of course. How may I help?'

Karin shows him the picture, which he examines for a long moment. 'I'm sorry, but no, I did not see these people yesterday.'

'Today?' Karin asks.

'No,' Niccolo says, echoed by Luisa, 'No.'

'Is there someone else here who might have seen them?' Mac asks.

'Rafaela was here yesterday and today, all week in fact,' Luisa offers. 'In the gift shop, there.' She points to the small glass-fronted room beside the ticket booth.

'Thank you,' Mac says, '*ciao*.'

'*Ciao*,' Niccolo returns the good-bye, but not Luisa, whose eyes follow them with concern. When Karin turns to look at the other woman, Mac pulls her forward. There is no time for emotional bonding, mother-to-mother commiseration, the kind of painfully self-indulgent wondering aloud he's noticed women have a tendency to fall into.

★　★　★

171

I don't like the way Mac keeps pulling me and I tug my hand away. 'Thank you.' I turn back to look at Luisa. '*Ciao.*'

'*Ciao.*' She waves and for some reason I feel a little better, just knowing she understands how we feel, why we've come so far. But I don't like the look of pity that materializes in her eyes. I turn on my heel and follow Mac into the gift shop.

'Rafaela?' he has already started. 'Do you speak English?'

'A bit.' The old woman sounds tentative, as if she has just exhausted her vocabulary. Beneath a bonnet of silver hair, her face is as grooved as a walnut. She wears a slight trace of pink lipstick, which reminds me that there is always hope.

'Our family.' I show her my phone, the picture, and she studies it. 'Have you seen them?'

It takes a moment but finally she understands. Shakes her head, shrugs her thick shoulders. 'No, no. *Mi dispiace.*'

'Are you sure? Look carefully. Please.'

'Thank you,' Mac says, dragging me out of the gift shop back into the light.

'You're hurting me.'

'She hasn't seen them, Karin. No one has.'

'But they were here.'

'That's what Giulia told us.'

'No luck?' Luisa is still there, standing by the ticket booth, waiting for her next tour.

'No.' My voice comes out a strained whisper. But I won't cry.

172

'Were there any cars left here overnight? A blue Peugeot?' Mac asks. Luisa turns to the girl in the ticket booth and questions her in Italian.

'No,' Luisa tells us, 'the car park was empty when she came in this morning.' A cloud shifts overhead, bathing her in a soft light. I notice her wedding ring, the lack of any other adornment except for plain gold earrings.

I nod and turn away quickly to hide an embarrassing surge of emotion. Walking along the path to the parking lot, Mac following, a glance to my left reminds me where we are: Su Nuraxi, the labyrinthine heap of stones that was once a castle and a fortress. You can see from here how many ins and outs and hiding places are enfolded in the rubble. I tell Mac, 'We should look.'

'No one saw them yesterday. They weren't here, Karin.'

'But we should *look*.' Because for some reason *we* are here, we were directed to this place, and I want to know why. It's not exactly under guard; anyone can walk right in without a tour guide, which tells me you could conceivably lose yourself unnoticed. I pivot off the path and walk across the grass. A knee-height rope barrier is easy to step over. The closer I get to the fortress, the drier the ground becomes until I'm walking in a swirl of brown dust.

'Sorry!' I hear Mac call out behind me and imagine Luisa shrugging her shoulders, her empathetic smile. She will know just what I'm doing

173

and why. I don't look back. I hear my husband's footsteps running up behind me and expect him to try to stop me, girding myself for an argument. Instead, he keeps pace as I pick up speed.

I navigate the mazelike piles of stone, each group tracing a circle on the ground with some walls high enough to evoke shelter. The closer we get to the tower, the better preserved and taller the walls are. You begin to see portals, built-in tables, benches, hearths. Gradually, a sense of daily life takes shape.

Swallowed into the tower's narrow entrance, I'm instantly cooled by a blast of ancient shadows on stones untouched by light for centuries. The damp intimacy of the tower's interior surprises me. I stop to wait for Mac to catch up. Just ahead, the darkness blossoms into light, briefly, before shadows overtake it. In the distance, an amber glow.

'Come on.' I take Mac's hand the moment he enters, pulling him along the narrow passage of hand-laid stones. We enter a circular room lit from above by an opening, an ancient skylight high above our heads through which air and light pour. It has to be three stories up, and the walls look impossibly strong. It's hard to conceive of how this was built by human hands.

'Let's move.' Now Mac's urging me forward through another passage so tight a pulse of claustrophobia beats in my ears. We pass through passage after passage, room after room. Sometimes an empty window, a skylight, an alcove, but nowhere an enclosed space four people might hide or lose themselves in if they wanted to (or didn't).

Finally we emerge into an open area, an inner courtyard at the heart of the fortress that has the feel of a communal gathering place. In the center is a heavy rusted grate bolted over a wide gaping hole edged in stone.

'Probably the well.' Mac joins me, peering into the dark abyss. 'Water collection would be important, it would be available to everyone.' Tugging on the immovable grate, he calls, 'Hello!' His voice reverberates far and deep, repeating itself, folding and bending and returning until the word loses shape and fades away.

'This place is a maze of empty stone rooms,' I admit. 'They're not here. You were right.'

We go back the way we came. Mac drives carefully, getting the hang of achieving just the right speed so the transmission won't fail us. I notice he's taking the mountainous curves with more confidence now, less anxiety, but I'm too disheartened to feel pleased.

Close to Capitana, my BlackBerry buzzes with a stream of e-mails, alerting me that we're back in network. No messages from Giulia. None from Enzio Greco or anyone with the police.

'I'd really like to know what that locksmith at Carrefour had to say.'

Mac agrees with a nod. 'Try Greco.'

The receptionist speaks to me in rapid-fire

Italian, saying something I don't understand. 'Please ask him to call us: Karin Schaeffer, Mac MacLeary,' I say as she hangs up the phone.

'We could stop by Giulia's place,' Mac suggests.

I look up her address in the home instructions the Rossis had e-mailed me, and plug it into the GPS.

The quiet street where Giulia lives is lined with whitewashed houses dripping bougainvillea. Thatched porches offer shade. A pair of children swerve their bikes out of the road when they see us coming and stop to watch us drive past.

'I don't see Thirty-seven,' I say, looking for Giulia's house number. 'Just Thirty-six and Thirty-eight.' An orchard fills acres of land opposite the even-numbered houses. 'The Rossis must have made a mistake with her address.'

'Google her, Karin.' Mac's voice is edgy in a way that tells me something new is bothering him. 'Google her name.'

I tap the browser icon, which fires into someone's unsecured network, and Google Giulia Porcu. A number of them come up, but none in Capitana or even Sardinia. We drive a mile in either direction, hunting for her house. On the way back, we stop to read names on mailboxes along the road. All are labeled to identify the homeowners and tenants, but none are Giulia Porcu.

'Maybe it's under her husband's name,' I say, 'or her boyfriend's name—'

'Or her girlfriend's name,' Mac interrupts.

'Maybe she's a lesbian, or single, or a polygamist, or lonely.'

'Or bad with numbers.'

'Or a liar.' Mac stops the car abruptly, kicking up a storm of dust that hovers in a cloud in front of our windshield, obscuring the view of pretty houses. The tendons in his neck stretch tight and he looks at me. 'Maybe Giulia doesn't exist. Maybe this is a wild goose chase. Maybe something's going on and we should stop spinning our wheels and figure out what it is.'

'But we talked to her, Mac.'

'We talked to *someone* who sent us to look for Mary and the kids someplace they apparently never went. We called a number on a list given to us by someone we've never seen. We don't even know why we're really here, Karin, do we?'

The way he says it: the chilling simplicity of the question. He's right. We have come all this way, far from home, armed with relatively little information. We are on an island where we don't speak the language, in the middle of a far-flung ocean. Why?

While Mac drives back to the house on Via Degli Oleandri, I try Enzio Greco again. This time, no one answers.

We pull to a stop in front of the house. No other car. No signs of life. The reminders of our family's absence resonate with the eerie silence of an approaching storm. Late afternoon sun arcs down the sky. You can see the waves of heat through the

177

windshield, the oven beyond our air-conditioned pod. The engine shuts off and immediately the car starts to heat up.

Mac grinds his teeth, sending muscled ripples along his jaw. Pulls out the car key, runs his thumb against the jagged metal edge, says, 'I'm not sure, but I'm starting to think it has something to do with Millerhausen.'

'*Millerhausen?*'

'The timing. Think about it.' As his eyes flicker across my face, I see what he means. This trip happened so fast and worked out so perfectly. Too perfectly. And now here we are, losing ourselves in what is starting to feel like a futile search for our family. It's easy to see how it could go on indefinitely, maneuvering our attention away from some unspecified prize in a classic bait and switch.

'You're thinking the London job was bogus,' I say, as it dawns on me: The assignment was too easy and paid too much. We should have been much more suspicious of it from the start.

'There was nothing going on with that guy. They were wasting my time on purpose. Whose idea was it for Mary and the kids to come here ahead of us?'

'Mine or Mary's, I think. It all happened so fast.'

'Godfrey Millerhausen,' Mac says, 'is rich enough to get Kroll to help him stop our investigation if he wanted to. *Why* would he want to? They dangled Europe in front of us like a juicy carrot.'

'And we bit.'

'I'm going to start digging around Millerhausen again. Find out what he's so keen to hide from his wife. From us. I have a feeling this is how we're going to find Mary and the kids.'

'I can't believe this is happening.'

'I'll start with Dan Stylos, shoot him another e-mail and see if he decides to answer this time.'

'He won't.'

'You're probably right.' Mac finds Stylos's number, and dials. When someone answers, he introduces himself as a long lost colleague of Stylos's; but before he has a chance to launch in, his eyes land on me with such weight my stomach jumps.

I mouth: 'What is it?'

'Stylos,' whispering, hand over the bottom of his phone, 'is *dead*.'

Stunned, I watch him take it in. Listen as he offers condolences. And then, he says, 'If you don't mind my asking, what name is the first Mrs Millerhausen going by these days? We all used to spend time together, back in the day. I've lost track of her, but she was close to Dan. I'm sure she'd like to know.'

After the call ends, he tells me: 'Goes by her maiden name now: Liz Braud. Where do you think she lives?'

'Don't make me guess.'

'Right here on Sardinia.'

I take a deep breath. 'How did Stylos die?'

'His secretary said he took a long weekend at his summer place in the Hamptons and never came back to work. They've been dredging the Long Island Sound. This morning, they found his body.'

Inside the house, we flick on lights. Setting up the laptop at the tiny table in the kitchen, we easily find her. Liz Braud owns a hotel up at the northern end of the island where the super-rich escape from the stresses of being, well, super-rich. Photographs of her twenty-room villa, L'Hotel del Riso e dell'Oblio, show an array of luxurious rooms and stunning views. Liz smiles out at the world from the proprietor's welcome page: a tall, thin woman with shoulder-length blond hair that's obviously dyed and much too neatly coiffed. An sapphire pendant dips into the cleavage of her over-tanned, liver-spotted skin. But it's her bright white smile that captures your attention, the friendly smile that beckons you to come visit her in paradise. According to the short biography beside her picture, she arrived on the island for a vacation ten years ago and never left. She named her inn L'Hotel del Riso e dell'Oblio, the Hotel of Laughter and Forgetting, after her favorite novel by Milan Kundera, *The Book of Laughter and Forgetting*. (Which dates her, I think, as much as her bleached hair and leathery skin.)

I dial the hotel's phone number and wait as the rolling ringtone repeats and repeats and repeats until finally a message in Italian answers. Hanging up, I say, 'Let's drive up there and talk to her. Right now.'

180

'No.' Mac's forehead compresses into an accordion of skin. 'We have to understand this first.'

'She *lives* here,' I argue. 'She must know something.'

'Exactly. Which is why we should know *more*.'

'It's a long trip; we can talk while we drive. I'll make calls. We'll figure it out.'

'I'll want you to go see her, but—'

'Me?'

'I'm heading back to New York.'

'Mac, hold it.'

I follow him out of the kitchen and up the stairs to our room, where he throws his suitcase on the bed and starts packing.

'You're *not* leaving me here alone.'

He crosses over to me, red and furious as if he can't move fast enough, can't think fast enough, can't explain fast enough. 'We won't find them unless one of us goes back home and figures out what's going on. That has to be me, because I started this, and I've got half the case filed away in my head. You have to stay here, work with the police, and when the time's right, *if* we decide it's a good idea, you'll pay a visit to Liz.'

'But—'

'We can't both leave without Mary and the kids.' His voice grows gentle, almost pleading. 'And I have to be the one who goes home.'

After passing through the security checkpoint at the Cagliari airport, Mac turns to blow Karin a final kiss. He knows she understands why he has to leave: This is her family, too, she's an investigator herself, and she realizes that they have to spread their resources; and they can't waste precious time. But the expression on her face displays a familiar anguish that worries him more than he cares to admit. He's spent half their marriage keeping her away from the slippery slope to that dark place that sometimes consumes her. He doesn't like leaving her here alone, to say the least, but what choice does he have? Mary and the children are most probably still on the island. Someone has to stay behind.

CHAPTER 11

Mary comes up behind Dathi, who is doing the dishes (again), places her hands on the girl's shoulders, and whispers, 'Try and relax.'

Startled, Dathi looks around. 'Why are you whispering?' she whispers back.

'I don't know.' Mary releases her full voice. 'I don't know.'

'That feels good.' Dathi stops washing dishes but lets the water run as Mary works the knots out of her muscles. 'Shall we take a walk on the beach today?'

'Great idea.'

They both start laughing, and then the heavy silence falls again. Joking doesn't change the fact that they're being held hostage and there won't be walks along the beach or anywhere else. Mary thinks of Karin, captive elsewhere, probably in England, and the helpless claustrophobia returns. Dark emotions tease her, trying to reach into her mind. She pushes them away, but it's getting harder by the hour. Silently she prays that Mac is out there, looking for them.

Ben moves his toys across the floor, where a shaft of sun from the ocean-facing window is making him too hot. If today is like yesterday – and why wouldn't it be? – he'll spend the afternoon inching alongside the shifting blade of shadow.

Fremont lies long-legged on the couch, staring at the ceiling, a book open on his stomach. As he's never been much of a reader, Mary wishes he had a guitar to play. Needless to say, they don't have access to a computer. It makes her nervous to realize how lost her teenage son is without music or Internet. Ben and Dathi are better at entertaining themselves; he, because he's still small; and she, because growing up mostly in India, she wasn't spoiled beyond repair.

'This is a test of our inner resources,' Mary reminds the children. The teenagers ignore the seed of wisdom but Ben looks at her, obviously having no idea what she's talking about. Nonetheless, his sweet, round face smiles. She smiles back.

Finished with the dishes, Dathi turns off the tap. 'If we had some ingredients, I could bake something.'

'In this heat?' Mary asks.

'It would be something to do.'

'And *eat*,' Fremont adds. 'I could really fucking go for some chocolate cake.'

'Free!'

'Which I'm not, Mom, as I keep reminding you.'

'Watch your language around Ben. Please.'

Fremont rolls his eyes. Without his acne

medication, a pustulous rash has broken out across his forehead. He hasn't bothered to pick his Afro and it's gotten dreadlocky. Mary can't decide if it looks shabby or if she likes it.

'How long, Mom?' He swings his legs off the couch and stands up, coiled with ruthless energy. 'Why don't we just walk the fuck out of here?'

'Well,' keeping her voice calm, 'I suggest we do that as soon as we get the chance. Until then, we're . . . stuck.' At the last moment, she edits out the harsher words on the tip of her tongue: *locked up like animals for the slaughter.* That's how it feels. But she can't possibly share her anxieties with the children.

'Why?' Her son stares at her, asking a familiar, unanswerable question.

'I don't know, but it's got to be some kind of mistake.' Another bending of what she's really thinking: This was no mistake.

Outside, Emiliana walks by carrying a package from her car toward the other house.

And then suddenly Mary remembers where she's seen that face before.

The photograph she found at the Rossis' house: Mario, Maria, Blaine Millerhausen, and another, older woman. Whose hair was different then, shorter and streaked blonde, not bleached. But the face: It's the same face.

Emiliana is the other woman in the picture.

On a powerful hunch, Mary bolts past Ben, past Fremont. At the window, she shouts, 'Liz!'

Emiliana stops. Turns. Faces Mary with an irradiated expression, bright sun shrinking her eyes to pebbles.

'Liz Millerhausen!'

'You know her?' Fremont joins his mother at the window.

'I want to talk to you, Liz! I want to know what this is all about.'

'How do you know her?'

'Whatever you're doing, it isn't going to work.'

'Mom, what are you talking about?'

'Free – shhh.'

The sound of their voices draws the other woman out of the adjoining house. Suddenly, one by one, the locks on the front door of their jail snap open.

Blaine Millerhausen, in cut-off shorts and a striped T-shirt, is preceded by a blast of wind off the sea.

Sitting in the airport parking lot, getting ready to drive away without Mac, the sound of a plane roaring overhead startles me. I press the button to lower my window and stick my head into the oven. The heat here is ridiculous. Up in the sky, a plane flies away. Another one approaches. In reality, Mac is probably still waiting to board but in my mind he's already gone.

Jane greets me: 'Trip to Via Degli Oleandri. Exit the parking lot and at the first intersection, turn right.' She sounds so reasonable. I hate her. Reaching out, I touch the small GPS screen until voice options appear. *Sean (Irish)* is what I select, demoting *Jane (American)*. I want a man's voice to remind me of Mac; an Irish voice to remind me of the impression he does of his late Irish father, which always makes me happy. A voice to remind me of the tone of Mac's parting directive, 'Someone has to stay behind,' and why. A voice to help me keep myself centered without the person upon whom I have grown to rely.

Slowing down to yield for traffic at the airport exit, the transmission does its thing. Cars piling up in a line behind me honk as I frantically try to reengage first gear. Takes a minute but I know it by feel when I finally find the sweet spot, gear-up and then we're off again – I'm off again, alone, into the thin midday traffic of a country I just met.

I could do it: drive straight up north, right now, and ask Liz Braud what she knows. But I can still hear Mac's No and see the knot of his face trying to unwind the confluence of people and events that led us here. Something tells me not to act alone particularly because I *am* alone. At this point, we don't know what's safe and what isn't. And he's right: If we're going to solve this, it will be as a team.

The drive from Cagliari feels long without Mac. But at least there aren't any cliffs. Once away from the congestion surrounding the airport and city, it's smooth sailing, kilometer after kilometer, mile after mile. Palm trees, beach clubs, and restaurants swoosh past, until eventually signs of tourism abate.

There, on my right, is Su Marigu, the restaurant where Mac and I ate dinner just last night. Farther down, I see the pot-bellied man who sells beach chairs and umbrellas out of his open van. A woman shakes a throw rug out a window. A man carries a plastic chair out of a stand-alone market and sits in the shade, watching the cars and vans and trucks go by. Each of these places, these actions, should be familiar enough, and yet they're not.

This gradual absorption of the place, the skins of newness that peel off one by one when you venture somewhere you've never been, that very element of mystery and surprise that makes traveling so good, now come at me like shards of subterfuge. Everything is different here – nothing recognizable. What will it take for me to understand this place, unravel it, all on my own, so I can figure out how to find my family?

If I stopped in one of the local stores, would I see a missing sign posted on the wall? Or are missing-persons investigations conducted differently here?

Why haven't I heard back from Enzio Greco? I know *he* exists: We sat with him just this morning, talked face-to-face.

I turn on the radio in the hope of understanding something. Understand nothing. Switch it off.

Adjust the air-conditioning higher.

Traffic thickens so quickly my pulse accelerates.

And then I realize it isn't traffic, it's a maroon van and a silver sports car: one tailgating me, the other beside me. From the corner of my eye I can see two men in the car to my left; a sandy-haired young man leans out the passenger window, heckling the tailgating driver behind me. In my rearview mirror, I see a thin man at the wheel of the van, some kind of tattoo curling over part of his face: a snake licking his jaw with a forked tongue. The passenger in the silver car hangs halfway out the window to give the finger to snake-face, laughing derisively before drawing himself back into the car.

Worried the gear will slip out again, my hands glue tight to the steering wheel, summoning an ability for precision driving I only hope I possess. On impulse I shout, 'Hey!' and then stop myself, not wanting to draw attention to the fact that I can't speak Italian. Identifying myself as an outsider in a situation like this seems like a very bad idea. I will have to at least learn how to curse in Italian, but meanwhile, I accelerate to get away from these drag-racing fools, putting a quick dozen feet between us, hoping, praying, this gimpy car won't fail me.

The silver car slips into position behind me, a maneuver I don't understand. And then, suddenly, the van swerves around and ahead.

Sandwiched between them, I panic and lean on my horn. Another couple of cars drive past without a problem. It's a struggle to maintain speed to avoid either crashing into the van or getting

189

rear-ended by the car or stalling into a spectacular collision, but I'm managing it, I think, *I'm doing it* . . . then, just as soon as that thought articulates itself, I feel the first hard jolt to my rear bumper.

A second jolt.

A third.

The left lane is free and clear and so, holding my speed, I nose my way toward it. The van drifts left, inexplicably opening the road in front of me. I race forward to get away from them, thinking, *I made it*, when suddenly I realize that both vehicles are now in hot pursuit . . . of me, or each other – it's impossible to tell.

Cars in front hear us coming and get out of the way. Cars behind are nowhere to be seen. Where are the traffic cops to put a stop to this? My foot is pressing against the floor now. Sweat pouring down my face.

And then, suddenly, the transmission fails and I'm in free fall.

Blaine, in the flesh, is a small woman, but she manages to fill the doorway. Her short dark hair is slicked back, frazzles of it curling into the humid air; she must have just come out of the shower, or had a swim. Her eyes narrow meanly, aimed at Mary like a pair of knives: 'Shut up.'

'I only said I wanted to talk to your mother. Just talk.' Mary forces her tone to stay level. She'll be the grown-up in the room if it kills her, and it might.

Blaine takes two steps in. Mary accommodates with two steps back, even though there's plenty of space between them. The young woman's energy is so harsh, so intense, you can feel it across the room. Mary hears Fremont coming up behind her. Dathi, in front of her, is frozen beside the refrigerator, near the door. Ben pretends to be oblivious, playing with his toys, not looking up, but Mary knows he's aware of everything that's happening and it breaks her heart.

'No one wants to talk to you,' Blaine says. 'You just do what we say. That's all you have to do.'

'These are children,' Mary argues.

Blaine's expression hardens. She doesn't respond. Maybe because she's too young, or too sheltered, to see how it matters.

'Aren't you comfortable?'

Mary and Fremont both turn toward the window, where Liz now stands by the iron scrollwork, which, at this time of the afternoon, drops a lurid shadow back onto the sand. This close, she looks softer, less brittle, more comfortable inside the loose mantle of her cruelly aging skin.

'Don't you have enough to eat?'

'Why did you kidnap us?' Mary asks.

'I borrowed you.'

Bullshit. Regulating herself, Mary counters, 'Borrowed?'

An ironic grin spreads across Liz's face. Mary wants to bash it off.

'For the time being,' Liz adds.

Fremont gives off such heat, such irate energy, Mary's surprised he hasn't told them to *fuck off* yet.

'How long?' Mary steps closer to the window, shortening the distance between herself and Liz Millerhausen, or whatever the woman calls herself now. When Mary had tried to find her at the beginning of the Millerhausen investigation, nothing had come up for her under her married name for at least a decade.

Liz shakes her head and doesn't answer.

'Why?' Mary, turning, asks Blaine.

'I told you, shut up.' Blaine takes a few menacing steps forward, as if she thinks she can use her body to intimidate Mary. But her approach only gives Mary an idea.

Every step is a kick, every kick is a step, she used to tell her students back when she taught Tai Chi. *Every movement is sacred. Waste nothing.*

'Don't talk to her,' Liz instructs Blaine. 'Come out of there.'

Blaine's face reddens. 'But Mom, they know—'

'I told you, leave this to me.'

The door is gaping open, closer now to Dathi than to Blaine. Mary doesn't dare to even glance at Dathi; she just hopes the girl can read her mind.

'Oh no!' Mary twists to the window and points out across the beach, where one of the guards stands sentry, watching them. The other guard is probably roaming the property. That's usually how it seems to work. So it will be a risk, Mary realizes, but a risk they'll have to take.

Liz twists around to look. Even the guard turns to see.

Mary roundhouse kick-steps forward once, stunning Blaine. The second kick knocks her down.

'Free, Dathi – *go*!' Mary shouts. She delivers a third kick to Blaine's hand as it comes up to grab her foot, which she uses as a lever to twist the young woman onto her stomach. She stands on Blaine's back to hold her down as she gags for air. Watches her brave teenagers dodge through the open door.

You're free now, Free, Mary thinks, exhilarated, but just for a moment.

A shot rings out across the beach.

Liz has vanished from the window.

Across the room, Ben now stands, his face scrunched in fear. Mary calculates how much time she'll need to run over, grab him and go, and knows there isn't a chance.

I struggle to engage the transmission. Skid. Right the car. Speed up. And then, finally, realize with tragic absurdity that I'm now racing against myself.

I decelerate enough to glance in my rearview mirror and watch the van and the car shrink into the distance.

They're no longer racing each other. No longer chasing me. I can't tell if they've stopped or if they're still driving; but what I do know is that

I've put a world of distance between me and them and *I'm safe, I'm safe, I'm safe.*

Liz stands in the doorway, beside one of the guards. Through clenched teeth she orders her daughter, 'You, get up.'

Blaine waits for Mary to remove her foot, which she does. Because of Ben. And because the guard has a rifle and a gun. She steps back and waits for Blaine to make the necessary efforts to stand and limp over to her mother.

'You,' Liz tells the guard, 'get the boy.'

Mary races over and snatches Ben. She tries to run with him to the nearest bedroom, but the guard reaches her in the hall.

'No!' Mary screams.

Ben bursts into tears, trying desperately to hang on.

'It's okay, it's going to be okay,' her voice wavers with false promises, trying and failing to kiss him good-bye and he's yanked out of her arms.

The front door slams shut, his wailing voice now a diminishing vapor. She crumbles to the floor as the locks turn one by one by one.

Click by click, it falls into place: how she found the photograph; how she e-mailed Mario Rossi, asking about Blaine, asking if he knew where they might find Blaine's mother.

How can it be that the Millerhausen women are on this island? What could they possibly want with Mary and the children?

194

What happened to Karin in London? And where is Mac?

What was that Kroll job really all about?

And then, as suddenly as she recognized that face, *she knows*.

Lacie Chen at Kroll threw them the Sardinia bone, figuring they'd jump at it, which they did – like trained dogs. They were handily gotten out of the way. But why?

CHAPTER 12

My hands won't stop shaking, despite a long glass of ice water, despite a glass of wine, despite an effort to breathe deeply and remind myself I survived what I've tried to convince myself was a random act of youthful stupidity. Apparently drag-racing young men are a thing of the world: You see them in Brooklyn; in Maplewood, where I used to live; in any and every town my peripatetic Army family moved to when I was a kid. Put people behind the wheel of a car and they act like . . . people. Which is exactly the problem.

It's just that those drivers seemed determined to crush me.

Sensations and images cascade through my mind: the unforgiving solidity of the pedal flat against the floor of the car, the certainty that I'm about to die when the transmission fails at one hundred fifty-three kilometers per hour. And the shaking gets worse. Squeezing shut my eyes, I force away the visceral rekindling of those terrifying moments. I have to move forward. Stay focused. Work with Mac. Do whatever it takes to help find Mary and the kids.

Are they lost? Hiding? Did something frighten them, too? Did something happen to them? And Dante, the locksmith, *who was murdered . . .* why? I think about the Millerhausens and wonder about Mac's suspicion that our family's disappearance somehow sprang out of that investigation. I know he'll start looking for answers the moment his plane lands in New York. Somehow we have to find a way to work as a long-distance team.

I press my mind forward, will my hands to steady themselves (which they refuse to do) and, standing in the quiet living room, consider where to begin. Looking around at the shelves crammed with Italian books, some graphic novels, DVDs, and CDs, I think about the Rossis. Who are they? How did we get here? Is Mac right – *is* Godfrey Millerhausen somehow involved? Kroll? Barclays?

Paranoia trickles through my veins, a kind of sticky scratching from the inside that makes me want to break through my skin to get to it. I take my empty glass and on my way through the kitchen grab the wine bottle and bring it with me.

Sheer amber curtains deaden the waning sun that filters into Mario Rossi's office. Turning on the overhead light, I take in our host's spacious workspace. Floor-to-ceiling built-in bookshelves are neatly organized with graphic novels, mostly in Italian but also other languages. French, German, English, Japanese. A pair of retro-looking cartoon posters are framed on one wall. Upon close inspection I see that both prints are number one of limited editions signed by Mario Rossi.

Trinkets from around the world adorn the shelves; apparently, the Rossis like to travel. A Buddhist shrine sits atop a file cabinet, with a half-burned stump of incense in a green porcelain dish, a book of matches beside it. I pick up the matchbook and decipher enough to see that it's from a restaurant in Cagliari. Pouring another glass of wine, I leave the bottle beside the shrine, pocket the matchbook, and open the top file drawer.

The drawers are crammed with papers from Mario's life as a graphic novelist. Shows. Sales. Supply receipts. Shipping details. Letters of inquiry. Notes of appreciation. Fan mail. Unpaid bills. His desk is similarly stocked with the stuff of a working artist: a computer with a sleek twenty-seven-inch monitor and abused-looking keyboard; Post-its and tape, a stapler, all the prosaic tools of someone who steers the ship of his work life from behind a desk. A quick swivel in his chair and you're facing a drafting table, white with ink stains and scratch marks up and down both sides.

A breeze pushes the curtains against my bare arm and my heart jumps as I realize a window was left open. I push aside the curtain and am relieved to see more iron bars behind the window, which is locked in place with just a two-inch opening. It occurs to me that this house is awfully secure for an off-a-country-road island hideaway.

Glass and bottle in tow, I return to the kitchen, where I sit with the laptop and research crime statistics for the area, which turn out to be among the lowest in Europe. But I also learn about the Camorra, the island's mafia, which predates the Sicilian Cosa Nostra. According to Wikipedia: *The Camorra is involved in money laundering, extortion, alien smuggling, robbery, blackmail, kidnapping, political corruption, and counterfeiting. Some believe it is now the strongest mafia in Italy.* I sit back, sipping my wine, thinking that over. If this is such a safe island, why do the Rossis need all their windows protected with iron guards? But Mario is an artist and from what I can make out, Maria, his wife, serves as his helper and muse and keeps their house and lives running. If not for the iron bars, the front gate, the heavy doors and windows, nothing about these people would feel suspicious. And their references, all of them, glowed.

A quick Google search answers my concern: It turns out the Rossis bought the place just five years ago. The previous owner is listed under a corporate name. Was it a Camorra hideout of some kind? Bad karma, as Mary might say. And thinking about her, about Ben and Dathi and Fremont, about Mac, my blood runs with that sticky feeling again. I scratch my arms up and down until red welts rise on my skin. Pour a third glass of wine but at the last minute decide not to drink it. I have to stay clear.

Evening finally siphons off the day's heat and delivers a mauve twilight. I stand on the porch and watch the kittens chase one another back and forth under the trellis that stretches from the front gate to the house. Their mother calmly watches. I envy her. And then, as if to appease me, one of the black kittens runs to me. I scoop him up and listen to his frantic purring a moment, thinking it will calm me. 'I love you, Ben,' I whisper to the kitten. His rib cage against my fingers, as I stroke him, feels disturbingly fragile. When I set him back down my hands start shaking again.

My mind ticks forward, to tomorrow, and a plan begins to develop. What to do while Mac works his end of things.

Because I can't just sit here. I have to keep moving. Thinking. Looking.

I make another fruitless attempt to call Enzio Greco. Then turn on the TV and flip channels, searching for a local news station that might be reporting a hunt for my family. But all I see are images of tourists lounging happily on beaches. Traffic reports. A tidal schedule. Weather.

After putting on a small pot of water so I can boil up some pasta – I'm not hungry, but I have to stay strong – I go upstairs to the roof with another load of the children's damp laundry. Piece by piece I remove and fold the bone-dry T-shirts, shorts, jeans, and socks, the girls' and boys' underwear, Mary's and Dathi's sundresses. Parched by the hot sun, the fabric is stiff in a way that feels unfamiliar, and the smell is also new: something exotic, floral, that I can't place.

A clothespin snaps out of my trembling fingers when I try to attach one of Ben's wet socks to the line. Bouncing to a landing on the rooftop, it splits at the curled metal joint. I toss the pieces into the bucket whose express purpose seems to be the collection of broken clothespins, judging by the dozen or so parts accumulated inside, and stand by the roof's low wall. Looking out over the cactus yard, the palm trees, the rooftops of the Rossis' neighbors, the vista of an island I don't understand. Looking toward an ocean I can't see from here but know is out there.

Dathi holds out her hand and pulls Fremont forward, urging, 'I think it's okay now.' In the dark, no one will see them. Tepid light from intermittent lampposts along this road offers visibility but also cover. And she thinks she sees, in the distance, one of those open-air tourist bars where they can blend in and maybe get a drink of water. No longer hitchhikers, they'll be visitors, part of the scenery.

His hand feels clammy and cold, though the air is still pretty warm. Extreme thirst makes her dizzy and from time to time she has to stop. They stand together until it passes.

'You all right?' he whispers.

'Yes.'

'I'm going to fucking die if I don't get something to drink soon.'

'Shhh.'

A small car that blends with the night comes toward them along the narrow road leading from what she thinks is a hotel. Nothing too big or fancy, from the look of it, and the sign at the head of the road, announcing the entrance to Matta Village, was plain. They stop walking and stiffen in the headlights of the passing car, but the driver doesn't slow down, doesn't seem to notice them. She breathes again when the car vanishes into the darkness behind them.

'Fuck,' he says.

'Shhh.'

She's run away before and knows how to move stealthily, quickly, quietly. In India she ran for days so that her greedy uncle and the trafficker he'd sold her to wouldn't find her. She is momentarily overcome by a surge of feeling at the recollection of how fast everything changed all at once. How her childhood ended: first Granny, her protector, dying of a heart attack; then Mommy, her lodestar, murdered in New York; then Karin, her rescuer, coming from nowhere, supplying her with an itinerary that in days transformed her into a (nearly real) American girl.

She will never forget opening Karin's e-mail in the broken-down place someone had the audacity to call a cybercafe, when it was just a shack selling computer time on a PC. Opening the e-mail and reading Karin's note and realizing that she wouldn't have to run forever, that she would be able to follow through with the plans her mother had put in place for her to travel to New York. It was a risk stopping to check her e-mail, leaving that kind of electronic footprint, not that she thought Uncle Ishat would ever think to look for her that way. But the trafficker might have, or someone else. At twelve years old she hadn't known exactly what she was up against, just that it was bad.

Now, a year and a half later, she not only remembers how to run, but also that sometimes you have to take risks along the way. They both know they can't keep going without something to drink, anything they can get their hands on.

Earlier, at the roadside café with its front wall open to the air, a few people sat at rusted tables with their cold drinks sparkling and sweating in the heat. As they approached, the woman behind the bar saw them coming out of a car – a car driven by a man who only spoke Italian, a man who couldn't even understand the world *help* – a couple of dark-skinned teenagers obviously hitching their way across the island. The unwelcoming look she gave them was dirtier than trash, but her judgmental expression wasn't the only thing they saw.

Behind her, a television perched on the bar was showing the news. The face of the white-haired man who visited Emiliana and Cosima the past two days filled the television screen with his name typed out along the bottom: *Enzio Greco,*

Commissario di Polizia. He seemed to be discussing something important, something grim – a death, because it showed a body being loaded into an ambulance, the ambulance driving away.

'Do you see that?' she'd asked him.

'Fuck yeah. Something's not right.'

'We better get out of here.'

They turned around and hitched another ride. And now here they are, in some place called Budoni, according to a sign they passed, creeping down the moonlit road in hope of a drink of water. They discussed it and both are afraid to risk asking anyone for help, because if that white-haired friend of Emiliana's is in on their kidnapping, it means they can't trust the police. It means they are really on their own.

First, they need water. Then, someplace safe to sleep in the dark. And after that, they will try to make their way south and get back to the house, in the hope that Karin and Mac arrived and are looking for them.

Saturday, July 14

I wake up sprawled on the bed, still in my clothes from yesterday. *The Lonely Planet* is spread open beside me, raised spine tenting the facedown book. I stretch, accidentally knock the book to the floor, swiftly pick it up and try to find my place. It's useless, but it doesn't matter. I know what I'm going to do. Last night I read for hours, trying to understand this island, hoping to develop an idea of where to begin. The two easiest places to hide, or be hidden, are crowds and wilderness. So I'll start with the largest, nearest city – Cagliari – and then branch out from there. It will also give me a chance to drop in on Enzio Greco at his office on the way.

Gentle morning sun pours through the big window, which I'd left open to the moon and stars and cool night air. In a climate like this you'd expect mosquitoes, but when I realized I wasn't getting bitten last night, I looked it up. According to the guidebook, Sardinia once festered with mosquitoes and malaria killed off huge numbers people. Hardly anyone visited the island. Then, sixty-five years ago, in a brutal but successful experiment, ten thousand tons of DDT were dumped on the island. Mosquitoes defeated, tourism took off; and now, Sardinia is a jet-setters playground, particularly in the north, where Liz Braud has her hotel.

Liz Braud: I itch to drive north and find her; but I promised Mac I'd wait.

The clock on the dresser across the room tells me that it's nearly eight A.M.

Mac hasn't contacted me or answered my calls.

Rolling off the bed, I stop in the bathroom to brush my teeth and splash water on my face. Feed the cats and kittens. Grab my purse and the car keys from downstairs, and head to town.

★ ★ ★

205

'The worried mama!' Enzio Greco greets me, rising from his desk and coming around to hug me. I've never been hugged by a police commissioner before. After a moment's hesitation, I hug him back, but it feels wrong so I pull away. Yes, I *am* a worried mama, but that's not all. I'm an investigator with nothing to hold on to, other than this white-haired old man, and that's not what I came for. I want action, information, leads, answers, results. I want my family back.

'Why haven't I seen a single sign anywhere? And nothing on TV? And what about Dante Serra? We haven't heard back from you about him. Did you find out what time he was at the house?'

'Please, sit.' Greco steers me into one of his visitor chairs, and then calls something out to the receptionist in Italian. A moment later she returns with a tiny cup of espresso for me. It's strong and acrid, burning my stomach as it goes down. My appetite is gone; I ate very little of the pasta I made last night and even these few sips of espresso threaten to come back up. I rest the cup on the edge of his desk, across which he has reseated himself, *the commissioner*, and watches me.

'A little better?'

'A little.' A lie.

'Let me explain to you. Of course we are searching. Perhaps you didn't notice the signs because you don't speak our language. If you can give us a photograph of your children and friend, it will be better for our signs and faxes, no?'

'Why didn't we do this yesterday?' I pull out my phone. Yesterday I was panicked, I wasn't thinking. Why didn't *he* think of this yesterday? Three photos showing Mary and the kids zap from my phone to his computer. He forwards them to someone else.

'Now, you see? This is why our collaboration is important. Two heads, they are better than one head, no?'

The thing is, I would have recognized their names in a sign. I would have seen something meaningful, even in a different language. But I decide not to challenge him. He'll get the photos into his alerts now; maybe it will make a difference. I can see that Enzio Greco is going to need supervision, like a child, and it irks me. How did this grandpa get to be police commissioner? Something more than his hugging me feels off-kilter. And the fixed way he's looking at me, smiling almost aggressively: fake smiling. I say nothing. I feel like a bad guest in a foreign land, pushy and demanding: the *typical obnoxious American* that has invited an unwelcoming attitude in so many corners of the world.

'Thank you,' I say, lamely.

'You asked me about Dante Serra. I should have called you, to calm you, to tell you that your locksmith Dante was not Dante *Serra.*'

'But the locksmith at Carrefour yesterday said it was.'

'He told you this?'

'Well, no, but the way he responded when we said the name. He was sad. His coworker was murdered. You could see it in his face.'

'You must understand, we Sardinians are an emotional bunch. We feel each other's pain. What you saw on that locksmith's face was sorrow for a fellow Sardinian, a fellow locksmith, not a personal coworker.'

'No. I'm sure.'

'Please, *signora*, put your mind to rest. I assure you, your family will be found. There is nothing like murder surrounding them. I understand completely your frustration. But trust me, all will be well.'

'What's the Carrefour locksmith's last name?'

'Piras,' he says without pause. 'It's Dante Piras who works for them. He is the Dante who visited your house. I spoke with him myself and he tells me your friend and children all were happy when he is there. He does his job. He goes. No problem.' Greco's shoulders rise and fall in a universal gesture of the *fait accompli*.

'Maybe if I could just talk to him, or to the person at Carrefour who sent him, maybe one of them could tell us exactly what Mary said. Something might click that could help us find them.'

'You speak no Italian.'

That silences me.

'Please, you must trust me. As they say on American television, "We are on it."' He hands

208

me a slip of paper with a phone number. 'My private mobile. Call me when you want. I will answer.'

I return the espresso cup to the receptionist on my way out, and she gives me the same chillingly courteous smile as her boss. I phony smile back. Not liking it here. Not trusting them. Unable to articulate exactly why. I step from the office's air-conditioning into the rising temperature outside, the instant accumulation of sweat like a wet cloth on my forehead. On the road to Cagliari, I consider sidetracking to Carrefour to speak to the locksmiths myself, but decide against it. Greco is right: I can't speak Italian, and he promised he's *on it* . . . so I'll let him be on it, and search on my own.

On a side street off Via Roma, edging the marina district of Cagliari, I struggle to nose into a tight parking spot shaded by a bank of trees. A man in baggy jeans and suspenders, carrying an accordion, sees me. Miming directions, he guides me into the narrow space. At last, I think, a friendly native. A thin layer of world-weary cynicism melts away. I remind myself that you just have to be somewhere long enough, find the right people. As I get out of the car, he starts to play a song, his fingers moving nimbly up and down the eccentric keyboard that seems charming in his hands. Wondering if this Italian minstrel hangs out here a lot, I pull out my phone and start searching for the photograph of Mary and the kids I've been showing around. I approach him, smiling, ready to ask – when suddenly he stops playing.

'Money, money,' he says.

'Excuse me?'

'Money, money.'

Is he reminding me that I have to buy a metered ticket to display in my windshield? 'I know,' I say. 'I'm going to. Thank you.'

He rubs his fingers together in the universal language of greed and opens his palm for a handout. The smile falls from his lips, shifting the mood from friendly to something else.

Hot with anger, I turn away and walk to the meter, where I fumble to discern which coins amount to the right number of Euros to rent the parking spot for the most amount of time possible. Behind me, accordion music, coming closer. Finally I start pushing coins, any coins, into the slot until I reach the two-hour limit. Dodging the accordionist, I slip the ticket into my window and lock the door.

Walking quickly past a gelateria, I spot a news-stand and buy copies of *L'Union Sarda* and the *International Herald Tribune*. The cafés on Via Roma are crowded with tourists. I want to escape Mr Money Money, so I turn right onto Via Lepanto and left onto Via Sardinia, where the cafés are smaller and quieter. I take a small outdoor table at the first place I come to and order a breakfast of fried eggs, meatballs, and toast, and American coffee, which I expect to be dreadful but turns out to be not too bad with milk and sugar. The meatballs trigger my appetite and after eating I feel a new, calmer energy shift through my exhausted body.

Café to café, store to store, restaurant to restaurant, hours dissolve along narrow, cobbled, medieval streets as I show anyone and everyone pictures of Mary, Dathi, Fremont, and Ben. 'Famiglia,' I say. 'Perso.' Lost.

Every two hours, I return to the car to feed the meter. By late afternoon, I've retreated from the pitiless sun beneath a swath of shade at another outdoor table at a café across from the Piazza della Costituzione, the monumental structure separating the old city from the new – or the extremely old from the less old. Antico Caffé sits on the corner of a busy intersection where I can watch car and foot traffic intersecting from five directions.

Adults, children, tourists, locals, wheelchairs, scooters, cars, motorcycles, buses, vans. I watch them all, the faces of people I don't recognize, one after another after another, hoping that one of them will come into exquisite focus and be Mary, or Dathi, or Fremont, or Ben – *my baby Ben*. I want and need to see him, all of them, so badly it hurts.

Everyone smiles but no one helps. *Money, money*, I think, disgusted with the accordion-laden beggar from this morning. First the mosquitoes ravaged

211

the island. Then rampant tourism hollowed out a different kind of agony.

A shift in light on the apricot walls announces the waning of the afternoon. Coffee devolves into wine. Before long I'm too bleary to consider getting in the car and driving home or anywhere else just yet.

I gather myself and abandon my table. Walking, searching all the new faces – they're always new, I never see anyone twice – I feel Mario Rossi's matchbook in my pocket. The one I took from his office last night. After another couple of hours scouring the old part of the city – showing the photographs, repeating, 'Famiglia,' 'Perso,' I hunt down the restaurant on the matchbook.

As I wait outside for my table for one, tanned visitors back from another day at the beach gather for their dinner. They look content and relaxed in this beautiful, historic place. Their happiness rankles me. The desperation with which I miss my children is sucking the air out of my lungs so gradually I hardly realize I'm barely breathing until light-headedness overtakes me. When the hostess calls my name and summons me to a little table tucked against the wall, I avert my eyes and keep my anguish to myself.

CHAPTER 13

The taxi jolts to a stop. Mac's eyes snap open. Lurching forward, he gazes sleepily out the window at a sunny urban street and hears the sounds of English. *American* English. A mother in red patent-leather clogs pushes a double stroller along the cracked side-walk. A couple of teenage boys bounce a basketball to the rhythm of their walking. A young girl with her ponytail poking out of a helmet scooters in front of a father jogging to keep up while he sips an iced Starbucks. Mac blinks, and remembers.

He is home, in Brooklyn.

The brownstone is bathed in shifting coins of glittering sunlight. Nothing looks amiss: no news-papers or flyers or mail or garbage left on the stoop. All the curtains are open onto windows turned mirrorlike by the bright day. The dense familiar quiet of his home beckons; but he can't go in uninvited, at least not until he's offered the Rossis a fair chance to explain themselves. He almost called them (again) right off the plane, but given that he already left a message and never heard back, it seemed like a better idea to just show up. It has occured to him that they might have reason to run if they knew he was coming.

'You all right back there?' the driver asks with a lilt of humor.

'Feeling a little hazy. Had to wait all night long for a connecting flight out of Rome.' He swipes his credit card, trying to focus on the tip menu.

'See, that's why I don't travel: It knocks you off-kilter. More trouble than it's worth, you ask me.'

'Can't argue with you there.' Yawning, Mac gets out of the cab and waits for the driver to pop the trunk. Hauls out his carry-on. Waves to the new neighbor, a young man who recently moved in across the street, while the cab drives away.

Leaving his luggage on the sidewalk, he climbs the stoop, rings the doorbell, and waits. After a few more tries, he calls his home number and listens as redundant clusters of unanswered rings echo through his house. He starts to dial Mario's cell number but stops himself, unsure how to proceed. Then he looks up Lacie Chen's office number, his thumb hovering over it, tempted to call her, too, and ask, *What the fuck, Lacie, what did you get us into, and why?*

Instead, he speed-dials Billy, hoping to give his friend fair warning that he's about to have a house-guest. The call goes straight to voice mail.

Suitcase wheels clattering behind him on the uneven sidewalk, Mac starts the fifteen-minute walk over to Billy's in Park Slope, his brain like an untamed animal now, hungrily gnawing the scant remains of information he rehashed at the airport last night, and then for hours on the plane. The Rossis: Whenever he thinks of them, doubt congeals like a cloud casting an amorphous shadow. He's been inside their house in Sardinia and they seem real enough, but are they? How did *they* get roped into making this trade? How much money did it take for them to suddenly turn over their home to strangers? Money. Is there anyone enough of it wouldn't tempt? It must be hard earning a living as a cartoonist. Mac wonders who Kroll, and Millerhausen, paid more to do the dance of musical homes: him or the Rossis.

The front windows of Billy's ground-floor apartment are wide open to the warm summer air, leeching noise from a radio alternating rap music with an announcer's staccato advertisement of something. Brake realignment at Pep Boys. Mac finds this strange because Billy's a big country music fan and has made a point to let everyone know how much he hates rap. He rings the doorbell twice.

Finally someone appears from the back of the apartment. Through the nearest window he sees that it isn't Billy, and in fact, now that he takes a close look inside, he realizes that the furniture is covered in drop cloths. The living-area walls look freshly painted white. A man in paint-splattered overalls and a ripped green T-shirt opens the door. A dribble of red paint looks like blood on his forehead.

'I'm a friend of Billy's. I'm guessing he's not here.'

'Staying with a friend.' A Russian accent. 'You can't reach him, right? I been trying to get him all morning, ask him about this red color in the bathroom. I dunno. Think he should take a look before I commit.'

'I'm surprised he's not doing his own painting.'

'Landlord's paying me. Water leak tore a hole in the kitchen ceiling, been a big project fixing it. Almost done.'

'You happen to know where he's staying?'

'With his partner, some strange name I can't remember.'

'Ladasha?'

The man grins. Nods. Snorts a laugh.

Ladasha answers on the second ring, using a friendly Saturday voice, not her official police greeting.

'*Ciao!*'

'Dash?'

'I see your name on my phone and I'm thinking here's my first call ever from Italy. A postcard would've been just fine, y'know.'

'I'm in Brooklyn.'

A pause. 'Why?'

'Is Billy there?'

Another pause and Billy's voice is in Mac's ear. 'What happened? Why are you back?'

Mac explains briefly. He listens while Billy holds the phone away from his ear to ask Ladasha if she

216

can put up another homeless investigator. To Mac's surprise, she doesn't hesitate, though Ladasha being Ladasha, she doesn't mince words, either. 'Tell him to get his ass over here *right now*. He can sleep in Devon's bed. And tell him we got lunch waiting.'

'She said—'

'I heard. You sure that was Ladasha?'

'Mmm-hmm,' Billy hums, but says nothing. Mac pictures Ladasha hovering by his friend's side, ready to intercept the conversation, but the image fades when it becomes impossible to imagine the woman at home. He has always only known her from the precinct, where her sour attitude doesn't trump kindness, it vanquishes it. The woman compartmentalizes better than anyone Mac has ever known. Karin once said that single mothers should rule the world and he half agrees. No one juggles time and responsibilities better than a determined woman jammed between the rock and hard place of love and survival. With two marriages and five kids under her belt, Ladasha manages her life like a CEO, gets to work on time, never misses a school play, has dinner on the table at a reason-able-enough time every night. But the woman is notoriously tough to work with. Blunt to the point of obnoxious, she takes no prisoners in her quest to get through a workday.

And another thing: Ladasha and Billy openly irritate each other. Of all the people he might have stayed with, why her? Mac contemplates that as he walks to the subway, realizing that the person he would have stayed with was off on a jaunt in Europe, and had loaned out his house to a couple of strangers.

Halfway through the newspaper he bought on his way to the subway, which snakes him in the direction of Bedford Stuyvesant, where Ladasha lives with her brood, Mac's eyes stop on a headline on the city pages:

Family Mourns as Pregnant Teen Is Buried

As he reads, he realizes that this is the missing girl he'd heard about on the radio on his way out to the Millerhausen mansion in Connecticut the first time he went. A terrible sadness flows through him as he learns that an autopsy revealed the seventeen-year-old's pregnancy.

In the photo beneath the headline, a woman about Mac's age weeps at the graveside of her murdered daughter, her face swollen and distorted from grief. Beside her stands her husband, his expression stoic; another daughter, long weedy hair hiding her face, hand gripping her mother's so tightly it looks as if they're trying to fuse their flesh; and a young boy, maybe eight, whose face shows an exquisitely painful mixture of puzzlement and boredom. For a moment Mac wonders if the boy is learning disabled. Which makes him think of the Millerhausen boys, one of whose outsized special needs sent his frantic mother into a tailspin at the prospect of a divorce. Just a week ago it seemed easy to decide that Cathy Millerhausen's worries were probably baseless. Now, he has to find out why they aren't, and he has to find out fast.

His head throbs. He hopes Ladasha has some ibuprofen in the house. He looks again at the graveside photograph of the boy mourning his sister and decides not to decide about this child based on a single snapshot. People process grief in mysterious ways, especially children. Losing his sister like that – the boy is probably in shock. Mac recalls the paralyzing emotion upon learning of his own parents' murders four years ago, a dream-like longing to run but you can't; if you run fast enough you could outwit this horrible thing, but *you can't*. He remembers when he finally understood what grief was: that you drowned in it, again and again. Remembers Karin's arms holding him up when his legs turned to rubber. The bottomlessness of his despair.

Mac finishes reading the article as the G train approaches the Bedford-Nostrand Avenues station, bringing himself up to date on what happened to the girl:

Alicia Griffin graduated from high school on June eighteenth. On the twenty-second, she went missing. On July ninth, her body was found in a shallow grave. And then, when Mac and Karin were traveling through England, the autopsy revealed another horrifying detail: Alicia was buried alive. From there, the story just got more outrageous, reporting that fetal DNA of the girl's baby was traced to a prisoner currently serving a fifty-year sentence for armed robbery at the Atlanta Penitentiary.

Mac happens to know that the Atlanta Pen is a high-security federal prison and if the guy was allowed conjugal visits, they'd be vetted high and low. Little chance someone not his wife would make it through, especially not a teenager. When did fiction start passing as news? Still, he reads on.

The inmate whose DNA proved he fathered the child has been charged with accessory to murder, on the assumption that somehow, and for some reason, he had arranged the girl's murder from afar. The police are combing prison visitation records, speculating that it could be to find out if the woman with whom the inmate had conjugal visits was not his wife but Alicia Griffin. Mac cringes: Tagged to fact, that's just the kind of innuendo with the power to incite a cascade of rumors damaging to a potential jury pool.

He folds the paper and holds it on his lap. Nice girl from the suburbs. Played soccer and didn't do drugs, according to her stricken friends. It doesn't make a lot of sense, but he's heard and seen worse. Tragic. Glad it's not his problem to solve. But still, he can't help thinking about it – the girl, his own parents – the sensation of hollowness when you comprehend that a meaningful life was brutally ended, usually because of someone else's helpless rage, or stupidity, or greed.

The train squeals into the station. Mac rolls his suitcase onto the platform, where a mohawked teenager is blasting soul music from a boom box the likes of which he hasn't seen for a decade. Beside him, a girl in hot pants, a translucent shirt smaller than her royal blue bra, and glittering silver sneakers dances like she's auditioning for something. Passing through the cloud of distorted music, Mac's headache is upgraded to the threat of a migraine.

The sun on Bedford Avenue is bright and hot but nowhere near as brutal as a typical day in Sardinia. Mac thinks of Karin. Digs for his phone and speed-dials while calculating the time difference: almost eight P.M. in Sardinia.

'You're home?' she greets him in a voice crackling with distance.

'I was. No one answered the door. No one answered the phone.'

'What now?'

'On my way to Dash's. Billy's place is getting painted. Apparently he's staying with her.'

'With Ladasha?' She laughs. 'How are you?'

'Tired but okay. You?'

'No, *grazie*,' she says to someone else. Then to Mac, 'Sorry, I'm in a restaurant in Cagliari. I found a book of matches from here in Mario Rossi's office and I had to eat somewhere, so I thought why not.'

'And?'

'I spent the day walking around, showing

221

everyone I could find the picture of Mary and the kids. I'm wasting my time.'

'What did Enzio Greco say? What's going on with that?'

'He told me the Dante who fixed the lock at our house has a different last name.'

'But the guy at Carrefour said—'

'I know, that's what I told Greco. He thinks the guy just didn't understand us, or we didn't understand him, or something.'

'It's possible.'

'The thing is, I haven't seen a single Missing sign anywhere, and I've been going all around. I haven't seen anything on the local news. It's like Greco isn't really trying. I don't get it.'

'Keep bugging him. You're good at that.'

'Ha ha. But I am.'

A small Chinese man tries to push a brochure for a massage parlor into Mac's hand. Mac waves him off and drags his suitcase forward, walking now as he talks to his wife. He turns onto Greene Avenue and starts looking for Ladasha's house number.

'I'm heading up to see Liz Braud tomorrow,' Karin tells him.

'Wait on that, *please*. I don't want you stepping into any snake pits you don't see.'

She doesn't answer, which could mean anything.

'Seriously—'

'How was the trip?' she interrupts. She's made up her mind. Maybe she's right; maybe it wouldn't hurt to drop in on Liz Braud, ask some innocuous questions, see what spills out.

'Had to wait all night long in the Rome airport for a connection to New York. I could have slept at home, with you.'

'You know we wouldn't have been able to sleep.'

It hurts him to think of her alone in the house in Capitana. He can imagine her desolation. Wonders how much she drank. Or if she stayed up on the Internet, frustrating herself. He hopes she didn't try driving anywhere in the dark, the roads there being so treacherous, especially with the unreliable transmission.

'How's the car holding up?'

She hesitates, then answers, 'Fine.'

'It stalled out.'

'No, it's fine.'

'How bad was it?'

'Mac, we have to keep our heads screwed on straight if we're going to manage this. No excessive worrying about the other one, okay? It won't help. We have to focus on finding them.'

'I know that.'

'I know you know that.'

But she was right: He was worried about her, and it was a distraction.

'I guess I should go in now.' He stands in front of Ladasha's brownstone, pots of red geraniums staggering up the stoop. Already this is a different Ladasha from the precinct, the one who wouldn't be caught dead with a flower.

'She knows you're coming?'

He rings the bell. 'She knows. Be careful, Karin.'

'I love you, too.'

A cascade of footsteps approaches the door, which swings open to the sight of a teenage girl still in her nightgown at two in the afternoon. Her untended straightened hair sticks out at crazy angles.

'You're not Tyrone,' she informs him.

'I'm Mac. Your mother's expecting me.'

'She didn't tell *me*.'

'I can see that.'

A boy about six, wearing shorts and nothing else, pushes his sister out of the way. 'Mama said let you in.'

'Thanks.'

'Hey, Aaron . . .' shouts a younger boy whose excitement fades from his expression at the sight of Mac standing on the stoop.

'Sorry, I'm Mac.'

The three children quickly disperse, leaving Mac alone on the foyer's worn Oriental carpet. A mass of shoes is piled beneath a No Shoes in the House sign. The smell of toast wafts in from another room.

Billy trots down the stairs, barefoot in shorts and a T-shirt, black eyepatch angled over his left eye, big smile welcoming Mac as if it's his own home. Billy's obvious ease in Ladasha's house throws Mac off guard a moment, but he bites his tongue. Pats Billy on the back, gladdened by the warmth of his friend's embrace.

224

'Hey, man.' Billy steers Mac through a dining room – long oak table beneath a chandelier he never would have guessed you'd find in Ladasha's home – and into a large kitchen, where the woman of the house stands before a stovetop, frying eggs.

'Best I can do on short notice,' she says.

'Dash.' Mac kisses her cheek – another first. 'Good to see you. Nice apron.'

She hits him with a plastic spatula, streaking oil on the shoulder of his T-shirt.

'Ouch!'

'Leave my apron out of it.' She smiles and her gold canine glimmers in the sunlight from her backyard-facing kitchen window. Outside, an orderly garden, plastic toy box, picnic table shaded by a green umbrella.

Mac puts the folded-open newspaper on the edge of a counter and helps Billy set the kitchen table. Digging for forks and knives, Mac asks, 'How many?'

'Six,' Billy tells him.

'Devon and Dwayne are away at Y camp.' Eggs sizzle as Ladasha starts to flip them in the hot pan. 'Don't think I could take a whole summer of their lip.'

'Still into baseball?' Mac recalls Ladasha rushing around the city, coordinating game schedules for the two different teams on which her nine- and twelve-year-old sons are devoted players.

'Oh, yeah. Let them stand on the ninety-five-degree-hot field if they want to, but count me out.

225

Coupla years Kwame and Erik gonna be old enough to go to sleep-away camp, too. But they're so sweet, I'd miss them.'

'Sweet *now*,' Billy suggests.

'True,' she flips another egg, 'true.'

'Your daughter's not interested in camp?' Mac asks, spacing half a dozen pairs of utensils around the table.

'Don't get her started on Latisha,' Billy mutters, folding napkins.

The eggs sizzle louder and hotter as Ladasha flips them quickly now, focusing hard on the oil-splattering pan. 'No, Tish isn't interested in camp. Only thing she's interested in these days is boys. I could kill her.'

Mac glances at Billy, who raises a brow, and wonders what's up. When the children appear at the table a few minutes later, he gets the picture pretty quickly. Latisha, who he remembers being Ladasha's pride and joy – the eldest and most responsible, a good student and sought-after babysitter – is wallowing in puberty. In the brief time since Mac arrived at the house, the fifteen-year-old has slathered on a full face of makeup and dressed in tight short-shorts and a shirt that hugs her front, leaving little to the imagination. Laser beams of tension shoot between mother and daughter throughout the meal. While Kwame and Erik chatter happily about toys, games, and friends, painstakingly buttering their own toast and cutting their own eggs, big sister scarfs down her food in minutes and is out the front door, her mother's 'Hey!' answered by the silence of Latisha's sudden departure.

Billy chuckles. Ladasha snaps the back of his head with the dish towel from her shoulder, but finally laughs, too.

'Wow,' Mac says. 'When did that happen?'

'Tenth grade.' Ladasha squeezes her mouth tight, shakes her head.

'Is this what we have to look forward to with Dathi?'

'Nah,' Billy says. 'Dathi's a different kind of kid.'

'Just you wait,' Ladasha warns. Then, to her sons, 'Aaron's mother called. They're meeting us at the playground, so hurry up and get ready.'

Eager to get outside, Kwame and Erik clear their places, their dishes clattering into the sink, and race out of the kitchen.

'Take a break,' Billy tells Ladasha, stopping her when she gets up to clear more dishes. 'We got this.'

She sits back down. Moments later, the two boys reappear in clean T-shirts and shorts, socks baggy around their ankles, sneakers loosely laced, the bills of their baseball caps forward and ready.

'Okay, Mama,' says Erik, the youngest.

Ladasha smiles. 'Here I come. Go wait by the front door.' But it's another minute before she moves. 'I don't know.' She glances between Billy and Mac. 'All these kids, I watch them grow, and they're just like their daddies. Tish, Devon, and Dwayne – got too much Daltry in 'em, that self-centered piece of scum. And these little guys, well, sweet as pie on a fall afternoon – just like Larry was. Just goes to show, you can divorce the man, but you can't divorce the gene pool.'

'What happened to Larry, if he was so sweet?' Billy asks her.

With a hard look, she tells him, 'Drunken fool.'

'Guess it's always something.'

'Well, look at you – forty-seven and never married. But maybe there's still hope for you yet.'

'Mama!' The boys are growing impatient by the door.

'Here I come,' she repeats.

Ladasha pushes herself up from the table. Retrieving her purse from the kitchen counter, she spots Mac's newspaper, folded open to the story about the teenager who was buried alive. She picks up the paper and waves it at her guests. 'I hate to say it, but this girl here? If her baby was gonna be anything like it's daddy, well, maybe she's better off. Least my kids' daddies aren't killers. Gotta keep it in perspective,' she tells herself, setting down the paper. 'My kids, guess they're not all that bad.'

'You're doing a great job with them, Dash,' Billy tells her.

'Well, you kinda gotta say that, don't you?' She winks at him. 'Unless you wanna get kicked to the street.' And she's gone.

Mac stacks the remaining plates, carries them

to the sink and returns for glasses while Billy collects the utensils.

'Leave it,' Billy stops his friend. 'You go up and get some sleep. Devon and Dwayne have the room at the top of the stairs. Bottom bunk is Devon's – Dash said to use that bed.'

'Doesn't want an old man falling out of the top bunk?'

'Who knows?'

'I don't want to sleep yet.' Mac cinches two glasses each in either hand, puts them in the sink, and starts to empty the dishwasher. 'There's too much to do – only I don't know where to start.'

'Then get yourself some more caffeine and sit down,' Billy insists. 'I'll clean, you talk. Come on. Catch me up with the details.'

Mac takes his friend's advice and pours himself another mug of coffee. Leaning against the counter near the sink, he fills Billy in on Kroll, London, Sardinia, and everything he can remember about the Millerhausen case.

'How long before the cops started looking for Mary and the kids?'

'Not soon enough. At first, the commissioner actually told us they probably got *lost*. Even now, Karin says she doesn't see any sign of a search. There's something going on, but I can't figure out what.'

'That woman, Julie—'

'Giulia. It's like she doesn't really exist. But we talked to someone.'

'Hey, man – you're here. Go ring your own doorbell. Ask those people about their friend, see what they tell you face-to-face.' Twitches, frozen pupils, shallow breathing: signs of lying you can only detect in person.

'I tried. Stood there like an idiot, ringing my own bell, calling my own landline. Either no one's home or no one's answering. I almost called my contact at Kroll, the one who threw us the home exchange. The thing is, I'm not sure where to start. Who to trust.'

'I hear you.' Billy dries his hands and joins Mac at the table, bringing along a notepad and a pen, a detective starting a new case. Even if it's not an official New York City case, Billy has access to police resources Mac doesn't. 'What about the wife?'

'Cathy. Haven't tried her yet, but I'd really like to talk to her.'

She answers on the second ring. 'If it isn't my very own private detective. I thought you put my case on hold.'

'On the contrary. I heard about your husband's colleague dying.'

'Poor Dan. I sat with his wife and her family last night. So tragic.'

'Can we meet?'

'When do you have in mind?'

CHAPTER 14

The sour smell of moldy cheese permeates the room along with something else: a cloying sweetness that won't be dessert, because they never provide any, so must be rot. Mary lies on the couch, her mind numb, her body tingly and weightless. She can't find the energy to deal with the bag of groceries left yesterday by one of the guards. Why do they think she needs food? It's just her now. She doesn't need much and couldn't eat anyway. Do they actually think she'll just continue on like before, preparing meals, eating, cleaning up, and again? All that was for the children. The effort of meals, talk, games, routines – it was all for them.

And now they're gone.

That gunshot after Fremont and Dathi ran out – who was hit?

Ben – where is he now?

How will she face Karin and Mac, knowing that her foolishness led to the children's scattering?

Something contracts inside Mary's chest. Her eyes fix on a shadow drifting across the ceiling as a cloud overlaps the sun outside. The cloud shifts and the ceiling lights up. She only realizes that her eyes have closed when the world is suddenly dark. She listens for something, anything, outside the window. But since yesterday, the only sound has been the door opening, the bag being set down, and the door closing again.

And she thinks. It's all she does now.

The Millerhausen women . . . what are they doing here, of all places? Clearly, they know the Rossis. *What can it possibly mean?*

Are Godfrey Millerhausen and his ex-wife in on something? Thus the Rossis' offer of their home. The overpaid job from Kroll. What is Godfrey trying to hide from Cathy? It can't be just an affair.

If only Mary hadn't found that photo, *if only* she hadn't asked the Rossis about it, the children would still be with her. She's convinced that her e-mail to the Rossis must have triggered panic that she was on the verge of making connections they didn't want her to make. *If only.* Karin and Mac would be here now. They'd all be together in the house on Via Degli Oleandri. They might have finished their vacation and gone home unsuspecting. Never looked at the Millerhausen case again. Moved on. Lived.

Millerhausen – Kroll – the Rossis – Liz and Blaine.

A shapeless map, in names, from New York to Sardinia to here.

★ ★ ★

Interstate 95 is slow-moving as always on a summer Saturday afternoon. Mac rides shotgun while Billy grinds his teeth and grips the wheel, holding the car back at twenty miles an hour. They've had the conversations about how it's going to take forever to get to the Millerhausens' house, how traffic sucks, how there are too many cars on the road, too many people in the world. Turned off the radio when they lost NPR and all the local stations had too many ads.

It's another slow hour before they pull up in front of the Millerhausen mansion, but the afternoon sun is still in full force. The long private road to the house feeds them into a circular drive, where Billy parks behind a midnight blue BMW.

The door is answered by a uniformed housekeeper, which surprises Mac. For some reason he'd thought Cathy Millerhausen was more enlightened than that, but then he only met her once.

'Mrs Millerhausen is expecting us,' Mac tells the woman, who reminds him of his late grandmother, Rose, for whom his sister Rosie is named. Grandma Rose was short and stout like this woman, with the same gray curls capping her head. Not a trace of makeup: *This is me, take it or leave it.*

Pulling her startled gaze off Billy's eyepatch, she says, 'Mrs M is around back with the boys. Follow me.'

The place is a funny mix of genteel and garish, as if decorated by an insecure designer trying to please a hybrid of Mrs Astor and the Donald. A giant ornate gilt-framed mirror hangs on the wall opposite the lip of a wide curving staircase. Professional photo portraits of the Millerhausen twins, starting from birth, are equidistantly spaced alongside the stairs. On their way through the massive front hall, Mac notices how alike Bobby and Ritchie are in their baby pictures and how their likeness transforms and digresses as they age. Now, at eight, one brother looks fit and alert, while the other is heavier, with a dull glaze over his eyes. He doesn't see a single picture of Godfrey Millerhausen's other child, a daughter now in her early twenties who, according to Mary's research, lives in Paris. When they veer around a center table holding an enormous vase of dramatic white flowers, Mac is hit with their peppery-sweet fragrance and thinks of Karin. She loves flowers but would probably balk at this outsized display.

Cathy and the boys are out by the pool: kidney shaped, a grassy distance from the columned portico at the back of the house. She lounges in a bathing suit and sheer coverup, watching Bobby jackknife off a diving board, piercing the water and gliding like a blade through butter. Ritchie sits on the edge of the pool, feet dangling in, and claps awkwardly with large hands.

'Wasn't that great, Ritchie?' Cathy singsongs to her boy.

He nods in agreement without turning to look at her. She smiles. Noticing her visitors, she stiffens and rises to greet them.

'Anya, will you bring us some iced tea, please?' she calls after the housekeeper.

Mac greets her. 'This is my good friend, Detective Billy Staples.'

Cathy eyes Billy's black patch.

Crashing out of the water, Bobby swims to the nearest ladder, lean and fast. Mac guesses he's good at all kinds of things. You'd have to be, as a twin, to compensate for the other one, who sits, lumpish, watching his brother, not turning to look at the visitors.

'Ahoy!' Bobby says. 'Mom, you didn't say a pirate was coming today.'

'I didn't know.'

'Is he from Somalia?'

From the corner of his eye, Mac can see Billy working hard not to react. Guess they don't see too many black guys wearing eyepatches in Greenwich. Even so, the boy is getting a pricey education; he should know better than to shout out stuff like that. But then again, entitlement starts young, especially in the top tier of the 1 percent.

'We're friends of your mother,' Mac says. 'Sorry to disappoint.'

'Bobby, take Ritchie inside and get on some dry clothes, why don't you?'

'*Mom—*'

'*I said—*'

'*Okay*. Come on, Ritchie.'

The boys trudge wet into the house, Cathy

watching them until they're out of view. 'I don't think they'll say anything. If they do, I'll tell Godfrey we have new gardeners. He won't question that.'

'I take it he's not home,' Mac says.

'In the city all weekend, working.' She rolls her eyes. 'Obviously he's really good at this. He has a lot of practice – he cheated with me when he was married to Liz.'

'We didn't see him with anyone. We would have noticed.'

'You,' she indicates Billy with her chin, 'were following Godfrey, too?'

'No, he means his regular work partners. I'm with the NYPD.'

'Karin, my wife, works with me, as does my assistant, Mary.'

'I see. Don't I recall you telling me you were all going away? To Europe?'

'They're still there. I came back.' A beat, and then he tells her: 'Mary and our children are missing.'

Cathy's face blanches. 'Please, sit down.'

Anya returns with a tray of iced teas edged with lemon slices, ice cubes glittering cold in the heat. Mac sips his greedily, only now realizing his thirst. He feels the prickly urgency of an undefined need: What does Cathy Millerhausen know that might help him find his family? What does she know that she doesn't realize is exceptionally important?

'Tell me,' she says. •

236

'We spent a few days alone in England, my wife and I, and when we got to Italy, they were gone.'

'You're sure they'd been there?'

He nods.

'Where in Italy?'

'Sardinia, near Cagliari.'

Her glass stops midway to her mouth. She stares at him.

'I'm aware,' he explains, 'that the first Mrs Millerhausen lives there now.'

'*He knows.*'

Just as Mac has come to suspect. 'How?'

'He sent you away so you'd stop investigating him. It must be worse than I thought.' Cathy's eyes narrow. 'Godfrey loves to play games. He once told me his car was picking me up to bring me to a restaurant for dinner. Instead, I was taken to JFK and put on a plane to the Bahamas. Godfrey was waiting for me at the Pink Sands. I had to buy a whole new wardrobe, and we had a good time, but I hated him for it. The children.'

'Who stayed with them?'

'No one in particular. The maids.'

'Why didn't he just ask you to plan out a vacation?'

'Partly because he knew I wouldn't leave Ritchie for that long. But also because Godfrey loves a challenge.'

'He's manipulative,' Mac says.

'That's a nice way to put it.' She smirks. 'He's

237

heartless. You didn't end up in Sardinia on vacation just by chance.'

'Who does he know at Kroll Investigations?'

'Only everyone.'

Mac and Billy stare at her, waiting for more.

'He uses them all the time; his money keeps them at his beck and call. Whatever he wants, they do for him. It's his candy store, that place. He asks, they give.'

'Kroll called me for a job, sent me to London, to Barclays. Put me on a bogus case. Overpaid me.'

'I wish you hadn't been so professional when you put my case on hold,' she says, a sharp glint in her eyes. 'If you'd told me all that then, I could have warned you.'

'I thought I was finally too old to be such a fool.'

'No one's too old to be a fool. Trust me. Not when you're dealing with people like my husband.'

'You still think he's having an affair.'

'I'm convinced of it.'

'But he's hiding it well.'

'That would be his style. He'll divorce me and hold me to the prenup. He'll let Ritchie flap in the wind the rest of that poor boy's life.'

'I just can't see why he would orchestrate all this – sending us overseas to get me off his scent – just to cover an affair.'

'I wouldn't put it past him.' Her fingertip hums around the edge of her glass.

'Collusion and abduction are pretty serious crimes,' Billy says. 'I'm not buying he'd go to all that trouble just to save some money in a divorce. He really that greedy?'

'Yes. And no.'

Mac glances at Billy, trying unsuccessfully to process the non-answer. But sometimes two things can be true at once. What had first seemed like an easy case suddenly wasn't – that much he knew for certain.

'Not to state the obvious,' Billy sits back, crossing his ankle over his knee, 'but there's definitely something else he doesn't want folks to know.'

'Any idea what's scaring him?' Mac asks Cathy.

'If I knew that, I wouldn't have needed you.'

'What about Dan Stylos? He was the one person I really wanted to talk to,' Mac explains, 'maybe because he wouldn't call me back.'

'Dan was a lovely guy. He had a family and . . .' Cathy's eyes tear up, she can't finish.

'How well did you know him?'

'Just from company get-togethers twice a year: the holiday party, and a summer barbecue we host for executives and their families. He always struck me as down-to-earth.'

'Any idea why he killed himself?'

'Why do you assume he killed himself?' she answers.

'Were Dan and your husband close?'

'They worked very closely together. I don't know how close they were personally. We never got together as couples. It was business between them, that's all.'

239

'And now he's dead, and I can't talk to him.'

Cathy nods, her eyes drifting closed. 'Oh God.'

Bobby and Ritchie wander back outside wearing neatly pressed khaki shorts and polo shirts that look pretty spiffy on Bobby and sad on Ritchie. Holding hands, Bobby leads his brother into a shed, and they emerge with matching butterfly nets.

Suddenly something occurs to Mac. 'Do twins run in the family?'

'Not mine,' Cathy answers. 'Godfrey's, possibly, but he was adopted, so we don't really know.'

Startled, Mac repeats, 'Adopted?'

'You didn't know?' Cathy asks.

'I wish I had.'

Billy looks at Mac. 'What's on your mind?'

'What Dash said before got me thinking. Genetics. You can't avoid them.'

'Dash?' Cathy asks.

'My partner,' Billy tells her. 'We're both staying with her. Long story.'

'What about twins?' Cathy asks. 'I'm not following.'

'Just curious. I feel like we've got to unravel this guy from the beginning.'

'Godfrey keeps his adoption certificate in the safe in his home office.' Cathy gets up, returning a few minutes later with a yellowed envelope with faded typed print across the front: CONFIDENTIAL ADOPTION RECORDS. 'Unravel away.'

It looks as if it's been opened and resealed,

with a thick glop of wax emblazoned with an elaborate *M*.

'Godfrey had that seal made. He thinks it's funny. I don't.'

'You've read this?'

'How could I? If I broke the seal he'd know, and I didn't want to go there. He made a big deal about feeling sensitive about being adopted and wanting the paperwork just to have it, blah blah blah.'

'Did you ask him if he's a twin?'

'I did.'

'And?'

'He said no.'

Mac taps the envelope against his open palm. 'Well, shall we?'

The boys return, swinging their butterfly nets. 'Mom,' Bobby is ecstatic, 'Ritchie caught one!'

'Not here.' She tells Mac. 'Do it somewhere else and let me know. I can't be directly involved.'

'You gave it to me.'

'You stole it.'

Mac grins. 'Don't know if I like this.'

'Go,' she insists, and adds in a whisper so her boys won't hear, 'And don't worry – you didn't steal it, I gave it to you. But do me a favor and cover your tracks – make it seem like you got it some other way.'

When they rise to leave, Mac thinks to ask her: 'How did he get this?'

'One guess.'

Kroll.

Walking back to Billy's car, Mac says, 'Well, this is a first. I get the information handed to me, but I have to go looking for it anyway.'

'Gotta keep up appearances, man.' Billy laughs, unlocking the doors with his remote.

Calling Lacie Chen at Kroll late on a Saturday afternoon proves as useless as you'd think it would be. Mac leaves a message anyway, and stares out the window at the thickening traffic as they head back into the city through the Bronx. Co-op City looms up around them in angry towers of windowed concrete, begging the usual question: Why? Mac always thinks of master developer Robert Moses when he travels this route, and ends up thinking about all the blighted projects, his mind zeroing in on the crime statistics, poverty, and desperation of those places. Why did anyone think it was a good idea? Didn't they realize that creating these soulless out-of-the-way boxes would only enhance segregation and consolidate hopelessness in an already downtrodden group of people? How was such a ruthless vision allowed to be realized on such scale? Whole tracts of neighborhoods were condemned for Moses's brutal urban reinventions throughout New York.

Money. That's why and that's how. 'Affordable housing' got society's *unsavory elements* out of sight and out of mind. Buried them alive in drab mono- tonous apartments they could just afford. Left them there. Money looked the other way as it drove past on the highways Moses built to slice off *neighborhoods where people could no longer safely go.* There are so many problems with that thought: Neighborhoods. People. Safety. So many ways to define and misinterpret all of them.

Finally they drive out of the worst of it and Mac rubs his eyes. Maybe he should never have read Jane Jacob's *The Death and Life of Great American Cities.* Maybe he shouldn't read so much, period. Maybe he shouldn't feed on information the way he does. Maybe ignorance is bliss.

Maybe he shouldn't have asked about twins.

Or opened that confidential envelope Cathy Millerhausen gave him.

Maybe he shouldn't have come back from Sardinia, leaving Karin alone in a kind of wilderness.

'How am I going to pretend I found out on my own that Millerhausen has a biological twin,' Mac asks Billy, 'and not waste time doing it?'

According to the adoption record, Godfrey Millerhausen was adopted as a *single identical twin,* meaning they were separated at birth and adopted by different families. The document gives no other information about Godfrey's brother.

One corner of Billy's mouth dimples. He shakes his head. 'Fuck that. Move forward, that's what I say. Seems your case is getting more interesting by the minute. Personally, I wouldn't wait, especially if I was just a P.I. – no system to come crashing down on your head.'

'Are you kidding? Millerhausen could sue me. Get my license revoked.'

'For what?'

'You heard her: She's afraid of him. She said she'd claim I stole the adoption record.'

'And then she said she wouldn't. Anyway, you've got a witness saying you didn't. A witness with a badge.'

The half-full liter of water they found in the trash by the beach entrance is better than anything Fremont has ever tasted before, and that's saying a lot for an American kid. He knows that. He knows now how spoiled he's been, even though he and his mom are always broke and live in a crummy part of the city and only really have each other, despite all that he *knows* how much he has in his life. Or had. Half white, half black, no money, a no one at the frayed edges of one of the world's biggest cities, he has/had the greatest life a kid could want. Just the fact that he's been spoiled: that so little can amount to so much in comparison to other people's situations. His mother never let him think they were poor; whatever he wanted, whatever he needed, he had. Somehow she got him his own laptop when he started middle school. Even gave him a very cool electric guitar for his fourteenth birthday. His eyes start to tear in the dark and he wipes them dry. He can't afford to deplete the fluids in his body. Every drop is precious.

'You finish it.' He hands Dathi the bottle. He can hear what's left splashing around inside the plastic container as she lifts the bottom high and tilts back her head. The last of the water gurgles into her mouth. In the moonlight, he can see spasms of her silvery neck swallowing efficiently and fast.

'Ahh.' She tosses the bottle aside. 'That is the best water I ever tasted. Even in India, I never went that long without a drink.'

Half a night and one full day, that's how long since they've had a drop of water. Luckily they managed to get some food earlier in the day when a family left uneaten sandwiches at a beachside café and, pretending to work there, Dathi sauntered up like she was clearing away their refuse and stuffed what she could under her shirt. And ran. They have found that she does best in the eyes of others when she's alone, but he does best when they're together. Either way, they both prefer each other's company and protection to wandering through Sardinia by themselves.

'How far do we have left?' she asks him.

'Dunno, but I'm thinking we're about halfway there.' After hiding all day, they hitched two good rides tonight that brought them this far. 'Capitana, near Cagliari,' is all they say. Even when one of the drivers spoke English, they didn't dare talk to him in case he decided to turn them over to the police. In case that white-haired commissioner got his hands on them and returned them to those fucking evil ladies. If they're caught, the four of them will be trapped together again, and no one will ever know where to find them.

He wonders how his mother and Ben are doing in the apartment, what she's telling him about their absence. He's so young he'll believe just about anything, which is kind of a relief, but still. The last couple of days together in the apartment they ganged up and told the kid so many lies it would put Pinocchio out of business. Created a whole fantasy about when he'd get to see his mom and dad again, how they were still on vacation but they'd moved houses. *Moved*. Yeah, right: try *kidnapped*. Ben's lucky not to understand what's going on. Not that the rest of them really have any idea.

'I have to pee,' she says. 'Be right back.'

She picks up the empty water bottle and drops it into the trash on her way to find a good place to hide so he won't see her, even in the dark, when she pulls her pants down. It wouldn't matter; she feels like a sister to him. But he respects her need for privacy. His mother taught him how to treat girls and he's glad she did.

He presses himself into a shadow while a car's bright headlights swing over him. There aren't too many cars on the road since it's the middle of the night. If Dathi were with him, they'd probably try to hitch a ride with this one, but he's not going anywhere without her.

The car stops, pauses and backs up. By the time

it reaches the spot where he sits cross-legged on the ground, alone, his pulse is beating at his ears.

When Dathi comes back, he isn't there. She was only gone five minutes.

'Free?' she whispers, and then more loudly: 'Fremont!'

Crickets saw into the silence.

She heard a car pass when she squatted behind the bushes, just one car. And she thought she heard voices but it sounded like a radio.

'Fremont, are you here?'

Another car comes along and she throws herself into a shadow falling from a group of trees. Loneliness trickles through her like poison. Maybe he, too, went to pee. Sitting in the moonlit darkness, she waits.

CHAPTER 15

Billy's desk at the Eight-four is littered with scribbled notes, a napkin from yesterday's lunch, random paper clips, and a stack of case files in manila folders ranging from crisply new to frayed from overuse. A photo of his sister and her family is taped to the side of a half-dead plant. It's nearly nine P.M. and the graveyard shift lives up to its name under the bleak fluorescent light that turns you deathly gray if you're white, black, or Hispanic. Bad lighting: the great equalizer. Mac isn't used to it anymore, and yet it feels familiar, even good (in a way), being back inside a detectives unit.

Finally Billy's cell rings with the payoff they've been waiting for: Carlos Lopez, his contact in Vital Records who owes him a favor, is a single guy lonely enough to go to the office on a Saturday night to pay up. Perfect timing, since the records office closes for the weekend, allowing Lopez to dig into his computer alone. Normally the process for getting the kind of information Mac and Billy are after – the name of an adoptee in a sealed adoption case from decades ago – requires a court order, which they could probably get eventually, but it would take too much time. If they're going to figure out what Godfrey Millerhausen is up to, what's at stake for him, *who he is*, they'll have to do it fast.

'Yeah, I hear you, Carlos, buddy,' Billy says, 'and trust me, no worries on that.'

Mac imagines the conversation on the other end of the line: *This is highly confidential. No one knows you heard it from me. And I won't give you any paperwork on it, just the names.*

'Wow, man, that's a lotta databases to check. Really grateful. Thanks.'

Billy ends the call and looks at Mac, who asks, 'Well?'

'Their parents were teenagers. Father was Jim Smith, listed as "student." Mother was Sue Smith, listed as "student." Both age fifteen. The twin boys were born in Florida and given up at birth. Nothing more on the birth parents.'

'How did the Millerhausens find a baby to adopt in Florida? They're an old New York family.'

Billy shrugs his shoulders. 'Who knows? They found themselves a white boy. Guess they were willing to travel.' He does not say it with bitterness, nor does Mac hear it with guilt.

'The brother?'

'Adopted by Ruth and Owen Moore of Jupiter, Florida. That's all I know.'

A Google search opens a floodgate.

They named him Dallas Wayne, for reasons

unknown. He was raised an only child. And he was not a good kid.

Dallas Wayne Moore's rap sheet stretches the proverbial mile, starting with muggings as a boy in Jupiter. Carjackings as a teenager earned him a stint in juvie from which he was released upon turning eighteen. As he grew into a man, he escalated to burglary, extortion, and identity theft. But it was an armed robbery of a Brinks armored truck that put him in the United States Penitentiary in Atlanta, Georgia, for fifty years on charges of felony robbery.

Billy finds an array of Dallas's mug shots on file in a federal prisoner database. He starts off handsome and tall with light brown hair, just like his twin brother Godfrey. But a life of crime took its toll; by the last mug shot on his way into the Atlanta Pen, he is torn and pocked and ravaged, with thinning frazzled hair and an old scar zippering down his left cheek. Mac thinks of the infamous Bulger brothers of Boston: One grows up to be a university president, the other one a boss of the Irish mob. That the same parents raised them makes it all the more inscrutable a divide.

'Oh Jesus,' Mac pushes closer to Billy to get a better look at the screen. 'Holy mother of God.'

Billy chuckles. 'Seriously?'

'Raised Catholic, can't shake it.' Mac's finger presses hard on one of the links. 'Read this.'

'Not a touch screen, buddy.'

Mac pulls his hand away, leaving a smudge atop

250

DNA of Murdered Pregnant Teen's Fetus Matched to Federal Prisoner Dallas Wayne Moore. He remembers now: The article he read about the girl's murder tied her to a prisoner in Atlanta.

Billy grabs the mouse and clicks on the first link of many. Each report is short and repeats the same scant bits of information that are so hard to believe, they went viral online. They stop reading after the first dozen when they realize they're not going to learn anything they don't already know about the case of Alicia Griffin. Mac recalls reading in the newspaper about the theory that she snuck into jail for conjugal visits, which doesn't make sense. It makes even less sense if you look at the latest mug shot of Dallas. It's impossible to believe that a good-looking, healthy, and by all accounts normal teenage girl would be attracted to such an ugly wreck thirty years older than her, or that anyone could believe they were married, or that they had ever even met.

'Godfrey plays God,' Mac says. 'Gives life, takes life.'

'Looks like he's good for that pregnant teenager's murder.'

Mac nods. 'I'm liking him for it big-time.'

'The Mrs doesn't know the half of what a bastard her husband really is.'

'Let's go after him, Billy.'

'There's no way I can be official on this – it's not a Brooklyn case. But I'll help you, under the radar, any way I can.'

251

'Thank you, brother.'

Billy laughs. 'Brother from another planet, right?'

'From *my* planet, make no mistake.'

Mac feels the rightness of this moment like an electric charge. Finally he has something to hold on to, to pull him forward. He knows who Godfrey Millerhausen is. Knows what he's trying to hide. That it's much more than just an affair.

And much more dangerous.

'I have to tell Karin about this. She needs to be careful.' Mac's fingers shake so hard he keeps missing the tiny button for Karin's speed-dial and has to try again and again.

'Give it to me.' Billy takes the phone, presses K, and hands it back to Mac.

He listens to her phone ring. It's early Sunday morning in Sardinia, about five o'clock; she won't be up now unless, like him, she's stopped sleeping regular hours. Thinking of sleep sends a wave of terrible exhaustion through him: He hasn't slept in two days, other than that brief nap in the taxi on his way in from the airport. Finally Karin's voice mail answers.

'Call me. It's important.' He almost blurts out *You aren't safe* but thinks better of it. He'll need to take her through this step by step. And he needs to know what's been happening on her end. Then they'll need to make a plan. Decide whether to trust the Sardinian police or involve the State Department.

He sends Karin an e-mail and then a text. Staring

at his phone, he waits for a quick response that doesn't come.

'They didn't count on me coming back here,' Mac says. 'I was supposed to stay in Sardinia. I should be there searching for my family right now. My family's supposed to be more important than anything else.'

'Which they are to you, man. I know that.'

'I was supposed to leave Millerhausen behind me. And maybe I should have. This is deep shit, Billy.'

'Well, you don't do what you're supposed to do. That makes you a good cop.'

'I'm not a cop anymore. Why am I here?'

Billy grabs Mac's hand, covering the silent phone, stilling the shaking. 'You're here because you were right. If you hadn't come back, Millerhausen was going to get away with murder. You did what you had to do. You did right.'

'If I hadn't come back, my family would probably reappear one day, just like they disappeared one day.'

'Like another magic trick by Godfrey Millerhausen? I seriously doubt that.'

'Karin—'

'Is more capable of taking care of herself than anyone I've ever known.'

'I have to go back now.'

'No, we have to finish this. First I'm calling a guy I know at the Bureau, see what he can tell us about how those geniuses matched DNA to an incarcerated prisoner and didn't wonder why. Then you're going to get some sleep before you lose your mind. And then we're going to go see what game your friend Godfrey Millerhausen is playing today.'

Sunday, July 15

When I try to make toast and the bread just sits there, I realize the electricity is out. The lights won't turn on. My BlackBerry still has charge left but the Wi-Fi isn't working: no new messages, e-mails, or texts since last night. Looking under the kitchen sink, I see that I accidentally left the hot-water switch in the on position all night long. When I came into the kitchen at two A.M. for a glass of water before going to bed, something must have blown the fuse. I flip the heater switch to the off position, eat my bread untoasted, drink a glass of orange juice from the tepid fridge. The food stirs the nauseous dread that has planted itself in my stomach; I wait a moment, close my eyes and let it pass, hoping the food will ultimately help. Food, and the six hours of sleep I managed last night, which is more than I've had in days and enough for what I have to do.

I feed the cat and kittens and, on my way through the yard, flip the switch in the breaker box. Nothing was on when the fuse blew last night so there's no need to go back into the house.

Sean, my Irish GPS companion, tells me that it

will be a four-and-a-half-hour drive to Palau, specifically to L'Hotel del Riso e Dell'Oblio – Liz Braud's Hotel of Laughter and Forgetting.

At this time of day the heat isn't too bad yet, and being Sunday, few people are out besides serious beachgoers. A perfect warmth hovers beneath the chalky blue sky. I drive with my window open, letting the wind engulf me.

The drive along the Arcu Sa Porta is mostly smooth sailing, easy to maintain just the right speed to keep the transmission in check. Then, suddenly, I'm faced with a steep ocean view and only then realize that I've been climbing a mountain for a minute or so, the grade gradually growing steeper. I'm forced to twist sharply left.

The gear slips. Used to it now, I pop it back in. A meditative sensation overtakes me as my tires nearly kiss the edge of the cliff. As I twist and turn along mountainous roads, I tap the GPS to hear Sean repeat his last direction, just so I can channel Mac and his Irish impersonations.

I miss him.

I want to go home.

I want my baby, Ben, and my daughter, Dathi. I want Mary and Fremont. I want my family back. And then I want to go home.

I drive as steadily as I can, relieved when the road straightens into farmland for a while. But then the mountainous terrain begins like a bad dream full of sparkling images – beautiful sights you want to reach out and touch, almost making you believe you could fly if you gave yourself half a chance. That gorgeous summer sky. The pristine beach a mile below. People, small as ants, taking in the sun. The water a crystal green that defines an emerald. Finally, the road flattens again. According to Sean, I am almost there.

Signs for inns and hotels and restaurants line the road into Olbia, south of Palau. Finally, I'm siphoned into a long private drive that opens into a parking area for L'Hotel del Riso e Dell'Oblio. Beyond the well-tended grounds, the glorious vegetation, the seductive palms and the pink stucco hotel lies a spectacular view of the sea. This is just the kind of sweet, perfect place you'd want to spend your honeymoon but could never afford.

At six A.M., Mac's BlackBerry startles him awake. He fumbles for the phone in the half-light of Devon and Dwayne's bedroom, taking the call without noticing the caller ID.

'Karin!'

'Is this Mac MacLeary?'

'Who is this?'

'Special Agent Jon Mercado, FBI. Returning your call.'

'My call?'

A pause – Mercado rereading the message – and he clarifies: 'Detective Billy Staples called and left your number as an alternate. His phone didn't pick up. It sounded important.'

'It is.' Righting himself on the edge of Devon's bed, Mac resets his groggy brain to semi-awake, and gives Mercado the basics.

The agent lets out a short puff of frustration. 'Yeah, when Moore's DNA matched, we all figured something went wrong with the test. I was personally about to submit it for a retest but was pulled back.'

'By who?'

'Special agent in charge. Section chief told him to shut it down.'

'So it came from pretty high up there.'

'Yup. I heard that loud and clear.'

'And you let it go.'

'What choice did I have? Guy's locked up for fifty years, anyway. He'll die in prison as it is.'

'But what about the girl who got killed? If Moore didn't do it, maybe someone wants to know who did.'

'I hear you, I really do. I guess Staples caught the case and—'

'He didn't catch it. There's no case. We were just wondering.'

'Who do you work for again?'

'Sorry, another call's coming in that I have to take. Thanks for your help.'

Mac hangs up, wishing another call *would* come in, yearning to hear Karin's voice. He hopes Special Agent Mercado won't mention the call to his superiors. Mac and Billy will need a little time to sort all this out, gather enough dots to connect

257

Godfrey Millerhausen and Kroll to Alicia's murder before alerting the authorities. They have to get this right, since Millerhausen seems to have all sorts of inside connections protecting him.

Mac taps his silent phone against his knee, watching the light outlining the pulled shade grow more vivid as the sun rises outside.

The front door of the hotel is flanked by pineapple palms. Inside the plush, crisply air-conditioned lobby, my BlackBerry comes alive with a series of beeps and vibrations that I ignore when a young short-haired woman behind the reception desk greets me with a smile. '*Ciao!*'

'Do you speak English?'

'American? Me too.' She has the perfect straight white teeth of a former braces wearer. Scanning an open calendar, she asks, 'Are you checking in?'

'You're not Blaine, by any chance, are you?' Karin thinks she recognizes the girl from her Facebook page, which lists her as living in Paris and mentions nothing about Sardinia.

Her smile fades. 'Wait just a minute.' She disappears into a back office, closing the door behind her. You can hear the low thrum of voices talking.

As I wait, two slender women in beach cover-ups and sun hats stride through the lobby. Their chatter sounds French. They pass through an arched door onto a porch where it appears that lunch is being served. Just beyond, the splashing sounds of a swimming pool. A pair of men in bathing shorts and T-shirts follow the women onto the porch.

The office door opens and Liz Braud appears, taller and tanner and richer than her guests. Her smile is less perfect but just as white as her daughter's, a vivid contrast with the black linen tunic she wears over white slacks. A large teardrop sapphire drops into her cleavage on a silver chain. I want to lunge at her, find out what she had to do with our family coming to this island, demand information about the whereabouts of Mary and the kids. But if I do, if I even indicate that I have suspicions, our meeting will end before it even begins.

'I'm Liz, the owner. I'm so very sorry, but we're all booked for the next five days.'

'I don't need a room.' I force a smile but really I want to stare at her: The deep lines from her eyes to her mouth evoke an intriguing range of emotional history. Laughter. And forgetting. She left a very different world behind to come here. This is a woman with a past. Extending my hand, I introduce myself. 'I have some personal questions, if you have a minute.' I glance at the younger woman.

'This is my daughter, Blaine.'

'I thought so.'

'Mom—' A sharp edge to Blaine's tone. Her mother ignores her.

'Have you had lunch?' Liz asks me.

'Not yet.'

I follow her out to the porch where we sit at a small table that appears to be reserved just for her; it occupies the best spot in the place, with both shade and a glorious view of the ocean. Steps down from the porch lead to a teardrop-shaped pool with a blue interior and a glassy surface reflecting brilliant sunlight. I glance at Liz's sapphire and wonder which came first, the place or the inspiration.

'*Due insalate e due tè fredi*,' she orders when a white-coated waiter appears.

I think she just ordered us salads. Clearly she's very much the boss here; I recognize her ordering for me as a gesture of power. I feel another rush of raw anger toward her, and remind myself to tread lightly. She scares me but I also find her audacity . . . interesting. Something about the tenor of her voice when she spoke Italian just now, a depth, rings a bell but I can't think of why.

Liz turns her attention back to me. 'Where are you from?'

'These days,' collecting myself, neutralizing my tone, 'New York City.'

'I miss Manhattan sometimes.'

'I live in Brooklyn, actually. With my husband, Mac. He's a private investigator and your ex-husband's wife recently hired him to do a job.'

An unhappy grin splits her face into two horizontal halves, suggesting at least one bout with plastic surgery. 'I should have guessed it was something like that.'

'What do you mean?'

'Cathy's having him followed, is that it?'

'She wants to know if he's unfaithful to her.'

'And he is, of course.' A smirk. 'Been there myself.'

'Not that Mac could tell. In fact, he stopped working on the job over a week ago, before we came here.'

Crossing her long legs at the knee, she rests her chin on a flattened palm and looks hard at me. 'Why *are* you here?'

'Vacation. That was the plan, anyway.'

'But why Sardinia? Not that I, of all people, need to be sold on the place.'

'We found a last-minute home exchange and, well, Sardinia looked irresistible.'

'It is, isn't it?'

The waiter delivers our salads and tall glittering iced teas. My stomach rumbles. After a brief queasy moment, I force myself to eat. The taste of salted boiled egg melts into my hunger.

'Where are you staying?' Liz sips her tea without taking her eyes off me.

'Capitana, near Cagliari.'

'That far south! My, you've come a long way to talk to me.'

'It's very important. My family—'

'Vincente!' she calls out to the nearest waiter. '*Pane, per favore.*'

Another waiter stops by to top off our water glasses, which we haven't touched. Vincente returns

261

with the bread. A pale couple on their way out of lunch stops to greet Liz with friendly smiles.

'What a lovely hotel,' the woman says in an English accent. 'We're so glad we found you. What a joy.'

'My pleasure,' Liz beams.

When the couple walks away, she tells me, 'They just arrived this morning. I like to make people happy. When I married Godfrey, I was young and poor. He swept me off my feet and completely changed my life. When he left me for Cathy, I was crushed. I came here to get away from my loneliness and never left. It was the best thing I ever did. When you fall in love, it's important to recognize it, grab on and hold on.'

'So you raised Blaine here?'

'Partly. She was nine when we came here eleven years ago. She has her own place in Paris, and dabbles in filmmaking. She's trying to grow up. She'll inherit the place eventually, though I'm not sure how long she'll choose to stay. One day she'll come into a lot of money. She'll have choices.'

'You must still be in touch with your ex-husband.'

She looks at me, startled.

'Because of your daughter, I mean.'

'Sometimes we talk, but not often. After we divorced, Godfrey bought a private plane and hired a pilot, partly to ferry Blaine around the world to see him. Not your usual visitation arrangement, but it worked for us.' She gazes past our cool slice of shade into the blazing blue sky.

'My family is missing,' I blurt out. 'They're somewhere here on the island. At least we think they are. That's why I wanted to talk to you.'

She looks convincingly shocked by my news. 'Missing?'

'They came here a couple of days before we did. We were in England, on business. When we arrived on Sardinia, our friend, her son and our kids were gone. We don't know what to think. But when we found out you live here, well, we didn't see how it could be a coincidence. So here I am.'

Her hand settles lightly on my arm, and she looks into my eyes. 'I understand, I would have wondered the same thing, but I promise you it's nothing *but* a coincidence. Unless you think they could be staying here at the hotel?'

'No, that doesn't make any sense. We have the house in Capitana. Why would they stay in a hotel? Why wouldn't they call us?' I lean forward and lay my hand atop hers: dry, papery skin that feels fragile but probably isn't. 'Do you have any idea why your ex-husband would want to send us here?'

'You told me you had a home exchange.'

'Maybe Godfrey had something to do with arranging it.'

'I haven't spoken to him in ages. Really, I haven't the foggiest idea. You went to the police, of course.'

'Right away.' The midday sun shifts overhead and a stifling mantle of heat descends on the porch.

She slides her hand out from beneath mine and rests it on the table beside her unused knife.

263

'They're looking. That's good. But I haven't heard anything about a missing American family.'

'That's the thing: The police don't seem to be trying very hard. My husband flew back to New York to get some answers. We think it might have something to do with Cathy's case against your ex-husband.'

'In what way?' A fly buzzes onto her untouched salad and she makes no effort to shoo it away. I realize that she has no intention of eating her food.

'Liz, can you think of any reason Godfrey would want to keep my husband from investigating him?'

'No, not really. Godfrey's *boring*. And believe me, he wasn't very good at hiding his affairs. If your husband didn't find a paramour, she doesn't exist. It's as simple as that.'

'You're sure?'

'As far as I know, dear, but I haven't lived with the man for a dozen years.'

'Then why—'

'Godfrey used to say that if he hadn't fallen into a vat of billions of dollars, he'd have ended up with a blue collar. He knows he only has so much to offer on his own. I've wondered myself if the money forced him into a life he wasn't suited for and stifled him from becoming a better person.'

'Are you saying he isn't capable of doing something worth hiding?'

'As I said, I don't really know him anymore.' She waves her hand at Vincente and orders us espressos. 'I can make a call for you, if you'd like.

I know a few people in the local police department and they can call down south to see what's going on.'

'My son is only five.' My eyes tear up and I look away.

'He'll turn up, dear.' Liz pats my hand. 'You'll see.'

I check messages with the motor running and the air-conditioning struggling to overtake the dense heat that's gathered inside the car. Mac has been trying to reach me for hours, it seems. I read his texts first, then his e-mails, and then listen to his phone messages. Apparently, the Godfrey Millerhausen emerging in New York is not the one remembered here at the hotel. Two different wives, two different men. My heart hammers so fast I can hear it as I press M for Mac.

Voice mail. With the eight-hour time difference it would be about six in the morning in New York. Mac's an early riser but he could be sleeping, or out of network, or . . . *Don't think the worst*, I tell myself. Even with the stakes now so precipitously high.

'Mac,' I say, 'I just got your messages. I'm up on the Costa Smerelda – just had lunch with Liz Braud. She says Godfrey's boring and not too smart. She says if he was cheating on Cathy you would have found out easily. I'm not sure whether to believe anything she says. I'm still at her hotel. I'll go back inside and see if she has anything else to—' Mac's voice mail cuts me off before I can finish.

As I turn to open my door, a red car driven by Liz, with Blaine as the passenger, drives out of the parking lot and is swiftly gone.

CHAPTER 16

'*C*arlos Lopez is dead.' Billy stands in the boys' doorway, a purplish shadow hanging beneath his one good eye. Still wearing yesterday's clothes, he looks like he's been up all night.

'Your guy in Vital Records?' Mac says, stunned. 'But you just talked to him.'

'Quiet!' Latisha shouts from her room.

'Watch your mouth!' Ladasha shouts from hers.

'I only said quiet!'

'And I only said watch your mouth!'

Billy pads into the room and shuts the door. Ladasha is right behind him, a short striped robe revealing more of her thighs than Mac ever hoped to see. He turns away but she barrels in unselfconsciously and stands between the men with her hands on her hips.

'What is this, the breakfast club? You guys know it's Sunday?'

'Sorry, Dash,' Billy says.

'Who's Carl Lopez?' She tightens her sash, shortening the robe even more. Her bright pink toenails sink into Devon and Dwayne's brown shag rug like neon pebbles buried on a beach.

'Carlos,' Billy says. 'He crashed his car on the way home from helping us last night.'

'Helping you what?' Ladasha asks. 'What case are we working that you called VR on a Saturday night?'

Mac interrupts: 'How'd you find out so fast?'

'Internal Affairs. They already checked his phone records and found my number incoming.'

'And you told them what?' Mac asks.

'*What is going on here?*'

'The truth. That I'm investigating a murder.'

'Listen to me! What murder? I'm standing here in my own house and I'm asking you what murder you're investigating without me, Billy?'

'The pregnant teenager,' Mac says. 'The one we were talking about yesterday.'

'That's not even our *state*,' she says. 'What the hell is going on here?'

'That case Mac had right before he left for Europe – Millerhausen? Turns out he's a separated-at-birth identical twin with the prisoner up for the murder.'

'Jesus-fucking-mother of God.'

'I hear you, Mama!' Latisha's shout echoes in the hallway outside the door.

'Go. Back. To. Bed. Tish. NOW.'

'Like anyone can sleep in this house!'

'Then get up and get dressed for church!'

'Yeah, *right*!'

'*Yeah*, right!'

Footsteps pound along the hallway and diminish down the stairs. Another door opens and closes and two pairs of lighter footsteps follow their big sister down to an early breakfast.

'And you think he lured you to Italy to get you off his trail.' Ladasha doesn't ask it as a question.

'Don't you?' Billy says.

'He wanted to get rid of his underage pregnant girlfriend without any chance of me watching,' Mac says, 'or snooping around and finding out about his twin. But I don't know why they'd mess with Mary and the kids. All I know is, they're gone. And Millerhausen's a murderer.'

'So this Lopez, he gave you something last night, and now he's dead.'

'Gave us names from the adoption records that led us to Dallas Wayne Moore.' Before she can ask *Who's Dallas Wayne Moore?* Billy adds, 'The identical twin sitting in prison.'

'Can't be your fault Lopez had an accident the night he helped you,' Ladasha tries. But all her goodwill won't ease the foreboding that's eating at Mac.

'I'd bet money someone ran him off the road.' Mac starts to sweat under his T-shirt. He desperately wants to rip it off, but not with Ladasha in the room. 'Someone found out he told us Moore has an identical twin.'

'While you all were sleeping,' Billy says, 'I talked

to the warden at the Atlanta Pen. Woke him the fuck up and asked him how it is one of his prisoners is charged for a murder two months ago when the man hasn't seen the light of day for years. You know what he told me?'

Mac and Ladasha stand by silently, watching Billy, who appears ready to erupt. Mac realizes Billy is on a collision course with Internal Affairs: He's gotten too far into a case that isn't remotely his; without a doubt, he will pay a price. Mac wonders if he made a mistake dragging Billy into this . . . but it's too late.

'Warden Thomas Allen Archibald says to me – he says, "That girl got in here on a conjugal visit with Moore. We checked it out, up and down, and it's a hard fact. The governor hasn't announced it to the press yet but he plans to." And then he tells me to take my nose out of places it doesn't belong.'

'So we're supposed to believe that a girl from Harrisburg, Pennsylvania, gets a conjugal visit with a prisoner in Atlanta, Georgia?' Bitter incredulity bleeds into Mac's tone. He's seen willful nonsense come out of the penal system before, outright corruption, but this one takes the cake. Obviously someone is vigorously washing someone else's hands.

'Now that's a nut you'll never crack,' Ladasha mutters. 'How they explaining that away?'

'They say she took a bus.'

'They got a record of that? Credit card or something?'

'She paid cash for her ticket.'

'So this teenage girl, nice kid from the suburbs in the Northeast, gets on a bus and heads down South to do the nasty with a gnarly prisoner old enough to be her daddy?' Ladasha rolls her eyes. 'Even *I* wouldn't buy that load of crap, and I don't have a high opinion of teenagers right at the moment.'

Mac paces to the window and looks at the quiet early-morning street, hot waves of anger and frustration roiling through his body. Godfrey Millerhausen doesn't care how many lives he ruins to save his own skin.

'Then,' Billy goes on, 'I hear from Detective Marv Kneeler, the brains in charge of the Alicia Griffin investigation in Harrisburg, you know, the folks who closed the case when someone decided it made sense the nice girl was impregnated and murdered by some con who's locked up in another state. Kneeler claims to believe that the con in Georgia arranged to have his little missy buried alive in Pennsylvania. Nutso.'

'You said it.' Ladasha crosses to Billy to pat his shoulder. 'You're doing good. But they're gonna fire you, you know that, right?'

He nods once, misery etched on his exhausted face.

'They found you pretty fast,' Mac says. 'How big is the network Millerhausen constructed to protect himself?'

'Now there's a good question.' Billy flips a chair

and sits down, facing Mac and Ladasha. 'Just what I'm wondering. I'm taking phone calls in the middle of the night from people who got their heads so far up their asses they can't think straight. I can tell you, they're scared we're asking questions. They want us to stop.'

'I wish you'd woken me up,' Mac says. 'I can't believe you let me sleep through all that.'

'You passed out on my desk last night. Twice.'

'I could have stayed awake.'

'You needed to sleep. I'm your friend, so I let you. Okay?' Billy's bloodshot eye fixes stubbornly on Mac, who backs down, realizing his friend was right and good to look out for him like that. Reminding himself to be grateful he has a friend like Billy.

'Thank you,' Mac says. 'But Billy, maybe it's time you leave this to me. Dash is right, this will hurt you. This is some deep, deep shit, and you're not authorized to dig. But I'm an independent operator, so I can do whatever I want.' Drops form across Mac's forehead. He wipes his face with both hands but the sweat just keeps gathering like a tight new skin trying to suffocate him.

'We'll see,' Billy says.

Suddenly Mac thinks of Karin. He has to warn her. He takes his phone and jabs the K, listening to the curl of sound summon his wife across the ocean.

★ ★ ★

Just at the moment my phone starts ringing, ten minutes south of Palau, a speeding silver sports car diverts me away from Sean's directions. My Irish guide falls silent before announcing his reroute, redirecting me along a road barely wide enough for two cars to pass each other. The ringing makes me nervous as I concentrate on keeping my speed steady. On the fifth ring, voice mail picks up. I drive through an old stone village with not a person in sight. It's midafternoon, siesta time. The deep quiet gives me the creeps. I'm surprised when another car pops into my rearview, but feel some comfort knowing I'm not alone as I drive out of the deserted village.

I take the only direction out: a single narrow road that leads me up the side of yet another mountain. The picturesque road edges cliffs where, if you dare to lift your attention from the slip of asphalt, you'll notice telltale signs of hidden passages to what the guidebook promises are some of the world's most spectacular beaches. I begin to know when I'm nearing another beach entrance because parked cars thicken along both sides of the road, making it harder to navigate.

A car comes around a bend behind me, suddenly, with bewildering determination: the same sports car that diverted me this way to begin with. And then, in one shocking moment, I recognize snake-face and know that the car is even more familiar than I first realized. Just two days ago, driving home from the airport, this same man drove a maroon van and drag-raced his friends in the silver car he's driving now. Raced each other until they'd sandwiched my car nearly to a pulp. I can still feel the savage thumps of the van hitting me from behind.

I take a deep breath and pick up my speed, body adrenalized, brain hyper-alert to every inch the car gains on me. He's following me, this time I'm sure of it.

And he wants to drive me off the road.

Suddenly I know something else. Liz Braud. Her voice. The bell that rang distantly in my mind when she spoke Italian at lunch finally resonates: It was Giulia Porcu's voice. The Giulia who won't call me back. The Giulia who doesn't exist.

Liz sent snake-face after me. Suddenly I know that, too.

Mac was right. It was stupid to go see her before we understood what we were dealing with. *Stupid.*

The road narrows and climbs until I'm driving alongside cliffs that plunge into the sea to my left.

Across from the entrance to a beach, an old man sits beneath an umbrella, selling pineapple slices from his open van. A boy about eight years old darts across the road, his mother's shrieking voice echoing in the canyon of beach, cliffs, and sky. I swerve to avoid the boy, and keep driving. My heart racing wildly now. In the rearview mirror I see the hysterical mother yank her son out of the road and clutch him to her body. The silver car flies past them.

My phone starts ringing again. I yearn to answer, to tell someone, hopefully Mac, *I'm in trouble, help me*. Instead, I ignore it and drive faster.

The road drops into a steep descent. I pick up speed without trying, and take a sharp turn right. Almost immediately another hairpin turn catches me by surprise. Clenching my teeth, I take it, swerving left, praying the transmission will hold.

And it does.

I don't see the silver car behind me anymore.

For a split second of joyous relief I actually believe history will repeat itself, that he's only playing with me again, that he's decided to back off. That he has nothing to do with Liz Braud or my missing family or any of this. That I imagined the whole thing.

Lifting my foot off the accelerator I gently tap the brake to slow the car, wondering, briefly, if I should go straight to the airport and get on a plane out to safety. Knowing that I can't leave until I find Mary and the children; there is just no way. But the chase is over, I promise myself, *it's over*, and as soon as the car and my brain slow down enough to think, I'll figure out what to do next.

The sports car blasts into view from behind a stone wedge jutting out of the mountainside. I accelerate so fast and hard I can feel the floor rise up under my foot. And then it happens: The transmission fails.

I know without thinking that I would rather die in the certainty of solid earth than a free fall through sky into water. I take in the sharp turn ahead, a flank of stone to my right, the sheer drop off the cliff to my left.

He speeds up behind me and in a moment that hovers outside time, a plan forms without calculation. I steer as steadily as I can as he gets closer, his malevolent chase unrelenting.

And then I turn sharply right, into a jagged outcropping of ancient rock.

The front of my car buckles in on itself and at the whoosh of the airbag deploying, like an accordion releasing a peal of sound, I think of the man in Cagliari who guided me into the parking spot with music and kindness and whose *money, money* brought me down to cold reality. And I realize something clearly as my eyes watch a movie unspool in front of me, an unreal image I don't believe at first: the silver car racing straight off the cliff into deep broad lush lovely unforgiving silence: and what I realize, what I know, is that *money, money* is at the root of all this: that Liz Braud will do whatever it takes to preserve her wealth, and her daughter's inheritance, so that they can continue living their idle dream: even steal my family: even protect her former husband from the rotten fruits of his bad behavior: even deprive Cathy Millerhausen's damaged son a life of scant promise: and as time distends into a strange eternity I don't know if the explosive crash I hear emanates from mountain or sea: is mine or his: if I'm alive or dead: I don't know. And in that last moment my mother-arms are filled with twins-who-aren't-twins, Ben, lost, Cece, long gone, and my heart cries for the past.

'I wish she would answer.' Mac pockets his phone and looks at Billy standing there holding two coffees from a deli a block away on Lexington Avenue.

'How many times did you dial her while I was getting these?'

Billy was gone all of ten minutes. Mac figures he tried Karin four, five times. He shrugs his shoulders.

'Stop worrying about her,' Billy says. 'You know Karin; she's like a cockroach, you couldn't kill her if you tried.'

Mac glares at his friend, who looks away in embarrassment. 'You think that makes me feel better?'

'I'm sorry, man. I'm such an asshole.'

'Got that right.'

'Here, take it.' Billy hands Mac his coffee, which emits a cloud of steam when the plastic top is lifted off.

Mac gazes into the lackadaisical Sunday morning traffic on Park Avenue, moving up and down the wide street split by a median bright with apricot begonias. Summer weekends, the Upper East Side deploys to the Hamptons and beyond; why swelter in Manhattan when you own a slice of beach and sky to escape to? Unless you can't avoid work, or there's something else in your life holding you back, or you're trying to escape something, or hide something.

Cathy Millerhausen told them Godfrey was in the city all weekend, working. Ironic, considering that the man inherited his wealth, and from the sound of it spends most of his time constructing head games to play on people he's supposed to love . . . and people he doesn't even know.

Mac wishes there was even half a chance he'd find Godfrey with another woman, but he knows he won't. It would be so much easier than the direction they're heading in: following the man's DNA into a teenager's grave in Pennsylvania. Earlier that morning, Mac and Billy (against Ladasha's boisterous disapproval) decided to take this head-on and confront the man, talk to him, see if revealing their knowledge of his twin might free some information about Mary and the kids. Pretend to barter information for freedom, which of course would be a lie, but whatever works. They've already gone to Millerhausen's office, hoping to find him at his desk, but the place was locked up tight.

By now they've been standing outside his apartment building for half an hour and the only movement in or out has been an older couple emerging from a chauffeured town car, two pieces of luggage handed from driver to doorman. Home from a trip. As the couple glides into the building, Mac sees the doorman put down their luggage and turn to them with a rubber-banded stack of letters and catalogs. Vacation mail. Suddenly he thinks of the envelope from Barclays Bank, incongruously addressed to Mario Rossi at Mac and Karin's Brooklyn address, which arrived right before they left for England. He recalls leaving the envelope at home so Rossi would find it. A prickly sensation beyond unease trickles through him, a disturbing certainty that the envelope contained payment for aiding and abetting what was about to befall the MacLeary-Shaeffer-Salter clan.

He can't wait any longer.

The Sunday-morning doorman at 740 Park Avenue is a uniformed professional who hides any awareness of the two loitering men drinking their coffee on the opposite curb until Mac breaks away and crosses the street. Billy follows. The doorman's eyes hitch onto them. He removes his hat, runs a handkerchief along his scalp, and replaces the hat atop a silver halo of hair making him look not so much bald as balding. Folding the handkerchief quickly and efficiently, he presses it back into the inside pocket of his blue blazer. Before Mac and Billy even reach him, he's got his *how can I help you* face on.

'Good morning,' says the man.

Mac nods. 'Morning.' This close, he can read the worn gold name tag: *Arturo Rodriguez*. 'Mr Rodriguez, I'm a private investigator, Mac MacLeary.' Rodriguez hesitates a moment before taking Mac's hand in a tentative greeting. 'This is my associate, Detective Billy Staples, NYPD, Brooklyn Eight-four.'

'Brooklyn?' He seems a little worried now, forehead tensing. 'I live in Brooklyn.' Thinking hard, as if trying to figure out what he might have done wrong that a pair of investigators would seek him out all the way up here. 'My son-in-law, maybe he—'

'Mr Rodriguez,' Mac says, 'this isn't about you. We're looking for Godfrey Millherhausen. Mrs Millerhausen sent us.'

'I been here since six A.M. Haven't seen any of the Millerhausens all morning. I could call up for you, if you want. But who knows, he might not even be home.'

'Thanks, that would be great.'

They stand back while Rodriguez is swallowed by the cool shade of the lobby, the soft soles of his shoes a whisper across the marble floor. A minute later, he returns with the news, 'I let it ring ten, twelve times. No one answered. Sorry.'

'Maybe he's still asleep,' Billy suggests.

'Maybe.'

'Thanks again,' Mac says, and they return to their position across the street. The coffee has grown tepid, approaching the temperature of the balmy July morning. Mac takes a long drink. 'We'll give it a little more time,' he says to Billy.

'Right.'

A woman in cargo shorts, with frizzy red hair pushed off her forehead by a purple bandana, walks past holding a bouquet of leashes, half a dozen dogs of various sizes creating chaos at her feet. A fluffy white bichon frise – Mac thinks that's what it is because it looks like something his brother's ex-girlfriend had – runs a crazy circle around Billy's legs.

'Whoa!' Laughing, he trips trying to untangle himself, sprinkling the snowy white dog with lukewarm coffee. It shakes its fur and the liquid splatters onto the dog walker's bare legs, blending with her copious freckles.

'Sorry!' She kneels to calm the frantic dog, instructing Billy, 'Walk left, then step out. I'll hold her still.'

'Hand me the other leashes.' Mac reaches out and she transfers multiple loops of nylon and leather to him. He holds tight while the dogs buck against the tradeoff.

By the time Billy is free, and Mac has returned the leashes to the flustered woman, and she has walked away with her unruly canine brood, Godfrey Millerhausen has crossed the sidewalk and is just now getting into a taxi. Pretending not to know anything, Arturo Rodriguez, professionally blind, deaf, and dumb, stares into empty space above the spine of begonias.

'Hey!' Mac bolts across the street. As the taxi begins its slide into the thin traffic, Godfrey Millerhausen turns a wide grin out the rear window, his eyes crinkled in amusement. *Catch me*, the eyes say, taunting, *if you think you can.*

He knew they were there. He knew all along.

Billy races to Mac's side. An empty taxi whizzes past, nearly hitting them where they stand, forcing them to leap onto the curb in front of 740 Park.

'Go to hell!' Mac shouts to the departing cab. Rodriguez doesn't even look.

CHAPTER 17

Dathi awakens with a rock digging into her back and shifts away from it in a half sleep. The skin on the right side of her face and arm are burned from the powerful afternoon sun. Cringing, she sits up. The rocky enclave where she took refuge this morning was shady when she curled up here after venturing, alone, away from the road where she last saw Fremont. She closes her eyes and inhales the biting air whipping off the sea, wondering how long she slept unprotected from the sun after the rock's shadow abandoned her. Hunger coils in her stomach like a venomous snake. When she opens her mouth to yawn, she gags on a blast of thirst.

Her body hurts like an old woman's must. Standing, dizziness overtakes her. She steadies herself and then walks along the hidden stony cleavage out to where the mountainside opens to the Tyrrhenian Sea. Mary occupied them with geography lessons while they waited for nothing in the apartment. Her cracked lips sting when she smiles, recalling Fremont's angry remark that they were a 'captive audience.' She had never heard of the

Tyrrhenian Sea, which is part of the Mediterranean Sea, according to Mary, who wanted them to know where they are. She wonders now how long Mary prepared for her and Fremont to escape, if Mary had thought much beyond that.

Standing beneath an eave of stone, she looks beyond a vegetation-crusted mountaintop at an endless blue ocean. By the movement of shadows, she guesses it's late afternoon, early evening. A good time to strike out in hope of food and water.

Retreading the mile she walked that morning, she finally reaches the little café she remembers tucked back from the road. She'd thought it might be a good place to return to later in the day when it was less likely she'd be noticed. All the lunch patrons have gone, and the waitress is busy clearing, carrying a loaded tray into the kitchen. A peripheral table boasts a half-eaten sandwich, a nearly full glass of water, and a folded newspaper. Darting forward while she has the chance, Dathi grabs it all and runs. The waitress shouts after her but doesn't bother following. What's the difference? A girl steals some trash off a table. It's not exactly news.

Not like the article she sees on the front of the paper when she hides herself in an improvised dining nook behind a cluster of bushes. Something about a tourist being arrested. The picture shows Fremont. And it says where he is.

★   ★   ★

The place stinks of piss and vomit and Fremont tries not to breathe but that's pretty much impossible. So he rations his breaths down to the bare minimum. The cop who got him was on his way home but didn't waste a minute delivering his off-duty catch to the nearest precinct, or whatever they call it here.

'Ah, you don't look comfortable.'

He looks up and sees the commissioner standing outside the cell, one craggy old hand with a big gold ring holding on to the bars like he might open the door. But he won't. That's obvious. The man smiles at him and he looks away.

'Cheer up. It could be worse.'

Anger surges and he can't hold back. He feels himself fuming in the way his mother always warns him against, telling him, 'Hold your temper, Free.' Yeah, right, *free*.

'What could be worse? I mean, why am I even here? Am I arrested or something? What for?'

'*Bighellonare*.'

'What the—'

'Loiter.'

'Loitering? Are you fucking kidding me? I was just sitting there!'

'*Sollecitazione*.'

'Like I understand what you're saying to me.'

'Solicitation.'

'You mean—'

'*Prostituzione*. Yes, it is illegal even here.'

285

'Why are you doing this? What do you have against us?'

'Me? Nothing.' The old man smiles, tips his white head in a silent *ciao*, and walks away.

Fremont jumps off the hard bench and grabs on to the bars with both hands, calling into the damp corridor, 'Who are you doing this *for*?' His voice echoes back at him. He shouts, 'What about Dathi? What did you do with her?'

The clanking of a heavy door banging shut reverberates back into the cell.

Mary's body feels heavier than yesterday. Her mind, lighter. The cushions, having molded themselves to her body by now, ensconce her in a hardening shell. Another grocery bag has been left inside the door beside the last two, and now the putrid smell is stronger, worse.

These past two days she has gone over it and over it in her mind, and now she believes that Fremont was shot when the teenagers escaped. Believes it in her soul. And she can't recover from that. And when she thinks about Dathi, a dark-skinned girl alone in a foreign country, she knows what will happen to her if it hasn't already. Ben is the only one she doesn't know about. How will she face Mac, not knowing what to tell him about Ben? How will she explain that she urged Dathi and Fremont into an escape that was only worth its first thrilling moments of freedom before they tripped into the dark unexpected pit that Mary should have known would await them alone in an unfamiliar place? She can't face Mac with any of that news. Or Karin, if she has found her way free of her own captivity. Mary has failed them so badly. Lost their children. And her own. She can't. She can't.

Her mind drifts in the silence, backward to a better time when Fremont was small and soft and all hers in every way. Before he started to curse her existence and pull away from her. Before all this.

When Fremont was a toddler, Mary used to charm him with songs and poems, just like any other mother. The ways in which they were different didn't bother her: that she was a single lesbian mother; that her son was half black at a time when mixed-race children made people uncomfortable. Mary was a free spirit and a rebel and she always, always looked below the surface. She dug her fingers into people's muscles when they were sore. Dug her nose into people's business when they were unreasonably inscrutable. Dug her mind into research when there was more she wanted to know.

When Fremont was three, it occurred to her to look up some of the ditties she constantly repeated to him. The Mother Goose rhymes turned out to be bloody doozies. Worst of all was the one she sang most, the eponymous rhyme:

Mary, Mary, quite contrary
How does your garden grow?
With silver bells and cockleshells
And pretty maids all in a row.

All her life she thought this Mary was so sweet and ornery and *her*. She used to chant it as a little girl, walking through her mother's garden, and later as a young woman trolling gay hangouts, looking for love in all the right places: *pretty maids all in a row.*

Well, Mary was Mary Tudor, the daughter of King Henry VIII. She earned the nickname Bloody Mary because, as a staunch Catholic, she filled the cemetery, her garden, with headless Protestants. The 'Maiden' was a troublesome beheading device used before the streamlined guillotine came along. 'Silver bells': thumbscrews. 'Cockleshells': torture devices attached to genitals.

Mary wonders why we say things we don't understand.

Why do we go places we don't know?

Why do we trust people we shouldn't?

Why do we take risks when we don't have to?

And when something goes wrong, why do we think of ourselves as innocent, when we're not?

Mary, Mary.
Guilty fool.

I stare at a white wall with an Italian *tourismo* poster showing a collage of stunning beaches, ancient nuraghi, and amber-lit restaurants with radiant glasses of wine. When I sit up, everything hurts. But nothing is broken and I'm not bleeding anywhere that I can see. I touch a bandage on my forehead.

A nurse in a white uniform stops in front of me, smiling, and says in a kindly voice, '*Sdraiarsi.*'

'I don't understand.' My voice sounds woozy.

'*Aspetti, vado a prendere il medico.*' She walks briskly away, chatting in Italian with another nurse who glances at me, nods, keeps walking.

I find my purse stashed on a shelf above the gurney wheels. Everything is there: wallet, keys, BlackBerry. I turn on my phone and an endless list of Mac's efforts to reach me scrolls down the screen, so many I can't count. My vision blurs a moment. I blink and the tiny letters come clear again. My phone chirps a few times with old incoming texts and the nearest nurse freezes, turns to me and snaps, '*Non e possibile utilizzare telefono.*'

I don't understand her words but her tone is clear enough. Given all the medical equipment buzzing around us, I'm guessing she just told me not to use my phone. I nod and turn it off.

Hospital staff bustles around, tending to patients in varying states of distress. I must have been in the emergency room's intake area for a while; they must have stabilized me, because no one's paying much attention to me anymore. I need to call Mac but don't want to cause cellular mayhem.

When a nurse comes by, I ask, '*Bagno?*' Bathroom.

'*Attraverso la porta, a sinistra e in fondo al corridoio a destra. Si può camminare bene?*'

No idea what she said. I smile. '*Grazie.*' I can feel her watching me as I head for the door. I turn right and pass beneath a sign reading *Uscita*. Exit. I've picked up a few things in my few days on the island.

Signs in the lobby tell me I'm in a hospital called Ospedale Giovanni Paolo II. Feeling faint, I stop in the gift shop to buy a bottle of water and a candy bar. While the girl gets my change, my gaze lands on a stack of local newspapers beside the register. The lead story features the headline TURISTA ARRESTATO. When I pick up the paper, the bottom folds down and I see a photograph of a handcuffed black man being led into a police station. A light-skinned black man, unlike the dark Africans you see here, the southern end of the island being a short boat ride from northern Tunisia. The man in the photo looks American or European. And he doesn't look much like a man; he looks like a boy, tall and gangly, like he hasn't finished growing. And his hair, the Afro . . . it's so familiar. The blue sneakers. The photo only shows the man-boy from behind, but caught in the act of turning around, you can see a shadow of profile in the side of his face.

Fremont. I feel so happy to see him. But not in

a newspaper, under a headline like that. I scan the article, but of course can't read it; and then a word jumps out: *prostituzione*.

'*Volete questo?*'

The girl sells me the paper by counting out the right number of coins from my change in her open palm, and returns the rest to me.

On my way to the exit I peruse the article for any information I can squeeze out of it, which isn't much. Apparently he was arrested for solicitation, which is ridiculous. He's been taken to a *Polizia di Stato*, a police station, in Olbia-Tempio, which suggests he was nearby when he was picked up. Liz Braud, again. She told me she would call her friend in the local police to ask for help. Does that mean the police are in on this, too? Is Fremont safer in custody? Or less safe? My mind reels. I wish I understood what I was up against, but even half understanding now is better than before, when nothing at all made sense.

What about Ben? Dathi? Mary? My eyes flick across the foreign words but nowhere do I see *bambino*, child, *ragazza*, girl, *donna*, woman. But I can't really tell. My heart pounds as I realize that maybe it wasn't such a mistake driving north today. Maybe it brought me close to my family, after all.

A taxi driver idling by the hospital entrance catches my eye and smiles. I don't know where this hospital is located in relation to Olbia-Tempio, and I don't care. I also don't care that it would be stupid for me to leave the hospital when I'm obviously in bad shape. But still . . .

'*Carabinieri, Decimo Nucleo Elicotteri,*' I read aloud from the newspaper. '*Olbia-Tempio.*' I'm not sure exactly what I said but he seems to understand. The way his face lights up, his expression of recognition, as if he knows exactly what I'm talking about, gives me hope.

'*Non è lontano. Prego, venite con me,*' he says, opening the back door of his taxi.

I get in and he drives us out of the parking lot, away from the hospital. In his rearview mirror I glimpse one of the ER nurses running out the front entrance, gesturing and shouting at someone. But she's too late; I made a clean getaway. When I grin, my face hurts. I pull out my phone and speed-dial Mac.

'Karin! Where are you?'

'It's a long story, I totaled the car, but I'm fine.'

'*What?*'

'I'm *fine.*' The effort needed to emphasize that one small word hurts, but I'm not telling Mac that. Not now.

'Karin, if you're—'

'I think I found Fremont.'

'Where?'

'The police have him on some bogus charge. I'm going there now.'

'Did you call Enzio Greco?'

'What for? He's incompetent. And I'm starting to worry he might be part of all this.'

292

'Jesus.'

'*He's* probably in on this, too.'

Mac doesn't laugh at my lame attempt at humor. His tone is urgent when he asks, 'What about the others?'

'Just Fremont.'

'It's a start. Are you really okay? You said you totaled the car.'

'Just wrecked the car, not myself. You got my message about Liz Braud?'

'She said her ex-husband's dull?'

'"Boring" is the word she used.'

'Cathy Millerhausen called him a "bastard." Says he's a master manipulator. He likes to play head games.'

'I believe Cathy,' I say. 'Whatever's going on, Liz is part of it. When I spoke to Giulia that time, I was really speaking to Liz.'

A heavy pause precedes, 'We should have thought of that.'

'As soon as I left Liz's hotel, I was followed. And Fremont was picked up nearby. What about Godfrey Millerhausen? You find anything useful?'

'Big-time. That missing teenage girl from Harrisburg—'

'The one in the news right before we left?'

'Yup. They found her: pregnant, buried alive.'

'Oh my God.'

'They're saying the fetus was fathered by an incarcerated felon.'

'That makes no sense at all.'

'Exactly. Guess who has an identical twin sitting in prison? *Godfrey Millerhausen.*'

As if a veil is ripped off, I see it now with sudden harsh clarity. 'He killed her to stop a paternity suit, which would have been worse than the divorce settlement in the prenup Cathy wants to uphold.'

'Cathy doesn't know the half of it. I feel bad for her. And her twins, I met them. The handicapped one—'

'Special needs, Mac.'

'He'll have a tough time in life without special ed and services. He's lucky he was born into money.'

'You turn over the evidence yet? Do they have Millerhausen in custody?'

'It's all circumstantial right now, but I'm working on it, then I'm heading back to Sardinia. The guy who pulled the adoption record for Billy was killed in a car crash last night.'

Hearing that, my insides quiver; the deaths are piling up. That poor girl, buried alive. Dan Stylos, falling off a boat. Dante Serra, shot and left in the trunk of his car. I can't stop seeing snake-face hurl off the cliff in a flash of silver. And now this guy dies in a crash.

'I have a few people to see and then I'll be with you, Karin. Hold tight. And *please* keep safe.'

We say good-bye reluctantly.

The creamy stucco buildings along Via Venafiorita would seem to belie the presence of a police station; but on this island, prosaic charm takes on a lush redundancy. Eventually you'd probably stop noticing. My driver pulls up in front of a modest building with its *Polizia di Stato* shingle hanging unobtrusively beside the door.

Just as I'm about to go inside, my phone rings. Enzio Greco. But can I trust him?

'Signora! You got my message?'

'No, I didn't.' If he called me, it would have shown up on the list of messages, along with Mac's and all the others. Greco is lying.

'I have some very good news for you. We found one of your family. The older boy.'

'I saw it in the paper.'

'Where are you now?'

I don't answer, realizing it might not be a good idea for him to know that I'm at the police station. 'Why did they arrest Fremont when he's listed as missing? Why would they do that?'

'Signora, please, stop worrying. I am here to help. Everything will be okeydokey.'

I cringe, wondering where he picked up that silly American colloquialism.

'Thank you, Commissioner.'

'Call me if—'

'Good-bye.'

Humid air creeps along the skin of my bare arms as I stand at a high counter behind which a uniformed receptionist-cop has his back to me, listening on the phone. A thick band of perspiration stripes the back of his shirt. He ends his call and turns to acknowledge me: 'How can I help?'

'How do you know I speak English?'

'You look English to me.' He smiles sheepishly.

'I'm American.'

'To me, the same.'

Opening the newspaper atop the counter, I say, 'This boy is Fremont Salter, he's my friend's son. We traveled here together. We're tourists, on vacation. There's been a terrible mistake. I need to arrange his release.'

'Will you wait?'

'Yes.'

When he returns a few minutes later, he's smiling. Hope trickles at the thought that soon I'll see Fremont and he can tell me what's been happening and where the others are. That this could be over. We could be on our way home.

'There is some complication and we must do some paperwork. We like to suggest you come back later. Even tomorrow. This will take some time.'

My heart sinks. 'Tomorrow?'

'Perhaps.'

It hits me suddenly: Enzio Greco knows I'm here. He must have tracked my cell phone.

'I want to see him *now*. He's just a boy. You can't do this!'

'Signora,' he says, 'I am very sorry, but here in our country we have our laws and rules. This boy is enough of a man to stay a night. Trust me, please.'

'No. I won't. I can't.' I walk around the reception counter and try to open the door to the back, where I assume the small-town station keeps its offices and a few holding cells. The smile drops off the man's face. He grips my arm and pain shoots through me. I wince. Pull my arm away. Fury rips through my brain.

'I'll call the American embassy. You can't do this.'

'You may call who you wish. But still, you must wait.' He positions himself behind the counter and avoids looking at me by pretending to do something on a desk I can't see.

'I'm not leaving until I see Fremont,' I say, standing in front of the counter, trying to stare him down. He ignores me and my fury builds.

Trolling the Internet on my BlackBerry, I find the phone number for the U.S. embassy in Rome. To my utter frustration, I reach a voice mail system that lands me in a message box. Explaining the urgency of my call, I leave all my details. Hang up.

And wait.

The small visitors' bench is too hard for me to sit on, my body hurts all over, so I pace or lean against a wall. I can still see Cathy Millerhausen walking down our Brooklyn block on a June morning, bringing much-needed new business to my husband, who I knew would dread another tedious infidelity case but would take it anyway. Bills: You have to pay them. But not like this. The cost for this job has been obscenely high. And all for a filthy-rich sociopath who doesn't want to be held accountable for his transgressions. To think that he got that teenage girl pregnant and then buried her alive makes the half-digested candy bar from the hospital gift shop work its way up my throat. I swallow it back down. Hating Godfrey Millerhausen, hating Liz Braud, regretting everything that's sprung from this, won't change a thing that's happened.

Finally I close my eyes to rest. Propped between a table and doorjamb, I realize I must have fallen asleep when the sound of the opening door startles me awake and it's night outside.

When Dathi walks in, my jaw drops.

CHAPTER 18

Mac plucks two flyers from the ironwork on his way up the stoop, Billy just behind him. You can hear the doorbell chime inside the house, but no one answers. He rings a second time. Knocks hard three times. Silence echoes from within. Finally he dials his home number and hears the landline ringing inside. After seven sets of rings, voice mail answers. He tries again, expecting the same, when Maria Rossi answers sounding out of breath.

'Hello?'

'Maria? This is Mac – Mac MacLeary.'

'I am just out of the shower. Did I miss your call before?'

'Yes, but that's okay. I wasn't sure you were home.'

'We are home, but we are about to go out. Mario is waiting for me. Can I help?'

It strikes Mac that she doesn't mention his family or that they're missing in Sardinia. Is it possible that Mario, her husband, didn't tell her all about it? 'No,' he says, guarding his tone, 'I just wanted to make sure everything's okay with the house.'

'Oh, yes, everything is fine. We love Brooklyn. And Capitana – all is well?'

'Yes,' Mac lies, 'all is well,' just to see how she'll answer.

'Beautiful. May we talk later? I must run. *Ciao!*'

Turning to Billy, Mac reports, 'She says she's in the house, acts like she doesn't know anything that's going on.'

'She doesn't exist, man.'

'Yeah, I'm kinda figuring that out.'

When Mac lets himself in, the first thing that hits him is the smell of rotting flesh. Gagging, he steps back through the door into the outside air for a moment to clear his nose of the stench: like someone died.

The putrid smell intensifies as they walk from the front hall into the living room. Not only is everything as neat as when they left it, but nothing looks touched at all. A sheen of dust has settled on the coffee table and along the edges of the bookshelves. Cat footprints pepper the dusty dining table. Mac is struck by the forlorn sensation of abandonment that permeates his home. Closer to the kitchen, the smell is markedly worse.

Steeling himself, he pushes open the kitchen door.

It's a moment before his mind can begin to articulate the bloodbath.

Tiny, slender bones strewn around.

Shredded pieces of furry skin stuck to the wall.

Half-dried entrails slopped on the floor.

Mac's stomach gurgles violently. He forcefully swallows it back down.

'This is twisted,' Billy mutters.

'What do they want from us?' Mac's eyes tear up, surprising him; he doesn't usually cry. It looks like someone brutally killed Justin, whose fur is mostly black. He doesn't see any sign of orange fur. Maybe Jeff got away.

Then he notices that, deposited into Jeff and Justin's food bowls are more bones, a wiry black tail, a small chewed over skull. Their water bowl is dry, filled only with bits of a decimated animal.

'I think it's a rat.' Then Mac sees what looks like a wing under the kitchen table. 'And a bird. They went hunting.'

'They do that sometimes?'

'Sometimes they bring in a mouse. Nothing like this. They'd have to be really hungry.'

The cat flap from the back door into the garden is encrusted with bloody feathers.

Holding the hem of his T-shirt over his nose, Mac goes to the kitchen window and looks outside. In the long shadow cast by the fence separating their back yard from the neighbor's, Jeff and Justin are curled near each other on the grass. Mac watches until he's sure they're breathing, and feels a swell of relief. 'I see them. They're asleep.'

Billy comes up beside him, his bent elbow covering his nose. 'Never thought I'd be so happy to see those guys. I don't even like cats. More of a dog guy.'

301

'No one's been feeding them,' Mac says.

'Nope.'

'The Rossis were never here. But that letter came to Mario before we left.'

'Where do you keep your cat food?'

'Cupboard below the toaster.'

Billy finds a mixing bowl and fills it with dry food, fills another large bowl with water, and sets them on a clean area of the floor for the cats to find when they wander back in.

Mac remembers leaving the Barclays letter for Mario Rossi on the kitchen counter, with the home instructions, which look untouched. But the envelope is gone. He checks the trash, which is as empty as when they left for England. But the three outside cans, one for regular garbage and two for recyling, have collected a variety of refuse, offerings from passersby.

He digs through the cans until he finds the ripped-open envelope from Barclays that arrived the day before they left for Sardinia. So the Rossis – or whoever the people are they've been talking to on the phone – came for the letter, opened it, and left.

'Did they even put it in the right bin?' Billy asks, standing on the top of the stoop.

'Nope.' Mac shakes his head.

'They didn't recycle it? Man, they could get a ticket for that.' Billy's hard laughter provokes an onslaught of conflicting emotion in Mac, whose eyes tear so quickly, he turns away.

As he tosses the envelope in the green can with the paper-recycling sticker on the side, Mac notices something inside the envelope and pulls it out of the garbage. Whoever opened it hastily ripped the check off the stub, leaving behind a wealth of information. 'Well, will you look at this.'

The friends stand side by side, reading the slip of paper which tells them that a check for twenty-five thousand dollars was issued by Barclays Bank on July fifth, and the check number.

'Not too bright for criminals.'

'Nope, not too bright.'

'They paid me more than the Rossis,' Mac says. 'At least that's something.'

'How the fuck did they pull this off? I mean, aren't you guys staying in those people's house in Italy?'

'Seems like it. Kroll – they're *good*.'

'Let's get you back to Sardinia.' Though Billy doesn't say it, Mac can hear in his friend's tone that he's starting to worry about Karin, too. 'Give me that chit. I'll follow up tomorrow when the bank's open.'

'There's just one more thing I have to do: I need to find the woman from Kroll and pin this down before I leave. No way can I let Millerhausen get away with this.'

'I can do that. You go.'

'No. She sat there and sold me a load of bullshit. I want to look her in the eye and make her tell me the truth.'

'Don't know what makes you think she will.'

'Do me a favor and book me a flight for tonight. I'll leave as soon as I'm done with her.'

Billy sighs. 'You know where to find her?'

There are plenty of Lacie Chens in cyberspace but only one who lives outside Chinatown. Billy pulls up in front of a worn-out looking tenement on East Seventy-seventh Street off Second Avenue on the Upper East Side of Manhattan. The front door has been painted gray so many times, over so many years, that its surface is as lumpy as cottage cheese.

'Nice address, crappy building,' Billy notes. 'She young?'

'Climbing the corporate ladder.'

'Think I see a parking spot opening up ahead.'

'No, drop me here. You're not coming with me.'

'I'm in this with you.'

'You're a cop. You'll have to tell her that. And she'll make a stink about not having a warrant. It's easier if I go alone.'

'All right, but I'll be waiting out here for you when you're ready. Your flight's at eight ten. I don't see you down here by four thirty, I'm coming in.'

'That's plenty of time.'

Mac slams the car door. Standing outside the building, he turns on his phone's audio recorder and positions it in the front pocket of his jeans. He rings Lacie Chen's buzzer. After a moment, her voice crackles: 'Yes?'

'Lacie, this is Mac MacLeary. I need to see you.'

'Who?'

'Mac MacLeary. You hired me for a job in London.'

'Oh, oh, right.'

'Will you buzz me in please?'

'Why are you here?' An inflection of anger in her tone now. 'This is my home. It's Sunday.'

'I understand that, but we need to talk.'

'Tomorrow, in my office.'

'Now.'

'I'm sorry, Mr MacLeary.' The intercom snaps off.

He buzzes again, forcefully.

'Go away!' she insists.

'The man you're working for is a murderer.' When she doesn't respond, Mac tries again. 'He told you to hire me to put me off the scent of his—'

A long shrill buzz interrupts him. A click announces that she has opened the door.

A rickety old elevator carries him to the eighth floor, where she's already waiting in the hall. Barefoot in a sleeveless black maternity dress, with her short blond hair a tousled mess, she looks as if she's either been roused from a nap or didn't bother pulling herself together today. Mac notices that her finger has swelled around her wedding ring. Without a word, she ushers him into her apartment, shuts and double-locks the door.

They've entered directly into a tidy narrow living room decorated in ubiquitous modern Ikea.

'Does anyone know you're here?' she asks, lowering herself with difficulty onto the nearest chair.

'No one.' Except Billy. But that's none of her business.

Her forehead crumples in thought. On a credenza opposite the door, Mac notices wedding photos: Lacie, slimmer and younger, in a white wedding gown beside a young man who looks half Asian.

'That's my husband, Rick.'

'He back from Dubai?'

'Not yet. I haven't seen him for so long. If he knew—'

'He doesn't have to know anything. I just want my family back. I want this to end.'

'Your family?' Her eyes cloud in bewilderment. Mac explains.

'All I was told was that we needed to get you far away. Distract you.'

'Why London?'

'We have a good working relationship with the folks at Barclays-London. It's also conveniently on the way to—'

'Why Sardinia?' he interrupts.

'It's just where we were able to find the right kind of house, with people willing to cooperate.'

'With the help of Liz Braud, no doubt.'

Her eyes flit away as she recognizes that he knows more than she ever told him. 'Look, I realized the point was to get you out of Godfrey Millerhausen's business, but that was all I knew. We do a lot of work for him. He's an excellent client. We like to help.'

'Who told you to do it?'

'My boss said it came from the director's office. We didn't need to follow up, just hire you, find you some place to stay, and Barclays-London would handle the rest.'

'Did you know Godfrey was cheating on his wife?'

A blush creeps along her freckled face. 'I knew.'

'And you're aware of the prenup Cathy has.'

'I knew it was wrong to help him get out of that, but he's a paying client, one of our best, and sometimes we . . .' Her voice trails off. 'I should have asked more questions.'

'You're right, you should have. You know who his girlfriend was?'

She nods at him with trembling lips. 'She was just a teenager.'

He glances at Lacie's belly. 'He buried her alive.'

Tears rush into her eyes. 'I try not to think about that. I try to pretend I didn't know anything about it. I need this promotion and there aren't any jobs out there right now and—'

'How did he meet her?'

'Are you going to tell the police about me?'

'They're going to have to know all the facts. You can explain yourself however you see fit.'

'I don't know if I can handle this.' Her voice

wavers, growing faint. 'This is such a bad time for this to happen.'

'Lacie, listen to me, you have no choice.'

Taking a deep breath, she tells him, 'Alicia interviewed to be a summer intern in his office. She wanted to study business when she got out of high school. He didn't even hire her, he just . . .'

'She lived in Pennsylvania. Did he go to her?'

Lacie shakes her head. 'She'd come to the city on some pretext. He'd take her to dinner and back to his apartment. It was just two or three times, I think.'

Neither of them speaks the obvious: It just takes once to get pregnant.

'She refused to get an abortion,' Lacie says in a near whisper. 'She was going to tell her parents. This is really horrible.'

'How involved is Liz Braud?'

She blinks. 'She arranged the house. That's all.'

'Mary and the kids are missing. They were in Sardinia, in the house, and then they vanished.'

'I don't know anything about that.'

'I'm going to ask you again: How involved is Liz Braud?'

'Look,' Lacie says, pale and exhausted – scared. 'Their daughter Blaine spends a lot of time with her mother on the island. We've done a little work for them, too. I always got the impression Godfrey and Liz were friendly. Maybe he roped her into something, but I honestly don't know what, or why. I don't know. Maybe we got in a little over

308

our heads when we agreed to help Godfrey out with this one. I don't know.'

'It sounds like a conspiracy,' Mac says, staring her in the eye. 'Doesn't it?'

She nods. But Mac wants the answer on the recording. He needs to nail this before getting on the plane, so the police will have something to work with beyond supposition. He knows from a past case that when it comes to identical twins, DNA evidence doesn't fly in court. They're going to need someone on the inside, like Lacie Chen, to map it all out for them so the players will get nervous and start to talk. When the people at Kroll and Barclays realize they're facing prison as accessories to murder, Godfrey Millerhausen's money won't look so irresistible.

'Say it,' he prompts.

'It does sound like that.'

'Like what?'

'A conspiracy,' she says, haltingly, and Mac's got what he came for.

'Good luck with your baby,' he says, 'and don't worry. One way or another, this is going to work out for you.'

All the color has drained from her skin; in her black dress, she looks ghostly. She struggles to get up. Mac stops her.

'I'll see myself out.'

'Wait. I know it's a little weird to ask, but would you mind taking the trash downstairs for me? It's kind of hard for me to move around, I've been putting it off all day, and pickup is in the morning. Since you're going anyway—'

'Happy to help.'

'Thanks. The cans are right outside the building.'

Mac looks over her bookshelves while she goes into the kitchen. Someone reads a lot of paperback mysteries, someone else reads nonfiction, politics, and science. He hears her moving around in the kitchen, the opening and closing of a cabinet, the clank of something, the rustle of a plastic bag. Finally she appears with a small but full plastic garbage bag loosely tied at the neck.

'Thanks,' she hands him the bag, 'I appreciate it. Sorry for the smell, but I've been stuck in here and I did some cooking and cleaning before.'

A wisp of ammonia leaks from the bag.

'Will you tell me where Liz Braud is hiding my family?' he tries again.

'I mean it. I don't know.' Her hands tremble when she unlocks the front door. He thinks he believes her but isn't sure.

'If you do know, Lacie, telling me is the right thing to do.'

'I swear to you: I do not know.'

Mac hears her locks snap shut behind him. He presses the button for the elevator and waits before deciding to walk down the seven flights, only to find that the stairwell door is locked; an illegal fire hazard, but nothing he can do about it right now. Finally he hears the old elevator clank to life, ascend, arrive. He steps inside and presses L for

Lobby. The elevator starts its belabored descent, and then comes to a sudden, grinding halt.

He presses the red emergency button, expecting a bell to sound, but hears nothing. He holds the button in, pressing hard, but evidently the alarm isn't working. He tries all the buttons but nothing reactivates the elevator. And his cell phone doesn't have a signal in here.

The elevator lights snap off, trapping Mac in darkness.

Enclosed in the elevator, the ammonia smell from the garbage bag grows increasingly poignant. As a burning sensation crawls up the inside of his nose, he thinks he smells bleach, too. Apparently when Lacie Chen cleans, she really gets down to business. Maybe not the brightest move to use such strong chemicals when you're pregnant.

A factoid from high-school science returns to him: Ammonia and bleach are a lethal combination.

He also recalls something Lacie told him the first time they met: that she dropped out of graduate school in chemical engineering.

The burning sensation crawls to the back of his throat, into his esophagus.

He drops the bag on the elevator floor and glass shatters. Fumes rush out.

Battling to keep his balance against an escalating sensation of dizziness and nausea, his fingertips search the ceiling until he locates the outline of the hatch. He jumps and manages to knock the cover open before landing so hard on the floor the elevator shakes. A powerful urge to close his eyes overtakes him. But he fights it. Stands against a weight like water pushing him down. Willing his mind to stay focused, to keep hold, he propels himself upward. Feels the inner edge of the open hatch and hangs on for dear life. He knows that if he doesn't make it out, she'll find his phone and delete the recording. And her confession will die with him in this elevator.

Gagging, lungs on fire, his muscles weaken and fail him twice before he manages to squeeze the upper half of his body up into the elevator shaft. He rests on the roof of the elevator, alternately coughing out poison and gulping in stale but miraculous air. With a final heave, he pulls himself all the way out, rolls onto his back and kicks shut the hatch door. His head sinks down into a cushion of irresistible rest. His eyes are so heavy, and his body feels so weak, and if he doesn't move the world stops spinning, and suddenly the urge to sleep is too powerful to refuse.

CHAPTER 19

My arms are around Dathi faster than I can think. She won't cry right away, I know that much about her at this point – she'll hold it until later, when she's alone in bed, and only then will she let me adequately comfort her – but personally I can't help emotion from seeping through the dread that has coated me in brittle armor.

Pulling away to look at my daughter's dirty, sunburned face, I ask, 'Where did they take you? Were you and Fremont together? Where's Ben? Where's Mary?'

Dathi's slender hand reaches up to caress the air in front of my bandaged forehead. 'What happened to *you*?'

'I was looking for you. I drove up north, and I had an accident, but I'm okay.' *Accident. Okay.* As if I could fool her.

The officer-receptionist stops pretending not to see me and watches us with bald curiosity. Dathi keeps her eyes off him but I sense her keen and growing discomfort. She stretches onto her toes and I lean my ear down to her lips. She whispers, 'We shouldn't be here, Karin.'

'Fremont's here,' I tell her. 'We have to—'

'Shhh.' She takes my hand and pulls me outside, into a night drained of heat.

'They arrested Fremont,' I explain. 'It was a mistake, I don't want you to worry, but we have to—' *stay here until we get him released*, I am about to say, when she reveals how much more she knows than I do.

'It wasn't a mistake that they arrested him.' Her large black eyes open to me, and I succumb, listening to this girl whose intelligence and wisdom have astounded me from the day we first met a year and a half ago. 'The police commissioner is Emiliana's friend. Emiliana is the lady who kept us locked in. Mary called her Liz.'

'Go on.'

'And her daughter, Cosima.'

'Blaine,' I tell her. 'Liz and Blaine.'

'Yes, Mary knew that, too. That's how Free and I escaped, we . . . Mary told us, and we . . .' She seems to run out of breath and gulps for air. I hold her in my arms until her breathing regulates, telling her to take the time she needs. After a moment, she pours out the whole story of the abduction. Puzzle pieces skitter into empty spots between what Mac and I have already figured out. From the sound of it, Dante the locksmith was never a part of this; he was just in the way, poor man.

'The person who took all of you in the van that day,' I ask. 'What did he look like?'

'He was tall, and he had a creepy tattoo of a snake coming up the back of his neck. He was smelly and mean. He kept sweating.'

Snake-face. But I don't want to tell Dathi about my own encounters with him; she's had enough scares for a lifetime. Later, I'll make it clear that he didn't survive his run-in with me, but I'm not sure she needs to know how close the race was. A sickening weightlessness overtakes me as I feel what it might have been like to be the one whose car sailed over the cliff. But it's a reductive fear I won't indulge in. It didn't happen. He died. I lived.

'Tell me about the commissioner.'

'He came every day. Sometimes he brought food. They'd stand outside and talk, and then he would drive away. Later Free and I saw on TV that he's the police commissioner. The news said he was helping to look for us. That's when we knew no one was looking at all.'

'Mac and I were looking.'

A smile blossoms on Dathi's anxious face. 'Where is Mac?'

'New York.'

She looks bewildered, even dismayed, and I brush a hand across her forehead, pushing away a clump of hair threatening to cover her lovely eyes. 'He went back to try and help us.'

'In New York?'

'All this seems to have something to do with the case he was working on before we left. Do you think you can take me to where Mary and Ben are?'

'I'm not sure, but I can try. I know it's north of here, because Free and I were trying to go south, back to Capitana. We were hoping to find you and Mac.'

'Good thinking.' I try to smile in encouragement, but the pain in my face feels raw and my muscles won't do it. 'Liz's hotel is pretty far north. Was she hiding you guys there?'

'There weren't any other people, just us and them and the guards. We were in a house right on the beach. It wasn't a hotel. It was very lonely.'

'She probably had you near the hotel so she could come and go easily.'

We have to return north, which means leaving Fremont behind in an uncertain situation. Given what Dathi just told me, confirming my suspicions about Enzio Greco, we can't go back inside. I've already left two urgent messages for the American embassy, but will anyone retrieve them at night?

'Dathi, honey, we're going to have to leave Free here for a while. I think he'll be safe as long as they keep him locked up.'

'But they're telling lies about him; they said—'

'I know.' So she saw the newspaper, too. It has to be how she found her way here, just like I did. 'It doesn't matter what they say. It gives them

316

cover to hold him, that's all. We'll get it sorted out, but I think right now we better see what we can do about getting Mary and Ben back.'

The door to the police station opens. The officer-receptionist steps out with the phoniest smile I've ever seen, and says, 'Signora, please, sergeant like see you.' Just at the moment, a taxi helpfully meanders up the road. I metronome my arm, we climb into the backseat, and babbling English I urge the driver onward before offering specific directions. Another officer comes out onto the sidewalk, obviously angry. He yells something at the officer-receptionist, who shrugs and throws up his hands.

'Karin,' Dathi's tone is urgent, 'Liz has two guards, and they have guns.'

'It's okay.' But even as I say it, I know it isn't okay. I have no idea how one exhausted woman and one frightened girl are going to pull off an unarmed rescue. 'We'll figure something out.' I remove the battery from my BlackBerry so Greco won't be able to find me so easily this time.

Convulsing, Mac awakens. He rolls out of his vomit to prevent himself from suffocating. Folds onto his knees, takes a few deep breaths to steady himself, and remembers. He's trapped inside the elevator shaft in Lacie Chen's apartment building. He wonders how much time has passed, if she's looking for him. If, perhaps, she might decide it's a good idea to release the elevator and summon it upwards – in which case he could be crushed at the top of the shaft.

Shaking, he stands up and feels around in the dark with his hands. Using the tepid light from his phone, he sees a paint-stenciled 6 on the wall about four feet above him, and a pair of closed doors. After studying the inside of the shaft, he thinks to check the time on his phone against the time he ended the recording of his conversation with Lacie. Seven minutes have elapsed. He pockets the phone and struggles to get a foothold on the slim ledge in front of the closed doors, just managing to hang on while he tries to pry open the doors with his fingers. Three of his nails split, but the pain shooting through his fingertips only heightens his rage and determination.

When he feels some give, a pulse of opening, he grunts. Wrests the doors apart to squeeze his body through. Launches himself into the sixth-floor hallway. It looks exactly like Lacie's hall two flights up, so he knows where the stairwell door will be but assumes it will also be locked. Or maybe not. Maybe it isn't the building's policy to lock tenants out of the stairwell. Maybe she's got someone helping her. Someone who locked the door and sabotaged the elevator. Heart thumping, forehead dripping, Mac runs along the hall and pushes the door open into the stairwell.

He takes the stairs two, three at a time, hurling himself down the flights in a fog of lingering dizziness. He has to get out of here. Has to get the recording to Billy. Has to get on that plane to Sardinia.

The door to the lobby appears to be locked, but when it gives a little at his hardest push he realizes that someone is standing on the other side, holding it shut. He hears a man groan with exertion and shoves as hard as he can. Finally his opponent's strength gives out and, as the door bursts open, a pot-bellied man in a green superintendent's uniform falls panting on the floor.

'*Two* hundred dollars, Jose,' Lacie's disembodied voice calls from high in the stairwell. 'Two fifty. Stop him!'

Jose grabs Mac's ankle and yanks him to the floor. But before he can settle, an explosion rips through the lobby. The building's front door crashes open, shattering glass against a row of battered metal mailboxes.

'Hands up!' Billy shouts.

'*Three* hundred, Jose!'

'I may be broke but I ain't crazy,' Jose mumbles, letting go of Mac's leg.

'Come on, man, get up and get out,' Billy orders his friend. 'You're not gonna miss that flight.'

'Arrest them. They tried to kill me.'

'I'll take care of them later.'

'Billy, she knows everything about Alicia Griffin's murder and Millerhausen's cover-up. We can't let her go.'

'No we can't,' a woman's loud, angry voice blasts into the lobby, 'and no we won't!' Ladasha is still dressed for Sunday church, but she's carrying a gun. Clearly Billy called her while he waited outside. 'Get him to the airport, Billy. I got this. Backup's on the way.'

Billy grabs Mac by the elbow and pulls him forward. As the door swings closed behind them, two squad cars with lights flashing screech to a stop. In the chaos of their approach he can hear Ladasha grumbling, 'Last time I take in house guests,' and then her voice firming into an unambiguous order: 'You! Up against the wall, hands behind your back! You too, get down here, *I said now*. Get yourself up against the wall best you can and don't try telling me your water broke 'cuz I can see you ain't wet!'

Two pairs of backup run in to help her make the arrests of Kroll's no-longer-climbing-the-corporate-ladder Lacie Chen and a building superintendent who sold himself out on the cheap, considering the high stakes of this game.

'I think she was only paying him a hundred bucks at first to rig the elevator to freeze,' Mac tells Billy as they dodge traffic to beat a yellow light. 'He got her up to two fifty before you shot your way in.'

'Practically won the lottery.'

Mac leans back and slides his BlackBerry out of his pocket so he can e-mail Billy the recording. 'Oops, accidentally reactivated the recorder. Looks like I just taped our conversation, too.'

'We say anything bad about Dash just now?'

'Not that I recall.'

'All right then,' Billy says with a chuckle. 'We're safe.'

Monday, July 16

After trying five places, we luck out and find a teal Citroën convertible for rent. The little car is in for repair because the top won't fully close, but after some vigorous negotiation with an English-speaking rental agent who insists the car is out of circulation, he decides he can, after all, compromise his standards for a hefty profit.

Following the eastern coast of the island northward, driving in the middle of the night, there's little traffic. But in near total darkness, the drive is challenging. And now, at nearly two A.M., with a while to go before we're anywhere near the vicinity of Liz Braud's hotel, I can't go on. A ruthless migraine has exploded in my head during the past hour. A molasseslike exhaustion tugs at me. I can hardly keep my eyes open. We pull the car off the side of the road outside Orosei.

Wishing we had sweaters or a blanket to ward off the night chill, I wrestle the top of the convertible into enough of a closed position to hold in some of our body heat. Dathi stretches out on the small backseat and I curl up in the front passenger seat, but give up trying to find a comfortable position. My body hurts everywhere from the accident. In the silver moonlight, I notice shadows like

321

tentacles circling my right upper arm: a wicked bruise making itself known. I wonder what else is hurt or damaged in my body that I can't see, where other bruises will show up when I take off my clothes in front of a pair of eyes. Mac's, I hope. I miss him. Where is he now? Why hasn't he called?

Hours later, bright morning sun wakes me before Dathi. I get out and try to stretch my arms and legs, but the cold stiffened my muscles and now it hurts to move even slightly. It also hurts to think: My headache is still pounding like a boom box with no off switch. Rummaging through my purse, I reaffirm the knowledge that I don't have any painkillers. I'm forty, a mother, old and experienced enough to know you should always carry essential supplies. But as with so many other things in my life, that I don't always follow common wisdom can hurt as often as it can help. 'We all stay in character,' my mother always says. I miss her. I want to call her. But if it's early morning here, it will be night in Brooklyn and she'll be fast asleep. I wonder if Mac saw or spoke with her when he was in New York. The feeling of homesickness that has taunted me these past few days twists through my stomach like a ravenous hunger. But then I look at Dathi sleeping in the backseat, one arm flung wide, bent knuckles brushing the floor of the car, and remind myself that I'm closer to home than I have been since we landed on this island.

I put the battery into my phone and check for

messages: nothing. Pop the battery back out. By now I know that there isn't network coverage this close to the coast unless you're someplace populated, a hotel or restaurant or store. That thought cements my decision to look for somewhere where I might also buy some aspirin or ibuprofen or anything to disempower the migraine. Keeping an eye on the car, I pee in some bushes off the side of the road. Then, as quietly as possible, I pull a seat belt over Dathi, buckling her in so I can drive and she can keep sleeping.

I find a *farmacia* in Orosei and peer through the plate-glass window filled with bottles of sunscreen and pictures of ice cream. A light is on in the back of the store, but the door is locked. I sag in disappointment. Then, as I stand there helplessly in the tender early-morning humidity – a yeasty trace of fresh bread hanging in the air – a woman appears, flipping on lights.

'*Entra.*' She opens the door.

The moment I'm inside her store, I slip the battery back into my phone and after a few seconds, it comes alive.

'*Cosa ti serve, signora?*' the woman asks. When I answer in English she shakes her head, shrugs apologetically, and walks away.

Standing in an aisle stocked with hair products, I check my messages. A text from Mac tells me he's on a plane that should land around noon. I smile so fast, pain buzz-saws through my face and my expression contorts into a wince I hope the

323

woman doesn't see. Another text from Mac hurls me down the dark side of my happy upswing: He wants me to know that no one has been staying at our house in Brooklyn and not to contact the Rossis, who may or may not be who they claimed to be, but either way are definitely a part of this. A third text informs me that Jeff and Justin are okay, just hungry, and they've been fed enough to last weeks. A fourth text reminds me how much he loves me.

There are also three messages from the American embassy. Trembling, I call back and immediately reach Sam Quester, the man who has been trying to find me all night.

'Ms. Schaeffer, finally. First, are you okay?'

'I'm fine. I'm with my daughter Dathi, but I had to leave our friend's son at the police station.'

'I know, but don't worry,' Sam urges in a deliberately calm tone that both pacifies and unnerves me. 'Fremont's being transferred to police headquarters in Cagliari. He's fine. He's going to be released, but we want to do it in liaison with our FBI attaché in Rome. Someone's flying in right now.'

'How much does the FBI know?' Because I want them to know everything, I want them to see every piece of this puzzle before they even arrive so that no more dangerous mistakes will be made.

'I'm not sure, but enough to jump when I called. Apparently an investigation's been triggered in New York, something big, but that's all I can say, and frankly, all I really know. From our end, we're reacting to an abduction of U.S. citizens and mobilizing to help the local police in Sardinia.'

'*No*,' I insist. 'The municipal police here are part of the problem.'

I explain as quickly and thoroughly as I can manage, telling him what I know about Enzo Greco's daily visits to Liz Braud.

'You're sure?'

'Definitely. It might be better if you don't alert the local cops to any of this.'

'This complicates it.' The deflation in Sam Quester's long sigh tells me it's too late, he's already told them. 'Where are you now?'

'Did you already inform the police?'

'I made an inquiry, yes.'

'I'm in a town called Orosei. Looking for some ibuprofen. I've got a wicked headache.'

'I bet you do. Can you hold tight right there and we'll come for you?'

'The thing is, I think my son Ben is somewhere north of here. He's only five and I'm desperate to find him. And Mary, our friend. I'm not sure where they are, exactly, but we've got to look. I'm really worried something else might happen especially now that the cat's out of the bag.' A bad metaphor, because it makes me think of Jeff and Justin, left alone to starve.

'Don't leave Orosei, Ms. Schaeffer. Please. Let us take over now.'

We listen to each other's stubborn silence, and

then I say, 'Thank you. I'll be keeping my phone off but I'll check for messages. Call me when you know something, please?'

'I promise.'

But that I did *not* promise to stay in town bubbles through my throbbing brain as I search the aisles for something that looks like a painkiller I recognize. Sitting still and waiting feels ridiculous and impossible. What if Sam Quester isn't really with the embassy? What if he knows Enzio Greco? How can I reasonably trust him – and just wait?

The proprietress finds me wandering the store's aisles, and asks, 'Help?'

'Ibuprofen.'

I follow her to a shelf from which she plucks a white-and-pink box of Brufen Plus. She looks at me like she can read my level of pain from the look of my face (which she probably can), taps the box and holds up two fingers. I pay at the register and also buy a bottle of water with which I immediately take two pills. On my way back to the car I stop for some bread and coffee at the *panetteria* down the street. When I return, Dathi is groggy but awake.

We sit in the car drinking our sweet, milky coffee and sharing the warm bread until we're full and alert enough to continue our journey north.

CHAPTER 20

J ust landed, getting through customs. Where r u?
San Teodoro, east coast. Driving north.
Dathi is with me.
On my way to intercept Fremont – local cops trans-
ferring him to army cops – greco has no power with
them. FBI/Rome mtg me there. Good news Dathi!!
She thinks they were held far north but cant
remember where. Looking.
Stay in touch.
U 2
Keep safe
U 2

The cop shop they take Fremont to this time is
in a bigger building in a bigger town. A red, white,
and green flag droops off a pole above the front
door; he recognizes the Italian national flag from
world history last year in tenth grade. He figured
things were improving when they stuck him in the
back of the squad car without cuffing him again,
but his wrists are still raw from when that jerk
cuffed and arrested him in the middle of the night.
No one's talked to him (except the commissioner,

that once). Just a few words in Italian. He has no idea what's going on. He's been worried sick over Dathi. Did they arrest her, too? He hasn't slept or eaten for two days and sometimes he thinks he's hallucinating. Last night he thought he heard Karin's voice shouting somewhere inside the backwoods police station where they held him in a damp cell overnight with nothing to eat except cheese with maggots jumping out of it. Not that he touched it. He wouldn't. But the guard thought it was pretty funny. Karin never came back to see him so he thinks he *was* hallucinating. Had to be. If she had really been there, she would have busted her way in. He knows her.

Four guards surround him up the steps into the building like he's some important prisoner. They still haven't recuffed him but they're also not letting him out of their sight. He hopes when school starts this fall someone assigns the old 'What Did You Do This Summer' essay they always gave in grade school. *I got kidnapped by a sweaty Italian freak and then arrested for nothing on a resort island in the middle of nowhere.* He never realized until right now how much he loves America. He can't wait to get on Facebook and tell his friends about this.

'Free!' someone shouts, and for a minute he believes it, that he's actually free, as in *poof!* the guards will go away and let him walk out of here. But no. He turns around and there is a face so familiar his eyes water like a baby's.

Mac. And another man, blond guy with frame-less glasses who also speaks American English . . . music to Fremont's ears. Mac looks like he hasn't shaved in a week and when he gets close the smell says he hasn't showered, either. But who cares? Fremont pushes aside the guards and guides himself straight into Mac's embrace.

'Hey, kid, you look okay. You okay?'

'I'm all right, I guess. Those fuckers.'

'Let's get you out of here for starters, then we'll talk.'

'Whatever.'

'This is Guy de Luca. FBI, based in Rome.'

Guy offers his hand to shake. 'Here to help.'

'So is this over? Can I leave?'

'Pretty soon.' Mac pats Fremont's back like he just brought in a home run. 'Guy's got a little more paperwork to take care of, then you're free.'

'I *am* Free.'

'You know what I mean.'

'Cool.'

'Hungry?'

'Is it hot in hell?'

Guy's phone rings. 'Hope this is the call I've been waiting for. Give me a minute, son.' He turns his back on them to talk to someone in Italian.

'I thought that guy was American.'

'He is,' Mac says, 'but he's based in Rome. He's bilingual.'

He likes the way the blond white guy called him *son*. He never knew his sperm donor but it feels good when a man in charge recognizes him as a fellow male on his way up. And it feels good, really good, being with Mac. In fact it feels awesome. The tears start forming again but that just won't do, not until he sees his mother. She'll probably make him cry when she sees him because his mom, she believes you've got to let it all out.

'Who's the FBI dude talking to?' he asks Mac.

'The police, I think.'

He feels lightheaded, knowing the cops can't be trusted, and tells Mac, 'Bad idea.' And then he tells him the rest of the story, and about the old man with white hair, Emiliana's good friend the police commissioner. Liz, as his mother called the woman. The tears are back, thinking of his mother, knowing how she must be worrying about him and that he has no way to reach her.

'I already know about the commissioner; Karin told me.'

'She knows?'

'She figured it out, then Dathi confirmed it.'

'She's with Dathi!' Relief floods him like morning sunshine.

'There are different police forces here, Free. The one the commissioner heads is the local cops. But the one we're dealing with now is the Carabinieri – the military police. They work nationally and locally, and they're our best bet. The FBI hooked us up with them right away, so now we're good.'

'You sure about that?'

'Sure as I can be.'

'Fuck I hope you're right.'

'Don't hesitate to watch your language,' Mac advises, and they both laugh. 'Free, what do you remember about the place they were holding you?'

'It was kind of a little house on the beach. When Dathi and I got out, we ran all the way up the road. I didn't see any signs. Nothing until we were near Olbia. It must be a big town because there was a lot of traffic, but it was a while before I noticed it, and we were heading south, so I guess we were somewhere north of Olbia. After that we decided it was better to travel in the dark.'

The midday sun is hot on our bare heads in the open convertible but the wind feels good with its cold, salty bite. If we'd taken a straight line from Orosei we'd have gotten past San Teodoro in a couple of hours at most. But our zigzag route has at least tripled our time on the road because we don't know our destination. Somewhere on a beach. The coast of Sardinia is all beaches, and the island is almost all coast. *Somewhere on a beach* could be practically anywhere. We have no idea where we're going, but Dathi is sure she'll know it when she sees it. There's no good reason not to give her the benefit of the doubt. And so we have investigated every unmarked dirt road we've stumbled on. Visited numerous dead ends. Gotten out and walked narrow footpaths to nowhere.

Finally something ignites her memory.

'There!' She points to a stack of seven

arrow-shaped signs, five blue and two brown. All but two indicate the same direction. 'We passed this intersection on our way down. The first night we were running.'

Seven signs. Seven choices. 'Do you remember which direction you were coming from when you saw this?' If she could track her movement backward, it would be a good start.

'That one: Olbia.' The sign on the top of the stack, directing us to the left.

I accelerate off the narrow beach road onto a newly paved road leading to town. We follow signs through winding streets into the heart of Olbia, a smaller city than Cagliari, less medieval and more Mediterranean, filled with tourists and businesses to serve them. Olbia is only a forty-five minute drive south from Palau, where Liz Braud has her hotel. My pulse quickens at the thought of how easy it would be to drive between the two locations.

Are Ben and Mary somewhere in Olbia?

Somewhere on a beach.

I want to yell, scream, argue, weep. *I need Ben*, to smell his powdery skin, to feel our cheeks fuse in perfect softness. If we don't find him soon, I think I'll lose my mind.

I prompt myself to take a deep breath.

Levitate above the nauseating panic.

Keep going.

Just keep going.

★ ★ ★

Mac watches Fremont, whose face is pressed up against the helicopter window, gazing at a distant landscape that looks like free-spirited earth-toned modern art. Wearing headphones to block the chopper's deafening racket, the teenager almost looks as if he's listening to music – except for a mask of apprehension transforming his young face into someone with worries beyond his years. What is the kid thinking and feeling right now, to have come to this? Searching for his mother from the sky. Knowing the outcome could be bad. And what he's already been through, not just this past week but during his life: to live with an identity defined largely by his creamy brown skin color, never knowing where a full half of his DNA originated, abiding the worldview of a devoted but idiosyncratic mother. He is loved. Mac can see in his fervent searching eyes that Fremont knows that. All the boy wants right now is his mother back. All Mac wants right now is Ben back. Once they have the rest of their family, they can be whole again.

The pilot steers them leftward, hugging the coast. Below them, a cluster of buildings comes into view: Monopoly pieces haphazardly tossed alongside a hard edge of land married to the brilliant blue sea.

'Olbia just below,' Guy de Luca shouts.

Mac and Fremont both lift an earphone, and Guy repeats himself. 'Olbia.'

Fremont looks down without recognition. Mac

watches the boy watch the earth pass below them. So far nothing has inspired his memory.

Fifteen minutes later, they land in Palau, ready to descend on Liz Braud's L'Hotel del Riso e dell'Oblio – a private investigator, an FBI attaché, a backup of Carabinieri, and a teenage boy who knows too much to be lied to. Laughter and forgetting: what gall. *Soon you won't have the luxury of laughing* or *forgetting*, Mac thinks, hopping out of the helicopter onto sunburnt, wind-whipped earth.

Waiting on the field are two red-striped black Alfa Romeos, the squad car of the Carabinieri. Four uniformed officers sit inside their cars until the winds from the copter's swirling blades die down.

Mac and Fremont travel together in the back of the nearest squad car. Guy de Luca rides in the other car. No one speaks, or sees much of the beauty rushing past them on the road. They are focused only on arrival.

They reach the entrance to the hotel with its towering palm trees heralding the pretty gravel road that leads to a masterfully elegant pink stucco inn with terraces down to pool and ocean. Mac glances at Fremont and notices the boy's hand shaking on his lap.

'It's going to be okay,' Mac tells him, not knowing if it will, or how any of this will play out. He reaches over to still the trembling hand. Fremont's fingers clasp his fervently, like any child grabbing hold, and Mac's heart shudders. If they can't arrive

334

in time to save Mary, if they can't arrive in time to save Ben, Fremont will be an orphan and so will Mac (all over again). Mac already lost both his parents to murder. He doesn't know if he can absorb the loss of his only biological child. Not at his age. Not at fifty. After a moment he realizes that Fremont isn't squeezing his hand in gratitude only, but in understanding support as well.

The cars pull up in sequence and park in front of the hotel. A gardener stops raking gravel to stare at the four police exiting their cars. Guy, Mac, and Fremont follow. A young woman with short dark hair, wearing a filmy magenta sundress over a white bikini, spots the cortege from the hotel's open front door. Mac recognizes Blaine Millerhausen from the photo Mary showed him that day in New York, standing on Madison Avenue, killing time on what he then thought of as a dead-end case, another paranoid wife determined to unearth a husband's imagined infidelity. How wrong he was. How wrong they all were.

If Mac's eyes don't deceive him, Blaine, barefoot, is wearing a diamond toe ring that releases a brilliant sparkle as she turns on her heel and vanishes inside the inn.

What will happen, he wonders as he follows the police and Guy de Luca up the steps to the entrance, between a pair of pineapple palms, when Cathy Millerhausen's prenup deprives Blaine of a hefty slice of her inheritance? And suddenly he knows exactly, to the dollar, why they are here.

It was always about how the financial legacy went down.

How many times has he heard stories about the interests of first wives and first children trumping second families? Something about the magic of your first child . . . a chill runs through Mac, thinking about Ben. And he knows.

Blaine Millerhausen's diamond toe ring is why they are here. Her ability to have whatever she wants. That's why Alicia Griffin had to die.

Mac breaks into a cold sweat thinking about the avarice, narcissism, and willfully delusional single-mindedness it took for Godfrey Millerhausen and Liz Braud to hurt so many people so their child could hold on to the maximum possible inheritance.

'What do you people want?' Liz Braud comes around the front desk, tall and poised, chin high as a queen's. Her blonded hair is swept off her forehead, pulled behind her ears in a brutal knot.

'Can you identify the people who held you captive?' Guy asks Fremont.

Close at Mac's side, Fremont points at Liz and Blaine. 'Right there, those ladies. Both of them.'

Liz holds her composure, tanned jaw clenched, nostrils thin with outrage. 'What makes you think you can march in here without warning and just—'

Guy interrupts her. 'This is an arrest. We can do it right here in the lobby or we can go somewhere more private. It's your choice.'

Her chilly eyes turn to him. 'And you are?'

'Special Agent Guy de Luca, FBI attaché, Rome office.' Guy rattles something off in Italian to the uniformed police and they circle Liz and Blaine, who cowers at her mother's side.

'What do you want?'

'Mary Salter and Ben MacLeary: Where are they?'

One corner of her mouth quivers. Guy waits, but she doesn't answer. Waves of hostility pass between them until finally he breaks the silence.

'You're under arrest for—'

'Let's do this in my office,' Liz says.

'Too late; you lost your chance. We can talk in the car on the way to the station.'

More Italian orders from Guy and both women's hands are shackled behind their backs with a variety of handcuff Mac has never seen before. These cuffs, a dangling infinity sign of chains tugged tight at their nexus, look more like jewelry. Offbeat low-end bracelets the likes of which the bejeweled Millerhausen women would never wear by choice.

As the officers escort the women through the lobby, under the gaping attention of their guests, Liz's focus snaps to Fremont.

'Your mother thinks you're dead,' she tells him, and then turns away before he can answer her to her face.

'You fucking, fucking, fucking . . .' Fremont stammers until Mac's steadying hand tries to stop an explosive tirade that won't get anyone anywhere.

337

'Easy, son,' Mac urges.

'Where is she?' Fremont shouts after the women. Neither one responds, so he throws his best grenade, just to hurt them: 'You're going to jail!'

Blaine twists around and winks. 'We'll see about that.'

'Your friend,' Fremont spits, 'the police commissioner, they already arrested him, he already told the cops everything!'

A spark of panic lights Blaine's eyes. The muscles at the back of the mother's neck grip her merciless spine. The moment is more satisfying than Mac would have thought.

'Then why did you ask us where your mother is, if you already know?' Blaine says with false calm.

Mac whispers to Fremont: 'Don't answer.'

Guy follows as the women are taken outside. Mac and Fremont watch from the front door as the Carabinieri drive off with their prisoners. When Guy's cell phone rings, he takes the call pacing the perimeter of the gravel driveway.

'That was a good one about the police commissioner,' Mac says to Fremont, whose body shivers in anger. 'Even if it isn't true. Yet.'

'But they're going to arrest that slimy dude, too, aren't they?'

'I'm sure they will if they can.'

'What does *that* mean?'

'They'll have to be careful how they handle the commissioner. There are always a lot of politics involved, and politics can be corrupt. We don't really know this country.'

Shaking his head, Fremont snorts agreement.

Half an hour later, while the chopper's blades kick up a fierce wind, Guy ends a phone call and shouts over the noise, 'The daughter broke and gave us the location. It's outside Olbia. We can be there in ten, fifteen minutes, depending on the airstream.'

'What about the guards?' Fremont asks. 'They have guns. They shot at me and Dathi when we ran away.'

'Liz Braud called them off. My contact confirmed they're on the run, and they're being sought. We're free and clear. Almost there, folks. Let's end this.'

Mac and Fremont share a cheer of unabashed joy.

Dathi holds my phone, reading aloud from the directions we managed to pull off Google maps in an unexpectedly wired café in a village whose name I never noticed. Somewhere outside Olbia. According to Mac's text, Mary and Ben are being held east of Golfo Aranci, a town nestled into the bend of an archipelago jutting into the Tyrrhenian Sea. His text also specified that the pair of armed guards Dathi told me about were gone. When I report this bit of information to Dathi, she says, 'Hurry, then.'

'Mac wants us to wait for him to get there,' I tell her, 'which should be soon.'

'As if you would, Karin.' A wicked smile lights her face. Truth is, I more than share the urgency of almost-being-there. There's no way we'll wait.

'Are you sure this is the road?' I ask her, skeptical because the farther we drive, the more adrift we are from any sign of civilization.

'That's what it says.' She gazes out the passenger window. 'Anyway, I don't see any other roads, do you?'

'No.'

From all appearances, Via Cala Moresca is a road to nowhere, a rough lane squeezed between ocean and wilderness. There are no signs. No intersections. Just the endless road.

Dathi bolts forward. 'Look, *there*.'

An unmarked turn to the right takes us along a brief road culminating in a fork.

'I think I see a house,' she says, '*there*, do you see it? And it's just about where the directions say it should be.'

Through a thicket of trees you can just make out the edge of a low building. Without taking time to decide, I fork to the left.

Mac leans back hard while the helicopter whirrs itself into an awkward but sufficient landing, making abrupt contact with the rocky soil on the outskirts of Golfo Aranci, in what appears to be a semiverdant wasteland of sandy earth and low brush between town and ocean. About a hundred feet away he sees a dusty road, abandoned except

340

for a black Alfa Romeo with a fine red stripe, a driver at the wheel and the motor running fast and loud and ready.

We circle in front of a one-story building that meets the other road, the one I didn't take at the fork. So both choices lead to the same destination. Great for making a quick escape, if you have to.

White-painted iron gates cover every window and door. A window facing the ocean is open, but I see no sign of movement or life inside. The deadly silence sends a curl of alarm through my body.

I crack open my door, and in the subtle movement of leaning to get out, a single gunshot rings into the quiet, obliterating our windshield. The bullet lands in the leather headrest, leaving an angry crater where, moments ago, my head had been.

'Get down!' I tell Dathi, as a second bullet pings the air.

We hunker beneath the dashboard. Whoever is shooting at us – you can hear his footsteps crossing gravel, coming closer.

'Karin,' Dathi whispers frantically, '*Karin.*'

I don't know how to respond, because it's true: If he finds us, we'll die. *When* he finds us; we couldn't be an easier target. He approaches with slow, taunting confidence, in no great hurry, because it's his game now.

'I thought the guards were gone,' she whispers.

'So did I.'

You can hear him brush up against the car. The car trembles against his weight.

And then . . . another shot breaks over us.

'Are you okay?' I whisper.

'Yes.'

Footsteps and male voices. I realize with an intense jolt of relief that it's English I'm hearing.

'Karin? Dathi?'

Mac's voice reaches me like a balm. I unfurl myself and there he is, leaning over the side of the convertible, staring at me. The sight of my husband after three long days and nights thrills me despite his ragged appearance. Fremont stands on the other side of the car, helping Dathi up. With them is a blond man I don't know; he looks crisp and professional, and somehow not Italian. A Glock 22 pistol dangles from his hand, a rifle is strapped over his shoulder. At his feet is the shooter: a black-clad guard, apparently dead.

Seeing Karin rise from the floor of the convertible, her head bandaged, arms bruised, Mac catches his breath. Once she's standing, he doesn't wait for words. He holds her. Drinks her in, the antiseptic smell of her, inhaling their reunion as he realizes she's been in a hospital.

'What happened to you?' he whispers in her ear.

'We have to find Ben.'

CHAPTER 21

At the sound of gunfire, Mary startles like a baby falling and plummets backward in time to the moment Fremont and Dathi made their escape. The shot that followed. The brutal certainty that one of them was killed.

When she manages to shift her legs off the couch and hoist her body around to sit up, a wave of dizziness overtakes her. She breathes into the weakness and hunger that she's given herself over to: the beautiful fragility of an untethered mind that allows you to fly through time to better places than this.

She's been back to her old apartment in Greenpoint, where she and Alma lived together, before they decided to have a baby. Where they put in all the fixtures with their own two hands so they could live in the loft for cheap. Where they earned a fixture fee from the next tenant, four years later, after they broke up and the baby they had together was really Mary's because she'd borne it and now she understood something fierce about motherhood and no way would she give up her son or even allow visitation rights to a woman who cheated on her, broke her heart. They split the fixture fee fifty-fifty, but it didn't mean anything. Not to Mary. She was heartbroken and alone, but loneliness never set in because she had Fremont. Fremont Salter. Her son. Her flesh and blood and namesake. The boy who would carry her forward into the universe. And she loved him so much that she couldn't regret her heartbreak, because without Alma she never would have journeyed into motherhood.

Life is a flow.

It comes at you and you ride it.

At the New York Aquarium that time, she told Free he was her baby dolphin, riding on her back. That they were a matched set. They belonged together.

'But I don't look like you, Mom,' he said. He was six.

'You look like me on the inside.' That got him thinking. 'The thing to always remember, Free, is that the world is a rainbow.'

Sitting on the couch, her head spins. The edge of the cushion digs into the bare underside of her knees and it hurts; her skin feels thin as rice paper against the harsh upholstery. She doesn't move. Her body smells of urine.

'It's us!' a girl's voice is shouting from outside. Sounds like Dathi. But Dathi is gone, so it couldn't be her. Gone or dead. It occurs to Mary that if Dathi was the one shot as the teenagers ran away, Fremont could still be alive. So no, it can't be

Dathi calling to her from outside the door. Because that would have to mean . . .

'Mary? Ben? Is anyone there?' That voice sounds like Karin's. Mary laughs. Now she knows she's hearing things.

Suddenly, there's another gunshot, this one painfully loud and so close she can feel its reverberations.

The door bursts open, letting in a rush of ocean air to create a buoyant cross breeze with the thwarted wind at the window. Two specters drift in, a woman and a girl, the female partnership of deliverance she always knew would greet her when the time came. But then, behind them, three other figures come into focus: men. And one of them is . . . can it be possible?

She stands on wobbly legs and opens her arms to her son. He rushes to her. The touch of him, the feel of his skin, his familiar smell beneath the caked-on grime, the tight way he holds her, is sustenance.

'I can't find Ben anywhere.' The bell of Dathi's voice, searching the house she knows too well.

Searching for Ben.

Mary's insides melt. This is the other moment she's been dreading. But she has to rise to this. These people, her friends, came all this way to help her. Now she has to help them with the little she knows, and so she gathers her will. 'They took him.'

'When?' Karin's face is bright red, and so are

her eyes: bloodshot webs, the whites barely showing. She's been hurt: the dirty bandage on her forehead; the grim purple bruises vining up her arms. She recalls the horrifying image of Karin lashed to a chair. But she's alive! *Fremont is alive, and Karin is alive*. If nothing else, Mary owes them the simple facts.

'Yesterday. The day before. I don't know. Right after Free and Dathi escaped.'

'Friday,' Karin says. 'Three days ago.'

Mary leans against Fremont, who holds her. When Karin's arms wrap around her, too, her guilt grows heavier. '*I'm so sorry.*'

'For what?' Karin's voice is soft, forgiving. 'You stayed with all the children. You took care of them.'

'I let them take Ben.'

'They were armed. How could you have stopped them?'

'I don't know, I don't know—'

'Shhh. You did your best.'

But what real value is doing your best when you've failed?

The other man gets on his phone, saying, 'Let me see what I can do,' and stalks outside to speak in private. Mary wonders who he is. She can tell from his authoritative tone that he's here to help, and feels a surge of borrowed energy.

'I found a photo in the house.' She clears her throat, raises her voice. 'It shows the Rossis with Blaine Millerhausen and an older woman, who turned out to be Liz, having a meal. They were obviously friends. I asked Mario Rossi about it in an e-mail, because I didn't know who the older woman was. I asked, since they knew Blaine, if they had any idea where her mother was. Never heard back. And then that man came and took us. The man with the hideous snake tattoo.'

'Why didn't you tell us about the photo when you found it?' An edge in Karin's tone.

Inwardly Mary winces as more regret slices through her, because it's true: She should have told them right away. She bears down on the pain and wills herself to answer honestly. 'I didn't want to worry you.'

Karin and Mac exchange a sharp glance, and he asks, 'Where's the photo?'

'In my purse, I think. Yes, I had it in my purse.'

'Where's your purse?'

'I don't know. It was in the van.'

The other man returns, the tight pinpricks of his sun-shocked eyes sounding an alarm. 'Both women confirm that the guard who took Ben handed him over to Commissioner Greco. They've got a GPS signal from Greco's cell phone, so if he's with his phone, looks like we've got him. And if Ben's still with him, we'll have him, too.'

CHAPTER 22

The helicopter seems to take us straight into the sun. In the row of seats behind the pilot and copilot, Dathi, Mac, and Guy de Luca gaze out the windows as we fly westward across the island to Capo Caccia, on the opposite shore. Mary sits between Fremont and me in the back row, clutching both our hands, and yet I feel lightheaded and eerily alone. What if Ben isn't with Enzio Greco anymore? What if we don't find my little boy? What then?

No one speaks. There's nothing to say except to voice panic and fear, and what's the point of that? No one dares tell me it will be all right when they can't possibly know if that's true. I know from running missing persons searches, back when I was a detective, that the hunt runs on a strange mix of fact and fiction. You pick up any lead you can and follow it. If it's worthless, you try another one. And again. Until, hopefully, one of them pans out. Already I can tell that the pattern of hysteria elicited by missing child alerts is no different here in Italy than back home in the States.

Minutes after the alert was finally issued

throughout all branches of the island's police force, calls started pouring in.

Someone saw a lost little boy at a resort hotel far north, in La Maddalena.

Someone saw a little boy wandering alone on a beach in Tortoli.

Someone saw a little boy being dragged by a woman who may not have been his mother in Quartu Sant'Elena.

Someone saw a little boy and girl sitting alone and dirty beside the road in Vilamar.

Sardinians and tourists alike had seen my Ben all over the island. And yet no one could accurately describe him. Good Samaritans' gut instincts abounded with false leads.

But then . . . an elderly woman respected in her village of Codrongianos had noticed a little boy with brown hair leaving a café two days earlier, crying and talking in a foreign language. Her curiosity was piqued when the boy was put into the back of a car with no child seat by a man with white hair who looked like someone she thought she'd seen on television a few times, though she couldn't place him. When the news broadcast the missing child alert with photos of Ben and Enzio Greco, she recognized the boy and the commissioner immediately.

Another woman, a British tourist staying in Mugoni, reported seeing an older white-haired Italian man speaking heavily accented English with a young boy. They were carrying a bag of what appeared to be groceries, and because a set of keys jangled in the man's hand she got the feeling they'd been shopping and were heading to their car.

And then, just this morning, a man walking along the cliff at Capo Caccia heard a boy and a man speaking a foreign language together inside the old lighthouse. He'd thought they were speaking English but could have been wrong. He didn't see either of them, but the boy sounded young.

If you look at a map, Codrongianos and Mugoni are reasonable stops on the way to Capo Caccia from Golfo Aranci, where Ben was pried from Mary's arms. Was he taken from one remote peninsula to another? When I think of the ruthless periphery of this island, I feel the worst kind of despair. I can still see the silver sports car racing over the cliff, hear the sound of its crash below. I still feel in my gut how easily it could have been me. If Ben is with Enzio Greco, what is his logic in sequestering him so close to the ocean?

And then it hits me: You can make a quicker escape from a shore than inland if you plan to leave by boat. In a rising panic, as we chopper across the sky toward the western edge of the island, I try to think of who Greco might want to pass my child off to in a last ditch attempt to pretend he has nothing to do with this. My mind races through possibilities: human traffickers, Somali pirates, who else? Who can possibly want that child as much as Mac and I do?

My body leans into Mary's as the helicopter

swerves left. Below, an isthmus of land dips into the sea.

'Guy?' I summon the agent's attention. 'Is that it down there?'

He speaks with the pilot before answering, simply, 'Yes.'

From this distance you can make out a square building on the farthest point of land jutting into the water.

'It doesn't look like a lighthouse,' I say.

'No, it doesn't.'

We're all heading into unknown territory together; even Guy de Luca doesn't know the lay of this land. An American living in Rome. Sardinia must be almost as foreign to him as it is to us, with the exception that he can speak the language and has official entry to anywhere he wants to go.

A single road comes into focus, zigzagging crazily toward the lighthouse. A procession of squad cars and an ambulance make their slow way along the bent road. I worry at the sight of the ambulance. Do the police have new information since we took off from Golfo Aranci? Or is it common procedure here, as at home, to arrive at a potential crime scene prepared?

Outside the lighthouse, a single car sits in a dusty parking area.

'It's so far down,' Dathi notes.

I say, 'It looks deserted from here.'

Mac and Fremont agree with a nod.

'If it's even open to tourists,' Guy explains, 'it

would probably be closed on Mondays. Most things are in Europe.'

As we descend, I can feel my center of gravity rapidly shift. Wind ricochets off the skin of the copter, jarring us right, then left, and right again, like an unsteadily spinning top. Beside me, Mary squeezes shut her eyes and presses back into her seat. Fremont and Dathi seem to hold their breath as they watch through the windows, their gazes unwavering as we plummet down toward an earth that seems to be speeding back up at us. We land on the rocky terrain with an angry thud. The chopper blades whip dry grass and loose stones into a tempest of unsettled earth, finally slowing enough for the copilot to unlatch the door.

Guy de Luca jumps out first, followed by Mac, Fremont, and Dathi. I don't like that the teenagers are here with us on this mission, but having worked so hard to find them, there's no way we're letting them out of our sight now. I help Mary out and down.

Capo Caccia is a stunning, intimidating piece of land surrounded by azure ocean on three sides. The end of the earth. In the blistering sun, wind assaults us from every angle.

'Looks like we got here first,' Guy says.

'Well, I'm not waiting.' Mac starts walking toward the lighthouse in the near distance. Guy follows.

Mary stands beside me, shivering in the heat. She looks so broken. 'Why don't you stay here with

Free and Dathi,' I suggest, 'and keep an eye on each other while we check out the lighthouse?'

'Good idea,' Fremont says. 'We'll watch her.'

Dathi agrees, 'That's right.'

'I'm fine. I want to help.' But the filament of Mary's voice is unconvincing.

'You are helping.' I kiss her cheek. 'Stay here with the kids.'

I pick my way along the stony ground in pursuit of Mac and Guy, who are circling the lighthouse now, looking for an open door or window. I reach Mac as the fourth window he tries groans open in its swollen wooden sash. Chips of soft wood and graying paint rain down as if the window hasn't been opened in years.

'Guy!' I call. 'We found a way in.'

Mac hoists himself up onto the window ledge, balancing to take a look in before pushing himself all the way through. I follow, the muscles in my bruised arms straining as my body cantilevers over the ledge and into an unfurnished room that smells dank and feels hollow. Landing on my hands, a pair of repeating slaps echoes through the room. My whole body hurts when I hit the floor. Guy arrives more gracefully, his movements and strength proving his relative youth; somehow, he lands on his feet.

'Split up or stay together?' Mac asks.

'We'll be faster if we split up,' I suggest.

'But safer if we stay together,' Guy says. 'Are either of you armed?'

'No,' Mac answers for both of us.

'I'll go first, then.' He slides his gun out of his hip holster.

There are three utilitarian rooms on the ground floor: the empty one we arrived into, a bare-bones kitchen, and a sitting room with a card table and three rickety folding chairs. Upstairs are two monastic bedrooms, each with a single bed, and a bathroom whose floor is missing a row of tiles down the middle like a gap toothed grin. A heavy pattern of mildew covers a flimsy white shower curtain half-obscuring a chipped porcelain tub. It's inside the tub that I see it, and my heart leaps into my throat: a little green plastic boat. The kind of bath toy you'd buy in a grocery store for a young child.

I lean in to pick it up, sure I smell the tang of recent soap. A new-looking price tag plasters the boat's underside. 'It's still wet.'

'Don't jump to conclusions,' Mac warns me.

But Guy catches my eye and seems to allow me the presumption that Ben might have recently bathed in this tub. This moldy tub. An appalling thought. I drop the boat into my purse.

There is no other sign that Ben might have been here. My head is pounding now; the headache is back. Leaning over the grimy sink, I turn on the tap and swallow enough water to chase down another pair of painkillers. We search through every room, opening closets, checking in corners and under beds, even opening kitchen cupboards.

There's no indication that anyone has spent a night or eaten a meal here for a long time. Except for the plastic boat.

'I don't know,' Guy says. The three of us stand together on the second floor landing by the top of the stairs. Dust kicked up by our presence dances in beams of strong sunlight shining through a hall window.

'We should check the grounds,' Mac suggests. I'm about to agree, and Guy has already started down the stairs, when we hear the sound of a scuffle outside.

Mac and I are at the window first, with Guy pressing between us. Outside, Dathi and Mary are running toward the cliff, where Fremont stands so close to the edge he appears almost to float in the sky. He's frantically waving to them, shouting something we can't hear from inside the lighthouse.

CHAPTER 23

'He's there!' Fremont shouts. 'I see him! He's there!'

Dathi's imagination conjures a broken doll, Ben or whoever *he* is, sprawled at the bottom of wherever *there* is.

'Ben,' Mary chants under her breath, 'Ben,' sounding excited, almost happy. But doesn't she realize that beyond that precipice there's just air and sky and nothingness?

Fremont watches Dathi help his mother struggle across the stony ground. She is showing him a side of her he hadn't expected to see for years: a woman who needs taking care of; a mother alone in the world except for her son. Watching her, he suddenly feels twenty-five and not sixteen. He feels like a man who should have told his mother to wait while they checked this out. They've got to get more food and water into her than the granola bar and half bottle of water she had in the helicopter; *but first they have to find Ben.* As he watches his friend help his weakened mother, a girl younger than him at thirteen yet older than him in so many ways, he adores her like a sister and believes they'll be friends for life.

He stands at the top of a path that was invisible until he was close enough to see that the cliff offered more than just a sheer drop-off. A broken signpost lies on the ground, announcing *Grotta di Nettuno. Attenzione!* Narrow stone stairs stagger down the side of the mountain, with nothing but a short barrier separating you from oblivion. Behind his mother he sees the front door of the lighthouse fling open. Karin, Mac, and Guy come running out.

He turns and watches as the man with white hair walks slowly up the stairs. The commissioner seems so confident that he's alone on the side of the mountain, so at ease with himself, that he pauses to glance at the horizon. But when he starts walking again and looks up, when he sees them, the startled expression on his face is priceless.

'You,' his mother shrieks, seeing the man who helped Emiliana and Cosima, Liz and Blaine, hold them captive. '*You.*'

Fremont grabs her arm so she won't fall into the opening of the stairs, but energy returns to her in such a hard blast that he loses his grip and she gets away. He follows. So does Dathi. Mary is running down the steps now, holding on to the barrier, moving faster than you'd think she could after days of solitary captivity.

'Where is Ben?' she shrieks in a voice he's never heard, a voice that sends chills through him. '*Where*

357

is he?' And he ages another five years as he understands how powerful guilt and remorse can be,
how and why his mother believes she failed Karin
and Mac, how she failed everyone, how her belief
that her own son was dead bankrupted her spirit
and stole her will to live and on top of it she may
have also killed her friends' son and that is just
too much, too much. As he chases his mother
down the steps on the side of the mountain, his
jaw grips so furiously he hears his teeth crack
inside his head. And outside his head he hears a
deafening explosion of wind.

Mac is first down the stairs, in front of Karin and
Guy, defying their understanding that the gun goes
first. But this is different. Because what Mac sees
in front of him – Mary and Fremont and Dathi
racing down the stairs, one chasing the other –
looks like sanity hurling itself into a vortex.

At the end of the stairs is a cave, Guy explained
upon translating the fallen sign: *Neptune's Grotto.
Careful!* Apparently it's a famous cave and a tourist
attraction, but because of the difficulty reaching
it, not too many people visit.

'Stop!' Mac shouts.

Behind him, Karin echoes, 'Mary, kids, *stop.*'

Nowhere else to run, Enzio Greco turns around
and hurries in the direction of the cave. But he
can't move fast enough.

Mary reaches him first.

To Mac's astonishment, instead of pushing

Greco aside, she leaps onto his back, toppling the old man onto the stone steps. He cries out in Italian, his incomprehensible words bouncing off the mountainside and echoing over the seascape in a haunting aria of fright.

Greco's hands grasp the stone barrier and he hauls himself partway up with Mary still fixed on his back. Her fingers claw at his throat, nostrils, mouth, eyes. He shouts something else in Italian. Guy yells back in Italian, repeating himself firmly, twice.

But it's too late.

Shrieking in agony as Mary's fingers work to penetrate his eyes, Greco stands suddenly, arching and spinning in an effort to buck her off.

'Mom, stop!' Fremont begs his mother, but she doesn't seem to hear him. She continues her attack as if driven by an inner motor.

'Mary, don't!' Dathi's plea mixes in the wind with Fremont's.

And Karin, again: 'Mary, *stop!*'

Mary's left hand detaches first, and then her left foot breaks free. With one hard twist of his body, Enzio Greco hurls her over the barrier. And then the wind takes her.

'No!' Fremont cries, hinged at the waist over the barrier, hurling his voice after her as if she might grab on to sound. *'Mommy, Mommy, no!'*

Mac stops running. Karin stops behind him. Dathi pushes past them to join her friend at the barrier, both of them reaching, reaching.

Behind and above them, on the lighthouse plateau, a battalion of cars arrives, their doors slamming, feet pounding forward, Italian police rushing down the stairs.

Mac and Karin together draw Fremont away from the barrier and anchor him against the craggy wall of the mountain as he collapses, shaking. Guy rushes past them in a fury, cocking his gun, aiming it at Greco with such a steady and determined hand that Mac believes the agent could make his mark running. Believes it, and wants him to. Never before has he felt such pure vengeance. Enzio Greco. Who served them espressos on their first visit to him when the family went missing. Convinced them he would help. Told them not to overworry. Smiled. Mac wonders how much Greco's cooperation cost the Millerhausens. And wants him dead.

Dathi is holding on to me so tightly it hurts, but I let her. Mac is mostly holding Fremont up, the boy is so tall and heavy, but all our arms are around him. There's no way Mary can have survived that fall. No way. And before the awful thought that Fremont is now an orphan can take hold, something else replaces it.

He is ours now.

He belongs to us and we'll never let go of him.

Guy de Luca stirs a cold breeze as he rushes past, red-faced, outraged, ready to kill. As uniformed cops stream down the stairs, a tendril of panic inches through me. Who owns these cops' loyalty? Law or lawlessness? Guy de Luca or Enzio Greco? But when I see a bright flint of disgrace paralyze Greco as he watches the parade of officers charge toward him, I recognize his bleak acknowledgment that no one is here to save him.

He lifts a leg over the barrier, straddles it, and looks down at the ocean.

And I know something else: He's going to jump.

But what if he's the only person who knows where Ben is now? What if my son isn't in the cave and we have to find him but only a dead man can tell us how?

'Where's Ben?' I shout, breaking free of my family and charging behind Guy, taking the vertiginous stairs two at a time. 'Where is he? *Tell us!*'

Greco swings his other leg over the barrier just before Guy reaches him. And trailing a cry that resonates with injustice – as if he's been pushed, as if somehow he's been forced into this – this choice between confession and death – he hurls himself into the abyss.

CHAPTER 24

The helicopter trolls cliffside, examining the seam where stone meets ocean, in search of Mary and Greco. Meanwhile, I follow Guy and Mac follows me the rest of the way down the stairs into the sea-level maw of the grotto. Frothy waves crash onto the stone landing that serves as the cave's entrance. When the tide is up, the cave must flood. A small child would be swept into the sea.

We enter through a gash in the mountainside and step into silvery shadows that darken the farther we go. Puddles of dormant seawater glimmer like scattered mirrors. Beyond a path defined by a single sagging rope boundary, a vast pool of water reflects a towering wedding cake of stalagmites dripping white with calcium formations. The high ceiling is swallowed by darkness.

'Ben!' My voice rises, folds, returns, repeats. 'Ben, sweetie, it's Mommy and Daddy. Are you here? Ben!'

'Ben!' Mac calls. 'Say something so we can hear you!'

The redundant chorus of echoes rounds in on

362

itself, its tight spiral boring into me. 'Ben!' I shout, feeling excruciatingly helpless. 'Ben, answer!' But if he is out there, if he's trying to answer, we'll never hear him in the cacophony of our own voices.

We continue into near total darkness.

'Why don't we have a flashlight?' I ask through a yoke of frustration.

Sounding as helpless as I feel, Mac answers, 'Why would we?'

'Shhh.' Guy's attempt to whisper echoes like coins strewn throughout the cavern. 'Listen.'

And I think: If we find him, and he's dead, I'm finished.

And if we don't find him, I'm lost.

And if we find him and he's alive, then this will be the second time in his short life he will have survived an abduction, and I swear we won't – Mac and I won't – ever tempt fate again. No more investigations that coax danger into our lives. We'll do something else, something useful, open a shop or learn a trade or write a book or something, anything, to keep a roof over our heads and our souls at peace and our bodies tucked safely at home with our children.

And then I hear it: the tiny echoes pulsing from afar.

'The wheels on the bus go round and round, round and round, round and round, the wheels on the bus go round and round, all about the town.'

'Ben!' I shout. 'Where are you?'

'Mommy?' His voice is high and sweet and frightened. '*Mommy?*' Panicked now, as if he isn't sure we're really here.

'Keep singing and we'll find you.'

'The wheels on the bus go round and round,' he begins, and repeats, and as the echoes multiply his voice seems to grow stronger and more insistent.

Hurrying now, we see a staircase down and take it. The echoes flatten as we descend and then the little voice inflates and multiplies again. Enough sunlight drops in from somewhere to elucidate a sepia chamber of stalactites dripping from the ceiling into dark glassy water, their spiked ends piercing the smooth surface.

'The wheels on the bus go round and round.' His song now is clear and high, ringing out close enough for the sound to resemble an actual voice and not a cruel suggestion that what you hear may or may not be an illusion.

'Ben!' I try again.

'Mommy,' says my little boy. 'I'm right here.'

'Oh my lord,' Mac mutters behind me. I can hear Guy's rhythmic breathing. Everything inside me goes still.

Ben sits alone on a flat shelf of stone at the opposite side of the grotto. I can just manage to see him through a crosshatch of murky sunlight and vivid shadows: my darling boy, sitting like it's rug time at school and he's waiting for his next instructions. He is starkly alone on his rock. No blanket. No food. No water, except for the seawater lapping the edges of his perch. That bastard left him here to drown or starve, to wither in a bewilderment of loneliness and fear.

'Ben,' I say in a diphthong of joy and panic. 'I see you, too.'

'Mommy,' he says thoughtfully, 'you don't sound like you.'

'I'm me, don't worry.' Trying to keep the tears out of my voice. 'Hold tight, sweetie pie, and we'll find our way over and get you.'

'Come now!' His keenness is a beacon that rises and repeats, convincing me that the blissful release moving through my blood like champagne bubbles is real.

'I'm on my way, baby. I'm on my way.'

CHAPTER 25

Sunday, July 22

remont gazes into the sky through the scratched window of the airplane that's taking us back to New York. Dathi, beside him, is engrossed in the book she bought yesterday in Rome. I sit beside her in the aisle seat, my arm extended across empty space so I can hold Ben's hand. Nestled in his father's lap, he's mesmerized by a cartoon on the miniature television screen. From this angle I only see pixilated blurs, but a flash of yellow tells me it's probably *Sesame Street*. He loves Big Bird.

I return to watching Fremont watch the sky. The elegant silhouette of his light brown cheek reminds me so much of Mary; he inherited the valentine shape of his mother's face. Everything reminds me of her lately. Her body still hasn't washed ashore, which according to the Italian Coast Guard will happen eventually, if it wasn't eaten by sharks. They explained that, when people fall, it can happen in many ways: you bounce down the ranks of stone until one stops you; you

366

roll into the water; or something snags a piece of your clothing and you dangle and probably, eventually, drop to the next level. Because traces of Mary's blood were found near the bottom of the cliffs, but not her body, the working theory is that she tumbled into the sea. During the week we stayed on, in Sardinia and then Rome, helping the authorities understand the knot of cases the best we could, we waited on tenterhooks for news of Mary. What if a passing boat rescued her? What if she washed ashore alive with amnesia? What if . . . what if . . .

I watch Fremont watch the sky, trying to see below the blanket of clouds into the ocean that swallowed his mother. Looking for her. He'll spend years waiting for her, I suspect. At the embassy in Rome we were told that after seven years, if she still hasn't been found, a death certificate will be issued. Small comfort being no comfort, essentially. All we know for sure is that she's gone.

The way I see it, when Enzio Greco hurled Mary over that barrier, she *flew*; Mary didn't do things in halves. She sailed over tiers of arid stone, was lifted like a feather by the wind and delivered into the embrace of a dazzling ocean. Part of me dares to think she enjoyed her sudden, if temporary, ability to fly. But mostly I'm horrified at the thought of her crashing into the cold water. Sometimes my skin hurts, thinking of it. Now, high above the Atlantic Ocean on our way home, a chill makes me feel raw inside and out. My thumb gently caresses the top of Ben's soft, plump hand, and I feel a little better, but only just.

Enzio Greco landed on a spiky outcropping of stone on his way down the side of Capo Caccia. His body was found easily, removed bloodily, and delivered by the Carabinieri to the military's medical examiner in Cagliari the same day of his suicide. No one is willing to trust the municipal police, of which Greco had been commissioner, with this case. The U.S. State Department is considering starting extradition procedures against Liz Braud and Blaine Millerhausen so they can face accessory to murder charges at home; but Italy wants them for the case they'll be building on conspiracy, abduction, and police corruption. The International Chamber of Commerce Commercial Crimes Services is launching a task force to determine whether to bring conspiracy charges against the Millerhausens, the Rossis, Lacie Chen, Ian Gelson, Kroll, and Barclays Bank. According to the newspapers, Italy's prime minister has been briefed on the matter. Untangling the interconnected cases, in three different countries, is expected to take years.

Back home in New York, Godfrey Millerhausen is under house arrest in his Park Avenue apartment, awaiting the progression of the legal cases against him. The check stub the Rossis left in the garbage can in Brooklyn was enough to trace the route of their money from Barclays to an offshore corporation in the Canary Islands owned by a subsidiary of Hauser International, the Millerhausen family company. As for the Rossis, it turns out they *are* real people: an artist and his wife who were friendly with Liz Braud and needed the money.

I look at Mac: eyelids closed, signs of age creeping along his face in a latticework of experience and wisdom and regret and hope and love. Or maybe I'm reflecting my own feelings onto him. I wonder if he's sleeping. He takes a deep breath, exhales slowly, and so do I.

When Cathy Millerhausen came walking down our block that June morning and hired Mac, like so many other husbands and wives had done before, to find out if her spouse was cheating on her, no one could have expected how difficult and painful the case would become. Or the price we would pay.

Mary. *Mary.* I miss you.

Fremont turns to glance at me and I hold his eyes.

Fremont is used to not having a father but he'll never get used to not having a mother. Her eyes were light brown with flecks of green and he can still see them if he concentrates. Karin's eyes are blue and unfamiliar at this close, calm distance. She's being so kind to him, and so is Mac. But will he ever look inside her eyes and see a mother?

Dathi can feel Fremont and Karin looking at each other above her head, where she is scrunched down in her seat, reading. Pretending to read. She knows how it is to be an orphan, knows it takes time to settle into your new life once it finds you. She still wonders sometimes how her karma led her to become the daughter of white Americans, but she's mostly used to it now. She remembers both her parents, but the bitter grief of losing them – first her father and then her mother – especially her mother – turned to mist and drifted away without her really noticing. Fremont will get there; she knows he will. In the meantime she'll be a sister to him. She wonders if now he might consider letting her join his band. She likes to sing. Her mother – her first mother, her real mother – used to call her 'my songbird.'

Mac's entire body aches. No matter how long he closes his eyes, rest won't come. He was never good at sleeping on planes.

He recalls the intensity of his boredom with his work this past year, how he hated taking the Millerhausen job because it was just like all the other cheating-spouse cases that paid his bills but drained his soul, how he took it for the money, how he dropped it like a hot potato when Kroll showed him a fatter slice of the money pie, how he jumped at it like a hungry bear. How it was like winning the lottery: a lucrative job and a vacation rolled into one. How he expected to return home spiritually renewed, with money in the bank. Well, he has the money. But he senses that his renewal will take a while longer than expected. Mary's loss has punched a gaping hole in him. And he has Fremont to worry about now: a teenage boy who knows nothing about fathers. Not that Mac knows much about teenage sons. He remembers reading that adolescent boys work hard rejecting their fathers, that a primal battle between males erupts in most homes. But Fremont has never had a father, so how will that work? Can a new father and son accept and reject each other at the same time?

Ben's weight on Mac's lap grounds him. And he thinks, Today is good. It could be better, but still, it's good enough.

They drag their wheeled luggage out of customs at JFK, and to Mac's relief, there he is: Billy, one-eyed and familiar, a head taller than most of the car-service drivers displaying handwritten signs with their clients' last names.

'Look!' Dathi waves.

'Pirate Bill,' Ben murmurs, briefly lifting his head from a nap on Mac's shoulder, a nap that makes him feel as heavily unwieldy as a fifty-pound sack of grain.

Smiling, Billy maneuvers around the throng of drivers.

'Thanks for coming,' Mac says.

'I thought a friendly face might come in handy.'

'Friendly?' Dathi reaches up to snap the elastic

band holding Billy's eye patch at its usual raffish angle.

'Down, girl,' Billy says, wrapping her in a hug.

He hugs or kisses or touches each of them, spending an extra moment with Fremont. Seeing his new son in the arms of his best friend is a comfort to Mac: together, the two men comprise a color wheel pinging with conflicts the teenager will no doubt continue to grapple with as he matures. Can't he have two fathers, one white and one black? Wouldn't that work better than one in this very particular case? When Dathi first joined them, Mac knew that their family wouldn't be conventional ever again, and it never bothered him; actually, he liked it. In a way, looking back, it was preparation for this.

Billy takes Fremont's and Dathi's backpacks off their shoulders, slinging them over his own, and then reaches for Karin's big suitcase. Empty-handed, Karin takes Mac's smaller suitcase so he can get a better grip on Ben.

'Follow me.' Tall and straight, as if unburdened by a ridiculous amount of luggage, Billy leads the way, nimbly avoiding anyone who straggles into his path. When his group lags too far behind, he stops and turns. 'Yo, you gotta step it up if we're gonna make it through this crowd.'

He leads them outside into a dark summer night of jet fumes and weary travelers. Halfway through short-term parking, he stops beside a clean white van.

'Did you rent that?' Mac asks. Billy's car is too small for a family this size.

'It's Dash's. Seats seven people. She loaned it to us for the night.'

'Nice of her.'

'Yeah, she's a softie.'

A snort of laughter escapes Karin. 'Right.'

Mac and Billy pause to look at her. She hasn't gotten to know Ladasha as a mother, in her home, as Mac did last week. Karin doesn't know the gentle side of that very tough woman. He'll explain about that later when time opens up the space for all those nuanced conversations; they'll be rehashing this summer for years to come.

Before I can get my key out of my purse, standing on our front stoop, the door swings open.

'Mom!' I throw my arms around her: peppery and sweet and blissfully familiar.

'I hope you don't mind' – she hugs me back – 'but I thought you might appreciate a welcome wagon.'

'You thought right.'

Mac carries Ben straight in the downstairs entrance, the fastest route to the bedrooms. After double-parking the van, Billy follows him with the luggage. Dathi and Fremont come up the stoop behind me and wait for the lovefest to end. But it doesn't: As soon as my mother releases me, her arms envelop Dathi.

'Hi, Pam,' Dathi coos.

'When are you going to start calling me Grandma?'

'Soon.'

How many times have I heard that same conversation between them? Mom knows as well as I do that Dathi will call her Grandma when, and if, she's ready.

I go inside but Fremont waits his turn: a good sign, I think. Mom hugs him longer than she hugged me or Dathi, which is exactly what I expect of her. She's heard all the news, knows all the facts, and will have prepared herself to add a grandchild to her growing brood. Doesn't matter that this one is taller than she is and has an Afro worthy of the sixties, or that he curses like a drunken sailor when he feels like it, or that his grades dipped in tenth grade and will probably dip even lower now that his emotional plate is overfull. Mom hugs him long and hard, gently patting his hair like she's neatening a halo.

Along with greeting us, Mom has also cleaned the kitchen, turning Mac's description of bloody carnage into an abstraction. A plate of homemade oatmeal cookies is warm and fragrant on the table, the whiff of cinnamon an indelible reminder that life goes on.

CHAPTER 26

Wednesday, July 25

Z accheus Mead Lane is graceful and silent, with strong limbs of old trees reaching to shade the winding road. Our green MINI Cooper with its checkerboard top doesn't fit in here, and I like that. I roll down my window, inhale the fresh air. It's not nearly as hot here as when we left Brooklyn an hour ago. The lush green peacefulness of this town is a beautiful and valuable thing, but I have to admit I'm more comfortable in more humble surroundings. Every now and then we pass a gated entrance signifying a grand house tucked behind the tall hedges. When we come to the Millerhausen mansion, Mac turns in between the forbidding stone columns that mark the entrance to their estate.

'What time is she expecting us?' Looking at my watch, I see it's almost three o'clock.

'She isn't.'

'Mac!'

'What, Karin, suddenly you're Miss Manners?'

'*Ms.* Manners.'

Mac chuckles. He knows I'm not one to follow rules, and he's right: I wouldn't have even thought about how rude it could seem dropping in unannounced if we weren't facing an enormous house with outsize hedges on either side of the front door. Money intimidates. I know that. And push that boundary away.

'The bushes look like space orbs,' I say, noting their perfect roundness.

'I didn't notice them the other times I was here.'

'Would you have noticed them now if I hadn't mentioned it?'

'Probably not.'

'See? You're not as observant as you think.'

He rings the bell and we wait.

'Maybe she's not home,' I say.

'If I was getting the kind of media attention she's been getting lately, I wouldn't leave my house for a month.' He rings again. This time footsteps approach.

'You're more *intuitive*,' I say, 'which is unusual in a man. And very nice.'

The open door releases a cool draft. Cathy Millerhausen is wearing a lime green sleeveless sundress and gold hoop earrings. I notice a large diamond ring paired with a wedding band, and am struck that she's still wearing them. Her arms are bright red with sunburn, the skin peeling off in chunks. I recognize the delicious perfume that wafted off her that time I passed her on our block.

376

'Mac and Karin.'

'I didn't know if you'd remember my name,' I say. I only met her that once, and it was brief.

'After what you've been through on my behalf?'

'I hope you don't mind us dropping in like this,' Mac says.

'Not at all. I can use some adult company. Please, come in.'

We follow her into a vast marble foyer. An occasional table holds a ridiculously huge vase of white orchids. A soccer ball and two pairs of muddy cleats are piled at the foot of an impressive staircase.

'Wow, it's hot out there. Can I get you some lemonade?'

'That sounds great,' Mac answers.

To reach the distant kitchen we pass through three other rooms; you can see why it took her so long to answer the door. Our route takes us by the familiar messy piles generated by any family: stacks of books on a coffee table, a puddle of dirty socks beside a plush chair, a candy wrapper on a couch cushion. The clutter surprises me. In a place like this, you'd assume disorder would be dealt with promptly by hired hands, and I wonder why the place isn't neater. She seems to notice my prying eyes.

'Had to let go of all the help,' she says. 'One of the housekeepers sold a story about us to a newspaper and I said *that's it*. I fired everyone that same day, gave them a generous severance, and my boys and I were all alone by dinnertime. Actually, it's been kind of nice.'

Mismatched twins, eating melting bowls of ice cream and playing a game of cards, sit catty-corner at a butcher-block island in the middle of a spacious mahogany and granite kitchen.

'Bobby, Ritchie, these are our friends Mac and Karin.'

I'm glad she called us friends. Of course she wouldn't have brought us this far into her house if she felt otherwise. Having never met her sons, at first I'm not sure which one's Bobby and which one's Ritchie. Both are blond, with eerily similar features. But it seems to me, in a measured leap of assumption, that the boy with sharp features, dexterously shuffling a deck of cards, is the one without special needs. And that the bulky one with untied sneaker laces, who seems to be in agony trying to stay on his stool, is the one with special needs. I know I'm right when the first one deals out two hands of cards, saying, 'Okay, Ritchie, let's try it again,' and Ritchie sweeps the cards off the butcher-block in a bout of frustration I didn't see coming. Bobby's temper starts to flare, until Cathy touches his shoulder. He collects himself.

'Ritchie,' she says gently, 'when Bobby gives you your cards, pick them up the way I showed you, okay?'

'Okay,' Ritchie says, nodding. His brother collects the cards off the floor and shuffles again.

'Sports work better,' Cathy takes three tall glasses down from a cabinet, 'but I thought they needed some time out of the sun.'

The appliances are so well hidden behind cabinetry facings you have to really look to notice them. Glowing brass pots and pans hang from a rack above the island more for decoration than utility, I suspect, as they're pretty far from the eight-burner restaurant-grade stove.

'I made this myself.' She hands us glasses of lemonade with mint leaves floating on top. The sour sweetness is cold and wonderful. 'The mint grows wild by the pool house. So what brings you so far from home?'

'Checking in,' Mac says.

'That's nice of you.'

'Customary at the end of a job.'

'No it isn't, but thanks, anyway.'

She's right, of course: Final payment is usually the last communication once a case is finished. But I know that Mac's been bothered by how he suspended her case to leave for Europe, how his own impatience (and mine) to get away might have added to her sense of betrayal. Even though our trip ultimately led to the real heart of Godfrey Millerhausen's culpability, that doesn't nullify Mac's sense of shame at how he tried to slough Cathy off when he thought she was just another jealous, paranoid wife.

Cathy pulls up a stool at the other end of the butcher block. We join her. The twins try and fail to get their card game under control, and give up. They finish their ice cream and Ritchie follows when Bobby leaves the kitchen.

'When does school start?' I ask. Ben starts first grade two days after Labor Day, but different states follow different calendars.

'Not soon enough,' Cathy cheerfully complains, 'for Bobby, anyway. Ritchie gets support all year. In fact Anita, his language specialist, is due any minute.'

'How are the divorce proceedings going?' Mac asks.

'Haven't started yet. My lawyer's trying to figure out if I'll be better off *not* divorcing Godfrey right now.' She notices my eyebrows shoot up. 'Strange, right? But if I can control Godfrey's personal wealth more effectively by staying married to him, then I can set up the trusts I need to face anything in Ritchie's future. I can work out guardianship for the twins in case something happens to me. I can get everything arranged the way it needs to be. And I can start a foundation to support research into his condition. That's something I'd really like to do.'

'That's a great idea,' I tell her.

She touches the back of Mac's hand. 'I admit this isn't how I thought things would end. But you see? You helped me. And maybe down the line you'll have helped a lot of other kids like Ritchie.'

Mac's eyes jitter away from Cathy's face, graze

the gleaming kitchen cabinets and land on me. I can see him struggling to hold back emotion.

The doorbell rings.

'That'll be Anita.' Cathy stands.

We go with her to the door and part ways with warm handshakes. 'Thank you,' she says, 'and keep in touch.'

A young woman carrying an overstuffed canvas bag greets Cathy on her way upstairs to look for Ritchie.

'If you see Bobby,' Cathy calls after her, 'tell him I'll play Go Fish with him while you work with Ritchie, or if he wants, I'll teach him Heads Up.'

'Isn't that poker?' I ask.

Cathy's eyes flash at me like I said something wrong. 'I'm surprised you've heard of it.'

'I was an Army brat. The moms killed a lot of time; they knew all the games. And some of them gambled. Heads Up was a tricky one.'

'It can be.'

If I'm not mistaken, she's blushing under her sunburn.

'Its just for two players, right?'

Mac says, 'I didn't know you *could* play poker with just two players.'

'It isn't easy, but you can.' Cathy opens the door, heat rushing in, stealing the dry coolness off my skin. 'Thanks for coming.'

Mac turns around to give her a hug, which bewilders me since the mood suddenly got very stiff. 'Be well,' he says, even going so far as to stroke her head a few times. Her blond hair gets snagged in his wedding ring, and he gently yanks it out. 'Sorry about that.'

'No problem. I'm sure I won't miss a few strands of hair.'

CHAPTER 27

Friday, August 10

Mac runs through Prospect Park, lungs heaving, knees throbbing, trying and failing to focus his attention on Sharon Jones's lyrics to *100 Days, 100 Nights*. But he can't stop thinking about Cathy Millerhausen. He turns up the volume, pushes his earbuds deeper in, tries to drown out Cathy so he can really take in Sharon's audaciously gorgeous R & B – to be born with a voice like that. He wants to be inspired by music, not sink back into the quicksand of the Millerhausen case. Karin is right: They both need to put their wretched summer behind them.

But how?

It's only August. Summer isn't over. And neither, apparently, is the case.

He dials up the volume until Sharon's voice explodes into raw, deafening sound. Rips out the earbuds. Stops running and crouches down to catch his breath.

How did he miss it?

Turns out Cathy Millerhausen used to be a dealer at a casino in Vegas. She had a very different kind of life before Godfrey Millerhausen strolled over to her table one early morning. He was no prize, except for the money. And except for her Connecticut-ready looks, and the odd fact that she turned out to be a good mother, she was no prize, either.

Not that a person's background needs to mean anything when you consider it in the framework of a crime. Legally, it shouldn't. But what if Mac had thought to learn more about Cathy when the case first started? What if Karin or Mary had thought about it? Would he have asked the Harrisburg detectives if *they* had learned anything about Cathy? Could a few easy questions have triggered a whole new direction . . . and possibly saved Mary's life?

Mac lifts the bottom of his T-shirt to dry his dripping forehead. Another runner lopes past him, looking as high on endorphins as Mac wants to be but can't seem to achieve. It's a kind of impotence, he thinks, to be unable to relax. Unable to stop thinking until you scrape every ugly possibility off the bottom of the problem.

The problem suddenly being, did Godfrey Millerhausen kill Alicia Griffin? Or did his crime stop at impregnating her? Does the fact that a victim was pregnant with a man's child at the time of her death, and that man had every reason to want to hide it, necessarily mean he's guilty of her murder?

No. But it looks that way. Godfrey would have seen it, too. When Mac wonders why Godfrey didn't just try to buy Cathy's silence about his affair with Alicia and her pregnancy – nullify the prenup, give his wife a lucrative divorce – it hits him: He probably did, and she probably refused, because she wants it all.

Why didn't Mac question her motive when she came to him that day? He knows the answer: Since he went private, he rarely questions the motives of his clients. He takes their money and does the job. Grins and bears it. Hopes life will take an interesting turn. Looks forward to time off.

Cathy's a charmer, that's for sure. She must have thrown her force field of suspended disbelief around the Harrisburg detectives, too. Because no one, *no one*, thought to look in her direction. Those idiots were even willing to believe that an incarcerated prisoner could impregnate a teenager in another state – were willing to close the case and go home.

Mac thinks of a documentary he once saw called *Paradise Lost: The Child Murders at Robin Hood Hills* and the two follow-up films tracking the case's progress over years. How three teenagers went to jail until DNA proved their innocence almost two decades later. How a judge and multiple juries overlooked a lack of corroborating evidence to irrefutably tie the suspects to the murders. The teenagers weren't perfect: they liked to get high, one was borderline retarded, one dressed all in black. That none of it meant they were killers was overlooked again and again. Two of the boys drew life sentences. The third went to death row. *And they were innocent.*

This case is different: Godfrey's DNA is the damning evidence against him. But it only proves he made the girl pregnant. Mac can't get that out of his mind.

Who *killed* her?

Mac dials up Pachelbel's Canon in D, replaces the earbuds and resumes his run to the gently braided sounds of violins and harpsichord. He thinks of Karin, how much he loves her, and his children, how much he loves them, and Cathy Millerhausen almost drifts away.

His phone vibrates in the back pocket of his shorts. He veers onto the grassy shoulder and comes to a stop.

'We're done,' Billy says.

'Are you breaking up with me?' Mac's attempt at humor wheezes out and becomes a cough.

'You okay?'

'Fine. I was just running.'

'Since when do you run?'

'Since lately. Need a way to get my mind off things.'

'Well stop running, brother, because I am here to ease your burden.'

'You sound like a preacher.' Mac laughs, but

mostly in relief, knowing that what he's been waiting for is coming. That he's about to find out whether he did the right thing by giving the FBI the strands of Cathy Millerhausen's hair that *accidentally* got snagged in his wedding ring. He'll find out whether it was worth pressuring Billy to stir up enough trouble to get them to exhume Alicia's body from her grave.

'Maybe that can be my next career,' Billy says, 'since this one's all but shot. Did I tell you Internal Affairs scheduled me for a sit-down in September? I can hear them greasing the guillotine.'

'I'm sorry, Billy.'

'Not your fault.'

'Yes it is. I dragged you into all this.'

'Yeah, well, maybe your punishment is that I'm gonna be your new partner.'

'That's not a punishment.'

'You say that now.'

'Come on, stop torturing me. Tell me the results.'

'The perfume the crime scene techs smelled in Alicia's grave when they dug her up the first time?'

'What about it?'

'They assumed it was Alicia's. But according to the parents, their daughter never wore perfume. She was allergic to it. The lab ran some tests and told us it was Joy.'

'I've heard of that.'

'Expensive stuff,' Billy says. 'Even if Alicia wore perfume, she couldn't have afforded that one. Unless Godfrey gave it to her.'

'Cathy Millerhausen wears a lot of perfume, I noticed.'

'Yup. And her credit-card records going way back say she should have bought stock in Joy.'

'It doesn't prove anything,' Mac says.

'They got a skin sample off a rock deep enough in the grave that weather didn't touch it. DNA matches Cathy Millerhausen's, and Joy's all mixed up with it. She must have tossed the rock into the hole. Maybe she tried to hit Alicia, knock her out or something, and missed.'

'Maybe.'

'Another thing. The feds also found out that Dan Stylos, the dude you were trying so hard to talk to when all this started, well, he passed a few friendly e-mails with Cathy in the weeks before he died. They agreed how sad it was about Alicia.'

Mac's gut drops with the confirmation that his recent suspicions are true. 'Cathy knew about Alicia all along.'

'And so did Stylos. Since Godfrey never hired Alicia as an intern, my guess is they were the only ones who knew. If you read all the e-mails, there's something threatening about them. Like she's saying to the guy, If you tell anyone that I know about this girl, well, *don't*.'

'Jesus.'

'So now they're thinking they might like her for Stylos's death, too.'

'Stylos fell off his boat and died.'

'And Alicia fell into a hole and died. Someone pushed them. And let's not forget Carlos Lopez crashing his car the night he unsealed the adoption record for me.'

'What does all this prove, though?' Mac says in despair. 'E-mails and perfume don't make a solid case.'

'Skin. In the grave.'

'A good defense lawyer can argue that a wife's skin is all over her husband's belongings. And her perfume, too.'

'What, you playing devil's advocate on me now? This was your idea. You got what you wanted.'

'I didn't want this.'

'What did you want, man?'

'I wanted it to be what we thought before – Godfrey Millerhausen, guilty as charged. I wanted it to end there. I wanted to come home and stop hating myself for getting Mary killed.'

'You didn't kill her. It wasn't you.'

Mac can't argue. It's how he feels.

'Cathy gave us lemonade when we went to her house last week. It was really good. I wanted to remember it that way. When I hugged her good-bye, I wanted it to be real.'

'You hugged her so you could take a hair sample. You told me so yourself.'

'I know. But I wanted to be wrong. I wanted to

not be such a coward and such a fool. I wanted to be a better detective.'

'Look,' Billy says, 'you *are* a good detective and you know it. Anyway, it's not about what we want. It's about what we get.'

Mac puts his iPod away and starts running again, this time in silence